THE LANDS OF DE GRESSIER

[signature]

05/21

The Lands of de Gressier

1913 - 1935

Charles Bunker

YOUCAXTON
PUBLICATIONS

ISBN 978-1-913425-32-6
Published by YouCaxton Publications 2020
YCBN: 01

YouCaxton Publications
www.youcaxton.co.uk

Cover art by: Timiarts Design
Typeset and cover design by Ella Knight Designs

Books in the de Gressier Series

Book One   The Lands of de Gressier   1913 – 1935
First Published 2020
Book Two   The Vines of de Gressier   1921 - 1958
Book Three   The Soul of de Gressier   1960 - 1977
Book Four   The Watches of de Gressier   1991 – 2014

The Lands of de Gressier - Family Tree

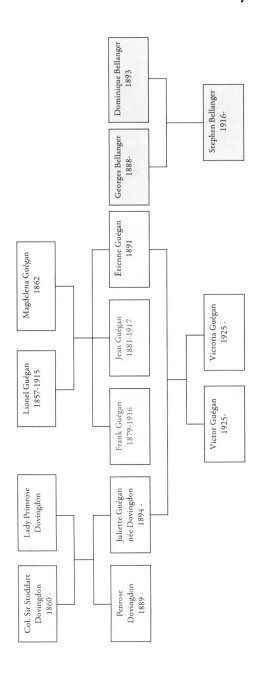

The Lands of de Gressier

This is a story which only the grandchildren can tell for they are not the secret keepers.

Prologue

Hertfordshire, England February 1925

HIS BODY WAS hunched, caused by a pain. Not a physical pain. Not a pain that the Colonel would admit to, but a pain which came from profound sadness.

He stared at the fire, deep in contemplation. His tweed suit was hanging as a crumpled sack from his shoulders, making it look as though it were a strewn pile of cloth with just a head poking through.

The Colonel mindlessly raised the tumbler to his lips and took a sip of whisky without noticing the taste. He rarely visited a pub, but when he did so it was always the same one, where he sat in the same chair, by the same fire, never quite feeling at home. It wasn't a class thing. He had always felt as comfortable with his soldiers, as with his officers. In many cases he preferred the company of his men, for they had an innate honesty, rarely found in the complexity of army politics. It was the overwhelming sense of sympathy, which came from his family's notoriety, which he now found embarrassing. Those of high society still shunned and set the Colonel aside, unless they needed his money, for even though the editorial in the Times reported that his son's actions were both justified and heroic, it was his running away which had left a stain on the family's name, and Col. Sir Stoddart Dovingdon hated it.

Jack Morris entered, allowing the pub doors to swing heavily. He paused for a fraction of a second, just long enough to make the room his own. He saw and walked straight towards the Colonel who, observing Jack's arrival, stood up. Within an instant the Colonel had risen to his full height, such that his body filled the tweed suit which now fitted him immaculately. In doing so, he created an unmistakable presence in the room; a commanding presence which came naturally from years of being in charge and issuing orders.

"What can I get you to drink?" asked the Colonel, as he moved towards the bar.

"A brandy, please," said Jack.

"A beer, please," said the Colonel to the barman, deliberately ignoring Jack's request.

"Pint or half?" asked the Barman.

"Pint," said Jack quickly. He was determined not to lose the banter which, despite their class difference, the two men found easy to share.

The Colonel admired Jack. He was sharp, quick-witted, and resourceful. He was of the new generation. A generation which, because they saw their fathers, brothers, uncles, and friends simply disappear into mist in the mass slaughter of the Great War, did not have the same respect for the class structures of the past. As a result, Jack conversed with dukes and dustmen with the same polite disdain.

The Colonel moved back to the table by the fire. Jack picked up the pint mug in his left hand and had a swig. He bent at the knee and lifted his suitcase using just the thumb, fourth and fifth fingers of his right hand, having lost the other two fingers to German shrapnel.

Pte. Jack Morris had served with the Hertfordshire Regiment, later to be given the honorary title of the Herts Guards because of their courage and determination on the battlefield. It was the Colonel who, through Jack's father, had insisted he joined the territorial forces; thus Jack's weekends, and two weeks in the summer, were spent training, or "playing at soldiers," as he and his pals would call it.

It was the army which gave Col. Dovingdon and Jack a kinsmanship which is only found in those that have served. The Colonel had retired after years of distinguished service. However, unlike Jack, he had seen no real action. He had been sent abroad many times, but the mere arrival of the British Army settled things down locally, and within months he was home again without a shot fired. He tried to re-join the army with the call up in 1914 but, then aged 50, he was considered too old, and those who he approached to "get involved again" considered him too curmudgeonly and his requests were quietly ignored.

At the start of World War 1, Jack went on parade with G Company on Hitchin Market Square and in November 1914 he left for France as part of the British Expeditionary Force. Jack never rose in rank. He was to be medically discharged as a result of injuries sustained on the first day of the Battle of Festubert in May 1915. These injuries included a large chunk of his right calf muscle sliced away, deafness in his right ear, as well as the two lost fingers.

Jack remembers little about the action which saw him hurt, except his desperate need to get back to his regiment with his rifle showing its trigger guard shot through. He remembered only too well being told how, in a war long gone-by, a soldier had been charged with cowardice as a result of a self-inflicted wound and had avoided the death penalty by the skin of his teeth. It was obvious from Jack's wounds that this was not the case, but he was desperate to prove it so. For this reason, it was not the dreadful pain which was the most pressing thing on Jack's mind as he was stretchered back behind their lines, but the need to have his gun by his side at all times.

Jack also had an unjustified sense of guilt. He never mentioned it, and no one else knew, but he was hurt without ever having fired a shot. He had never seen an enemy soldier to shoot at. As a result, he never felt he had done 'his bit'. It was this simple fact which always made him the first to answer the call when an 'army man' wanted something done.

"Are you ready?" said the Colonel pulling out an envelope from his inside jacket pocket and placing its contents on the table.

Jack pulled out a worn padded stool from under the table and sat down. He picked up the envelope and looked inside. "First Class!" he said in surprise.

"Yes, this is important."

The Colonel also handed over five, one hundred French franc

notes, eight crisp five-pound notes, and six Thomas Cook travellers' cheques, each worth five pounds: a small fortune.

"As agreed," said the Colonel, "another twenty pounds when you get back. Tonight, you will stay at the Savoy Hotel in the Strand. Tomorrow morning you'll catch the boat train from Waterloo to Paris where you will stay the night in the George V Hotel on the Champs Elysée. Both hotels have already been paid for. The next day you will catch the train to Bordeaux from the Gare d'Austerlitz. How you get from Bordeaux to Château de Gressier is for you to work out. It is all written down here, including Miss Juliette's address."

Jack nodded his understanding. He had already heard these instructions a couple of times before. His only worry was how unsuited he felt to the posh places the Colonel had booked him into.

"Do you have your passport? Show it to me," ordered the Colonel.

Jack produced his brand-new passport, acquired just for the occasion.

"How's your French?" enquired the Colonel, handing back the document unopened.

"Only what I learnt when I was last there. But don't worry, I'll manage."

There was nothing left for the two men to say.

"Time to go," said the Colonel, standing up and putting on his trench-like overcoat.

Jack slowly gathered up the papers and money on the table. He folded and sorted them neatly, then slipped them into his inner jacket pocket. He reached down and picked up his suitcase. He looked up to see the Colonel was already at the front door.

They walked out into the damp and darkness. The orange and blue beams of the gaslights brushed the drizzle which put the town square into a mellow focus. They gave out a hue of warmth which concealed the coldness of the early evening.

Petards Jewellers was on the other side of the square and its display windows were bathed in a soft yellow from its recently installed electric lights. The Colonel strode across the cobbles, allowing Jack to follow, and with the doorbell tinkling as it opened, they both went inside.

"Good Evening Colonel," said Lionel Petard. "I've just finished. I'm sure you will be pleased."

Lionel was a big man who wore thin framed spectacles pinched on the end of his nose. He was spotlessly dressed wearing a neat well-pressed green apron, which he put on clean each morning. Lionel did everything slowly and deliberately, typical of a craftsman who had learnt not to rush. He knew that the time he patiently invested into creating something beautiful paled into insignificance when compared to the sense of satisfaction he felt at making something which he intended should last one thousand years.

Lionel handed over two packages.

The Colonel opened each box and placed the contents side by side on the dark green velvet cloth that covered part of the counter. He was delighted. Two full Hunter gold pocket watches beautifully and very delicately engraved with the family crest; and below one crest was engraved the name Victor, and below the other, the name Victoria.

The Colonel stroked each of the watches slowly and carefully. It was as though he was transposing all his love, loss and grief into these two tiny objects to be carried to his two grandchildren, and with them went his greatest wish, that his daughter would come back to him.

"Please take this letter with you," said the Colonel at the last minute, handing Jack an envelope marked with only one name, that of Juliette. "Can you please make sure she gets it? It's very important to me," he added. From the way the Colonel spoke, Jack knew that, despite the incredible value of the two watches, the letter was the most important thing he wanted delivered.

Chapter 1

Cambridge 1913 - 1914

MISS JULIETTE VICTORIA Dovingdon had a sense of anticipation but no excitement as she walked through the large wooden gates, for she expected to be there. She had convinced herself that it was nothing special. Just another step in the path she had ordained for herself. There had, of course, been battles, mainly with her father, who was not convinced of the merits of educating women, but her agreement to do a year at finishing school in Switzerland and France first, had provided the coup de grâce.

The last battle had been about travelling to Cambridge University on her own. She knew she couldn't bear her mother's fussing, or the arrogant dismissal by her father of her efforts, which would have accompanied them. They had stopped delivering her to boarding school, on the first day of term, years ago, and during her finishing year, she had managed to navigate to, and around, Paris, Rome, Vienna and Venice without difficulty, so there was no reason why they had to come. No, Juliette had to make this journey on her own. Her original plan was to take the train, but another compromise was found. It was agreed that their chauffeur would deliver her to Girton College and carry her things to her room.

A small queue had gathered outside the porters' lodge of Girton College when Juliette arrived. She knew from the outset that it had to be Girton and not Newnham, the other women's college in Cambridge, because she felt an affinity to the place, for the original college was in her home town, very close to the lavender fields where she had ridden her pony on very many occasions as a young girl.

"Why did you choose Girton?" asked Dorothy Wrinch, who was also starting that term. She was standing in the queue behind Juliette.

"What are you going to read?" Dorothy asked before Juliette had been able to formulate an answer to her first question. Over the next sixty years, Wrinch was to become a leading academic in mathematics as a biochemical theorist.

"Just think," burst out Wrinch, "we'll get to go to Bertrand Russell's lectures!"

Juliette tried to ignore the excitable monologue and answered the first question. "Because it follows the same curriculum and timetable as the men," she said. "It's the college's conviction that men and women are equal," she added, as an afterthought.

"Oh my!" exclaimed Wrinch, "a suffragette in our midst; how very exciting!"

"A suffragist," corrected Juliette. "I'm sure we'd get a better, quicker result if the sisterhood acted peacefully. You know the suffragette's flag?" Juliette continued strongly.

Wrinch nodded,

"You know the colour green in their flag is for hope, purple for dignity and white for purity," said Juliette. "Well it seems to me that Emily Davidson forgot about dignity when she threw herself in front of the King's horse on Derby day." She was referring to an event a few months before in which Davidson had been killed. The 'accident' had been taken into the nation's psyche as Pathé News had made sure that the event was shown in every cinema throughout the land.

Wrinch nodded her approval again, more strongly this time as did several other girls who had gathered around and engaged in the conversation without actually saying anything.

A bowler-hatted porter led the two women to their rooms, on the same staircase, identified by their names painted above each doorway.

There was a formal dinner the first evening when, by candlelight, Emily Jones, Mistress of Girton College, told those assembled what was expected of them: no frivolities, no romance, just hard work and academic excellence.

To avert their attention away from matters of the heart and flesh, they were told that, despite having given the largest single donation to help Emily Davies build Girton College, Barbara Bodichon was never able to achieve the status in society which she richly deserved because she was illegitimate. Juliette, with those around her, quietly discussed the contradiction of this reasoning, for if an illegitimate woman could be responsible for helping to create such a college, then perhaps the sins of the flesh, could not be that disastrous. But Miss Jones made one other thing clear as she spoke: as far as Girton was concerned, the company of men was not to be enjoyed. They were the competition to be surpassed in every way.

That evening, the new women of Girton College enjoyed the process of meeting new friends, wondering how they were going to find their way around, and how the whole place was organised, for it was all so very confusing. Irrespective of the anxiety caused by it all being new to them, each woman felt that their futures were set and bright.

Very quickly Juliette settled in and loved every minute of Cambridge. The work was hard, impossibly hard at some points, as she learnt, tested and proved the theorems of the great mathematicians, but it was when she was introduced to the work of Newton that her passion for astro-physics was born.

As the winter moved in and the days got shorter, the time spent in tutorials, lectures, reading books and writing essays increased, such that there was little time for the frivolities which Juliette had hoped would adorn university life. She had expected a work-hard, play-hard environment but, because the logic of mathematics and astrophysics played to the strengths of Juliette's mind, the work dominated every aspect of her waking and dreaming moments. However, she also found it all too clinical, without any emotion or passion and so, as spring came and the days grew warmer, Juliette gravitated towards a new group of friends, some of whom would later become famous. Nicknamed the neo-pagans, she sat quietly on the edge of a group which included such people as Rupert Brooke, Virginia Woolf and Ludwig Wittgenstein as they debated and wrote pamphlets and poetry about love, feminism, pacifism and their attitudes towards sexual freedom; but it was all just a little too avant-garde for Juliette. While these young men of Cambridge teased and flirted with her outrageously, growing up with an elder brother and his friends, had given Juliette more than enough confidence to deal with the testosterone of youth.

Juliette was pleased with her first year's exam results, which were better than she had expected and so, basking in a modicum of success, she stayed on at Cambridge for a few days doing very little but reading for pleasure and lazing about with friends under the summer sun on the banks of the River Cam. For Juliette it was truly an idyllic time. She could not have been happier.

The same could not have been said of Juliette's mother, Lady Primrose Harriet Dovingdon, whose first and only priority was to find Juliette a husband. As a result, Juliette was faced with a summer social calendar, put together by her mother, which was as arduous as anything she had to cope with at Cambridge. Juliette had 'come out' the year before at the Queen Charlotte Ball and fully participated in that summer's social season, but to her mother's chagrin, no beau had attached himself to Juliette's delights. So once again, every social event was meticulously organised, even to the point of Lady Dovingdon insisting that Juliette attend the Queen Charlotte Ball for the second year, even though it was on the same day as her exams. Under no circumstances was a university in the fens going to get in the way of the serious business of finding Juliette a husband.

The Eton v Harrow cricket match, Wimbledon men's finals, Gold Cup day at Royal Ascot, and Henley Royal Regatta were all attended, with Juliette's elder brother, Penrose, being press-ganged into sacrificing rare holidays to be her chaperone. Each event required a new dress, hat, and a fitting beforehand. And so it was that Juliette dutifully pranced through June and July 1914 for the eligible young bachelors of the day to admire, as though she were a young foal in an auction ring seeking a bidder. She found it all faintly ridiculous, as not only was finding a husband a long way from her thoughts, but every day throughout July the men she was with talked excitedly of war with Germany, and how quickly they would win. Marriage was far from their thoughts, too.

As the men talked of war, Juliette made a point of reading every quality newspaper studying the commentary and analysis. She found it hard to believe the assassination of Archduke Ferdinand in Sarajevo was going to bring down the European order as easily as a gust of wind brings down a house of cards. Every time she questioned her father about the logic of what was happening, for it seemed to her to have no logic at all, he would dismiss her enquiries condescendingly, telling her it was not the place of women to trouble their heads with the affairs of state.

Penrose was far more helpful in explaining what was happening, but as war grew ever closer, he had to work inordinately long hours at his job in the Treasury as confidence in the British economy's ability to afford a war rapidly waned, just at the time when the government needed to raise the money to pay for it.

Juliette was no soothsayer, but she was convinced that her country had dream-walked into war. She was equally certain that within a short time the pieces on the chess board would inevitably be moved into stalemate, for while Great Britain might eventually defeat Germany, she was not sure what it would win.

When Juliette returned to Cambridge in October 1914, it was quite different from the previous year. Within the hallowed walls of Girton, not much had changed, but throughout the rest of the university there was a noticeable difference, for the exuberance of youth had gone. Not only was the intake of new undergraduates much reduced, because so many had delayed their entry so as to enlist straight into the army, but the ranks of those already there were depleted, having also joined up, 'not wishing to miss a great party'.

As the autumn of 1914 drifted into the chill of winter, and with depressing reports of fighting in Belgium and France starting to fill the newspapers, the mood in Cambridge began to change as the euphoria of an early victory evaporated and then stultified into the realisation that war was a deadly serious business and it was going to take a very long time to win.

Juliette thought nothing of the war during the Michaelmas term, as she was consumed by a passion for her work and a determination to do just as well in her second year-end exams. The change in mood passed her by. At the end of term, Juliette travelled home to spend a few days idly with her parents as they prepared for Christmas. This time, her father's previously dismissive attitude had changed, for he had become quite proud of her achievements. For the first time, he included her in the discussions of his business and the inventions of the time which had, over recent years, made him a lot of money.

Juliette's mother was equally as proud, but for a different reason. Over the last two years, Juliette had developed from a schoolgirl into a confident and beautiful woman. Her hair was now worn short, in accordance with the fashion of the day, and this gave her face an exquisite, elflike quality. So, while she still looked like delicate porcelain, Juliette's self-belief allowed her to radiate laughter and joy in almost every circumstance.

Penrose arrived home for the holidays two days before Christmas. He was completely exhausted, so he proceeded to sleep non-stop, only becoming compos mentis late on Christmas Eve. Juliette listened carefully as he and her father debated the alternative tactics for victory. For the first time she discovered that the war was not going well. She sat uncomfortably, saying nothing, as her father and Penrose contemplated, out loud, the best way to make money out of the situation, for they were both certain that money could be made from this war. It had ever been so.

Nevertheless, very slowly, over the Christmas break, a frostiness started to pervade the whole household as Penrose said nothing about joining up, while each day his father expected him to ask for his help in getting a commission in his old regiment. On the day Penrose returned to London, and Juliette returned to Cambridge, their father was so angry with both of them that he refused to say good-bye. They were in league together against him, as they always had been, he thought.

On her return to Cambridge, Juliette thought little about the war or of the curmudgeonly mood of her father, focusing only on her work; that was until she received a letter from Penrose.

Chapter 2

England 1914

DAVID VICTOR PENROSE Dovingdon was put down for Eton with a flourish and excitement in the week he was born. The Dovingdons had been at Eton for three generations and it was a foregone conclusion that Penrose, as he was always called, would be the next. That was until Bertram Pollock was appointed headmaster of Wellington College just a couple of years after Penrose was born. Pollock and Col. Dovingdon were good friends, albeit Pollock was deeply religious and Dovingdon was not. They were members of the same London Club and shared an interest in the battles of the Boer War, but most importantly they were both keen members of the Royal Institute with a complete fascination in the new sciences of the day. And so it was that, rather than being the fourth generation of Dovingdons to go to Eton, Penrose was the first generation to go to Wellington.

Much to his father's disappointment, Penrose served his early years at Wellington without distinction; one of the also-rans of the school. He excelled at being in the middle of everything, never doing too little, or too much, to be noticed. Even his chosen position on the rugby field as full back was deliberate. It was a nice, easy position which kept him away from the ball as long as possible. All was to change one Saturday afternoon when Wellington was playing Cranleigh School at home. Suddenly and without warning, Penrose was put down to play in the under sixteens second team because the regular incumbent was injured.

As usual, Penrose hugged the 10-yard goal line until there was a break by one of Cranleigh's second row forwards. With his head down and ball in hand, a huge boy was thundering like a charging bull towards the goalposts. Every sinew was bursting as he was intent on scoring a try. Penrose knew his duty. He had no alternative but to put himself between the charging bull and the goal line. Penrose knew it would hurt, but with his arms outstretched, and jumping from side to side in expectation of a last-minute swerve, he stood his ground. In a nanosecond, two gladiators were born. Penrose crouched down in anticipation and then their bodies crashed together with a huge groan as air was forcefully exhaled from both opponents.

Penrose was thrown backwards, but in the process he grabbed his opponent's shirt with both hands and held on in a vice-like grip. The second-row player went over the top of him and crashed facedown into the hard pitch, releasing the ball in the process. It bounced in Penrose's direction. He picked it up and looked around. Play had virtually stopped as everyone on the field expected a try. Now his job was to kick the ball into touch where a new set play would begin, but Penrose's blood was up. Having survived, he felt he had to do something to prove himself and so he started to run. Not with his head down, as he had been told, but with his head up and watching his opponents. He found a speed which he had never sought before and swerving, stopping, bluff-passing, and with the occasional rapid acceleration, he ran through the field, only being brought down five yards before the opponent's goal line. The ball was quickly scooped up by a fellow team mate who took six large strides before touching it down, the winning try was scored. But everyone knew that this was really Penrose's try.

Watching, just for those few minutes, was Penrose's young, unmarried assistant housemaster called Piers Goulding. He taught Penrose mathematics, coached the second rugby team and every Wednesday afternoon he came on military parade as Capt. Goulding of the school's Officer Training Corps. The next week things happened to Penrose. He was called for training with the second team and put into the position of a blind side wing forward. In Goulding's maths class, his desk was moved from the back to the front row. In the Officer Training Corps, he was made up to corporal in his squad; all because Goulding had concluded that Penrose was capable but lazy.

It was Penrose's failure, through sheer absent-mindedness, to turn up to a rehearsal for the inter-house singing competition the following week, which was to bring Goulding and Penrose closer together.

Goulding's passion was cryptology. He loved anything to do with ciphers and codes. He had read mathematics at Oxford and stayed on for a further year to specialise in code breaking, but penury had forced him to leave and take up a teaching post at Wellington. Yet his fascination with the subject never ended. Consequently, his detentions always required the latest miscreant to try and break a code; sometimes taken from history and on other occasions from ones which he had personally devised. Goulding didn't expect anyone to come up with the correct answer. Instead he insisted on seeing pages and pages of workings showing what effort had gone into their failure.

Penrose's punishment was an exercise using the Caesar cipher which simply changed the order of the letters of the alphabet so that no word could be made out. It took most boys over an hour to work through the problem, but Penrose had it solved and checked through in less than ten minutes. Penrose cursed himself, as instead of sitting still for the rest of the fifty minutes pretending to work, he gave the result to Goulding who, instead of applauding his work, set him the task of cracking one of his own codes. About ninety minutes later, Penrose arrived in Goulding's study looking pleased with himself as he handed over the first verse of the school song. Goulding was aghast. It should not have been possible to crack that code and certainly not that quickly.

"How did you do it?" asked Goulding.

"You said it was one of yours, didn't you, sir?" said Penrose.

Goulding nodded.

"I thought sir, if it was one of yours, it would be based around solving a series of simultaneous equations because that's your interest, but nothing seemed to fit. It made no sense. I then wondered why you'd told me to write on the copy of the Economist you gave me. It was a strange thing to do. The giveaway, if I may say so sir, were the two letters 'EC', at the start and then the date and then the page number. With this information, I guessed you'd given me a one-time code pad, which you did. I thought you would use the Caesar Code or something like that to put it on top of the one-time pad, but you didn't, which thankfully made it easy or at least, just saved me some time."

"How do you know of the Caesar Code?" said Goulding.

"My father was in the army, sir. It's the kind of thing he made sure I knew," replied Penrose. "Once I had the first three words it was obvious that it came from the school song. Then all I had to do was work out how many letters you had used to find out how far into the song you had gone."

"Well done Penrose, off you go," said Goulding, as he sat feeling totally deflated. A code he had enjoyed developing was cracked by a school boy in less than a couple of hours. What made it worse was that, within a couple of hours, every boy in the school would know the way into the code so he couldn't use it for detention again.

"It was good fun, sir. So much better than the homework you normally set," said Penrose, trying to pay a compliment.

When Penrose had gone, Goulding reached into his case, drew out his record book and examined Penrose's performance during the year. The boy had achieved top marks in virtually every test, or written work he'd set. The next day, in the staffroom, Goulding went round every one of Penrose's other teachers to discover the same thing. No one really took any notice of him as he sat quietly in class giving the appearance of daydreaming, and yet his marks were always near to the top of the class, but never at the top.

"You know he speaks French fluently," said his French master. "Damn waste of time coming to my lessons. His father said something about a career in the Foreign Office; had him taught to speak French like a native."

At the beginning of the next school year, Penrose found himself moved into the top forms and a marked man. He was no longer able to loaf about. Things were now expected of him in every sense, and as happened on that fateful afternoon on the rugby field, Wellington School discovered that when things were expected of him, Penrose put in just the right amount of effort to succeed.

It was Goulding who encouraged Penrose to apply for Oxford but, although no Dovingdon had been to university before, Penrose considered Cambridge to be in the family history, for no other reason than it was so close to where they lived. So it was, aged 18, that Penrose went up to Downing College to read mathematics and he loved it. There was a freedom to study unbound by a classroom timetable.

At Cambridge, Penrose played rugby but was not good enough to get a Blue, tried his hand at rowing and decided it was only for masochists and, as at Wellington, he shied away from being the centre of attention, seeking to be liked but not popular.

The bargain with his father, on going to Cambridge, was that he would continue his French lessons and join the OTC; ever hopeful that one day Penrose would change his mind and decide to take a commission in his regiment. As Penrose had learnt from a young age, a bargain with Col. Dovingdon was not a bargain but an instruction, and so with his Certificate A from the OTC at Wellington he joined Cambridge OTC, charged with getting his Certificate B.

Penrose was a very reluctant soldier and therefore not a good one. He called it 'playing at war' and the hours of drilling, saluting, stripping guns and map reading were of no interest to him. On the other hand, he found battlefield theory fascinating and yet, whenever they went on manoeuvres to put the theory into practice, he found it total chaos. He had no clue as to what was actually going on. At summer camp, usually at Aldershot barracks, he would find himself in some mock battlefield which would last all day, never knowing who his enemy was, where he was supposed to be going, and least of all, who was in charge. He could not understand why the events on a battlefield could not be worked out like a game of chess, giving a weighting to each of the pieces and working out what move your opponent would make in response to your own. He began to understand the joy his father got from playing toy soldiers and refighting battles of history to show how the outcome might have been different. If Penrose were to do any soldiering, it would have to be around the tactics of war, not in the field of battle, as that was all too damn confusing.

In his last year at Cambridge, there were the usual competing approaches from the Foreign Office, the Colonial Offices and East India Company, often as a result of lobbying by his father, whose passion for maintaining the British Empire knew no bounds. Instead, Penrose took a position in the Treasury. It was a semi-compromise, going into Government which his father wanted, and doing something with maths which he wanted. However, he very quickly found that the Treasury had nothing to do with mathematics or, to be correct, had something to do with only one branch of it: namely, arithmetic and only then with the signs of plus, minus and percent.

The work at the Treasury was dull and set within a hierarchical structure which was stupefying. The pay was poor. Penrose would not have been able to enjoy London and his country pursuits if it weren't for the generous allowance he received from his trust fund set up by his father. Life was made bearable by invitations to the estates of friends of his father and even more enjoyable if a minister from another government department happened to be staying too, as the civil service rules of the day permitted Penrose to stay until the minister left. However, just as with his father, it was the work of the Royal Institution where Penrose found his stimulation. It's programme of study and lectures constantly gave him something to look forward to.

While Penrose looked outside his work for stimulation, it was becoming apparent that the Government's planning was focused towards one primary area, winning an arms race with Germany, or more precisely a naval race for control of the seas. In the melee, papers were written and rewritten, published, distributed, and left unread as the great ship of state sailed on regardless of the consequences. Penrose found it all too depressing to bear.

As with all great events, Penrose would always remember exactly where he was when he heard that war had been declared. Like all his colleagues in the Treasury, other than going to hear Sir Edward Grey's speech in the House of Commons, Penrose had not left No 11 Downing Street since hearing Foreign Office reports that the German army had crossed into Belgium, on its way to France. Being just a corridor from the Cabinet Room, and the Prime Minister, Penrose watched history unfold as a note was issued to the German Ambassador demanding the German Government recognize the neutrality of Belgium. It gave an ultimatum that their army had to leave that country by midnight on 3rd August. The German Ambassador gave no such assurances, instead he argued that Germany had invaded because they had unimpeachable evidence that France intended to attack Germany via Belgium.

Penrose was sitting with senior civil servants, and Members of Parliament serving in the Treasury team, in the office of the Chancellor of the Exchequer when David Lloyd George came into his room. He stood very still and slowly the conversations stopped. His face was engraved with an exhausted grief. Then, in a very somber tone, he said, "Gentlemen, I am sorry to announce we have received no assurance from Germany that they will respect the neutrality of Belgium by tonight's deadline. As a result, the Foreign Office has issued a statement declaring that a state of war will exist between Great Britain and Germany as from 11pm tonight. Further, Winston has just reported that the Admiralty has signaled all ships and establishments under the White Ensign telling them to commence hostilities against Germany. Gentlemen, I suggest we all go home. There is no more to be done tonight."

Penrose looked at the date. It was 4th August. He looked at the clock. It was exactly one-minute past eleven o'clock; sixty seconds after midnight in Germany. He felt a cold chill go down his spine which contrasted with the general excitement in the room. "Six months at most," said one. "More like six weeks," said another. Penrose's chill fell into a deep gloom as he wondered whether any of these people really knew what this was going to mean. He could contain the professional diffidence expected of senior civil servants no longer.

"There will be no quick win," said Penrose firmly, desperately trying to control his anger. "Germany will lose, there will be no doubt. It cannot fight a war on two fronts and expect to win. It was Napoleon's greatest mistake. Clearly no one in Germany has studied history. Watch what happens, the war we are now fighting will enable Russia to make a land grab up to and including parts of Germany. You wait and see, this war is going to divide Europe into two. It will end up pitting Britain and France against Russia. There is not going to be a good outcome."

The room went silent.

"Gentlemen," said Lloyd George, "it really is time to go home. Goodnight."

It was nearly two o'clock in the morning when Penrose finally left his desk. The night air was warm, so he decided to walk to help clear the putrid secondhand cigar and cigarette smoke from his lungs. As the fresh air hit him, he realised how very tired he was. In the previous few days he had helped to lead the Treasury Team responsible for dealing with the biggest run on the Bank of England in its history, and now the country was at war. He found it hard to believe.

As Penrose walked across Green Park, he was asking and answering the same questions as everyone else. Why has Germany done this? This war doesn't involve Belgium, or France, and certainly has nothing to do with us. It's a German-Russian war. However hard he questioned himself, the answer was always the same. It's that damn stupid treaty between France and Russia where each promised to protect the other. They both feared Germany's military might and, each knowing that it could not win a war on two fronts, had decided that they should form an alliance to keep the peace. While good in theory, it failed to take account of the personality of Kaiser Frederick Wilhelm II, the expectation that he would act logically and the pride of the German army. Hell, men are such damn fools, thought Penrose.

Chapter 3

London January 1915

MUCH TO COL. Dovingdon's continued disgust, Penrose didn't sign up when war was announced. The government needed money to fight the war which meant that lines of credit had to be arranged with countries of the Empire. As Penrose was to say to many a governor general, "Great Britain now needs a return on its investment," and it was their job, and Penrose's job, to get that return.

Right from the start, Penrose meticulously followed the fortunes of the British Expeditionary Force. By early September 1914, the German army was just 30 miles from Paris. Penrose read everything which was written about the French and the BEF's decisive victory at the Battle of the Marne which gave immediate hope that it would be a quick war. However, there then followed a race north to the sea as the Allied and German armies tried to outflank each other. With the Germans taking control of Antwerp, Penrose followed the BEF as it returned to fight the first Battle of Ypres between mid-October and mid-November and then when winter came both sides started to dig in. The two armies had fought themselves to a standstill with the BEF losing over 58,000 men. By the start of winter, Penrose came to dread opening The Times in the morning in case he learnt of the death of another of his chums from school or university. It was already a depressingly long list and getting longer.

Penrose discussed joining up many times with his work colleagues, who told him he was needed where he was. His father's view was quite different. It was his duty to take 'the King's shilling', he told Penrose immediately war was declared and the sooner he got on with it so much the better. As far as Col. Dovingdon was concerned, Penrose should join the Hampshire's, his regiment, there was none other. One phone call to the Colonel and a commission would be his.

Throughout Christmas and the New Year, Penrose's father fumed and then got angry at his son's failure to join up. The trouble was that Penrose saw little purpose in him storming a machine gun post and being shot with the first bullet. It had happened to him all too often in the mock battles he fought in the OTC[1]. He knew he was capable of a better contribution, but he didn't quite know what. Penrose's solution came when his clerk told him that he was leaving.

"I'm joining the Royal Engineers," said the clerk.

"Why the Sappers?" asked Penrose enquiringly.

"'Cause it's where the brains is, sir. They build the railways and things over there. I've always been good at maths. It's why I were given this job 'ere. Always 'ave been, and they need mathematicians to work out how to build things, so seems the place for me."

Penrose nodded approvingly.

"The place for you too, sir, if I may say so. It's 'em what 'ave the signals an' given how keen you are on coding...." The sentence was left unfinished.

Penrose thanked the clerk, wished him well, and thought little more about their conversation, for he had draft documents in front of him which had to be completed and issued in time for that afternoon's London bank clearing.

That night, Penrose dined alone at Found House, his father's house, in Mayfair. It was now a depressing place. Only the housekeeper was employed. The rest of the household had left to support the war effort. This meant that most of the house was shut and cold. Since the war started, the Colonel rarely came to London and when he did, he preferred to stay at his club where he had the company of others. Without the big fires in the drawing room, dining room and hall, the house seemed damp and a chill set about the place which made it singularly uninviting.

After he had eaten, Penrose retired to his bedroom, warmed with a roaring coal fire, and started to write the letters which he had been composing in his thoughts while he ate. His first letter was to the Colonel of the Royal Engineers, telling of his OTC certificates from

---

[1] Officer Training Corp

Wellington and Cambridge and seeking a commission. He took pains to explain his specialist knowledge of ciphers and coding. His next letter was addressed to the Permanent Secretary to HM Treasury, tendering his resignation with immediate effect. He then wrote to his father. Penrose found this a difficult letter to write as he knew his choice of regiment would not find favour. His letter to Juliette, his sister, scampered across the pages in a flood of fact and emotion.

Penrose stoked the fire and moved to sit closer to it. With more heat coming into the room, he started to draft a letter to his mother. He found this the most difficult letter to compose and after three false starts, with the earlier drafts thrown into the fire, he retired to lie on his bed where he quickly fell asleep.

Two days later, he had a letter from Major General Sir George Scott-Moncrieff telling him that, upon completion of his basic training, he would be commissioned as a Second Lieutenant. In the next post came a letter from the adjutant with a kit list, a joining date which was in three days' time, and instructions to report at Chatham Barracks. The only job he did not have to do which was on the list was to open an account at Child & Co. Bank, 1 Fleet Street, London for his pay and rations as, on the days that he and Juliette were born, their father had opened bank accounts for them at this very branch.

The following day Penrose handed in his letter of resignation. It caused an immediate rumpus. After a wigging from the Permanent Secretary and being told in no uncertain terms that he was deserting his post, Penrose was instructed to see the Chancellor of the Exchequer and explain himself.

David Lloyd George shook Penrose warmly by the hand and together the two men moved to the armchairs positioned in front of the fire. Lloyd George beckoned Penrose to sit, which he did.

"Look, Dovingdon," said Lloyd George, his welsh accent being accentuated for effect. "We can't have you going off like this. The war is being fought here too. The money for this bloody thing has got to come from somewhere and it's chaps like you who find that somewhere. You cannot leave, do I make myself clear?"

Penrose liked Lloyd George. He identified with many of his Liberal policies. He'd been chancellor for nearly seven years and, as a result, he towered above the department with a force of character and statesmanship which was rarely seen in government, but for all that Penrose never truly trusted him.

"Certainly sir," said Penrose. "The trouble is I've already accepted a commission with the Royal Engineers and if I don't report as instructed then I'll be charged as being absent without leave or, even worse, a deserter."

Lloyd George grunted a few words which Penrose didn't hear.

"Major General Scott-Moncrieff will no doubt assign me back to you, if you ask him."

Lloyd George grunted another few words which left Penrose both confused and embarrassed as again he didn't catch what was being said.

"You really don't need me now Maynard Keynes is back in our midst," said Penrose trying to find a way out. It was now obvious to him that Lloyd George couldn't care whether Penrose stayed or left. He was just doing his Permanent Secretary's bidding, as politicians have done from the moment the civil service was established, and probably long before then. "He is already doing the job of two of us," he added.

"Keynes, Maynard Keynes," repeated the Chancellor, who grunted one more time and then looked down at his papers. Nothing more was said. In the silence, Penrose knew that the meeting was over and so was his career as a civil servant.

The next morning, Penrose was up early with a feeling of freedom not felt since he left Cambridge. He had two days to prepare and in his usual methodical style he wrote, and then worked his way through a jobs list. At his tailor's he was told it would take six weeks before he could have a uniform. "We are a bit busy at the moment," said the Master Tailor apologetically. He was advised to try Harrods. Nevertheless, he placed an order, and then did as had been suggested.

At Harrods, Penrose purchased everything on his kit list including a service revolver, taking a perverse pleasure in charging everything to his father's account, except for a small portable camera with several rolls of film which, as it was a fun thing to have, he paid for himself. Finally, there was the visit to the family solicitor to draw up a Will; a few specific legacies to some chums but with everything else going to Juliette, his sister.

In the rush, Penrose didn't get back home to see his mother and explain in person his reasons for joining up. With guilt pouring through every vein, he wrote to her. He found it incredibly difficult to express the feeling of love he had for her, his joy of the life which she had given him and that she need have no fear that he was about to throw it away needlessly. *I am sure I will be able to make some difference, albeit right now I know not how*, he wrote, *but I would not be able to look myself in the mirror each morning if I did not try.*

Penrose also wrote again to his father who, very unusually, had accepted his choice of regiment with magnanimity but only on the condition that Penrose carried his great-grandfather's silver tipped officer's cane wherever he went. It had been given to Col. Dovingdon by his father when he took his commission and he now wanted Penrose to have it. Penrose thanked him for his gift and made the promise about the cane as asked. He also thanked his father for the offer of providing him with a man servant, which had been made in the same letter. Penrose turned it down explaining that he thought the Army would be able to provide him with a batman at the appropriate time. In reality, Penrose thought that he would have enough difficulty in the months and years ahead looking after himself. The last thing he needed was the responsibility of looking after a manservant. It was now obvious that those who had set off only six months before with dinner jackets and golf clubs, in great optimism that this would be over by Christmas, were now seriously mistaken.

Chapter 4

Cambridge January 1915

PENROSE'S LETTER TO Juliette was short, no more than two sides. He wrote to say he was leaving his job in the Treasury and taking a commission. It was time to prove to himself that he was equal to any other man. It was more important to him that he support his old chums in a role where he might be of some assistance, rather than writing another bureaucratic paper on some mindless issue which would never be read. But it was the last sentence which upset Juliette the most. *Please look after Mama and Papa*, he wrote. *I am sure Papa will be furious, for I am not joining his regiment, but*, he added, *I am sure they will do better without me, for I am not the best of soldiers.*

As Juliette sat in the library trying to concentrate on proving the equation she had been set by her tutors, her mind was elsewhere. The discussions over Christmas had shown to her that things were not going well, and now Penrose was asking her to look after Mama and Papa. He wouldn't be doing this if he thought everything was going to be all right. This small request made Juliette feel as though her world was on the precipice of some almighty change, but she could not work out precisely what, for hadn't they promised that this war would be won in six months?

Just after lunch, Juliette left her desk, donned her coat and scarf as, although the sun was bright in the sky, it was chilly outside. She started to walk with no particular route in mind, she first headed towards the city centre. A brisk purposeful pace took her walk along the backs of the colleges, then a footpath up to Lammas Land where she headed for the Grantchester Grind and through Grantchester Meadows. Juliette rarely walked on her own, always seeking company, as she liked to talk as she walked, but this time Juliette needed silence to think. By mid-afternoon she had arrived at The Orchard Tea Garden in Grantchester from where she made her way to Orchard House. It was an 'up river resort' well known to varsity men and women because it was where Mrs Stevenson served her famous afternoon teas of scones, cream, and jam. It was also where she took in lodgers, the most notable being Rupert Brooke who, on Winston Churchill's introduction, had joined the navy just fifteen months before. In four short months, he would be dead.

In the warmth of Mrs Stevenson's kitchen, Juliette removed her coat, scarf, and hat, and sitting at the scrubbed kitchen table, ordered tea for one. She said little, for she was still mourning the loss of an important concept, one that had been with her all her life, namely her brother would always be there for her. Now, he had deliberately decided to put his life at risk and in the process was sacrificing her future too. She did not see it as an heroic or unselfish act. To the contrary, it was, she thought, the most selfish thing he could possibly do.

As Mrs Stevenson warmed the scones and decanted jam and cream onto a plate, Juliette began to think through the issues for herself. She had read the papers and heard many opinions, but with mathematical theorems filling her every waking moment, none of it had really taken her attention. However, now that her brother was involved, she realised it was something she needed to think about, and hard.

With tea made and scones set out on a tray, Mrs Stevenson beckoned Juliette to follow her into the drawing room where she placed the tray on a table by the fire and then left Juliette deep in her own thoughts. Juliette was pleased to see her hostess go, for although she meant no harm and was only trying to be polite and entertaining, Juliette found her conversation banal when compared to the life and death situations that her brother and hundreds of thousands of other men were facing. Above all, what Juliette hated most of all was having her train of thought interrupted by a monologue which politeness required her to acknowledge.

It was dark outside when Juliette came out of her tranced state of deep thought and contemplation.

"Do you think you can call a cab to take me back to Girton, please?"

asked Juliette as she walked into the kitchen. "It's too late and too dark to walk back, and I must be back before lock-up," she added.

While she waited for the cab, which Mr Stephenson had to walk to the phone box in the village to order, Juliette engaged Mrs Stephenson in the conversation she was reluctant to have earlier. She knew what she had to do and was now comfortable in her decision.

Back at college, it took Juliette some time to find her friends who were cooking crumpets and teacakes in front of the fire in the common room. Their chatter was accompanied by 'La donna è mobile' from Verdi's opera Rigoletto. It was being played on the piano, slightly slower than normal and with the lightest of touch, by one of their number who had the remarkable ability to adapt and play any piece of music, making it suitable for the mood of the occasion. Juliette said nothing as she was enthralled by the sight of fingers dancing magically across the keys producing a sound which was both recognisable and unique.

When the piano playing came to an end, there was a silence, after which there was the sound of spontaneous applause from the gathered few. It was just at this moment Juliette announced her decision - she was leaving at the end of term.

The room fell silent.

"Why?" shrilled the chorus.

"Are you pregnant?" asked someone impertinently, immediately lowering the tone, while nevertheless saying what everyone else was wondering.

"No, of course not," retorted Juliette firmly. "We should all leave and become nurses. It's the one thing we can do to help with the war."

They all started to speak at once; different conversations were taking place all at the same time with everyone joining in each. The themes were broadly the same. Everyone thought it a good idea but after the exams, when their research was finished, after their degrees were completed and, of course, the war would be won by the time they finished their training. The negatives then came in a torrent. The uniforms were dreadful, dealing with bedpans would be ghastly, but then there were the men. They bantered over the glamour and the hardship well after Juliette had decided to head to her bedroom.

The next morning, Juliette rose early and, well before breakfast, she had written and posted her letter to the matron of the London Hospital, applying for a nurse training contract.

Chapter 5

Chatham England January 1915

PENROSE JOINED THE Royal Engineers at their Regimental Headquarters in Chatham. He was one of around fifty men assigned to an officer training squad. Some, like him, found their commission came 'in the post' as a result of their OTC experience, but most of the men were from the ranks who, given the urgent need for officers, had been identified as suitable material for officer training and would, on passing out, become a Temporary Gentleman for the duration of the war.

For ten weeks Penrose marched, was yelled at, stripped guns, and ran assault courses, bayonetted sandbags to smithereens and did hours of fieldcraft. In fact, he did everything which he hated about his OTC days at Wellington and Cambridge, but this hatred was reinforced ten times over, not least because it was for real. He found some consolation in the fact that he was not being trained at Aldershot, which was the training centre for the Yeomanry. This meant he had 'no bloody horse' to worry about, albeit years before he had been trained to ride at full charge at the gallop with his sword drawn. To both his surprise and chagrin, there was nothing in his course on the strategies and tactics of battle or war. But then, as he thought about this, it only added to further disquiet, for as any reader of newspaper reports, and competent in mathematics, could have worked out, as a lowly subaltern, his chances were not good.

At the end of his training, Penrose was ordered to join the Royal Engineers Reserve Battalion Signals Service; in particular, a new unit responsible for building and maintaining battlefield telephone systems. Penrose knew nothing about telephones, other than how to use them. With a deep depression descending upon him he made an appointment to see the Lieutenant-Colonel of his training unit to explain that coding and decoding of secret messages was his interest at Cambridge and that was what he joined up to do.

"Sir, I've been instructed to join the Royal Engineers Signals," said Penrose, by way of introduction to the discussion he wanted to have.

"Yes," said the Colonel with a smile of approval on his face. "I thought you'd like that given your interest in communications."

"Sir," said Penrose, "I thought I would be assigned to code-breaking as that was my speciality at Cambridge."

"Speak any German?" asked the Colonel.

"No, sir."

"Of course not," said the Colonel. "Damn stupid question."

"I'm fluent in French," said Penrose in dissent.

"Good man, but you can't break many German codes if you can't speak German, can you? So I thought the best place for you was with the Signals. Next best thing, don't you think?" said the Colonel, who then added, to make sure there was no debate, "Request denied."

Penrose had spent too long fighting his father to know that when one of his generation made a decision, there would be no going back, particularly when the plans were already in motion.

"Thank you, sir, most grateful, sir," said Penrose. He stood to attention, saluted and dismissed himself. And so he discovered first-hand how the decisions of war were made.

The Colonel returned to his desk, and without forethought, picked up a red ink pen and fatefully wrote on the front of Penrose's personnel file, 'Speaks fluent French'.

Chapter 6

London January 1915

IT WAS THE smell which struck Juliette the most. As she walked through the front door of The London Hospital she was unprepared for the stinging of disinfectant and carbolic as they hit her nostrils. This made her feel unduly nervous. Not a feeling she was used to. She couldn't quite work out how it was that when she went up to Girton, she did so in a state of composed excitement, and yet she was arriving here in a state of fear.

Juliette was pointed in the direction of Matron's office and there she sat outside with hat and gloves alongside several other girls all seeking a training contract. Juliette tried to compare herself to the others without speaking to them. She examined their clothes and faces for clues, but nothing gave her an idea of the competition or her ranking within it.

The interview with Matron was fierce. The wit and clever repartee which saw her through her Cambridge interviews had no wash with issues of nursing.

"Miss Dovingdon, we are not interested in knowledge for the sake of knowledge, but knowledge for the sake of its application," said Matron Lūckes. "If you want to research, to get more knowledge, then you should go and read medicine," she rebuked, to a poorly answered question. "We are about nursing and that is a specialist skill. Some of it is learnt, but most of it should be intuitive. It should come from being a caring person, without that attribute you are not suitable to do this job. Now, tell me about the medications you've administered when you cared for someone who was poorly."

This question left Juliette quite speechless for she had no answer. She had never looked after anyone who was unwell. As she failed to answer each question satisfactorily, Juliette cursed herself for the lack of preparation. She left the room feeling very inadequate. It appeared that getting into The London was harder than getting into Cambridge.

Juliette caught the train back to Cambridge suitably chastised. She began to think that nursing was not the career for her. Perhaps she should change her course at Cambridge and read medicine. Would this be possible? she wondered.

Juliette's solution came in the post a few days later when she was offered the job of trainee nurse starting her probation on a new additional course The London was starting on Monday, 1st February 1915. If she passed the exams, then seventy weeks later she would be allowed to start work on the ward where her training would continue. In addition to the formal letter came a short, handwritten note from Matron expressing her delight at Juliette's decision to become a nurse, saying that she couldn't think of anything better than for men to have her tending their wounds.

If the interview with Eva Lūckes was tough, it was nothing like the feeling of dread Juliette had at telling Mistress Jones that she was leaving Girton. The reception she got was completely different from the one she had expected. Jones fully understood. She regretted that Juliette would not stay until the end of the academic year, but she was a Girton Woman who would be welcomed back as soon as the war was over.

Juliette did as she was told and reported to The London Hospital School of Nursing on the Saturday afternoon before she was due to start her training on the Monday. It was bitterly cold and however hard she wrapped up she could not stop the chill digging deep into her bones. The trainee nurses' quarters were damp and cold. The geysers, which were supposed to provide hot running water, didn't work, and were never to work all the time she was there. However, Juliette's biggest shock was finding that, rather than having a room to herself, as she had at Cambridge, she was sleeping in a dormitory with eleven others.

On the Monday morning, Juliette and her new classmates, resplendent in ill-fitting and uncomfortable uniforms, gathered in the hall waiting to be greeted by Matron. They each studied the large hand bell which, before the days of anaesthetics, used to be rung when an operation was about to start as an instruction for all orderlies to come to the operating theatre to hold down the conscious patient. Thank God things had improved since those days, each quietly thought to themselves.

The first days in the classroom were incredibly strict and regimented. They were taught how to make beds with hospital corners, carry out bed baths and dress wounds. Alongside the scrubbing and cleaning, which was to be engraved in each of their eternal memories as part of the personal hygiene course, there were lessons in anatomy, physiology, general medicine and nursing care. Juliette found each of her classes fascinating. It was the first time she had realised the complexity of the human body and that held within it as much fascination as she had found in her studies of the universe.

There was one fact she could not ignore; it was that she was working incredibly hard. At the end of each day, she was physically exhausted and the little time she had off was spent catching up on her personal administration. There was, she found, no time for a private life.

Chapter 7

France June 1915

SITTING ON THE camp bed, Penrose read from his orders for the third or maybe the fourth time. After completing another 14-week training course with the Signals Service in Chatham, he had travelled constantly for three wearisome days, in a dismal mist of chaos and confusion, to join his new Company.

He had enjoyed his time learning the new technologies of telephone and wireless and the communication strategies from HQ, through Brigades down to gun batteries while, at the same time, becoming perplexed at the 50% casualty rate amongst the men sent out to repair the telephone lines damaged by enemy shelling and the movement of troops.

Penrose had spent the night before in a transit camp just outside Le Havre and from 6 am he had been on board a crowded train which travelled at speeds which made him think it faster to walk. Now, in this tented city in Étaples with 100,000 other soldiers, each in transit and waiting to join their regiment, Penrose was feeling tired and lonely, and with his kit still at the mercy of the British Expeditionary Forces transport system, he was feeling fed up. Now, with his new orders in hand, he was also both perplexed and confused.

He was to return to England and report to the Balloon Training Centre at Upper Grove House, Roehampton. There was no explanation. Accompanying his orders, was notice of his promotion to Captain; a matter which Penrose found completely ironic since he had not commanded a single man since joining up.

Penrose resolved to relax and stay where he was. That night he would dine in the officers' mess and in the morning he would track down the rest of his kit. Once found, he would take the next available boat home, but this time from Étaples. Another train journey of the sort he had getting here was more than he could contemplate, and certainly not before he'd had a good meal.

Chapter 8

Roehampton, England July 1915

AT THE BALLOON Training School, Penrose was greeted by a large, middle-aged gentleman who, from the size of his waxed handlebar moustache, had an air of an extravagant extravert about him. A fact which was reinforced by the strange mixture of uniforms he was wearing.

"Welcome to the Lovers. Bet you know nothing about this," said Captain Banks, introducing himself. He spoke with a booming voice, which suggested everything was a bit of a laugh. "Wing Commander Maitland sends his compliments. He's not here at the moment so he's asked me to look after you."

"Thank you," said Penrose perfunctorily. "I am completely in the dark."

"In fact, he's rarely here. Damn good chap, but he spends his time in London on committees trying to get training for flying machines properly organised," explained Banks.

"Oh."

"Do you speak French?"

"Yes, passably well."

"Explains it."

"Explains what?"

"Your posting. You're to command a Balloon Company. Don't know which one exactly, but it comprises two KBSs, Numbers 27 and 32 I think, not sure."

"What's a KBS?" enquired Penrose.

"They're at the southern edge of the line alongside the French," continued Banks, ignoring Penrose's question. "They almost abut each other. You'll spot for the French too." He paused. "Kite Balloon Section," he then said, answering Penrose question after a moment's contemplation. The ignorance behind it made Banks wonder about the wits of the man in front of him. "Well, they're supposed to have two sections but at the moment it only comprises about one and a half," he continued.

"Oh," said Penrose, none the wiser.

"They've not had a lot of luck recently."

"Who, us or the French?" said Penrose, wondering what 'not a lot of luck' meant in reality. Then he asked, "But what am I doing here?"

"You're going to be a balloonic. You're going to learn how to fly a balloon," replied Banks.

"What?"

"You're a Cambridge man, aren't you?" questioned Banks, concerned at Penrose's lack of understanding of his general situation.

Penrose just nodded, and then added, "Downing, read maths."

"You've got to learn everything about these things, even how to pilot them," said Banks, incorrectly categorising Penrose as a boffin with little practical common sense.

"Jesus!" exclaimed Penrose.

"Don't worry, it's not hard, we can teach you everything you need to know in about three, may be five, days, but given this is the army, we've got fourteen weeks."

"Why so long?"

"I don't know, but haven't you noticed how every training course in the army lasts at least 10 weeks?" he added, sarcastically.

Penrose hadn't.

"It's all terribly easy. You make hydrogen. You pump hydrogen into the balloon. The balloon goes up 'cause hydrogen is lighter than air. You're in the basket underneath which goes up too. When you're at about three or four thousand feet, you have a good look around to see what's happening. You get winched down and report what you've seen. Nothing to it, really."

"Only two things about that," said Penrose. "Hydrogen is darn dangerous, pretty flammable stuff if I remember my school chemistry, and don't we spot for the artillery to make sure they hit their target? And isn't there's something about the enemy not liking our balloons in the sky and trying to shoot them down?"

"Yes, something like that, probably explains why it takes fourteen weeks," said Banks who was now more confident of Penrose than he had been a few moments before. "No one's really ever told me," he added, shaking his head. "We find we make it up as we go along. It's more fun that way. Come on, let me show you to your room. Oh, you'll need this," said Banks throwing him a book.

Penrose caught it and read the cover, 'A Manual on Military Ballooning.' He looked up in surprise.

"Yeh, we even balloon by numbers!" retorted Banks, reading Penrose's thoughts.

"You said, as we were introduced, welcome to the Lovers. What is that all about?" asked Penrose.

"It's what we've nicknamed ourselves, after some gunnery officer came here and demanded that we train balloonists to get up close to the front, fly higher and fly longer. He said all we had to do was to train you 'to provide what every woman requires from her lover; closer, longer, higher'. Well, since then it's been a bit of a motto."

Penrose snorted in amusement.

Over the fourteen weeks, Penrose discovered that Banks' jocular naivety belied an enormous knowledge of ballooning, artillery, aeroplanes and the fieldcraft of spotting. Although he had never served at the front in any campaign, Banks ran masterclasses in the effective use of balloons in battle.

The ballooning course was as intense as any Penrose had ever attended. He was one of three officers in his squad of 30 men, the rest of whom were NCOs, and all were training to be pilots or spotters. They would be flying the new Drachen kite balloons. Strictly, they were still in the process of being trialled, but their improvement over the notoriously unstable spherical balloons meant that they were already in practical use. These kite balloons were easily identified, being shaped like a large sausage with another sausage wrapped around its back to half-way under its belly and with a tail fin. There was not a thing about ballooning which Penrose didn't learn. He learnt the work of the riggers, sewing and sticking the seams of the balloon together, and rope and wire splicing, so that he knew how to inspect the work of the most junior of soldiers, for it was impressed upon them, many times, that their lives could depend upon it.

Penrose's first flight was from Farnborough Common. The balloon handling party walked the balloon out from the hanger onto the common and as the wicker basket rose from the ground he became concerned as to how small it was and how low its sides were; it would be far too easy to fall out, he thought. However, as they rose higher over the Surrey countryside, Penrose relaxed and simply marvelled at the views below. He was seeing the world as a bird saw it and he found it the most exciting thing he had ever done. He had a new passion and if this was going to take him to war, then bring it on.

Chapter 9

London August 1915

JULIETTE LOVED NURSING. Although the work was hard and the regime tough, she couldn't remember ever being so fulfilled. She was constantly busy dealing with an ever-growing number of very sick men, mainly Canadian soldiers, badly asphyxiated, some with lost eyesight, as a result of suffering chlorine gas shell attacks as they defended a very small, but strategically important, area of ground known as Hill 60, near Ypres, in the early part of May.

Just as she had been all her life, once Juliette got interested in a subject, she became slightly obsessive about it, needing to know everything there was to know about it. As a result, she read beyond the basic curriculum, which she found easy to grasp, and became known as a bit of a 'smart alec' among her contemporaries. It also meant that, at the end of each day, Juliette was both physically and mentally exhausted. However, it was the capture of Nurse Edith Cavell which was to change the course of Juliette's life for ever.

Cavell had been a pupil at the London Nursing School and was matron of Berkendael Medical Institute, a hospital and nurses training school, in Brussels. She used it as a staging post to help numerous British, French and Belgian soldiers, who were stranded behind enemy lines, escape in to neutral Holland. On 5th August 1915 she had been arrested by the Germans on the charge of spying and had been tricked into giving a full confession of her activities. Apart from this, the only evidence the Germans had was a battered UK post-card from a returned soldier thanking Edith for her help. After a two-day trial, Edith was found guilty of treason and sentenced to death.

The indignities of shooting a woman for treason riled the sense of British fair play. It was the discussion of the moment as the papers wrote of the representations being made by the Americans and Spanish to spare her life, but to the young women probationer nurses of the London Nursing School, not enough was being done.

"We have to do something," said one probationer.

"She's one of us," said another.

Juliette watched as the mood developed, not making any contribution for there seemed no obvious solution.

Firmly and authoritatively, Judith Perfett, one of Juliette's colleagues, summed up. "It seems to me that, apart from launching a raiding party, there is only one thing we can do. The papers are saying that her best chance is with the Americans getting the Germans to give her clemency. Her next best chance is getting Field Marshal Sir John French to agree to a prisoner exchange which includes her."

"He'll never agree to that," a voice chipped in.

"Maybe, but we have to try. It's the one thing we can do," said another voice.

"How do we get to see Field Marshal French? He's in France and very unlikely to see us," commented a third voice.

"We write, all of us," said another probationer, enthusiastically.

"But he won't get them; the letters will be stopped before they get to him."

"We have to see him. There must be a way?"

Juliette joined the conversation. "I'll ask Lord Cecil to make an introduction. I'm sure Field Marshal French will see us then."

"Who are you talking about?" said another voice, louder than the rest. "Do you mean Lord Robert Cecil in the government?"

"Yes, I know him. At least, we've been introduced. I went to a party and stayed at Hatfield House in my coming-out year. I've been a few times."

"You've come out?" screamed all of the girls together. "You've been to Buckingham Palace and curtsied in front of the King?" asked another, just to make sure she had it right.

Juliette nodded, not wanting to say anything more. Although she wore exactly the same uniform as everyone else, she could not help radiate a difference which, over the months, had been ignored by her peers, as she found happiness in their company and they in hers. They all knew she had been to Cambridge and was better educated than them, but her mistakes as a probationary nurse were as bad, if not worse, than everyone else's, and this made her one of them. But once again, through these few words, they were all reminded that Juliette was different, for her speech and deportment were of a 'toff'. For some, it explained more of the person they already knew. For others, there was a sense of betrayal giving rise to an immediate feeling of hostility; of having a spy in their midst. Juliette reddened up in an overwhelming sense of embarrassment, something she had not done for very many a year.

It was to prove a fatal remark, for group planning took over. Juliette was to write to Lord Cecil asking whether he would be so kind as to write to Field Marshal French introducing her, as she would be in Saint-Omer and it would be a pleasure to meet him. Judith Perfett, one of Juliette's louder, pluckier colleagues who had suggested the idea, would accompany her. They would both take overdue holiday to go. There was a suggestion of a whip-round to pay for it, but Juliette, ever embarrassed by the subject of money, said she had enough for both of them.

That night, Juliette and Judith went to bed wondering what on earth they had got themselves into, but each was too worried about accusations of cowardice by their colleagues to say or do anything other than that planned.

Chapter 10

France September 1915

"WE ARE ALL equals in the eyes of the Lord," repeated Juliette to herself, almost as a mantra, as she and Judith climbed the steps to General Sir John French's Headquarters in Saint-Omer. Any hopes Juliette had of Lord Cecil ignoring her request for an introduction, were banished almost by return of post with a handwritten letter acceding to her request and wishing her a safe trip.

Juliette and Judith took enormous care over their appearance for their meeting with Sir John. It provided a much-needed boost to their confidence. They had starched and pressed, and pressed again, their uniforms with particular attention to their white aprons and the white collars and cuffs of their dresses. The creases to the veils of their white caps were perfectly formed such that their head dresses rested squarely across the back of their shoulders.

The place Sir John had requisitioned to lead the largest army in history was much smaller and far more modest than Juliette had expected.

After much waiting, Juliette and Judith were shown into a large room. French was sitting at one end, and as he saw the two ladies come in, he stood and walked to greet them. As he moved, Juliette noticed that he walked with an imperiousness worthy of a man who was described as the most capable cavalry commander of his generation. She found this odd, as it was being widely reported that the President of France had described French as 'a plodding engineer who was not very military in appearance'. Except, if French had not been so highly regarded, he would have been dismissed from the army long ago; firstly for an affair with another officer's wife and then for an affair with an Indian railway mogul's wife, He was notorious for carrying on a series of affairs with beautiful mistresses among the higher echelons of British society, of which Mrs Winifred Bennett was the latest and living with him in Saint-Omer.

"I didn't know that gloves went with a nurse's uniform," French observed casually, as he shook their hands and introduced himself.

"We wear them when we're on parade," said Judith confidently.

"I've inspected nurse parades before, and I can't remember seeing white gloves. Have we Parker?" He asked of his manservant.

"Perhaps, you haven't had the honour of inspecting the nurses of The London Hospital," said Judith tartly.

"Perhaps you are right," conceded French. "Please, take a seat," he instructed as he returned to his desk to look for the papers relevant to the meeting.

"I have a letter here from Cecil introducing you," said French aimlessly, as he read the letter feeling a little perplexed as it didn't say why. "If I may say, he keeps very fine company. How do you know Robert?"

"We're family friends," Juliette replied.

"His letter doesn't say why he wants me to see you."

"We have come to ask for your help for Nurse Cavell," said Judith abruptly.

They had debated long and hard about what they would say and how they would say it, and now, contrary to all their plans, Judith had come straight out with it.

"That's quite impossible," responded French, with frustration in his voice.

"We just need your guidance and instruction, sir," said Juliette, speaking softly to try and recover from what was a bad start.

"We are happy to be at your service to do anything you ask to help free Nurse Cavell," said Judith, following Juliette's conciliatory tone.

"As I said, it's quite impossible." He paused. "Ladies admittedly last year hasn't gone well for us. The problems we had with our high explosive shells are no secret, but this is a war we are about to start winning. It is a war we are sure to win."

"If we can't do anything, surely you must be able to help with a prisoner exchange. I am told the Americans will facilitate if you agree," said Juliette, in an imploring tone.

"Please understand, it is simply not possible for me to swap a civilian non-combatant for a German combatant. Can't you see that puts one man extra into their fields whereas I get none? In a war of attrition, each man counts," he added.

"But," interjected Judith, "this means you are valuing a man's life more than a woman's."

"Nurse Perfett," French said angrily. "What do you think I do all day? I have to put some men's lives at greater risk than others. It's not nice but it's the only way...." He paused for thought and then continued, ".... the only way we will win this war. We are at war. You understand that?" he added crossly.

Juliette and Judith were shocked by the force of their rebuke, for he was, of course, right. He had a dreadful responsibility.

"We have the Americans trying to do their best for Nurse Cavell," continued French, in a much gentler tone. "As a result, this matter has become highly political. Please believe me when I say that I have not been tardy, but understand, there is nothing here that you or I can do."

"If we can't do anything here, is there something we should be doing somewhere else?" asked Judith very cautiously.

"No! the debate is closed," said French firmly. "The future of Nurse Cavell is in the hands of others; but there is another matter." His tone changed immediately as did his subject. It was as though he had switched off one personality and switched on another. "There is a serious shortage of nurses at our clearing hospitals. If you can work there, then this will free up a couple medics to work at our ADSs; every little bit helps."

"ADSs?"

"Advanced Dressing Stations. These take the wounded men from the RAPs[2] on the battlefields, patch them up and send 'em off to hospital. You will save more than one life there," he said with a hint of sarcasm. They both nodded wisely, although neither of them knew what an RAP was either.

"Sir," said Judith, "we are under a tutelage contract with The London Hospital that will be expensive and difficult to break."

---

[2] Regimental Aid Post

"If you agree, I will arrange for Matron to be written to and the situation explained. I'm sure she will understand."

Juliette and Judith looked at each other and smiled a knowing smile.

"Carlton will liaise. He will deal with everything, ladies," said French waving in the direction of an officer. He stood up and returned to his desk. The meeting was over.

Carlton led Judith and Juliette outside and into the small library where they had been placed to wait when they first arrived. "Quite fortunate," he said, "as Miss Becher, Matron in Chief of the QAIMNS, is meeting with the General in two days' time. We'll arrange for you to see her and she can sign you up then."

Juliette knew of the Queen Alexander Imperial Military Nursing Service. Her initial plan had been to become a QAIMNS nurse, but because they had set a minimum age qualification of twenty-five, she did not apply. However, Carlton's obvious enthusiasm for the meeting meant she said nothing of what appeared to be an immediate problem.

"What are you doing tonight?" asked Carlton.

"We're staying in the same lodgings as last night," said Judith.

"We were expecting to be here just for today, going home tomorrow," continued Juliette.

"And it's frightfully expensive. I think they are charging double because we're from England and obviously not with the army," added Judith.

Carlton nodded in appreciation. "Here's the plan," he said. "You will dine with us in the evenings until you've seen Miss Becher. I will arrange for your lodgings to be commandeered while you are here. This means you only pay the agreed army rate. I presume you are sharing a room?"

They nodded in unison.

"Good, I will arrange for a driver to take you back there now and collect you at 6.30pm this evening. We don't dine here. There's not enough room. I'm sure Mrs Bennett will be delighted to have your company."

Juliette just hoped that Carlton did not hear her intake of breath at the mention of Mrs Bennett, for how was she going to explain this to her mother?

Juliette and Judith spent the next two days enjoying Saint-Omer. During the day they wore their civilian clothes so as to keep their uniforms clean and smart for the dinners in the evening. Mrs Bennett was a delightful hostess, and despite the formalities of the evening, Juliette could quite see why General French would want her around him. She had that lightness of touch which meant that, for those few moments when they were together, he was able to forget the terrible burden which had been placed on him.

Judith was petrified by the thought of a formal dinner. She had never experienced an event like that before, but with instructions to follow everything Juliette did, and not to argue any point, she found, to her surprise, she was enjoying herself, being the attention of many an admiring officer.

The interview with Miss Ethel Hope Becher took place at Sir John's HQ where she had ensconced herself as though she had every right to be there. She, too, had trained at The London Hospital under Miss Lückes, and from her stern appearance it became immediately obvious to Juliette and Judith that Miss Becher appeared to mirror herself on their nemesis. Miss Becher had seen service in South Africa and was about to retire when she was asked to take over as Matron-in-Chief. As with Sir John, Juliette and Judith could see that the responsibilities weighed heavily on her shoulders.

It was The London Hospital and training under Miss Lückes which provided the common bond between the interviewer and interviewees. It allowed Becher to proceed in a strangely informal manner with questions, not designed to catch them out, but simply to understand their level of experience. They also worked out together that they had just managed to complete six months of service in a home hospital, which was the minimum requirement before a nurse could work overseas. There were only two sticky moments. The first was when Becher asked their ages and then quickly retorted "don't answer that," adding quickly afterwards, "We are about to reduce that as we need more recruits." The other was when she asked why they didn't join the VADs.[3]

---

[3] Voluntary Aid Detachment – volunteer nurses.

The look on Juliette's face said it all. "I only ever apply for the best," she said.

Becher's response was to make it clear that, in joining the QAIMNS, they would be subject to military law and military discipline and the penalties which came with them.

"There is one other thing," said Judith. "I am under an indenture with The London Hospital which requires that I have to pay them back for my training if I don't work in their hospital."

"So am I," said Juliette.

"Yes, but you can afford to pay them back. I can't," said Judith sourly.

"When I write to Miss Lückes for references, I will explain that you will be completing your training with us and request, no insist, that she releases you from all your obligations. Does she know you are here?"

"No," they responded in unison.

"Then please write to her as a matter of priority, explain the circumstances, and offer your resignation."

The two girls nodded. Miss Becher rang the bell which was on an occasional table close to her armchair. The appearance of a white-coated orderly signalled the interview was over.

"Where and when do you want us to report?" asked Judith.

"Oh, we haven't covered that, have we?" said Becher. She looked down at her papers, selected two pages which she studied carefully and then said, "General Hospital No 3 in Le Tréport; they're quite busy and could do with some extra help. It's in a newly built hotel on the clifftop; quite pleasant. Report there the day after tomorrow. They will be expecting you."

Chapter 11

France September 1915

Dear Ma and Pa,

I am sure my handwriting on an honour envelope will have surprised you. It will be even more of a shock when I tell you I have enrolled in the QAIMNS and will be in France for the duration of the war. I cannot tell you, until I get home, how I came to be here and why I have to stay, but you have to believe me when I say that none of this was planned.

Judith Perfett, from The London, came with me and is staying too. She is marvellous. Honestly, the best friend anyone could have. Her surname, when mispronounced, is exactly the way she is. Sometimes I think she would make an excellent wife for Penrose. She's so much brighter and much less snooty than his normal women friends.

Our first posting has been to a General Hospital right on the seafront. I'm not allowed to say where, but we are a long way from the front, so there is no danger. The first few days have proven the work to be long and hard but incredibly rewarding. I'm still expected to study for my nursing exams, although there is no time for lectures and no books to study from.

On the first two nights we were in France, we dined with General French and Mrs Winifred Bennett. As I sat at the table, I knew how strongly you, Mama, would disapprove but Mrs Bennett was so kind, particularly to Judith, who is not used to such grand company. She is a lovely looking woman, very tall and attractive with a huge sense of fun, so I do not think we should judge her too harshly for supporting our host, on whom there is a tremendous burden.

Please send my love to Penrose. I worry about him so.

Your ever-loving daughter,
Juliette
Ps. Mummy, will you please collect my things from The London.
I have written to Matron so she knows what has happened. I will
need my nurse's uniforms and some ordinary clothes. If you think
boarding school and not Ascot, then you will know what to pack. I
will write with my postal address very shortly. Thank you x

Chapter 12

England September 1915

THE WEATHER OF late spring and early summer 1915 meant that Penrose could not get the requisite number of flights, so it was not until mid-August that he passed out of his ballooning course. He had nothing like the required number of hours in the air to be a pilot; nevertheless, he was deemed competent to take charge of a Kite Balloon Section and was promoted to the rank of Major. Penrose was not sure why, but it added to the mystery of everything that was happening to him. He felt he was the least deserving, and certainly the least trained, major in the whole of the British army.

Penrose was given five days' leave which he spent very quietly with his parents, for there was no one around. The pride that Col. Stoddart Dovingdon felt in Penrose's achievement was only matched by the anger he felt towards Juliette for absconding without his, or Matron's, permission. Penrose would have sworn that, if she were much younger and at home, his father would have put Juliette across his knee for playing truant. Penrose was entirely the opposite. He was enormously proud of her, but secretly so, for to have said any words of support would have been akin to blasphemy.

Col. Dovingdon and Penrose had few conversations about the advantages of balloons in battle, for they were immediately self-evident. The Colonel was far more interested in the future of the aeroplane and whether Penrose should learn to fly, which Penrose rejected, saying that he had spent too long in training and it was time for him to get into the fight.

In the evening of his last night at home, Dovingdon shared with Penrose the investment opportunities which were on his desk.

"Do you know one in four men wears a wristwatch?" said the

Colonel as he passed a copy of an investment prospectus for H. Williamson, a watch making company, to Penrose, "And the other three are planning on buying one. It's going to be a huge business."

"As long as the watches are buried with those that die," said Penrose, in a sarcastic throwaway comment. However, that totally whimsical remark meant that the prospectus went mistakenly into the bin, with nearly all the others, for an investment in H. Williamson would have provided an exceptionally good return.

"We've been offered the licence to the UK rights to the hookless fastener by the Universal Fastener Company of New Jersey in the States," continued Dovingdon throwing what would become known as the zip to his son. Penrose played with it. He recognised its ingenuity, but when told it was a replacement for the button and its likely cost, he, like his father, was certain it would not catch on.

"This is one I am going to go for," said the Colonel emphatically, passing over another investment document. "It's a business I understand. We've made most of our money by investing in steel and in glass making. This is just an extension. It's rustless steel. I think some people call it stainless steel. If you add chromium and carbon in just the right measure to a steel alloy, it doesn't rust, and the army is desperately keen to have it."

Penrose listened as his father waxed lyrical about the products and projects he was investing in and the way he structured his investments. He went to bed that night enthused about his father's investment business. For the first time, he thought he might like to do something like that when the war was over.

Chapter 13

France October 1915

PENROSE MADE HIS way through the trenches, very conscious of his undeserved promotion to major. It was a hard and arduous journey as the ground was sodden underfoot, sapping his energy. He kept tripping over trench boards and ladders as he worked his way through men who formally moved aside to let him pass. As part of the Royal Flying Corps, he had made his way into France through their base at Saint-Omer racecourse, completely oblivious to the celebrity treatment which had been enjoyed by his sister earlier at army HQ.

Penrose had travelled by horse-drawn cart to the front and now, with a haversack and kit pack weighing him down, he struggled on, making something of a spectacle, for it was rare to see an officer on his own carrying his kit bag, let alone one of his rank. They had servants or batmen to do that. Strangely, Penrose felt obliged to turn down every offer of help which came from every sergeant he passed to prove something to them and to himself.

Occasionally, Penrose stopped to ask the way and each time the response was a mere grunt and a point in the general direction. The feeling of despondency amongst the men was as palpable as it was worrying. On the last occasion he asked the way, Penrose was pointed back in the direction he had come and so it was that he found his way to the dugout of 32nd Kite Balloon Section.

It was past dusk and turning quickly into night as Penrose entered the dugout. He stood in the door for some time observing the scene before him until he was spotted and a voice shouted "Attention." There was a scramble as men slowly rose from the floor, their chairs, their beds, and their slumbers, only moving faster to get to attention when Penrose came into their gaze. The air was damp and stale, but it was exhaustion which oozed out from every one of the men's pores. Behind those eyes, which he could see in the half light of just a few candles, there was a darkness. It was as though each man's character had been lost in numbness.

The scruffy voice which shouted attention had come from a small, stocky, balding man who was clearly older than the rest. He had sergeant's markings on his arms and from his presence he was clearly in charge.

"Is this the HQ 32 KBS?" asked Penrose, taking off his helmet.

"Yes sir," replied the sergeant.

"Good," said Penrose. "Stand the men at ease sergeant and carry on."

The sergeant bellowed the instruction as though he were on a parade ground, more in an effort to impress Penrose that he was in charge of his troop than it was to allow them to return to whatever it was that they were doing. But there was little immediate movement, because each was studying their new commanding officer and wondering if he was going to be better or worse, but most importantly, luckier than the last.

"Do I have any quarters, sergeant?" asked Penrose.

The sergeant pointed to a curtain, and without saying anything, led Penrose further into the dugout. Behind the curtain was a bed, a desk, a table with some very rudimentary washing equipment, a makeshift cupboard and a set of shelves made from stacked bricks and planks. Although it was wet outside, the earth walls of the dugout were dry and warm. From the way in which everything was neatly organised, it was, for its previous occupant, clearly a prized hideout from the chaos going on beyond the curtains.

"Sorry sir," said the sergeant, as both their eyes alighted at the same time on a bundle of personal effects on the chair by the side of the desk. "We haven't had instructions on what to do with Captain Chivers' things."

"Captain Chivers?" said Penrose, tipping his head slightly in an enquiring manner.

"Yes sir, the officer before you."

"What happened to Captain Chivers?" enquired Penrose, desperate to learn more about Chivers' fate, but more importantly what he was supposed to be doing.

"Didn't make it, sir. We wasn't able to get him landed before Jerry shot him down. You see sir, the Captain wouldn't jump, sir. Trouble was sir, Captain Trowton before him died from jumping." The sergeant paused and then asked: "You a jumper, sir?"

Penrose ignored the question for he had not considered the issue before. "How many officers have you had?" he enquired, becoming very conscious that he outranked the two previous incumbents.

"You'll be the fourth in the last year, sir. It's a bad spot here for officers."

"And what is it we do precisely?" said Penrose.

The sergeant looked amazed. "You don't know, sir?" he asked.

Penrose didn't reply. Instead he asked, "Where are the junior officers? I am supposed to have three lieutenants," he said, in the hope that one of them would be on hand to give him the briefing he had been promised.

"Mr Holmes is on compassionate leave, sir. In Blighty on a sevener, back in a couple of days. Mr. Conwright is in hospital, pneumonia we think, but don't really know. Quack came up, beg pardon sir, doctor came up on an inspection and sent him packing pronto. Mr. Gray is with 27 Section in Ypres."

"Oh," said Penrose now completely nonplussed by the news. He walked to the chair behind the desk and sat down. The lights from the candles in the main area of the dugout cast a very faint shadow across the mud walls of his anteroom. As he moved, Penrose spotted the stub of a candle, glued by wax onto a saucer, perched in a hollow dug into the earth wall of his chamber.

"Do you have a match, sergeant?" said Penrose.

"Light for the officer," bellowed the sergeant.

Immediately the candle stub was lit a glow was thrown around the room, for behind the candle, were tens of pieces of broken mirror. They had been stuck onto the mud, assembled as a mosaic, causing the light to sparkle in all directions as the flame flickered. Penrose moved forward to study it, for this was no mirror stuffed behind a candle to give more light, but some painstaking work designed to give joy, which it certainly did.

"Who did this?" asked Penrose, pointing to the work of art with his helmet, which was still in his hands.

"Major Finton, sir. You'd 'ave known him as Lord Finton. Our first commanding officer when we was set up," said the sergeant.

Penrose had never heard of either Lord or Major Finton before, but all the same, nodded as though he knew his name.

There was a silence. Sergeant Wilkinson didn't like silences, especially when he was with those who he considered to be of superior class.

"We spot for the southern edge," said the sergeant, responding to the question Penrose had asked some time ago. "Every day we send up the blinking balloon and report movements, but mainly we give coordinates for the gunners to gun. We tell them whether they're too short, too long, too far one way or too far the other, but we're in a bit of a phoney war here, sir. We send a few rounds over to tell Jerry we're still here and they send a few rounds back. It's all a bleedin' waste of time."

"Yes, I understand all that," said Penrose curtly, for he knew his duties. "What's your name, sergeant?" he asked.

"Sorry sir, 204710 Sergeant Wilkinson," he responded, standing to attention. He then stood quite still as he watched Penrose remove his trench coat and start to settle in. He was wondering whether he should go or stay, for it was clear to him that Penrose's mind was elsewhere.

"Thank you, sergeant," said Penrose, turning around to address him. "I'm ...," he stopped himself for he had not spoken of his new rank before. "I'm Major Dovingdon, your new commanding officer; stand easy."

"Sir, we also run to and from the French," said Wilkinson. "We're supposed to spot for them too, but we have no way of communicating with their artillery ... that's if they had any 'ere," he added sarcastically. "It explains why we're away from the main battlefields, out on a limb. The French, they're about three quarters of a mile away over there," and he waved in an odd direction.

"You speak Frog, sir?" asked Wilkinson.

"Yes, sergeant, I speak French," said Penrose, the expression in his voice showing disapproval of the derogatory term.

"They all spoke French before y'us. It's why you're 'ere sir. It's 'cus you speak Frog."

"I speak French sergeant, not Frog," said Penrose firmly. "Please, let us not use that expression about our allies."

There was a pause, for Penrose was now beginning to put in place the missing information as to why exactly he was here.

"What's this about running?" asked Penrose, placing his helmet on the desk so he could take off his haversack, as suddenly it felt very heavy.

"We run for three days and they run for three days and we pass messages to each other. I don't know what the messages say. It's always top secret. Seems the officers give each other reports on enemy positions."

"Who runs?" said Penrose. "And where to?" he added, now completely confused.

"We run to the French side and they run to our side."

"Aren't our trenches side by side – together?"

"Oh, no sir. There's just under a mile between the end of our line and the beginning of theirs."

"Are you saying that we are at the edge of an unprotected flank, sergeant?"

"It's the higher-ups, sir. They don't want us mixing with the Frogs."

Penrose raised his eyebrows and sighed in disapproval as Wilkinson continued in the same breath, "Beg pardon, sir, I believe the expression they use is 'an unreliable influence'. I think they worry about the French ..." he paused, "... revolting, sir." Wilkinson smiled as he enjoyed his own pun, and Penrose smiled back. At that moment, these two men knew they would get on well.

"A phone connection is too much, I suppose?" said Penrose.

"Can get listened into, and in any case, I'm told the wires keep getting broken. I think it's been suggested many times before, but no one pays any notice to us out here. Sometimes," said Wilkinson reflectively, "I think we are fighting our own little war."

Penrose decided it was time to bring the conversation to an end. "This is what we are going to do," he said. "I'm going to take one hour out to prepare myself. Then you are going to give me a briefing on the men. It will take no more than one hour, then in the morning, at 10.00 hours, I'm going to do an inspection."

"The balloon is due up at 10 am," said Wilkinson.

"On whose orders?" asked Penrose, perplexed.

"Don't know sir. It always goes up at ten hundred hours. Bloody stupid if you ask me 'cause Jerry knows when to come for us. Clockwork Charlie we call 'im. It also brings a ton of flak 'cause we've shot at 'em and then they fire back at us. It's all such a predictable fuck up."

"Then tomorrow the balloon will go up at twelve hundred hours. There will be a late inspection at 10 am. From the glance I had of the men earlier I think they're going to need longer to get ready than usual, don't you? I don't want to be putting men on report on my first day, do I, sergeant?"

"No sir, good idea sir," said Wilkinson.

"One-hour sergeant," said Penrose, and with that Wilkinson was dismissed.

"Sergeant," called Penrose, just as he was leaving. "Sorry to trouble you," he shouted "but how about a cup of tea? And take those, please," he said, pointing to a bundle belonging to the former occupant. "Make sure that they are returned to Captain Chivers' family."

"Sir, there's a nice pistol in there with quite a lot of ammo. It would be best if that stayed here. You never know. Came with Captain Trowton and Captain Chivers said it should stay."

"Doesn't seem a very lucky pistol to me," said Penrose, thinking of its recent history.

"Think of it as third time lucky, sir," Wilkinson replied quickly. "We're a bit short of helmets and a bit poor on boots, and some of his cooking stuff will be very useful unless you brought some in your kit."

"All right, sergeant," said Penrose, knowing he was beaten in this debate. "I'll have the pistol and ammo. You separate out the rest of the kit into what you want to keep and what should be returned. Make a list of everything that is being kept and I will make sure that Captain Chivers' family is paid for what we keep. If I explain that this is in the best interests of the war effort, I'm sure they'll accept that."

"I'm sure they will, sir," said Wilkinson, who left the Webley

Revolver in its officer's leather pouch and a bundle of ammunition lying on the bed. He then backed out of the room carrying the personal effects of a man whom he had really liked but was no more.

At last Penrose felt able to make this small place his. He placed his helmet over a metal bar which had been banged deep into the earth to create a coat peg and off came his trench coat which he placed on top.

"Sir, sergeant suggested you might like a cup of tea," came a voice from behind, and with that Penrose was presented with a delicate china cup on a saucer and a small silver tray. "Sorry sir, no milk or sugar."

"Thank you," said Penrose who was surprised to find country house service at the front, "and you are?"

"Private Cable, sir. I came out as Lord Finton's man. It was His Lordship who set up this unit. After he was shot, I joined up and became batman to Captain Trowton and then Captain Chivers.

"Doesn't seem a very lucky job, does it?" said Penrose, enquiringly.

Cable took that remark to be referring to his job, whereas Penrose was referring to his own position, as he was somewhat in disbelief at the news he was hearing.

"It's okay sir," said Cable. "Every one of them was a gentleman, treated me jolly well.

"By the way sir," said Cable pointing to the china cup and saucer. "They came out with Major Finton. I didn't return them home sir because I knew he wouldn't want me to until after we've won. Whenever Major Finton bollocked, pardon expression sir, bollocked someone, he always gave them a nice cuppa tea after. You know, 'fined one shilling and have a cup of tea'. Been a bit of a Company tradition ever since."

"Erm," said Penrose, "I don't think it is one I will be following."

Penrose took the tea and thanked Cable in a manner which made it clear that he was being dismissed. He sat on the bed and sipped at the hot tea. The sharpness of the tannin bit into his taste buds. Nevertheless, it was good and it gave him the revival he needed.

Wilkinson's briefing lasted much longer than the hour, as he insisted on telling Penrose an anecdote about each of the men under his new command, so it was much later than planned when he blew out the candle and his cabin was plunged into darkness. His last thought, as he drifted into sub-consciousness, was the effort which had gone into making sure that, as far as 32 KBS was concerned, the war was fought with as much comfort as possible. He wasn't sure what he expected, but it was not this. It was as though each of the officers before him had resigned themselves to the fact that the war was going to be a long haul and they were determined to make the best of a bad job.

Chapter 14

France October 1915

Note to reader: Those not interested in Penrose's active service in World War 1 may miss this chapter.

PENROSE WOKE MUCH later than he intended. He set no alarm, and since he had given no instructions as to what time he should be woken, Cable allowed him to sleep. However, as soon as Penrose was awake, Cable produced a cup of tea, a basin of hot water, soap and someone else's shaving kit. His boots, which had been cleaned of yesterday's mud and dirt, now shone. Cable knew how to make himself invaluable. Breakfast comprised a couple of very tough dried biscuits and another cup of tea, after which Penrose decided it was time he went for a walkabout.

As Penrose stood at the entrance to the dugout, he discovered it was a beautifully crisp clear morning. More importantly, he could see that the entrance was not facing the trenches as he thought it did the night before, but rose through a few steps into a clearing between some trees. The shelling, which had pounded some distance away through the night, had stopped, and although men were everywhere, each going about his duty, there was an eerie silence. It was going to be a warm day and hopefully the sun would dry out the dampness of yesterday. Penrose was just about to move off when he heard some coughing behind him. He turned around.

"Excuse me sir," said the man with the cough, who stood to attention and then saluted. "Sergeant Wilkinson sends his compliments but was wondering if you would like to be shown around. Might be best sir, can't have you being shot sir, not on your first day."

Penrose looked at the man. From Wilkinson's briefing the night before he knew he was being addressed by Sergeant Castleigh.

"You'll recognise him straight away sir, because he talks posh like you," said Wilkinson and he was right. Penrose was also told that Castleigh looked young, too young to be a sergeant, which he did. "Very bright man," said Wilkinson of Castleigh. What he did not say was that this tall, thin, wire-framed man was incredibly strong, and most importantly, he feared no one. He got the respect of his men not by putting whoever challenged him on a charge but by rising to the challenge and whipping the poor sod into a pulp with the strength of a punch from a bare knuckle fighter; all contrary to King's Regulations, but when you box for Durham University, as Castleigh did before the war, you learn a trick or two. It was quick and simple justice, easily understood by the men who never complained.

"Yes sergeant, that would be helpful," said Penrose.

"I need to get my weapon, sir," said Castleigh, "Can I suggest you do the same, sir?"

Penrose nodded remembering Wilkinson's words of the night before. "Best soldier you'll ever meet, sir. He's a natural; one of the few who can read the land."

Penrose, very conscious he had a lot to learn, collected his pistol, checked it for bullets and switched on the safety catch. "OK, let's go for a walkabout."

Chapter 15

France October 1915

Dear Ma and Pa,

I have discovered I am no Florence Nightingale. I thought this at The London but now it has been proven. I have been moved from the wards to work with the surgeons in the operating theatre. It is so transformative. The operating theatre is a place where order is made out of chaos. Everything has a beginning and an end. The men arrive dirty and in such bad condition and they leave clean with a chance of recovery. It suits me so much better.

The amputations are awful, but that is not as bad as the stomach and chest wounds where the agony is immense and the chance of recovery so very slight. The discipline is unbearably rigorous; worse than at The London. They make no allowances that there is a war on and we are working such long hours. Though we are supposed to get time off, we never get it, because there is so much to do and we are so short of people to do it.

Judith is wonderful. I think I have found my very best friend in the world. She's always there to help long after she has completed her own jobs.

I am a long way from the front and therefore remain safe. I am very well looked after.

Please tell me about Penrose. I do worry about him.

Your ever-loving daughter,

Juliette

Chapter 16

France October 1915

Note to reader: Those not interested in Penrose's active service in World War 1 may miss this chapter.

PENROSE APPEARED ON the parade ground exactly two minutes before the parade was due to start. He stood at the side, watching what was happening. Unusually, he had paid particular attention to the way he looked. He knew over one hundred pairs of eyes would be upon him. He was a little nervous as it was the first ever inspection he had carried out. He had been on parade many times but never in this role.

Penrose moved into the centre stage at exactly 10 am at which point Sgt. Wilkinson shouted, "Parade, parade attention." The word was elongated but on the sound of 'shun' and the men's feet coming together on the wet grass, a grey horse appeared at a canter from one of the tracks coming through the woods. The horse slowed down at the edge of the parade, broke into a trot and then came to a halt just a few yards from Penrose. The rider dismounted, marched up to Penrose where he stopped, stamped his feet, came to attention, and saluted.

"The Colonel sends his compliments, sir. He wants to know why the balloon hasn't gone up."

Penrose returned the salute, looked at the Sergeant Major and deliberately took his time before answering. "Sergeant Major," said Penrose, "we both know that is not true."

The Sergeant Major said nothing, for he was bewildered by the challenge. He had moulded every officer before him and none had challenged him straight out, as Penrose had just done.

After a period of silence, in which each expected the other to speak, Penrose provided an explanation. "Sergeant Major, the parade started at exactly 10 am when you appeared. Exactly the time when, historically, the balloon has gone up. Ipso facto, the Colonel cannot have known that the balloon had not gone up at the time you left him. Accordingly, Sergeant Major, the Colonel cannot have sent his compliments with the question you asked. I presume it is you who wants to know?"

"Sir," said the Sergeant Major, without providing further comment while absorbing the possibility that this officer was sharper than the others before him. "Sir, why are we having a parade and not putting up the balloon per standing orders?"

"Because, Sergeant Major, it is what I ordered and I expect my orders to be obeyed," said Penrose sharply.

"Sir, the Hun will be over any moment now. To parade all the men right now is unwise; it's too dangerous."

"Thank you, Sergeant Major. If you would care to take time, you will notice that the guns are manned and only C and D troop are on parade. The others are on perimeter watch. I think, in the circumstances, proper precautions have been taken."

The Sergeant Major stood stunned, for he knew that, despite being a major, Penrose was very much a rookie officer and for him to have behaved with such battlefield skill was unheard of. Penrose allowed him time to wallow in his discomfort, while being secretly grateful for the advice he received from Sergeants Wilkinson and Castleigh during his informal morning tour. He was learning fast. He had to.

"May I carry on, Sergeant Major?" said Penrose, allowing obvious sarcasm to creep into his voice to show his disapproval of the distraction.

"Sir."

The parade continued without further issue. Instructions for haircuts were given, rifles ordered to be re-cleaned and re-inspected. Penrose made a point of putting no man on a charge. Just at the moment the parade had been dismissed and with the field emptying, there was a shout of Jerry at 10 o'clock. Where's 10 o'clock wondered

Penrose, for he had no concept as to where 12 o'clock[4] was. Did anyone else know? Immediately the shout was up, two German aeroplanes, nicked named 'balloon busters' came into view. Their sound travelled before them. The battery of guns started firing while Penrose stood staring as shells exploded around the planes with little puffs of smoke and a muffled sound following some tenths of a second later. The Lewis and Vickers machine guns, issued to defend the balloons, streamed lead into the air. No plane was hit but Penrose took delight in the way his company reacted and went to war without him giving any instructions; each sergeant leading his troop as though he were an officer.

The planes flew on, then turned around and flew back. On their return journey they were greeted again by Penrose's guns; this time causing the planes to weave through the air. It was all jolly exciting, but a little disconcerting given the number of shots fired and their failure to hit their target.

When in the officers' tent surrounded by his non-commissioned officers, Penrose congratulated them on the turnout, making sure that his remarks were qualified as being 'acceptable in the circumstances' and then in a light-hearted way, enquired as to whether the guns had ever hit a German plane. The way those around him jocularly dismissed the notion worried him. Being one of those expected to go skywards, he found the fact that he had little or no protection from his ground guns a matter of grave concern. He was told that other KBS guns had managed to shoot down German planes, but not them. Their best efforts seemed to comprise putting holes in their own balloon; a poor situation which needed rectification, he noted without comment.

Penrose took his first battlefield balloon flight at 12 noon precisely. He gave no orders. He just granted permission to carry on when asked. The professionalism of those he was commanding impressed him. His pilot was Corporal Stanner and even though he had 1,000 hours of airtime he, like nearly all the pilots under Penrose's command, had

---

[4] The clock method is used to identify targets where directions are related to hours on a clock face and 12 o'clock is straight ahead.

not yet achieved the 1,600 hours necessary to be qualified and get his wings. Nevertheless, immediately the corporal stepped into the balloon, he was in charge. Even though he was of much lower rank, Penrose had to follow his every order.

"Cast off," shouted the corporal, and with that all the riggers holding the stays of the balloon let go. The balloon rose quite quickly until it caught the weight of the winch cable, unlocked to free wheel, and with the grasping sound of the winch fading away, Penrose floated into the air. The sky was bright and beautifully clear, albeit very cold.

"It's much better we go up now rather than in the morning," shouted the corporal, "as the sun is now in the south, and moving behind us, we can see so much further. When they send us up first thing, we are looking east into the sunrise and it's damn difficult to see anything."

Penrose nodded in appreciation. Once again, he thought he was ascending into heaven. He loved being so high, seeing the world as though he were a bird. Normally there was a quiet whistle as the wind blew through the guide ropes or a squeak as the basket strained under their weight, but today there was no wind, the sky was blue and bright, and the conditions were just perfect. Penrose took time to reflect for, if there were no war, this would be the best job in the world. The beauty before Penrose's eyes was mesmerising. It meant that he was not paying attention to the detail as he should.

As they climbed higher, Penrose was fascinated by the symmetry of what he saw below him. The English and French held the high ground with their trench lines jiggering in and out across the top of Célieux Ridge along which he could easily see a chain of five woods each almost abutting the trench line. He could immediately see why the trench lines had been placed where they were because each of the woods made a natural defensive barrier. Penrose had already been told that each wood was exactly 1,500 metres square, just under one-mile square, with 1,500 metres of free land between them. It meant that the distance between the northern and southern edges of the chain of woods of Célieux Ridge was just over eight miles long and, from this height, he could see every part of it.

The trees had been planted well over a hundred years before as a present from the farmer to his four sons. The middle wood behind the British line had been reserved by the farmer for himself. Exactly in the middle there was a clear area of 1,000 metres square which, before the war, had been set to lawn. It was where the farmer used to hide himself away from the trials and tribulations of the day. But with the lack of attention, it had become a paddock. It was where Penrose had inspected his company earlier that day.

"Cotta's Patch, sir," said Cpl. Stan Stanner, pointing out their parade ground. Penrose nodded.

As they rose, Penrose noticed there was an unfamiliar uniformity about the area which puzzled him. It was not like England where roads, hedgerows, ditches, streams and rivers did not run straight but meandered across the countryside in an unplanned muddle. Penrose contemplated the fields below him for it looked as though it had all been engineered by the kind of person who couldn't bear a crooked picture on the wall. But then, as he remembered his French history, one thousand years of marching armies, and the tidy minds of the French, he had his answer.

"The French trenches, sir," said Cpl. Stanner pointing. Penrose nodded again. From this height it was easy to see why the British and French had decided that this was the point where their lines were not to meet for no attack was going to be made from the north or the south through those woods. For the Germans to attack from the east would mean a long charge across open fields and then up the sharp incline of Célieux Ridge. It would be sheer murder to give such a command.

"So our trenches are in front of the three woods to the north and the French trenches are in front of the two woods to the south?" Penrose asked in clarification.

Stanner nodded.

Penrose looked directly to the east and just a few metres away from the zig-zag of British and French lines was a straight road running north to south which would have made an excellent supply route, except it was high on the skyline and far too easy a target.

"By controlling the Ridge, we can observe almost everything to the East," continued Stanner proudly, at the same time pointing into the distance at the village of Mivry and its impressive church tower and steeple.

"Mivry's pretty much deserted now," he continued. "We are fairly certain there are no Germans there, only a handful of locals, but look behind, further east, at the small town of Mincé. A garrison of Germans occupy that. It should have no real strategic importance, except there is a railway line ending there."

"Single or double line?" asked Penrose.

"Single up to the head but then it leads into a spaghetti of sidings." Stanner paused. "When we are up here, we pay particular attention to what's going on there, as they've occupied that town for a reason, haven't they, sir?"

They both looked at each other.

"You can be certain of that," said Penrose, bemused by Stanner's reference to spaghetti.

Stanner pointed west, behind the French guarded woods, and in the distance, towards the small village of Coeur de Foucy which was the headquarters of the neighbouring French reserve company. It was easy to assume that, with the church situated at the crossroads and with the white tents in the surrounding fields, the village would be an obvious target, but the topography of Célieux Ridge meant that the village could not be seen from the German lines. Although it had been attacked, it meant that the attempts were sporadic and the village had remained largely undamaged by the German guns.

"If you look to the North West, you will see the town of Archez," continued Stanner. "It's where our RHQ[5] is based."

Penrose strained his eyes but could see nothing obvious, although with his field glasses he spotted, through the midday haze, what he thought was the seat of all those that ruled over them. It was the British and German lines which fascinated him as, at some points, they looked only inches apart. Furthermore, as he looked into the distance the two lines seemed to merge into one, making all those who observed it, appreciate the illogicality of the war and wonder what it was really all about.

---

[5] Regimental Headquarters

While they were climbing to the agreed height of 4,000 feet, Stanner was working hard plotting each and every change in their view. The smallest of details was important because it gave a clue as to what was happening on the enemy side. Any movement of any carriage or freight car on the railway line was noted and every truck or car movement was recorded, for this information was the lifeblood of the intelligence officer. The corporal worked hard with his pencil, drawing neat sketches of roads and land with a cross recording each change.

"How do you remember what was there before and what has changed?" asked Penrose.

"I box, as I was taught, sir. "

"Box?" asked Penrose.

"Yes sir, it's what all observers do." Penrose shook his head in bewilderment which encouraged the corporal to go on and explain.

"You take an area which you box in; a bit like choosing the edges of a picture frame. You see that church, the crossroads, the wood and the barn?"

Penrose nodded as he followed Stanner's hand pointing to the objects in the distance.

"Now you stare inside that box so as to remember everything in it. You then close your eyes and you imprint onto your mind exactly what you have seen. Some do it in colour, sir, but most of us do it in black and white."

It was obvious from his expression that Penrose was struggling.

"At the start, you might find it best to join your thumb and forefinger from each hand to make the box, bit like the frame of a picture," said Stanner demonstrating as he spoke.

Penrose did as he was told. He stared and studied hard and then closed his eyes covering them with his hand as he tried to imprint the vision which he had seen before him. Nothing happened. He stared again, this time taking a smaller frame which was no bigger than a small drawing-room painting. He studied the picture in more precise detail, slowly engraving, in the darkness of his mind, the picture he saw before him. By the time he had finished, in Penrose's memory was a picture, a mixture of black, white and sepia with the odd spots of colour. Penrose wondered why he had not been taught this trick at Balloon School and, still struggling, he questioned how good he was going to be at doing this. Hopefully, it would be something that would come with practice. In fact, like all trained spotters, Penrose would soon be able to recall that picture, and many others he would create in his mind, even weeks and years later.

Suddenly, Penrose was overtaken by a deep penetrating cold, for the basket, which only came up to their waist, provided no protection from the elements. Even though the sun was up, there was a very cold wind coming from the north and it was freezing him to the core. His body was now hurting. He wanted to go down to get warm.

"How much longer do you need, corporal?"

"None, sir, I was done ages ago. Ready to go down when you are."

"Yes, I'm ready."

"It's been a long flight, sir. We aren't usually up this long unless we're spotting for our guns in which case we can be up here at least a couple of hours and sometimes nearly all day."

Penrose picked up the 'phone and gave the order to winch them down. As they descended, he kept checking to make sure that his mind picture was fixed and not fading. Every time he thought it was lost it reappeared as though it were a dream. This war had already taught him an awful lot, he thought.

Penrose was greeted on his return to his bunker by an order from HQ instructing him to report to his Regimental Colonel the very next day.

Chapter 17

France October 1915

Dear Ma and Pa,

Thank you for your letter. I was so pleased to hear that Penrose was back in England even if it was only for a little while.

My job has changed since I last wrote. Dr Barclay, the surgeon I worked with in the hospital, got moved to a Casualty Clearing Station because he was needed more there. It seemed right I should go too. It means I'm closer to the front but in no danger. The danger is at the Regimental Aid Posts. I go to those occasionally but only when there is no sign of fighting, just the shelling which never ends.

When I first arrived, I was hopelessly frozen to the spot when I saw badly injured men arrive from the battlefield, but soon you get the hang of what to do and while the nervousness and anxiety never leave, the fear which initially stopped me from doing my job has, I am pleased to say, now passed.

Sometimes I look after the wounded men on their journey by ambulance to the hospital, but because it has not stopped raining and everything has turned to mud, it makes the conditions both harsh and difficult. It is on these occasions that I realise I am becoming quite a suffragette, as it would be far more sensible if I could wear trousers like the men. We've all shortened our dresses a little, but they are still too long so remain inconvenient and impractical.

I have decided that I'm going to study medicine when I get back to Cambridge. Perhaps it is only when you have looked inside the body that you really discover what a fascinating instrument it is. Too much is taken for granted. I particularly want to research why some men die and others do not. We have men with the worst of injuries who should die but do not, and others who are not badly hurt but somehow give up the fight and die. I can see no obvious pattern and it makes no sense. If you could find some general medical and surgery books to send me, then perhaps I can make a start on those studies now.

Judith is marvellous. Honestly, she is the best friend anyone could have. I do not know what I would do if she was not here to keep my spirits up. All the officers love her. She could have the pick of any of them.

Please send my love to Penrose and ask him to write. I worry about him so.

Your ever-loving daughter,
Juliette

Chapter 18

The Somme, France October 1915

Note to reader: Those not interested in Penrose's active service in World War 1 may miss this chapter.

WITH A BORROWED horse, Penrose made his way to his regimental HQ. He was grateful for the detailed instructions on how to get there for it was a long way, as he had seen from the sky the day before. The regiment had requisitioned an old country château for the war. It was once a statement of the wealth of the owner but now, with a large number of tents in the ground to deal with an expanded number of people, it looked faded and worn.

As Penrose walked through the front door into the large hall, it appeared that everyone around him seemed to know what they were doing and were busy doing it; whereas Penrose was certain that he did not. It confirmed Penrose's perplexity at a system which, on his signing up, had taken control of his life, moved him hither and thither, promoted him at each stage of the way, and had now given him a job for which he knew he was singularly unqualified.

Penrose was shown into a large drawing room where there was a strong fire burning gently in the grate. It was a warm and welcoming sight on another bright but very cold day. Penrose was warm from the exertions of his journey, so with his greatcoat removed, he sat in a leather chair placed around an occasional table in what, he observed, had become the officers' mess. A soldier, immaculately dressed in a white jacket, enquired what he would like to drink, but before Penrose could contemplate an answer he was told that the Colonel would see him now.

Penrose knocked and waited, didn't hear any response, knocked again, waited a little longer and then decided to walk in. Penrose came to attention, saluted and then waited. The Colonel assiduously watched his every move. "Major Dovingdon reporting, sir," said Penrose making a deliberate point of speaking and not shouting.

The Colonel had taken over the former drawing room as his office into which he had moved the dining table to give himself an enormous desk. Scattered around the edge there were a few dining room chairs and, from the marks on the wall, it was clear that the former occupiers had taken into storage a large number of paintings.

Col. Bertrand Jones loved being a soldier, but he hated war. In his entire career he had never been to war before and now his hatred of war, and in particular this war, was beginning to pervade all his thoughts and actions. He did not, he kept telling himself, join the army to kill people. He just wanted to play sport, see the world and have an adventure. He never took soldiering seriously. It was something which had to be done to keep his men occupied while he played. Anything and everything about soldiering was tedious. It was with a natural skill that he selected damn good soldiers as his non-commissioned officers and made sure that they were close at hand with every one of his promotions. It was why a gentle whisper in the Colonel's ear from his NCOs of long standing could have such a profound effect. The only bit of soldiering Jones liked was practising cavalry charges. He found them incredibly exhilarating, galloping full speed, sword drawn, horses all around him, yelling like a true trooper. It was better than any hunt or chase and Jones would take his men anywhere if there was a charge they could join, for he strongly believed that tedium killed the soul of any soldier as effectively as any bullet.

Jones had also worked out that there were two ways to get on in life; either by being damn good at what you do, which required an awful lot of hard work and luck, and he was never going to work hard at being a soldier, or by making sure that you have all the right friends and connections, and to this end, Jones worked as hard on keeping and maintaining contacts as some others did on their soldiering. By making sure he was involved in everything, and responsible for nothing, Jones excelled at War Office politics; that was until he got this post, where, he had now concluded, he was unfortunately responsible for everything! It was perhaps why his first question to Penrose was, "Do you know the Minister for Munitions, David Lloyd George?"

"Yes sir," Penrose replied. "I was in the Treasury when he was Chancellor of the Exchequer. We were together the night war was declared.""

"Do you know Lord Asquith?"

"The Prime Minister? Yes sir."

"Do you know Sir Edward Grey?"

"Yes sir, I was in a meeting with him the day before war was declared."

"Do you know General, Sir John French?"

"No sir."

"It appears your sister does."

"You surprise me," said Penrose.

"Is your sister Miss Juliette Dovingdon?"

"Yes sir."

"She knows Sir John," said Col. Jones firmly. "They met last month in Saint-Omer."

Penrose chose not to comment as the news came as a complete surprise. She had said nothing to him about meeting him.

"Kings Regulations and Orders 1912, Section 212 requires you to report personally to me on joining your unit. Why did you not do so?" asked the Colonel, deliberately changing tactics.

"I presented myself here, sir, at 8:00 am on 10th October to report as required. I was told by one of your staff officers, I don't remember his name, to take up my post and that you would call for me at the most convenient moment. I am assuming this is that moment."

"What's this about you disobeying standing orders?" said the Colonel abruptly, not wanting to be put off by what was clearly a satisfactory answer to his first line of attack.

"Sir, I'm not aware of any orders that I have disobeyed," said Penrose, having already armed himself with the answer. Instinct had rightly told him that there would be a rapport between the Colonel and the RSM which would require careful management.

"The balloon going up at 10.00 am every morning, as instructed."

"Sir, I took command of my unit at midnight on 10th October. I have received no orders from you since. I have checked standing orders and there are no instructions there fixing flight times. I have checked with my three sergeants and each has confirmed that there are no written instructions on when the balloons should fly, but then ...." Penrose took a short breath. "It does not surprise me because no commanding officer would want to deliberately put his soldiers at risk."

Col. Jones had dealt with more crap and bullshit from his officers and men than would fill a farm yard. He had learnt that the longer he allowed someone to speak, the more they would either hang themselves in their own guilt or prove their worth. He therefore deliberately remained silent, in effect giving Penrose permission to fill the void.

"Two officers and two observers have been killed in the last eight months and each incident coincides with the balloon going up at 10.00 hours. Even if we put the balloon up in a different place within an area of two square miles, they would quickly find us. We are damn bad at shooting down their attacking aeroplanes. My gunners have not shot down one German plane since they were formed, so while it's dangerous for them, it's damn dangerous for us. Importantly, it means we can't do our most crucial job, sir. The best time for launching our spotting flights is either just before sunrise so we can report immediately on overnight movements, or in the afternoon, when the sun is behind us, as that substantially improves our view. Under my command the balloon will be going up at different times but far more often. I assure you sir, you will get the same intelligence coverage, if not better, and we will always be there to spot for the gunners."

The Colonel said nothing. He squeezed his lips together and nodded in appreciation. If there was an order, Penrose was now sure it had been cancelled.

"And the French?" said the Colonel. "What's happening with them?"

"I haven't met my French counterpart yet. We still receive and send written messages which we pass immediately to HQ."

"Very important, those meetings," said the Colonel. This time it was Penrose who allowed the silence to fill the room as he had no idea of the real purpose of these exchanges.

"At HQ, we get told complete rubbish by the French. They tell us what they think we would like to hear, not the truth; makes it bloody difficult when you can't trust your allies."

Penrose smiled at the hypocrisy, as only two or three weeks before the start of the war a delegation from the French Ministry of Finance called on the British government asking them to support the French franc as part of the war effort. Penrose had been in the meetings telling the French that the British government would do everything it could to support their currency, despite knowing damn well that they didn't have the reserves to help themselves, let alone the French franc. More importantly, the British government was doing everything to try and keep the peace between Germany and France and therefore to take sides by supporting the franc would have sabotaged those efforts. "It's a diplomatic lie," he remembered Sir Edward Grey saying at the time, "and they never count."

"It's through your network we get to hear exactly what is going on, or at least we get a better understanding," continued the Colonel.

"What?" said Penrose in disbelief. "We are using this to spy on the French?"

"Mais oui," said the Colonel, breaking into schoolboy French, "but be assured that they are using it to spy on us too."

"Are we worried about that?" asked Penrose.

"No, the French hate the Germans more than us. For that reason, we have no fear in telling them the truth, however bad. Whatever our chaps say will only support what we have already said."

"But sir, idle chatter kills," protested Penrose.

"Not this time, dear boy, idle chatter saves lives."

"Is there anything you need?" said the Colonel changing the subject.

"No sir."

"Good, because I couldn't have got it for you," he retorted sharply. "Have you met your junior officers?"

"No sir. Mr. Holmes is on compassionate leave; Mr. Conwright is in sick bay and Mr. Gray is with 27 KBS which I have yet to find. I will make their acquaintance shortly. I've had good briefings from the sergeants, so I feel equipped to get started."

"Major, your promotion was necessary so your rank was above that of your French counterpart. It was no longer appropriate to have a Captain parlaying with a French Captain. Please don't think your rank makes you a wise or superior soldier. You know nothing of this war, or its burden, and have a lot to learn. I am instructing you to proceed cautiously. The Colonel slowed his voice and he spoke a little louder. "And, make sure you take advice from those who have been here longer than you."

It was as un-oblique an instruction for Penrose to do as his RSM suggested as had ever been given to any officer. At least it explained Penrose's rank which, until that moment, had been a complete mystery to him, although it didn't explain why the two officers before him had only carried the rank of captain.

"One last question, if I may," said Penrose.

The Colonel looked up.

"I have a sense that, at Célieux Ridge, we are fighting a bit of a phoney war. Is this right?"

The Colonel stared intently, for the question displayed a perception which none of Penrose's predecessors had previously shown, albeit that it was actively discussed by the junior officers and NCOs[6] who were stationed there.

"Three times a week," continued Penrose, "our guns fire ten rounds each towards the German lines in Mivry and Mincé, plus whatever is needed to try and shoot down whatever flies overhead to protect our balloon. They fire a similar number of rounds back. Most of theirs go into the woods; very rarely do they score a hit on our line. Neither of us is trying to move forwards."

"From Célieux Ridge we can control the volume of traffic on the railway line going into Mincé," explained the Colonel. "Our assessment is that it is very unlikely that the Germans will want to take the Ridge because the cost in lives will be too high for a limited strategic gain. However, even though you might rarely use it, you always make sure you have a lock on your back door, don't you?" The Colonel paused. "In any case, it keeps the French happy and it's a good place to put the reserve KBS when you are up to full complement."

The Colonel nodded to indicate that was the end of his answer.

---

[6] Non-Commissioned Officer i.e. Sergeant or Corporal.

"I'm sure you want to get back to your men, so I won't delay you," he said. The interview was over.

Penrose saluted and left. After he had closed the door behind him, he stood for a moment looking into the hallway and wondering what had just gone on. He was dismayed at the way he had been dismissed as he was expecting to dine that evening in the officers' mess. For the past 24 hours, he had been looking forward to a bath, a properly cooked hot dinner, and most importantly, some clean sheets.

"Survived your first interview?" said the Staff Officer who appeared as if it were his job to rescue each child just after they had been chastised by the headmaster. "No shouting?" he continued.

"No shouting," repeated Penrose.

"We were expecting you to get a royal bollocking for not sending up your balloon on time. He is a stickler for punctuality."

"No bollocking," confirmed Penrose, bewildered that such a small issue should appear to be so widely known.

"Are you dining tonight?" asked the Staff Officer.

"I wasn't invited. In fact, I was semi-ordered back to my men."

"Aah, so you won then."

"Won" said Penrose, becoming aware that he was constantly repeating what had been said to him immediately before.

"If you get a bollocking you tend to get invited to dinner to show no hard feelings. Prove yourself right and your reward is being right."

"Very perverse," commented Penrose, then he remembered what Pte. Cable had said about Major Finton, 'fined one shilling and have a cup of tea'. Is this the way the war is going to be won, he wondered.

"Would you like a bath and something hot to eat before you go back?" asked the staff officer.

Penrose nodded wistfully before being led away by the same officer, who chatted gaily about nothing as he led him to an enormous bathroom at the top of the Château. There another white jacketed orderly appeared with towels, washing and shaving kit.

Penrose soaked in the bath. With his hair washed and his face muscles relaxing under a hot towel, he reflected on how very strange his first few days at the front had been. There was gunfire but he had seen no actual fighting. There was a determination to maintain a standard, just as though they were at home, which seemed to deny there was a war. He was also perplexed for he had an overwhelming sense that underneath there was a change taking place for, in the trenches, there was an intermingling of class which appeared to him to put an unfair burden on the conscripted man. Penrose thought of his French history and wondered whether war led to revolution or revolution led to war. He could not remember. As he soaked in the tub, the water getting slowly colder, he wondered for the future of Great Britain once the war was won ..., if it was won.

"I'm surprised to see you," said Sgt. Wilkinson on Penrose's return. "I thought the Colonel would have invited you to dinner."

"Well, we're both wrong on that one," said Penrose.

"Balloon up at 10.00 hours tomorrow, sir?" asked Wilkinson.

"No sergeant, per the rota, please."

"Lieutenants Holmes and Conwright are back. Shall I send them to see you?" asked Wilkinson, while simultaneously contemplating that the RSM's training of Major Penrose Dovingdon was probably going to take longer than usual.

Penrose nodded and went into his cabin within the dugout and closed the dividing curtains. He threw his things on the bed, sat down at his desk and then it dawned on him. In a world of chaos and uncertainty he liked this cabin, as here, in this smell of dust and dirt, he was wrapped in a womb of peace and quiet.

First Lieutenant Denis Holmes and Second Lieutenant Clifford Conwright presented themselves together. They were told to stand easy. The first thing that struck Penrose was how incredibly young they were. The second thing was how alike they looked. They could have been twin brothers. Both were tall, wiry and willowy with wide brown eyes and smile lines replaced by a no-nonsense facial expression made sterner by their young moustaches. The only noticeable difference was the colour of their hair.

"Which of you," asked Penrose, "wacked one of the men, took him out with a with a couple of punches?"

Conwright stamped his foot, stood to attention, and said "sir" acknowledging his responsibility for the deed.

"No punching the men, please," said Penrose, almost informally.

"Won't happen again," said Conwright. "Won't need to. Every man knows where he stands with me. For the sake of all the men he 'ad to be taken down, sir. He was a big bullying bastard."

"And where do they stand with you?" asked Penrose, sharply.

"I won't ask them to do anything I won't do myself."

"How did you know, sir?" asked Conwright bemused, because of the incredibly short time Penrose had been with them.

"I didn't," said Penrose, "It's a trick I learnt from an RSM at summer camp years ago. There's always a punch-up somewhere and he said the sooner you know about it the better off you will be, and where better to start than at the top."

"Sgt. Castleigh's been known to, er, well once he took a man out for refusing to follow orders," added Holmes. "He's a good fighter, is Castleigh."

"Hell Holmes! What are you setting up here, a Conwright v Castleigh boxing match?" protested Penrose.

"Not a bad idea," said Conwright. "Might be fun since we're both from County Durham."

"No!" said Penrose firmly, thinking that a boxing match between one of his officers and one of his NCOs was far from fun. "For God's sake, sit down," he commanded.

"You should watch Castleigh," continued Conwright. "He was at Durham University too, a bit after me. He joined up when the war started. Bright enough to be an officer."

This caused Penrose to study Conwright, then he looked at Holmes and then back at Conwright. There really was no difference between them except the colour of their hair and now Conwright's accent which was clearly Geordie in its tone. It was this differentiating feature that made one an officer and a gentleman and the other an officer and a TG; a Temporary Gentleman. The notion that somebody could be a temporary gentleman offended Penrose's logic for there was nothing temporary about Conwright.

As he thought of Conwright, the words of Shakespeare's Henry V came into his mind, for they were some of the most favourite words of his father. He then spoke without thinking that he was being listened to, "We few, we happy few, we band of brothers".

"For he today that sheds his blood with me, shall be my brother," continued Conwright as naturally as if the two were in conversation. They looked at each other and smiled the smile of comrades in arms.

There then followed a couple of hours of general chitchat, in low voices so that they would not be overheard, as Pte. Eric Cable served them with tea, cocoa and dry biscuits.

"If yous were at HQ you would be having one of these," said Cable as he handed out brandy served in china tea cups. "Given how well you did at HQ today, seems a shame you should miss out," he added.

"It would appear that the back channels are alive and well in this army," commented Penrose.

"Yes sir, possibly sir; if I may say so sir, well done, bloody suicide otherwise," said Cable, beaming with praise.

"Thank you," said Penrose not knowing whether he was more pleased by Cable's ability to summon up a cup of brandy, or the fact that the ranks had heard he had done a good job.

"I think it's time I contacted my French counterpart. When do we take over the running?" asked Penrose, as the brandy reminded him of his meeting with the Colonel that morning.

"Tomorrow," said Holmes. "They do Mondays, Tuesdays and Wednesdays and we do Thursdays, Fridays, and Saturdays."

"Sundays?" asked Penrose.

"Church Parade day, sir," said Holmes and Conwright in unison, with the appropriate degree of sarcasm slipping into their voices. Penrose jerked back his head in acknowledgement of a stupid question.

Chapter 19

Normandy, France November 1915

Dear Ma and Pa,

Thank you for your letter and for the books. How clever of you to choose exactly what I have to study.

I have had five days' leave for the first time since I arrived in France. I am at the seaside a long way from the front. I have found what should be a lovely hotel because it is so very pretty, and the food is good, but the experience fails because everyone is so disagreeable. I think the only reason they tolerate me is because I speak to them in French, but every request has the response of a puff or a sigh which is very off-putting. I find it strange how quickly my ear and French tongue comes back to me. It is such a beautiful sounding language.

I am sorry I have not come home, but the journey is so hard and long and I just did not have the energy to make the trip. Yesterday, I slept for most of the day. I went for a long walk along the beach in the late afternoon and then slept some more. Today, I am now feeling fully rested and am much happier. When I arrived here, I felt like a fully stretched rubber band but now I am back to my normal self, although I'm not sure anyone involved in this war will ever be back to normal again.

I apologise for not writing as often as I should, but somehow it seems selfish of me to be writing my own letters when there are badly injured men who want letters written home. Honestly, you would be so proud of every one of the men serving. Of course they complain, but it comes with a sense of humour, sometimes so clever, that it can only make you laugh.

Away from the seashore, and the constant crashing of the waves, there is complete silence. At first I found it very disturbing as it was the first time in a long time that I was not shaken or disturbed by gunfire or bursting shells. It is truly strange how you get used to these things. The men tell me that, in the morning, they hear bird song as the birds gather for their winter migration, but it is a sound which I've never heard, just the whiz-bangs.

I am finding this war quite confusing, because at the Clearing Station, I see what can only be described as total war, men so badly hurt and injured. Then there is civilian life where I am now, where the issues of the war are so far away that they appear to be having no effect whatsoever. You would not know there is a war here at all. In between these two situations, there is the General Hospital which is almost factory-like in its discipline and order. It is, as I imagine HQ, cold, clinical, and efficient. I find it impossible to reconcile these three vastly different experiences.

I am really sad that I don't see Judith now. She got moved to a bigger hospital where she has been put in charge of a large ward. I still hear about her because she is so popular. I am told she has found an excellent way of dealing with malingerers. She tells them that they've got Reginlams Disease (anagram for malingers). It has a very painful cure which has to be administered without painkillers. She says they are just as likely to die from the cure as the disease. She is surprised how quickly they get better. I have a plan that she and Penrose are to get married. I have told her this and forbidden her to marry anyone else, although she has loads of offers. One day soon I will introduce her to him.

It will be difficult to travel home in the winter, but I will come in the spring when I get my next leave.

Your ever-loving daughter,
Juliette

Chapter 20

The Somme, France November 1915

THERE HAD BEEN a deep frost the night before which had caused the sun's rays to twinkle in the ice before it melted and then evaporated. There was also a slight fog in the air. Penrose made his way across Cotta's Patch to the agreed assembly point which was at the edge of a path, cutting between the trees, which would take them down the hill and through the woods westward until they came to a field which would lead on to the road to Coeur de Foucy and French company's HQ.

Lt. Holmes, Sgt. Macksey, a corporal and seven squaddies had already gathered and were stamping their feet in the cold and mist of exhaled breath when Penrose arrived. He was the last.

"Do we usually have this number?" asked Penrose, protesting at the size of the squad brought together for what he had naively imagined was a simple walk.

"No sir," said Holmes, "but the RSM has made it clear that under no circumstances are you to be captured."

"You know things, sir," interrupted Macksey. The irony of this was not lost on Penrose, who was only too aware of how little he knew.

They walked at a brisk pace, made easier because the mud was slightly harder and crisper than the energy absorbing sludge it had been just a few days earlier. They made it quickly through the woods and then onto the path which continued straight on, between two ploughed fields, until it reached the road.

At the road's edge, Holmes gave his instructions. "Every 10 seconds, we break cover and run for it sir. We're running for just over two and a half miles. The rendezvous point is at the T Junction to the village. We don't stop. We've been attacked too often by snipers to take any risks."

"Snipers, behind our lines? Ten seconds?" repeated Penrose.

"Yes, and yes. We always do ten seconds. Fifteen seconds is too long. He can always get another shot in fifteen seconds."

"Where is he firing from?" asked Penrose, perplexed as the road was well below the sight of the German lines.

"We think the sniper fires from the woods over there." The Sergeant pointed in the general direction of the woods on the French side.

"Aren't those supposed to be under French control?" asked Penrose. "Are you telling me we suffer from German snipers in the French lines?"

"To be fair sir," said Holmes, "they have the same problem as us. Patrols and snipers penetrate our backline too, not in Cotta's Patch because the wood surrounding that is too thin, but from the woods to the north of that. There's no consistency about what they do which makes it very difficult to catch them.

"How often does this happen?"

"About every 8 to 12 weeks. It's very random. We can go months without a problem. We think a patrol takes a sniper in and then gets out, leaving him behind. After every attack we and the French search like mad but we never find him. He only ever makes one attack and then goes silently away. He's a skilful bastard."

Penrose absorbed the unwelcome news. He had no idea of the dangers involved in what he previously thought was going to be a stroll through some woods and fields of France.

"Sir," said Macksey, bringing Penrose back to reality. "Can I suggest you leave your raincoat and backpack here? It's a long run. It will slow you down." Penrose observed that everyone else had already done as Macksey had suggested.

Lt. Holmes touched everyone and gave them a number. They instinctively knew it was their order on the run. Penrose was number four. Better than being three, he thought. He guessed that number three was always the victim. He made a mental note to check. Each man strapped his rifle over his shoulder and behind his back so that his hands were free. Penrose had no rifle, but he checked his pistol at his side to make sure it was secure.

Lt. Holmes looked at each man in his squad and they touched eyes.

Nothing was said. There was telepathy which indicated a readiness.

"Go," shouted Holmes and he ran off at an extremely fast pace. He knew it was his job to lead and leading meant going first. Number Two shouted his seconds out loud, ... "Eight, nine, ten," and then he was gone too, setting out determinedly behind the first runner. Penrose watched Number Three leave and started counting himself.

"One, two, three."

His adrenaline was burning fast. He tried hard to slow down his counting.

"Four, five, six."

Those three seconds seemed interminable.

"Seven, eight, nine."

He couldn't wait a moment longer, for just like a greyhound at the opening of the trap, Penrose was out with a bound running for all his worth. After a couple of hundred yards, he realised he couldn't run the whole distance at the speed he had set himself. It was hard going. After just half a mile, he was past the line of the woods at the back of Cotta's Patch and in open fields. Penrose's heart was in his mouth. He wanted to stop. He needed to stop but he knew his future leadership was dependent upon completing this run without shame. Every pace was now hurting him. The cold morning air was biting into the back of his throat and his boots were chafing his feet as he had not tied them tightly enough. Penrose's body started to slow down in response, but his mind kicked it back into shape. One, two, three, four, he said to himself. One, two, three, four. Each number coinciding with his foot hitting the ground.

Penrose threw back his head to try and get more air into his lungs. As he did so, he saw a small flash come from the forest edge and then, in slow motion, he saw Number Three twist and fall to the ground. It was only after he saw him fall that he heard the single shot.

Penrose ran faster for he was certain that the second shot would come in his direction. He stared at where he had seen the first flash, in anticipation of a second one. His eyes turned to Number Three who was on the ground yelling in screams of pain. So sure was Penrose that he was about to be hit that he threw himself to the ground ignominiously sliding into Number Three's body.

"I need your gun, give me your gun!" yelled Penrose.

Number Three was in too much pain to take any notice. Penrose grabbed the rifle and tried to fight it off him, but his writhing made it impossible.

"I need your rifle, give me your rifle!" yelled Penrose again, but Number Three was so overtaken by pain that he didn't hear, nor could he help.

Penrose grabbed the rifle and tried to fight it off him, but it would not come free. Penrose reached deep into his trouser pocket and pulled out a large penknife purchased from Harrods especially for the war. It had been sharpened to a razor's edge in the tedious hours on the train to the front but nevertheless it was not an easy match for the canvas strap which had to be sawn through until it was free. At that moment, Number Five was beside him.

"He's over there," shouted Penrose, "at the edge of the forest, about one yard to the right of the third fence post." He pointed in the direction. "I saw the flash. He's definitely there."

Sgt. Macksey, the Corporal and the five squaddies were soon with them. In very quick order they were all firing, laying down lead in the direction Penrose had identified as the target. No one was looking after Number Three. Each knew the drill. They had to make the area safe and only then could they look after casualties.

Penrose's mind slowed down as he deliberately lifted the sights up on the rifle he had freed from Number Three and with a few clicks set it to the 800-yard range, which he estimated to be the distance to the edge of the woods. He started to fire. His target was the exact spot where he was sure the shot had come from.

Further down the road Penrose could see that Holmes and Number Two had joined up and were together.

"Corporal, take him, and him with you," said Penrose pointing to two soldiers. "Join up with Mr Holmes. His squad is to attack on my order." The corporal's face turned ashen as he absorbed the news.

"Don't worry, we will give you covering fire until you get to Holmes. Just wait a moment."

Penrose retrieved his field glasses from inside his blouse, realising that he had badly bruised his chest by landing on them as he hit the ground. Very carefully, he studied the target area through his binoculars. There were no obvious sniper signs to be seen.

"Wait for my order, rapid fire to the edge of the woods," said Penrose. "Gentlemen," he continued, speaking rapidly to the Corporal and the two soldiers. "On my order you are to join Mr. Holmes and his squad. Once there, you will group to attack the enemy position."

There was an obvious tension made much worse by the yells of Number Three.

"Rapid fire!" yelled Penrose at which point Sgt. Macksey and the three soldiers staying behind climbed out from the minimum shelter they had found in the ditch at the edge of the field and started firing into the hedgerow.

"Go!" yelled Penrose, at which point the Corporal and his squad of two soldiers charged down the road to where Holmes had set up his base.

Once the Corporal and his soldiers were with Holmes, Penrose shouted, "Cease fire!"

Using fieldcraft signals, Penrose gave instructions for Holmes to charge the sniper's spot. He felt a pang of cowardice in not taking the charge himself, but he knew it was the right decision. Sadly, in this war, Holmes was deemed more expendable than him.

Once again, on Penrose's orders, Macksey and his soldiers fired into the woods. Just a few seconds later, Holmes and his soldiers were up and running full pelt to where the sniper had taken his shot. Penrose watched through his binoculars as the attack was pressed home past the fence posts and into the wood, but there was no enemy in the area where Penrose was certain the sniper had been. He had melted away.

Once Holmes and his soldiers had gone into the woods there was a rush to help Number Three. He was as white as a sheet and visibly shaking. His cries of agony had ceased as the pain had been replaced by a white fog.

"What's your name?" asked Penrose.

"Flagstaff, Jimmy Flagstaff," his voice faded as numbness overcame his obvious fear of dying.

"We're going to get you out of here, Flagstaff. Once we get you to the dressing station, you'll be as right as rain," said Penrose. "You'll be all right. Don't give up!" he said firmly. It was almost an instruction.

"Sergeant, look after Flagstaff. Use this squad of three to get him to the French village as fast as you can. I'm sure he will get the fastest attention there." Macksey looked at Penrose, nodded but said nothing. It was obvious that Flagstaff was in a very bad way.

Penrose left the group working out how to transport Flagstaff and jogged the 800 odd yards to where the attack group were assembled. They had found the coop where the sniper had hidden up, his place given away by a single bullet casing lying on the ground. He had escaped into the woods where, now hidden deep in the undergrowth and without a dog to track him, he would be impossible to find.

Back at the road, they eventually regrouped under Lt. Holmes' command and marched as a squad towards the village of Coeur de Foucy. As they marched, Penrose reflected on what had just happened and on his own performance. All those hours of running around fields as a schoolboy and undergraduate soldier, and then latterly at training camp, had paid off. He had surprised himself how easily he found it to take command, whereas on exercise it was the last thing he had wanted to do. He concluded that he'd done okay. Maybe not as well as a major should have done, but then no one had taught him that role let alone the role of a captain. As Col. Jones had told him just days before, and as he suspected, his rank was a farce. He still had a lot to learn about this war.

Penrose and his party met up with Sgt. Macksey and his group just as they were entering the village. Flagstaff was unconscious with all colour drained from his face. They quickly had him in the hands of French doctors and nurses who moved into a routine which they had done many times before.

Holmes led Penrose to a large white tent pitched in the garden of the farmhouse. "Capitaine Guégan, may I introduce you to Major Dovingdon," he said formally, as they passed through the canvas opening.

"Welcome Major," said Guégan, as he rose from his canvas chair and saluted.

Penrose stepped forward, returned the salute, and as they shook hands he said, with a perfect French accent, "Ravi de faire votre connaissance, monsieur le Capitaine."

Capt. Étienne Guégan was surprised, as no one above the rank of lieutenant had presented themselves to him before. It had always been the practice for the visiting lieutenant to present himself to the commanding officer and then be dismissed to talk to his equal rank and exchange reports. Guégan offered Penrose a seat comprising two bullet chests, one on top of the other. He then walked around the trestle table and came and sat opposite him on a similar structure.

"Perhaps Lieutenant Holmes would like to adjourn to his usual tasks?" said Guégan, who returned the compliment by speaking in perfect English.

Penrose had been nervous about his language skills, but hearing French spoken throughout the village, he was surprised how easily his French came flooding back to him, despite not having spoken it fluently for well over 18 months.

The two men spoke openly. Each told how they had learnt the other's language, while carefully studying their opposite number. Both noticed the other had a precision of movement, not realising that they were each subconsciously mimicking the other's behaviour to put them more at ease. They both spoke softly and calmly, choosing their words carefully and taking care over their pronunciation.

They first talked of Flagstaff's shooting and the problem of the German sniper.

"One man - one bullet every eight to twelve weeks causes a lot of chaos and extra work, never mind the loss of a man. And we can't catch him?" asked Penrose.

"No, we've tried, very many times and in different ways. We think he sometimes takes days to get into position," said Étienne, before adding, "It's a damn clever way to fight a war. I darn well hope we're doing the same thing to them."

Penrose nodded in agreement.

"Major, its twelve-thirty," said Étienne, "would you like to join me for lunch?"

Penrose was shocked. He had no idea of the time. Where had the last six hours gone? He could explain two hours, but some four hours of his life had disappeared into a time warp which he could not grasp.

"Capitaine, that would be very kind, thank you," replied Penrose, "but there is one thing I must insist on first. It is called 'home rules'.

It's well established in the diplomatic service. I think when in the French sector we should speak French, and when in the British sector we should speak English."

Étienne smiled and they sealed the deal in a handshake before moving into the farmhouse where a small table for two had been set up in a large room. Lieutenant Holmes was already at a table being entertained by his equal-ranking host. As Penrose placed his knees under the red and white checked waxed tablecloth, he felt a sense of civilisation rarely enjoyed elsewhere at the front.

Over lunch of onion soup and lamb stew, followed by a local French cheese, Penrose found his tastebuds were being excited as they had never been before. Until that moment he would have sworn that the Reform Club's lamb cutlets were the best in the world. Right now, with his senses heightened by war, he wasn't so sure. The only thing detracting was the local wine. It lacked the appropriate smoothness and was therefore a little rough on the palate. Nevertheless, two large glasses had the desired effect of relaxing him into a warm glow.

The two men started to talk frankly. Penrose explained his new appointment and he could truthfully say that he knew nothing, so it was Étienne who did the talking as Penrose asked question after question so as to fill the gaps in his knowledge. Étienne was generous, making sure each question was answered as fully as possible.

They both debated when the war might end. Neither would hazard a guess. Each agreed that men with single action rifles charging men with machine guns was not going to bring victory, just slaughter.

"We cannot keep sending a hundred men to storm a well dug-in machine-gun post for it to be captured by the 99th man," said Étienne. "We need new technology and we need it fast," he added.

Penrose agreed, and as he did so, he immediately foresaw the problem of reporting what was being said. They were clearly of the same mind, but taken out of context this might be interpreted as being subversive of the war effort. Penrose could dress up his views and report them as being Étienne's, who could do exactly the same thing. Penrose explained the dilemma.

Étienne had thought of the problem long before. "It seemed to me it was the reason why we commanders never met," he replied.

"Perhaps it explains why the conversations have always been between our subordinates."

"Then perhaps, this time, we should agree a common communiqué?" he asked.

Étienne nodded, "I think it would be wise." They both smiled and with it a friendship was sealed.

Étienne and Penrose were joined after lunch by Holmes and his opposite number. They agreed a common report, and this set two items firmly on the agenda: a plan to deal with the sniper and getting a telephone line installed between the two command posts.

Chapter 21

The Somme, France December 1915

Dear Ma and Pa,

Thank you for the letter and the parcel. It is starting to get very cold here and the extra layers of clothes will help keep me warm.

The good news is that I have passed my exams. I am now a fully qualified nurse. Thanks to Dr. Barclay I got two stages of promotion straight away to Sister. It now means I get paid for the job I have been doing ever since I left the hospital.

I didn't know that there was an extra allowance of two shillings and sixpence for each week I worked at a General Clearing Station. I should have been getting paid this long ago, but now my pay has been reviewed, following my promotion, I get paid this too. When I asked about back-pay, I was told it was something the QAIMNS didn't do, whereas it happens all the time for the VADS.

I know it is impolite to talk of money, and I even shocked myself by asking for back-pay, but it is common talk here as it is the one thing that everyone finds is consistently wrong. Sometimes it is better to talk of this than the war. It is very levelling. Socially, England is not going to be the same afterwards.

The best bit of being qualified is the change of uniform. It now gives me all the outward signs of authority rather than having always to fight to prove myself. I had learnt how to be very unpleasant to get my own way, particularly with the young officers who were so used to giving instructions that they would ignore me. Now I am of equal rank, I automatically get treated as an equal.

I saw Judith for a couple of hours a few days ago. We had such a giggle. It was as though we had never been apart. Judith passed her exams too, but I feel sorry for her as she only got made a staff nurse.

She really is a Nurse Nightingale, so much better and caring than me. I cannot help but think it was my rank which saw me unfairly promoted above her. When I asked Matron about it, for I felt very uncomfortable, she said it was just because of my theatre experience and they had a vacancy.

I know I should come home but it is a long way to travel and the men need us so much. When I get time off I just want to get into the countryside and sleep. We will have time enough together when this war is over, but I do miss you all.

Please send my love to Penrose.

Your ever-loving daughter,

Juliette

Chapter 22

The Somme, France November and December 1915

Note to reader: Those not interested in Penrose's active service history in World War 1 may miss this chapter.

TWO DAYS AFTER Flagstaff had been shot, Penrose made his way to his Regimental HQ. This time more confident in his position, for he had done as he was told and listened to his officers and NCOs. He had concluded that his job was neither complex nor too dangerous. It simply needed application and common sense and those, he felt, he could easily provide.

Penrose had three tasks in mind. Firstly, to make clear how strategically vulnerable 32 KBS's command post at Cotta's Patch was. Penrose explained, to an infuriated intelligence officer, how the gap between each of the woods along Célieux Ridge controlled the high ground and therefore its strategic importance for, once taken, it would give the Germans a commanding position for their guns to fire westwards and for their army to sweep into Paris. It was obvious, if you knew the ground, but far less obvious when all you had were lines on a map. Penrose was told both firmly, and with some anger, that the Germans were not going to waste valuable men trying to capture some woods and that he should leave the planning to them. If he was concerned, then it was his responsibility to plan his defences along Célieux Ridge accordingly.

The second thing Penrose did was to organise a telephone line to be run from his command post at Cotta's Patch to French HQ in Coeur de Foucy so as to avoid the needless running of messages. It was such a waste of manpower. More importantly, if they were attacked then a runner was not going to allow the French enough time to respond; and hadn't he just been instructed to 'plan his defences accordingly'.

Penrose's training as a telephone engineer enabled him to plan the route and work out exactly what was required. Then, starting with a fellow officer on the same training course, he created a network of contacts until he had agreement from all involved that a phone line would be laid. Penrose followed up his telephone order with a letter written on Regimental HQ headed paper, which he signed with his name and rank for good measure. He didn't care that he might not have the necessary authority. In fact, Penrose had no idea of his authority levels at all. He would just report what he had done in the usual way and see what happened.

Thirdly, he had to find his other balloon section. It was out there somewhere, but he did not know where. By pulling rank to get his way, and in the process exasperating the intelligence officer even more, Penrose eventually located an approximate position for 27 KBS. It was just as he was getting ready to leave that the news of Jim Flagstaff's death the night before arrived at Regimental HQ.

Penrose took the news badly. It was the first death he had been responsible for in this war and he found it hurt, really hurt. Another telephone call traced the name and address of Flagstaff's next of kin and then, with a heavy heart, Penrose sat down to write to Flagstaff's parents, commiserating at their loss and saying what a fine soldier he had been. He was just finishing his letter when the colonel's adjutant came to see him.

"Can I suggest you think twice about sending that letter," said the adjutant, who went on to tell him that many more were likely to die under his command and it wasn't going to be possible to write to all the next of kin. If he started now, he would never be able to stop, for those that didn't get a letter would be slighted. "I seriously caution you against it," he said.

Penrose folded the letter for it was complete but unsigned. "Thank you," he said. "They are wise words which I will need to think about," and with that he tapped the letter into an envelope which he placed in his small rucksack.

Penrose arrived at Foucaucort late into the evening. He was

dropped off at a command post where he grabbed a bunk bed, a bite to eat and had an uncomfortable night's sleep. In the morning he washed and shaved with a borrowed razor and, after he had asked around, it soon became clear that no one knew where 27 KBS was, other than when it was in the sky. It was, therefore, by line of sight that Penrose eventually found the other balloon section of which he was in charge.

Second Lieutenant Michael Gray was the least likely soldier in the whole of the British Expeditionary Force. On first impressions, it was impossible to believe he was an officer. He was slovenly and shabby with a natural slouch. He was reminiscent of a slothful child who could never keep his shirt tucked in. There was no doubt that Gray would have been bullied at school and the only reason he found it easier in a KBS Section of the British Army was that everyone seemed to ignore him. He liked this just fine.

Penrose introduced himself as his commanding officer, at which point Gray wilted in front of his eyes.

"Let's go a little way away from here and chatter," said Penrose. "Can you organise some tea?"

They moved away from the main group and gathered around the Renault winch lorry, which raised and lowered the balloon, and settled into some canvas chairs.

"When did you last have some leave?" asked Penrose, his senses telling him that the man in front of him was exhausted.

"Since I came to France, fifteen months ago? Never, I haven't been on leave," he said, answering his own question. Gray then added, "I've not even been relieved; not once," so as to emphasise the point.

"When did you get your training in ballooning?" asked Penrose.

"I haven't," said Gray. "Everyone else has been trained but me. I think they call my training on-the-job."

"Have you not been trained as a pilot or observer?"

"Good God no! Although with 1,746 hours of flying under my belt I think I know what I am doing by now," he added with strange diffidence, given it was a huge amount of time in the air.

"But you don't have your wings?"

"I know, it's a shame. It's just out here, no one thinks about us. If I do my job and give HQ what they need, then they are happy and we get left alone. I like it that way."

"What about the rest of your section?" asked Penrose.

Gray described the abilities of his three sergeants which he said kept the section all together.

"Have they been on leave?"

"Oh yes," replied Gray confidently, "everyone else gets their leave when due, except me. I make sure it's so."

"Do you know where your personnel file is?" asked Penrose. "It's just I haven't seen it."

"Nor the three or four officers before you," said Gray, his voice showing a resigned tone of accepted incompetence.

"The important thing," added Gray, changing the conversation away from him, "is we are at half strength. All the men work double shifts and we have to commandeer soldiers from other units as riggers if we are to get into the air. It works quite well, but sometimes it means we can't go flying in areas where HQ wants us to."

Penrose nodded, thinking that commandeering men was an ingenious solution, for a lot of the time the riggers didn't have enough to do and bored men create trouble.

"We are also terribly short of spares. Sometimes it's days before we get what we need to keep us in the air," continued Gray. "At the moment we are only flying by cannibalising 10 KBS's balloon." He paused, and then added, almost as a throwaway comment, "I don't know why they don't merge them with us, then, at least, we'd have one decent section."

Penrose observed but didn't pick up on the comment. Instead, he changed the subject asking, by way of winding up the conversation, "What did you do before the war?"

"I was a lecturer at King's College."

"Cambridge?" interjected Penrose.

"No, London. I lectured in ancient history," he added. "Not a lot to do with this bloody war."

Penrose nodded in appreciation and smiled a bit. "You'll get a 10-day furlough to go back to England immediately I can get you relieved. I expect that to be within the next five days. After that you'll come back to 32 KBS for a while."

Tears started to well up in Gray's eyes, further proving to Penrose that this man was totally exhausted. It also prompted him to leave. "Stay here," he said. "I will go and talk to your men alone." Penrose emphasised the last word as it would give Gray time to regain his composure.

Penrose introduced himself to the three sergeants, shook their hands and thanked them for the job they were doing. He deliberately asked very few questions, allowing the men to speak. As they spoke, he weighed up each man in front of him. Each was worthy of promotion, he concluded, as they looked as though each was prepared to go further than the usual mile. As with most squads, it was the NCOs that kept everything together, and looking at Gray, Penrose was certain that this was the case with 27 KBS.

As he traipsed back to his command post, Penrose felt sorry for Gray. He was the kind of officer you didn't want around. Intuitively, you didn't quite trust him as you knew, at some stage, he was going to foul up, and most likely at the moment when you least needed it to happen, except he hadn't fouled up so far.

Lt. Holmes was sent immediately to replace Gray, who went on leave. While he was away, Penrose tracked down Gray's personal file which had been sitting for months in a pending tray in the Royal Army Pay Corps. It had been discovered that he had been underpaid since arriving in France. No one would decide to pay him what he was due each week in case it brought up a question of the past, and no one was going to deal with a past mistake if the soldier didn't shout about it. The trouble was Gray never bothered to find out about his entitlements, just trusting the army to have it right. Penrose decided that Gray's back pay was not his battle. Instead, he insisted the file be sent to him and in the process, it took away the back-pay problem, at least until another day, if ever. Penrose did a spot check of Gray's logbook comparing it against those that flew with him and concluded that he had flown enough hours as Pilot-in-Command to get his wings. As no one in either section had more flying time, Penrose recommended that Gray be certified as a qualified pilot and promoted to a first lieutenant. Both recommendations were immediately accepted.

Penrose insisted that 10 KBS be merged into 27 KBS under his command, arguing that, since 27 KBS had a working balloon, it should be that way round. The captain commanding 10 KBS made the usual fuss, saying he should take command of 27 KBS, but Penrose responded by pulling rank, arguing that he was the senior officer and he expected his recommendation to be supported. It was, with one minor amendment. 10 KBS was not to be disbanded. It was to be brought back into operation under Penrose's command as soon as possible.

It was due to Penrose's unorthodox approach to problem solving, and thanks to Captain Banks, Penrose's former instructor at the Kite Balloon Training School in Roehampton, that 10 KBS was quickly flying again. Banks' skills as Penrose's scavenger-in-chief, and chief dispatcher of parts from England, would have been the envy of every other KBS in the war if they had known about it.

Penrose worked hard blending his junior officers, NCOs and men across all three sections so each had a full complement. However, just as soon as this had been completed, Penrose was ordered to release one quarter of his officers and one third of his NCOs and men to go to the front. The NCOs were selected by ballot. Once the NCOs were known, two of the officers voted to go with them, as they had been together since the war started. The NCOs then chose the men they wanted to take with them for no other reason than you had to trust the man next to you and this meant selecting the best. In short, the fat and heavy stayed behind, their weight a useful asset for a rigger. The slim and fit would soon be going over the top in the biggest battle ever fought by the British Army. It was a dreadful few days as friends said goodbye to each other.

It was a routine which Kite Balloon Sections were to suffer throughout the war. New men would join a KBS and almost immediately after they were trained and had settled in, there would be an instruction to transfer a certain number to the front. Nevertheless, through hard work and effort the balloons continued to fly

As the New Year came, Penrose was certain that, thanks to his officers and NCOs, his three sections were fit for war. For the first time he felt confident of their place and contribution to the fight.

There was just one thing going wrong, of which Penrose was blindly unaware. He had discovered that back channels were the most effective way of getting anything done. He found it much easier to get forgiven than get permission, so he didn't bother. Instead he chose to report what he had done. However often he was chastised by the Colonel for not going through the proper channels, Penrose's determination to get things done meant he determinedly ignored the rule book. It was making him very unpopular with the staff officers at Regimental HQ, who saw it as their job to control this war. An arrogant major, promoted three stations above his proper rank, not doing as he was told, was not going to be tolerated.

Chapter 23

Paris and Verdun, France February 1916

GÉNÉRALE PHILIPPE PÉTAIN, Commander of the 2nd French Army, was not the only one being entertained in the Hotel Terminus near the Gare du Nord on the evening of 23rd February 1916.

Earlier that evening, Capitaine Étienne Guégan had enjoyed a lustful liaison with the eldest daughter of a successful Parisian florist. He was now sleeping the sleep of the satisfied. While downstairs Lt. Colonel Bernard Serrigny was making history demanding to know Pétain's room number because, as he said to the hotel owner, "the life of France is at stake." The Battle of Verdun had started and Serrigny had urgent instructions for Pétain. He was to report to Générale Joseph Joffre, Commander-in-Chief of the French army, at 8 am. But nothing was so urgent as to stop Pétain from returning to the woman who was discreetly hiding herself under a blanket for what he later fondly recalled as "a memorable evening."

Five days before, Étienne had also been instructed to be at Supreme Headquarters at 8 am on 24th February to receive his new instructions. Immediately he arrived, he knew that whatever they had planned for him was being rapidly changed. As with every officer who had been through Saint-Cyr Military Academy, Étienne knew the importance of Verdun to the future of France. It was directly on the east-west route from Germany to Paris, and if defeated, then Paris would fall. The city's heroic resistance to the German invasion in the Franco-Prussian War, some 45 years earlier, had made it a military case study in defence.

As a result, Verdun had become the centrepiece of a defence system intended to stop any future German invasion with a series of concentric fortified rings built of concrete and steel; except, no one had told the Germans that it was impenetrable. So, after using 850 guns firing shells and poisonous gas into the city's defences, the German Fifth Army went into attack, overwhelming the Région Fortifée de Verdun, causing its commander to order a withdrawal.

Pétain's orders that morning were simple. He was to take his Second Army into the Battle of Verdun and fast. Étienne was to go with him as an aide-de-camp. Later that morning, in a small convoy of cars, Étienne travelled with Pétain and Serrigny to Souilly, 9 miles south of Verdun. There he was instructed to set up the Second Army's headquarters in the commandeered Town Hall while Pétain went forward to survey the situation. Pétain found the situation at the front desperate. On his return to Souilly, Pétain phoned every corps and divisional commander saying that he was in charge and under no circumstances was there to be a retreat.

To add to the problems, there was no suitable railway to get supplies into Verdun. So, while Pétain focused his attention on coordinating his artillery fire so that their shells were concentrated on specific targets to do the most damage, Étienne spent 20 hours each day supporting two engineering officers, Major Richard and Capitaine Doumenc. They were in the process of successfully commandeering a fleet of 3,500 motor trucks from throughout France to bring reinforcements to the front: 190,000 men and 22,000 tonnes of munitions in the first two weeks of the battle. It all travelled on a single-track road from the town of Bar-le-Duc, 30 miles south-west of Verdun. One vehicle started its journey every fourteen seconds, on a road later immortalised by the patriotic French as the Voie Sacrée (sacred way); a road along which 2.3 million Frenchmen would eventually be taken into battle.

Pétain's greatest complaint was that his guns were firing blind. The Germans had air superiority and he was without balloons. In response, Étienne wrote two letters: the first to Penrose asking him politely whether he would urgently dispatch one of his balloon sections to Verdun and to come himself as they would need a French speaker. The second letter, which was signed by Pétain, went straight to Penrose's Colonel. It formerly requested that Major Dovingdon, and at least one of his balloon sections, be assigned to the French Second Army for a period of not less than 12 weeks.

There was a terse meeting between Penrose and his Colonel in which it was agreed that 10 KBS would be despatched because it had recently been equipped with a new Caquot Balloon, and British army pride could not let the French see they were using anything but the best.

The Caquot Balloon had three tail fins which were not filled with hydrogen. Instead, as the balloon rose higher, its tail fins captured the increase in wind speed which acted as a brake on any sudden movement. The balloon itself was huge; over 80 feet long and over 22 feet wide and with 25,000 cubic feet of gas inside. When inflated, it took 48 men in a balloon-handling party to control it. The best thing was that it could fly as high as 4,500 feet, which meant that, with binoculars, a spotter could see 25 miles into the distance.

Lt. Holmes was promoted to Captain and put in charge of 10 KBS. With a new Scammel Winch mounted onto the chassis of a three-ton Leyland Truck, a new Portable Silicon Plant to make the hydrogen, five nurse balloons to store the hydrogen, two lorries with a full complement of NCOs and half a squad of riggers, the newest and best equipped KBS section of the British Army went, in the freezing cold, to help defend Verdun and block the German's route to Paris. Penrose followed three days behind, for he still had 27 and 32 KBS to manage but, because he was travelling light, he arrived at their destination at the same time as Holmes.

Unlike their first meeting, there was nothing refined about Étienne and Penrose's reunion in Souilly. The situation was dire and the look on Étienne's face told it so. A series of suitable launch sites, which had good road links, were quickly agreed. Penrose explained how the French were to provide their own spotters and how soldiers in the vicinity were to be conscripted as riggers at the time of a launch and landing. Étienne agreed, and wrote, in his own hand, a letter which required anyone to whomever it was presented to offer the holder 'every assistance'. It was then signed by Colonel Bernard Serrigny.

Penrose saw Holmes settled into his first site, gave some basic instructions to the French spotters and left Holmes to, what was to become, a bloodbath for his pilots and spotters. Immediately, they were airborne they came under vicious attacks from both German aeroplanes and artillery. It was not until the summer, when there were fifteen Escadrons de Vol[7] in the air over Verdun, and the French had won air supremacy, did the blood bath stop. Holmes stayed in Verdun, with all the men of KBS, without any leave until the battle was won at the end of December 1916, by which time they were all fluent French speakers. Many years after the war, and at the insistence of Colonel Bernard Serrigny, Holmes was awarded the Legion of Honour for his valour and gallantry during the Battle of Verdun.

While Penrose visited Holmes regularly, and used his influence with Étienne to make sure that 10 KBS was properly supplied, the focus of the British Army in the spring and summer of 1916 was directed at urgently relieving the French at Verdun with a 'big summer push'. Penrose was ordered to move 32 KBS from their comfortable position on Célieux Ridge, and together with 27 KBS, he found that, with his men and equipment, he was continuously ordered up and down the front, gathering intelligence ready for what was to become the Battle of the Somme.

[7] Flight squadrons.

Chapter 24

The Somme, France July 1916

THE PLANNING FOR the Battle of the Somme was meticulous. A five-day artillery bombardment would cut through and demolish the barbed wire defences in front of the German lines so as to make sure they were out of the way when the troops attacked. These shells would also destroy the Germans in their trenches and bunkers allowing the Allies to advance across a very wide front and take over the German lines, as their soldiers would either have died or retreated.

Penrose's two balloons were high in the sky on 1st July 1916 when the bombardment ended and the whistles blew. With binoculars forced into their eye sockets, his pilots and observers watched as the British soldiers below, with their bayonets fixed to their Lee Enfield rifles, climbed from the trenches and moved into no man's land.

Only the shelling had not destroyed the barbed wire as planned. Even worse, the German soldiers had not been killed or dislodged as expected, so when the barrage stopped, they merely scrambled from their defences back to their machine guns and rifle points where, not needing to aim, they fired into line upon line of British khaki, which was walking, not running, towards them as ordered.

For the French Sixth Army, the first day of the Battle of the Somme was a success as they forced the Germans from their position. For the British, it was a disaster with 20,000 men dead and 37,000 badly injured.

Penrose immediately debriefed his pilots and observers, who were still visibly shaking, not just from the dreadful cold at 3,500 feet, but from the memory of the sights in their binoculars.

"Why didn't they run, sir?" asked one.

"If only they had run they would have been at the German lines before they'd had time to emerge from their foxholes. They would then have had some chance," added another, his voice breaking with emotion.

Reporting failure is never easy. When Penrose wrote a report which laid the blame for the slaughter directly at the order for the soldiers to walk and not run, while being possibly right, it was not his wisest of moves. Unknown to Penrose, it made him a marked man with all those who had seen 'the walk don't run order' and didn't question it. It was the portent for his downfall.

Chapter 25

The Somme, France Summer and Autumn 1916

PENROSE AND JULIETTE'S experiences during the many Battles of the Somme could not have been more different.

From the air and the planning table, Penrose saw things as being neat, clean and orderly, albeit there was carnage on the ground. Up at a height of 4,000 feet, the pilot and observer were protected from the distress below; just as a walker is unaware of the suffering of the insects he has just trodden upon.

Penrose did not take time to think of what was happening in reality, for when he did he became quite emotional and unable to command. Those emotional moments had to be kept for when he was on his own. Instead, he concentrated all his efforts on keeping his balloons flying, and his men as safe as he could, while providing accurate reports to the artillery, and intelligence flowing to HQ.

It was also a fact that Penrose had been very lucky. For while his balloons had been shot down, and his guns and base badly shelled, his casualties during the Battle of the Somme had been light and not once in his sight.

For Juliette, the battle was one long stream of destroyed bodies, damaged minds and emotional distress. Working in the operating theatre in a Casualty Clearing Station, she was truly into the blood and gore of war. Over the weeks of the Battle of the Somme, she was to see more dead bodies than many an undertaker sees in a whole career.

Her biggest distress, and the one which provided a lifetime of nightmares, was the immediate triage of the injured men; sorting between those who needed an urgent operation, those too ill to be saved who, instead, would be nursed and kept out of pain until their death, and those who would be patched up and sent back to the front.

It was the faces of the young men triaged to die who would return in a nightmare. On many occasions, she was tempted to double or treble the dose of morphine to put them out of their misery, but she never did, and later, would always wonder why.

After her shift, but there was no shift because there was too much to do, she would write letters home for the dying, spoken with their last breaths. It was while doing this that she would observe life after life slowly ebbing away until it was gone; just a body left there in death. It was the letters of those men with young children which broke Juliette's heart, but like every other nurse, she was determined not to cry; for no man wants a woman's tears to be their last sight on earth.

Chapter 26

The Somme, France November 1916

Dear Ma and Pa,

Judith is coming home for Christmas and she kindly offered to post this letter when she gets to England. Knowing our letters are read by censors means we are always very careful about what we write. We are fighting for freedom but it appears not the freedom for our letters to remain private.

For the first time I can tell you the true conditions. They are exactly as the papers say and are truly awful. We are working and fighting in a sea of mud caused by the incessant rain. It is impossible for our soldiers to move forward over the ground because of the clods of mud on their boots and yet, time and time again, they are sent out to charge some machine gun post or line. They might have some chance if they could run but when you can hardly move one foot in front of the other then they become like statues and too easy a target. This whole thing is mindless. You cannot order endless men to run into walls of flying steel and not expect our world to alter. It's crazy.

When I am not in theatre I get moved constantly between dressing stations and the hospital. All the ambulances have had their glass removed, even from the headlights, to make them safer because the flying glass from an explosion kills. Instead we are now frozen to death in a hypothermia caused by exposure to the cold and rain.

Our men are incredibly brave, but we cannot go on asking them to fight in this way. We would treat a rabid dog better. There is an inhumanity going on here which you would not believe unless you actually saw it.

When this is over, as surely one day it will be, I will not allow it to happen ever again. I am determined to be a political activist in the cause of pacifism. I know there will be many German and English soldiers who will feel exactly like me. It cannot happen again.

To win this war we need better inventions. Papa this is your area. I hope you are working night and day to bring these about. Until we have a better way of charging their trenches then there will be no end to this mayhem and in this I am only saying what everyone else is.

We are in a living hell and it appears that there is no exit. I don't know when I will come home. I have applied for Christmas leave but I don't know if I will get it.

I know that, if I were to leave here, even for a little while, I would feel terribly guilty and that would make me very poor company. I also wonder if I were to leave, would I ever be able to force myself to come back. I just don't know if I am that strong. All I do know is that, with all the work we have to do, to be away from here would not be right.

Your ever-loving daughter,
Juliette

Chapter 27

Normandy, France December 1916

Dear Ma and Pa,

I am so sorry I am not home for Christmas again this year. I was not able to get a travel pass home.

I was so thrilled to learn that Penrose will be with you. I saw him for a little while in November, and apart from being tired, he was well. He appears to have a job he likes, although he tells me that he is in permanent trouble with his Colonel which cannot be good. Do talk to him about the Trust for his Company as he talked constantly about the problems that the war was causing his soldiers' families, particularly those who have been bereaved or have serious injuries. He worries about them so.

I am sorry if my last letter upset you. It was written at a particularly bad time. Everything has slowed down now because the weather is so bad and so the fighting is less and so are the casualties.

This must have been the fastest year in Christendom for I do not know where it has gone. For certain, it has truly been an annus horribilis for all of us. I pray that 1917 is so much better, but at the moment I cannot see how.

I am working on Christmas Day and Boxing Day so I have taken my leave in advance and am back at the Guillaume's Hotel on the Normandy coastline again. Honestly, the first time I came here they were so surly and unfriendly that you would have been mad to come back, except I did. Now they treat me as one of their family. They warm my room and have filled it with wonderful home-made Christmas decorations. Before I used to have to eat on my own; now I join the family for dinner. I am sure my honoured guest status is because I speak reasonable French. At last, those lessons Pa insisted on me taking have proved beneficial!

The first thing I did when I got here was to have a hot bath. I thought I had kept myself clean, as so much attention is paid to the subject, but the bath water was so dirty I paid M. Guillaume extra so I could have a second hot bath. It was only after that did I feel like a lady again. We try so very hard to keep everything spotlessly clean in hospital as this is the only way we can stop infections spreading. We wash, we scrub and we boil everything, but everything that comes out here and starts as bright white ends up as a dull grey. There is not a soldier who comes in wounded from the front who does not have to be immediately treated for lice. I am sure my veins are now coursing with the flow of French soil amongst my red blood corpuscles.

Being at the seaside at this time of year is not much fun, but the countryside reminds me so much of home that I am beginning to love the place. I think I will come here on my honeymoon if, one day, I am lucky enough to find a man who wants to marry me.

Thank you for the medical books. I am not getting a moment to read them, but they are proving an especially useful resource for all the medical team in the hospital. Honestly, we see more different diseases in one week than a GP would see in one year.

Your ever-loving daughter.

Juliette

Chapter 28

Lydd, England January – March 1917

Note to reader: Those not interested in Penrose's active service in World War 1 may miss this chapter.

VERY SLOWLY PENROSE started to seethe. Not only did he outrank everyone on the course he had been sent, but he knew more about balloons and their use in artillery range spotting than any of the lecturers. After all, it was precisely what his three kite balloon sections had been doing for the last two years.

What made matters worse was that it was winter, and he was in Lydd; a place surrounded by Romney Marsh with its flat and low-lying wetlands. It meant it was permanently damp and dingy with a miserable micro-climate of mist and fog,

Lydd was a long-established military town with the Royal Garrison in Artillery and the School of Siege Artillery Brigade well entrenched in their barracks. It was not a place you would choose to be in January 1917 except for three things. It was away from the fighting. It gave an opportunity to sleep in a bed, and finally, the chance of hot regular meals. All pleasures rarely enjoyed by a soldier at the front.

It should, therefore, have been with a degree of anticipation and relief that Penrose turned up on the first day, except his Colonel had denied him the extended leave which was due to him before attending such a course. It meant he could only spend a few days with his parents over Christmas. It was, therefore, with a large degree of pique that, on 2nd January 1917, Penrose reported to the School of Siege Artillery to attend a course to be jointly delivered by the No 2 Royal Flying Corps Balloon School.

"Sorry about all this," said the Squadron Leader who was leading the course, by way of opening a conversation with Penrose on the third evening of his course.

"Eh," replied Penrose, sulking in the corner of the officers' mess nursing a warm beer.

"All this is a bit of a waste of time for you," continued the Squadron Leader.

Penrose nodded, and then grimaced in agreement.

"I thought we would be doing a lot of flying but there is nothing about flying in the whole programme," said Penrose in a way which made his complaint sound less so.

"What made you think that?" asked the Squadron Leader.

"It's what the adjutant said. My Colonel thought aeroplane spotting was the future, more accurate than balloon spotting and wanted me to find out."

"We'd all assumed you'd been sent here because you'd dropped a bit of a bollock," continued the Squadron Leader, with an unusual degree of honesty. "It's why most officers who are as knowledgeable as you end up here. Their HQ wants them out of the way for a week or two to let things settle down."

"Oh," said Penrose, a bit hurt. "I've done my time at the front. There's no balloonic who's not done his bit," said Penrose firmly,

"Yes, sorry, of course. You know what I mean."

Penrose decided not to take umbrage at the remark and to keep his indiscretion with his Colonel to himself. "Can a spotter plane in the air bring accurate pinpoint shell fire on a target?" he asked, in an attempt to change the subject.

"Yes, yes," said the Squadron Leader excitedly. "Transportable radios were first trialled in aeroplanes in 1914. Last year, a lot of work was done to improve them. In the trials, they used the same clock and 25-yard concentric rings to direct gun fire which you balloonists use now. I'm sure they're only months away from being perfected, and then, when the pilot can speak to the ground, it will be fantastic."

"And now?" asked Penrose.

"What, the sexton and signal method?"

Penrose nodded, not having a clue at what the man was talking about.

"Not too good at the moment. It's a bit too hit and miss if you will excuse the pun. We know what height the spotter plane is flying at, and using a sexton focused on the plane, we can measure its angle from the ground when it signals that it's above the target. Then, it's a simple matter of trigonometry to work out the distance and then set the correct trajectory. After all, we already know the bearing. The only trouble is that altimeters aren't that accurate. At the height they're flying between 8,000 and 12,000 feet, they can be out by five hundred feet, plus or minus a bit, and that can make a huge difference to the firing range."

"A two-month course to learn what you have told me in less than one minute doesn't really equate, does it?" commented Penrose.

"The main problem is that our planes can never stay over the target long enough. They either get fired at by enemy guns on the ground or there's soon an air battle with the Germans which sees our guys driven off target and unable to signal."

"So it doesn't work?" said Penrose, dejectedly summing up the conversation

"Not yet, but it will. Look at the intelligence we are now getting from aerial photographs. We can now see whether we're hitting the target or not."

"It's not instant. Too much firepower is wasted. When in the air, a balloon communicating directly with its guns can be deadly accurate," commented Penrose, arguing the case for a job he had been doing.

"It's strange your adjutant expected you to be flying," said the Squadron Leader. "He wasn't expecting you to get your wings, was he?"

"No, I don't think so," said Penrose perplexed at the question. I was told I would be spotting from Avro's 540Js or maybe DeHaviland D.H.9As. The adjutant was surprisingly specific about that."

"That's good; otherwise you really would have fouled up!"

"Why?"

"We don't broadcast this, but life expectancy is not good for new pilots at the moment. The rumour is that average flying time from the first combat mission to first crash or being shot down is less than two hours. Some say it's as short as ninety minutes."

"Jesus, that's not good," commented Penrose. "It is only our aeroplanes which give my balloons any form of protection. We're bloody hopeless at shooting down the German planes with our guns on the ground, although with the new shells, we're getting much better."

"That's good," said the Squadron Leader, welcoming all support for the new flying machines. "You don't think you've been booked on the wrong course, do you? It's just there is a newly established TDS in Lydd and that's exactly what they fly."

"TDS?" puzzled Penrose.

"Training Depot Stations; they teach cadets to fly."

"I don't know," said Penrose slightly perplexed. "However, I think you and I agree that I'm wasting my time here."

"I know the course commander there. I'll talk to him in the morning," and with those few words the Squadron Leader got up and left Penrose to finish his beer in peace.

By mid-morning the next day, Penrose was packed and waiting in the officers' mess for a car to take him to his correct placement; to learn to be an observer, some would say spotter, at Lydd TDS. An earlier phone call to the TDS had established that a major, whose name they had never learnt, had not turned up to take his reserved place on the course. It was immediately concluded that there had been an almighty administrative cock-up, and so with the agreement of all parties, Penrose was to be re-assigned to TDS Lydd and with it, Miss Drew Stubman came into his life.

Chapter 29

Lydd, England January – March 1917

DREW STUBMAN'S CONTRIBUTION to the war effort was as a volunteer driver for the Royal Flying Corps. On this day her instructions were straightforward. She had to collect a major from the Royal Garrison Barracks and take him to the aerodrome and tents which comprised TDS Lydd.[8]

From the moment Penrose saw Drew, he was smitten, for she had the widest and brightest emerald green eyes of anyone he had ever seen. He was completely mesmerised by the way they sparkled in a watery glaze. Each eye seemed just like an engagement ring twinkling in its setting of diamonds. He knew he was staring but he couldn't stop. He was only glad she was staring straight back noticing his deep brown eyes, made softer by some very thin crow's lines which had developed in recent months. Whichever way he looked, whether into her thick orangey red hair which flowed smoothly with the turn of her head, or to her neat and tiny nose which made her cheekbones seem more pronounced, or to her beautifully balanced mouth which could only emit a smile, his gaze always came back to her eyes. Through them, he could see into her soul and in that moment, he instinctively knew everything about her.

For a man who had paid little or no attention to women over the years, this was a complete shock. Penrose was captivated, and with it came both a joy and a fear; but the fear was worse. All Penrose's confidence evaporated in the worry that she might reject him.

It was because of her beauty that Penrose decided to sit in the front seat next to Drew, rather than in his usual position in the back, as she

---

[8] Training Depot Station where cadets are taught to fly.

chauffeured him to the TDS. He was very conscious that he had never been driven by a woman before, and although he found it very strange, he quickly and condescendingly concluded, without saying anything, that there was no reason to object. Her driving skills were as able as any man.

Penrose was not the kind of man Drew would have chosen as her suitor, even if she wanted one, which she didn't. Firstly, there was the age difference between them, but more importantly, Penrose was from what she would call 'old money', the landed rich who had no reason to work because they could live off their investments. Instead, they took positions in government to further their own interests. It was this class which Drew had learnt to dislike intensely.

Drew's father was a remarkably successful publican. He had built up, and traded on, pub after pub in and around Portsmouth and Gosport until he owned three of the largest around the naval base. It was where the sailors would spend their pay during their shore leave, and with it their money flowed to him, so his family wanted for nothing. Seeking better for his only child than he'd ever had himself, he paid for Drew to be tutored and then educated at Roedean School near Brighton; for wasn't his money as good as anyone else's?

Except Drew was never accepted as an equal by her fellow pupils. They were mainly the daughters of the landed rich and professional classes. This meant that, while Drew had acquaintances, she had no true friends. It was not the fact that, at the end of term, Drew would return to the flat above her father's largest pub while her fellow pupils would go to their gardened homes which upset her. It was more the expectation of her fellow pupils which rankled. It was their feeling of right, and of being right, which jarred. While Drew's contemporaries felt they had an entitlement to be at one of the best girls' schools in the country and have everything they wanted and more, she felt she was exceptionally fortunate. Each of her fellow pupils would ask for, and usually get from their parents, anything they wanted. Drew would never ask her father for anything. The Stubman philosophy was that everything had to be worked for. Very slowly, term after term, Drew started to build a resentment against her fellow pupils which she would later admit turned into resentment against a class which thought itself better, but without any justifiable reason.

At the end of her last term at Roedean, Drew's class was taken, as a treat, to see George Bernard Shaw's play Pygmalion which was enjoying its first run in the theatre. She immediately identified herself with Eliza Doolittle; no longer fit to be a barmaid of her parents' class, and yet not suitable to be the wife of a gentleman. She was, she concluded, an inbetweener too. Someone who was going to have to make her way outside the class structures of the day. Except, unknown to Drew, those class structures were dissolving in front of her very eyes, as evidenced by the fact that she was in uniform and driving officers.

Squadron Leader Nicholas Badenoch was younger than Penrose, but the war had aged him badly. He suffered permanent nightmares from the memories of everyone he had trained who, through the misfortunes of war, were never going to come back. This made him a virulent taskmaster as he was determined that no one was going to die because he hadn't trained them properly.

Penrose and Badenoch saluted each other formally and then shook hands. Penrose smiled, but no warmth was returned.

"I hope you don't think you've come here for a spot of R&R," said Badenoch, abruptly.

Penrose looked perplexed.

"When you're in an aeroplane at six thousand feet, you're on your own. Everyone has to be able to do everyone else's job. Even as an observer, you still have to know the rudiments of navigation to get home again, how to fly the plane to get you there, and then you have to be able to land; skills which will save your life. Parachuted, I presume?" There was a fierceness in Badenoch's voice

"Once or twice," replied Penrose, deliberately deciding not to elaborate.

"Got your log book?"

It was with those last few words, and a nod of approval, that Penrose was introduced to the pleasures of flying, and the misery of air sickness, which he found he could only control by flying on an empty stomach. Balloons were notorious for making people airsick but not Penrose. It was the slow up-and-down motion of an ill-trimmed plane, just as a boat riding the waves, which was more than his stomach could bear.

In late January and throughout February, when in the few hours of daylight it wasn't raining, snowing or blowing a gale, Penrose learnt what he needed to be an observer. He found it easy as it was what he had done for almost two years. Navigation, which seemed to cause most people problems, he sailed through having done a ship's navigation course between school and university, in a one-time boyhood dream of going to sea. The only difference was the wind direction, and not the tide, which had to be factored into the calculations.

After a few hours of learning to fly straight and level, climb and descend and turn without losing height, Penrose was taught how to land. This took him into flying circuits, and what had become known as bumps, as he spent hours taking off, flying a rectangular course around the airfield, landing and then taking off again without stopping.

When Penrose wasn't flying or in a lesson, he would deliberately seek out Drew, whose days never seemed to end. She was always there first thing in the morning when he reported to the crew room, and she was always there extremely late into the evenings. He would always make it look as though their meeting was casual, by co-incidence, but once together, he would study her face, her slim wrists, delicate hands, small feet and dainty ankles. He could swear that, if he were an artist, he would be able to paint her from memory. Sadly for Penrose, she showed no particular interest in him.

The first real conversation they had was when Drew learnt that Penrose and his sister had both been to Cambridge University. It was on learning this that Drew's ambition to go to university was rekindled with a passion which, over the months Penrose was in Lydd, became obsessional. Their conversations were all about Cambridge and the opportunities it provided. It was these which convinced Drew, whether fairly or not, that Roedean had dismissed a university career for her on snobbery grounds; no publican's daughter was going to be their representative in the hallowed halls of Oxford or Cambridge University. Drew had to know everything there was about winning a place. If she could, through Penrose, meet his sister, then this might lead to her being introduced to her college, then who knows? All Drew knew was that a cold call was never going to do it.

"Is your sister a suffragette?" asked Drew, in all seriousness at the start of their first real conversation.

"I haven't asked her," said Penrose, surprised at the question. "I'm sure she is. In fact, I'd be really surprised if she isn't. Why do you ask?"

"I'm definitely a suffragette," said Drew defiantly. "Do you think that would preclude me from going to Cambridge?"

"Good God, no," said Penrose wholeheartedly. "I would imagine it's a pre-requisite. What do you want to study?"

"I don't know what the subject is called exactly," Drew said. "It's a mix of anthropology and political philosophy. For example, take President Lincoln's Gettysburg address." She started to recite it by heart:

"Four score and seven years ago our fathers brought forth on this continent a new nation, conceived in liberty, and dedicated to the proposition that all men are created equal."

Drew stopped, thought for a moment, smiled weakly at Penrose and then continued.

"That we here highly resolve that these dead shall not have died in vain—that this nation, under God, shall have a new birth of freedom—and that government of the people, by the people, for the people, shall not perish from the earth."

"In speaking for those men then, he was also speaking for our men now, wasn't he?" she asked.

"How the hell do you know that?" said Penrose beaming, if not a little perplexed. "That's impressive, very impressive," he continued. Penrose knew of the Gettysburg address but had never read it, let alone heard anyone recite it.

"You see that's what I want to study. Things are happening now, and things were happening then. They need to be thought about. I want to be with the people who are doing the thinking." There was a passion, almost a sense of desperation in her voice.

"Why was it, before John Locke wrote The Age of Enlightenment, did we fail 'to hold these truths to be self-evident, that all men are created equal, that they are endowed by their Creator with certain unalienable Rights, that among these are Life, Liberty and the pursuit of Happiness?'" asked Drew quoting from the American Declaration of Independence.

She paused as she saw Penrose's expression change from one of perplexity to one of consternation. "I'd have loved to have been around at that time, to hear Thomas Jefferson and James Wilson discuss the draft of the constitution of the USA. Wouldn't you?"

Penrose nodded weakly, for he had no contribution to make. It was a subject in which he was uncomfortably out of his depth.

"Have you read Thomas Paine's book 'The Rights of Man'?" she asked.

"No. I'm sorry, I haven't."

"What about Edmund Burke's 'Reflections of the Revolution in France'?"

"No, I've not read that either," said Penrose apologetically.

"What about Karl Marx?"

"That one passed me by too, but in my defence, to carry around a copy of Das Kapital in the Treasury would not have been career enhancing."

"We are on the verge of another major revolution, as big as happened in the USA and in France, and you're not thinking about these things?" asked Drew, disappointment creeping into her voice.

"Before the war I was thinking about these things, but from the economic not political aspect. I spent many hours in discussion with John Maynard Keynes and he is developing some interesting philosophies." Then Penrose added tartly, "Since the war started I'm afraid my focus has been on keeping my men and myself alive."

"It won't stave off the revolution unless there's a material redistribution of wealth," continued Drew, completely ignoring Penrose's defence. "But that's not going to happen, or if it does, it's gonna make us all poorer."

"How do you work that out?" asked Penrose, for while he agreed, he was interested in Drew's reasoning.

"It's obvious, in a period of uncertainty, the rich, no not just the rich, everyone stops spending out of fear. You only have to look at my father's business and multiply his customers' actions a million times, and when people stop spending, the jobs go."

"How old are you, if I may ask?" enquired Penrose, completely disconcerted that he was having a profound monetary policy conversation with one who was not only obviously young, but also a woman.

"Nineteen, why?" Drew replied casually, while thinking about the next point she wanted to make. "The only solution is that as wealth grows, the poor must get to keep a bigger share of that growth than the rich. "Have you read Adam Smith's book the 'Wealth of Nations'?" she asked.

Penrose was tempted to lie. It was one of the books he should have read at Cambridge. Instead, he attended a lecture where the book was discussed in detail. From that, his knowledge was condensed onto one sheet of paper ready for revision at exam time. Instead of answering he chose to ask a question.

"When did you read all of this?"

"The last couple of years when I was at school. Do you really know none of this?" asked Drew.

"I'm afraid it wasn't covered in my maths lectures," said Penrose defensively, beginning to feel that Drew was proving to be well out of his league.

"But you were in the Treasury, making big decisions. How can you have done that without some philosophical position?"

"Because my job was to keep the banking system alive, and when there's a run on the Bank of England, as there was in the week just before war was declared, then there is only one focus: to get the Old Lady all the money she needs."

Penrose then changed his tone from being defensive to being authoritarian. "If you want to know what will bring about revolution faster than anything else, it will be a collapse in the banking system, and that's what I helped stop just before this damnable war started."

"I'm sorry," said Drew, feeling suitably chastised. "I didn't realise."

In normal circumstances, Penrose would have pressed home his advantage but this was far from such a case as, in front of him, was someone who, from all appearances, could be described as only a girl, and yet was debating with the knowledge base and sophistication typical of his former colleagues in the Treasury.

"So how do you get the poor to keep a bigger share of the growth in wealth?" he asked.

"Are you asking or testing?" responded Drew, her voice much calmer and quieter than before.

"Asking, I'm interested," he replied, responding in her lower tone.

"Two ways: Trade Unions; if workers organise themselves better then they will be able to get better pay. It happened in my dad's pubs once. He'd have been quite happy to have sacked all his staff, the lot of 'em, and hire a new lot, but he couldn't risk his sacked barmen standing outside sending his customers elsewhere. He knew he would never get them back, so he forked out. It's a fact, they are the best paid pub workers for miles around, and with that he gets the best, most loyal staff."

"And the other way?" prompted Penrose.

"Taxation: we tax the rich more," said Drew. "Say 50% or 60% of their income and then the Government spends this money on projects which create well-paid jobs."

"You sound like Maynard-Keynes. He works in the Treasury. He's a great one for public spending. You should meet him."

"Yes! I would like that," responded Drew, a bit too eagerly.

Unknown to Penrose, it was that one small remark which invited Drew to become putty in his hands, for he was already putty in hers.

That night in his bed, Penrose cursed, for he had once been told that it was improper for a man to marry a woman who was younger than half his age plus seven years. He was thirty which meant that Drew was much too young for him. In the dark of the night, and with some mental arithmetic, that he checked three or four times, he worked out that when he was thirty-six, she would be twenty-five. He knew he couldn't wait that long. He knew the imponderables were on her side, not his. Was she attracted to him and if so, would she wait? Penrose did not know the answer, but he knew he could do something to influence the waiting game. Unable to sleep, Penrose wrote to Juliette introducing Drew to her, explaining she wanted to go up to Cambridge and needed help.

Likewise, Drew was lying in bed thinking of Penrose. He was OK handsome she decided. Not ugly, but not so pretty that he fancied himself. The fact that he was from the upper middle class and moneyed should have put her off. Yet, having sat at the centre of government, he knew far more about how things worked than her. He had attentively listened to her opinions and had respected them. It was this she found exceptionally appealing, for no man had done that before. He was clearly successful. Marriage never came into her mind, for he was much too old, but she was sure they could become good friends. In fact, she planned on it.

For the rest of Penrose's course, he instinctively migrated toward Drew and they grew closer together. Penrose delighted in her ability to find fun and giggle at almost anything. He found this quite addictive because she literally lightened his otherwise heavy heart.

Drew, who was more circumspect, found her heart race just a little faster each time Penrose was first near her, only to slow down a few seconds later as they renewed their familiarity. It was his kindness, gentleness and calm confidence which she found compellingly attractive; so different to the other, wildly excited, kids surrounding her, who were also learning to fly, and in their immaturity thought that this made them God's gift to women.

Chapter 30

Lydd, England March 1917

TIME AND TIME again Penrose asked Drew out, offering all kinds of chaperone arrangements, but she would not accept. It wasn't that she refused because she didn't want to go. It was always circumstances which gave her a valid reason to turn him down each time, until his last day, when she agreed to afternoon tea in Rye; just far enough away from Lydd to give them some privacy.

Penrose made sure he was early, as his sister had impressed upon him how much she hated walking into a restaurant and not finding her host there. It was, she explained, why women were always late; so as to avoid the embarrassment of sitting at a table on their own, dreading that some lothario might come up and introduce themselves.

Penrose didn't recognise Drew straightaway for she was out of uniform and he had never imagined her another way. He watched with mild curiosity while the maître d' took the coat of a woman at the entrance, only realising some seconds later that it was her.

She was wearing an elegantly tailored light navy blue dress, buttoned from the waist to high neck line with a modest collar. Around her neck was a single string of pearls. The long sleeves of the dress were accompanied by short white gloves. Around one wrist she wore a delicate platinum wristwatch and around the other were three strings of matching pearls. There was an elegance not earlier permitted by her ill-fitting uniform.

As the maître d' walked Drew slowly to their table, Penrose stood up to greet her. He could not help but notice that others in the room turned to look at her, or more importantly, that there was an entirely different woman in front of him, looking far more petite than she had ever looked before. However, there was one thing which, for all her sophistication, hadn't changed, for frustrated at the maître d's slow pace she was bouncing behind, trying to get past, as though she was in a rush to impart some news, which she was. As a result, there was no intimate greeting between them.

"Have you heard? Have you heard?" she asked excitedly, speaking as though she was out of breath.

"Heard what?"

"The Russian Revolution, it's started. I told you it would."

"You did," agreed Penrose, taking her hand, and kissing her perfunctorily on the cheek, as one might with a long-standing family friend. In her excitement, she was oblivious to the fact that the maître d' had drawn back a chair and was waiting patiently for her.

"The Tsar is gone. He's abdicated," she said, as she sat down. "I knew he would go. It was only a matter of time."

"I know, its damnably bad news," said Penrose.

"No, it's not," said Drew defiantly. "It's good news. It means the people of Russia can be free to decide how they're ruled. There's no new Tsar because he abdicated for his son too."

Penrose nodded, already appreciative of the fact. "In a revolutionary state, the Russians will not be able to organise themselves to fight a war against Germany. You can be sure that they will sue for peace. This means that all the German troops on the Eastern Front will now be transferred to fight us on the Western Front. It's hard enough as it is, and if that happens, as I am sure it will, then it will become damnably hard."

"Oh ... yes," acknowledged Drew, slumping in her chair. "I'm sorry. I should have thought."

"It was always the Germans' strategy to win a quick war against France in the west, before taking on Russia. The fact that Germany is fighting a war on two fronts, and England and its Empire have come into the fray to help France and Belgium, is the only reason it hasn't won to date."

"There's an alternative viewpoint," said Drew, recovering from her earlier defeat. "That is Germany will re-enforce its campaign in the East because it will now be an easy win for them."

"No, that's not going to happen," said Penrose firmly. "Let's remember, this war only started so Germany could give Russia a smack on the nose. They've done that. They'll be glad that the war with Russia is about to end so they can concentrate on fighting us. Was this point not made in your newspaper?" asked Penrose somewhat mockingly. He knew how Drew, the most eclectic of readers, delighted in diligently studying almost every daily newspaper, as she didn't trust any one of them to tell her the truth.

"Do you think this will lead to the King abdicating?" Drew asked, but then not allowing him to reply, she answered the question for herself in the negative.

They ordered as Drew continued chatting away, excitedly trying to analyse the changing events. Meanwhile, Penrose was only half listening for his mind was focusing on the delicacy of her beauty. He knew she was pretty, but with her hair up and back she radiated a finesse he had not seen before. Then, when his mind was back on what she was saying, they started chatting animatedly about anything and everything, as though they were lifelong friends who'd just met up after a long time apart.

After a while, and in response to a tease by Penrose as to how hard it had been to get her on her own, Drew said, "It's not that I didn't want to go out with you, because I did. It's just that I'm not going out with anyone until this war is over, but with you leaving and with us being friends, well, it seemed right that we should say goodbye nicely."

"That's good, 'cause as soon as this war is over, I'm coming back to marry you," said Penrose without a thought. He felt totally foolish immediately the words had left his lips. Thank God, he thought, it sounded more like a statement and not a proposal.

Drew threw back her head and laughed a silent laugh. It was not a cruel laugh, but in the assumption that Penrose was teasing her. "There's been many an airman who has said that," she replied in the same teasing vein.

Penrose said no more. Instead, he quietly resolved that, if he survived, she would be his bride.

It was dark when they left the tea rooms. Penrose walked her to her car and there, after he had opened her door, they stood holding hands. They looked at each other, saying nothing, knowing that this might be the last time they met. They also knew that this was exactly what the other was thinking.

Penrose removed his cap and leaned forward and they kissed. It was the sweetest, gentlest touch of lips which each allowed to linger. In doing so, they sealed their relationship, for Drew felt a warmth on her chest and a weakness in her legs that she had never felt before, and with these feelings she knew, just knew, she had found her future husband.

Penrose watched and waved as Drew drove off. At the exit to the car park she stopped for a while. Her mind was not only racing but she felt a true sense of fear that she'd never experienced before. Having found the most exciting touch she'd ever felt, she had a dread that it might possibly be lost to her forever, and she couldn't bear that. After a few moments, her mind was made up. Yes, Major David Victor Penrose Dovingdon would be her husband. With no further glance in his direction, she was gone.

Chapter 31

France April 1917

Note to reader: Those not interested in Penrose's active service in World War 1 may miss this chapter.

PENROSE EMBARKED AT Folkestone, bound, for Boulogne, after five days' leave which he had spent with his parents. He told them of his love of flying and how it was what he was going to do when the war was over. The course, and Drew, had given him a new perspective and with time at home he was more relaxed and comfortable with himself than he had been for a long time. He found it strange to be looking forward to going back to the war, but he wanted to be with his men. He needed to get them through this.

As a senior officer, he had been allocated his own cabin on the troop ship but, like all those who put their safety first, he chose to be on deck. Although much colder, it was worth bearing, for it gave a sense of freedom and a much greater chance of not drowning should the boat be hit by a torpedo.

As the boat zigzagged across the Channel, so as to avoid enemy mines, and in the process making the journey much longer, Penrose strode the deck wondering whether others had seen in him what he now knew, but had not been able to recognise before. He had previously worked himself to a point of intolerable exhaustion. It was why he had become unbearable to his fellow officers.

From the moment Penrose had taken his command, there had been constant demands from officers above him. The majority of these were routine and administrative, took up an inordinate amount of time, and yet came with a demand for urgent action which seemed far from warranted. The minority of orders, those which would actually progress the war, always put the lives of the men under his command at risk. They were the ones he didn't want to receive or give, and each time they came he felt the responsibility terribly.

Penrose recognised the tipping point. He had not had a nervous breakdown from shell shock, as suffered by those constantly under bombardment on the frontline, but from the ever-growing frustration of having responsibility without any real power. It had come to the point where he had stopped requesting from senior officers. Instead, he started to instruct them, and if they did not do as he asked, he simply went around them.

As night fell, and the spray from the ship, crashing into the waves, soaked those on deck, Penrose reflected on his last fight with his Colonel. Penrose had ordered and taken under his command a motorcycle and sidecar equipped to lay telephone cables. He might move his balloons, and the artillery might move their guns, but they were both useless unless they could talk to each other. While the guns and balloons could move daily, it could take days to process a chit through signals to get the two units to talk to each other, by which time they might have moved again. It was why he needed, had ordered, and taken into his charge his own telephone laying equipment. It was when the Colonel of the Royal Engineers Signals complained to Penrose's commanding officer about Penrose purloining equipment, which should be exclusively for their use, that his anger overflowed in a demonstrable loss of temper.

Penrose had been summoned to see the Colonel both for a telling off and to be ordered to hand back the motorcycle and sidecar. Penrose was told, in no uncertain terms, that his action gave rise to a risk of a telephone exchange being overloaded, at which point the entire communication network would fail, putting the whole war effort at risk. Complete nonsense, argued Penrose vehemently and without any grace, reminding his Colonel that he had trained with the signals and knew how telephone exchanges worked. It took only a few moments of technical argument by Penrose to prove that the risk was vastly exaggerated.

"If there is a risk of an exchange overload then it is a complete failure of planning on their part and they should be told as much," said Penrose firmly.

"But it still leaves the fact that you have some of their kit which has to go back to them," said his Colonel.

"I ordered it especially to serve all KBSs," said Penrose defensively. "We damn well need it!"

"Yes, without any authority and by taking one of the machines they had on order," replied the Colonel, determined not to be beaten

"If I send it back, it will put my men's lives at risk," said Penrose crossly. "I have to have the guns working all the time if I'm to protect my balloons. They cannot be out of action, even for a day. It's you who needs the daily intelligence and we need their guns out of action," argued Penrose, his voice getting louder and louder.

"What if I order you to send them back?" asked the Colonel.

"Then it looks as though I'll be facing a Court Marshal," replied Penrose, using a tactic he had successfully used before, getting even more agitated as he said it.

"Then it looks as though you will," responded the Colonel sharply, "for you will be getting a written order to this effect and I expect it to be obeyed."

Penrose could not remember what he said in response, but it was loud, threatening and very ungentlemanly. As a result, he was dismissed and ordered back to his unit.

The grapevine very quickly heard of the bust up and the reason for it, which didn't help, as each man in each KBS was one hundred percent behind Penrose, only adding to the tension and the rumour mill. Three days later, four pieces of paper arrived by special courier for Penrose's attention. Everyone knew that these were orders from the Colonel. They waited with bated breath to see what they said.

The first paper was an order, specifying that it was not to be questioned, demanding the return of the motor-cycle and sidecar to the Reserve Signals Regiment within thirty days. The second piece of paper was a copy of a requisition of a motor-cycle and sidecar for Penrose's Company signed by the Colonel. The third was an order giving permission for the laying of cables between the guns and balloons, with instructions that the cables should only be connected to the exchange by a trained signals man. Interesting wording, thought Penrose, because that covered him. Finally, there was an order to attend the advance balloon course in Lydd. As soon as Penrose had read through his orders, he had a new respect for his Colonel. Wise old owl, he thought, as he realised he had been deliberately sent away to avoid a conflict. Now, as he sailed the seas back to France he resolved to apply the same wisdom in dealing with his men.

Penrose had already decided to find his Balloon Sections before reporting back to Regimental HQ, so he travelled via the officer clubs in Hazebrouck where he met up with 27 KBS to be told that they had been renamed 44 KBS. Someone somewhere had decided that all naval balloon sections should have all odd numbers and the army all even numbers. The navy, claiming to be the senior service, demanded the right to have 1 KBS. Who has the time, not only to think of these things, but issue the orders as well, wondered Penrose crossly, as he received an update on his sections. The news was not good.

The general consensus was that the new Caquot balloons were a considerable improvement on the old Drachen balloons, but the recent death toll had been dreadful.

Right from the start of the war it had been an unwritten rule that you did not bring your balloon down if you were just being fired at, but there had been a noticeable improvement in the accuracy of the shelling from German guns and the firepower of their aeroplanes. Now his balloons were being hit regularly, causing them to descend in various stages of distress. Nevertheless, now the artillery had discovered the usefulness of balloons in directing fire, his pilots and observers were being asked to spend as much as eight hours aloft at any one time, and in April, at 4,000 feet, the temperature was never less than minus ten degrees below freezing.

In addition, he heard how his troops were constantly having mustard gas shells fired in their direction which meant that they had to work with gas masks on and were constrained for air.

Penrose was told how on one occasion a balloon cable had been shot through by enemy fire causing the balloon to fly free. The pilot and the observer parachuted out before the balloon flew across the German lines but the pilot's parachute failed to open.

He also heard that an unlucky hit on 10 KBS's hydrogen store had caused a huge number of casualties as the pressured canisters, and its nurse balloons, full of gas exploded in a ball of fire throwing out shrapnel in all directions. All those in the immediate vicinity were killed, while others suffered appalling burns, both from the fire and from caustic soda which was thrown in all directions when their container drums burst.

There had not been a change in the fundamentals of this '*game*' of war. Both sides would send up their balloons and then direct their fire on their enemy's guns and balloons until the other side's guns or balloons were knocked out. For both sets of guns, it remained a war of speed and accuracy, where improvements in the technology of killing, and practice, were making both sides more lethal. A war where you saw the death and damage the enemy did to you but not the damage you did to them.

Penrose left Hazebrouck very conscious that the problems which he had left behind in January were now firmly back with him.

In the Officers' Club at Bailleul, before he caught up with his junior officers from 10 KBS, Penrose quietly contemplated the letters he now had to write to the relatives of the dead under his command. Last year he had only written five letters of condolence, yet just three months into this new year, he was facing the task of writing ten times as many.

Just after they sat down to dinner, Penrose was handed a wine list in a solid leather folder with 'Officers' Club in Bailleul' embossed in heavy gilt. In that second, the old anger was back inside him and he threw it on the table in total disgust.

"What the bloody hell's going on?" he shouted. "How can it be?" he demanded of his fellow officers in general, his voice rising, "that someone, somewhere has a job to produce this, with fucking gold lettering?" He picked up the wine list again and waved it around. "Why aren't they fighting this fucking war?" he demanded.

It was the first time he had used the f-word in his life. Others in the mess looked around disapprovingly, at which point Penrose nodded an apology to his fellow diners. He sank into his chair in despair. This was no longer a war which had to be won so we could all go home. It had become permanent; almost an institution, breeding its own longevity!

The report from 32 KBS was similar. What had started out as a soft war for balloonics was now proving very tough indeed. As his officers spoke, Penrose felt a sense of guilt about being away from his men during such tough times, although he didn't know how he would have made it better. It just gave him one purpose, to do his damnedest to keep his men safe and alive so they could get home to their families when it was all over.

It was with the knowledge gained at Hazebrouck and Bailleul that Penrose duly reported to his Colonel. He had already written an apology after his last outburst and perhaps this was why he got a much warmer reception than he expected. Nevertheless, Penrose started the meeting repeating his fulsome apology, although perhaps it wasn't necessary because the Colonel seemed genuinely pleased to have him back.

Penrose reported that aeroplane flight would only work for bombardment targeting when they were equipped with radios, but they would always have limited time in the air. For these two reasons, it made them less effective than balloons for artillery targeting.

"Write it up, dear boy," was the Colonel's response, for he had already worked it out. "Only sent you on that bloody course to make sure you weren't around to disobey my orders," he acknowledged. "Also, I needed to get you out of here after that report of yours claiming that the order to walk not run, on the first day of the Battle of Albert[9], had resulted in a huge number of unnecessary deaths. As you can imagine, it made you very unpopular with all those that were involved in giving that instruction."

Penrose hadn't imagined, because he was unaware that his report of the observation of others had caused such a problem. He hadn't been making any accusations, just reporting the facts as his men saw them.

"We lost 57,000 men on that first day, 20,000 killed," said the Colonel. He paused and looked at the ground. The responsibility of rank weighed heavily on his shoulders. "Bloody shame, bloody shame," he added, shaking his head in despair, "but we won't make the same mistake next time. They'll be damn well ordered to run!"

---

[9] The Battle of Albert is the name given to the first of the Battles of the Somme in 1916

Penrose smiled weakly for he didn't know what to say.

"We're planning another big push in the summer around the Ypres salient," said the Colonel. "I've put 36 KBS under your command and sent it up to Poperinge, so you'll have three balloons in that sector. I've made 32 KBS the reserve section for the time being and ordered it back to Célieux Ridge to nursemaid the bloody French."

Penrose grimaced his agreement at the same time as quietly cursing. Ypres was over 75 miles to the north of Célieux Ridge. His burden had just been multiplied many times.

"I need three of your KBSs in the air nearly all the time," ordered the Colonel. "There's a lot of preparation work to be done."

"Yes sir," said Penrose weakly.

"We have to make it happen this time." There was dogged determination in the Colonel's voice. "If the Germans do move troops from the Eastern Front, as they could do at any moment, it will make things very sticky. It's why we have to attack, and attack now."

It was with those words that Penrose was dismissed. Just as he was leaving, the Colonel suddenly barked at him, "Where are your medals?"

"I don't have any medals, sir."

"Of course you've got medals! Where's your Pip, the Mons Star?"

"Not eligible, sir, didn't join until after ..." Penrose didn't want to use the word retreat as that was defeatist talk known to upset.

"I thought you were one of us, *the Old Contemptibles?*"

"No sir."

"How come you have the rank of Major?"

"I think it's one of those strange fortunes, or misfortunes, of war, sir, depending on the way you look at it. It's because I speak fluent French."

"Ah, yes," said the Colonel, remembering his original orders. "Nevertheless, we've made a passably good soldier of you, haven't we?" he said, as he looked down and started to concentrate on his writing.

There was no need to reply. The meeting was at an end.

Chapter 32

France April 1917

My Dear Drew,
I have arrived safely in France and re-joined my unit.

I saw my Colonel who was most kind and surprisingly pleased to see me back. My soldiers suffered very badly while I was away, so I had the horrible job of writing far too many letters to loved ones back home. Despite the losses, morale seems good. I think it is having some spring sunshine on our backs which helps.

I have written to my sister introducing you as promised and have told her about your interest in going to Cambridge. I am sure she will write but it might be some time because her work means she gets very little spare time.

I wonder whether you realise we saw each other every single day for the three months I was in Lydd; sometimes two or three times a day. I have to admit I have thought about you every day since then; some days many times. I do miss you so.

When we said our goodbyes, I said clumsily that I would be coming back to marry you. It was, of course, an inappropriate thing to say given our age difference. I do hope I didn't offend you. I apologise if I did. Since then I have thought about what I said further. I am told, but I don't know why, that a woman should never marry a man if she is younger than half his age plus seven years. This is where we are now but, in a few years, when you are twenty-five, then these guidelines would work and you would not be embarrassed by marrying one so old.

It might seem a long time, but Cambridge is unlikely to offer you a place if you are married and it will take three years to get your degree so that is half the time gone.

I have been thinking about what I might do after the war that could keep me near Cambridge. I am sure aviation is going to be the next big thing and with the number of hours I have logged up, I am sure I could quite quickly become a commercial aviator. What do you think?

Would you be so kind as to introduce me to your father when I next have leave? I would so like to meet him.

Fondly yours,

Penrose

PS: I read the 'Age of Reason' on the boat back. What a time to be alive when, in a few words, it was possible to set out the arguments for an enduring political philosophy. I can now understand why you want to study this at Cambridge.

Chapter 33

France August 1917

Dear Ma and Pa,

Thank you for your letters. They bring so much comfort. I am sorry I don't write as often as I should, but I hope you get the postcards letting you know I am safe.

It was lovely to be at home over Easter, to get some sun and see England in spring was truly heartening. War denudes even the trees and hedgerows of any form of life and everything can look so bleak.

To think on Good Friday, when we were in church together praying for the war to end, the American Congress was voting to join the war! It renews your faith in God, and prayer, for with their troops now arriving, it doesn't matter about the Russians. I am sure we are bound to win, and everyone here feels the same.

It was truly lovely to see you both looking so well.

As you will have read from the newspapers, the last few weeks have been very tough. My job has changed once again. I am now in charge of a much bigger station. I moved to stay with Dr Barclay. Honestly, I think I am in love with him and him with me. But don't worry, it's not the marrying kind of love, for Eden is already married; it's a bit like the love I have for Penrose. In any case, he needs me, for while he is an outstanding CMO[10], very caring and capable, he is hopeless at everything else.

Here we have a ward of just over 60 beds and the wounds are so awfully bad. Heads smashed to pieces, arms, legs, and feet blown off, shots to the lungs and stomach with pus just pouring out. Sometimes it seems impossible to know how to even begin putting these soldiers back together again. These are sights no one should ever see or hear.

---

[10] Chief Medical Officer

I hear nothing from Penrose. Only what you, and a young woman called Drew, tell me. Has he told you about Drew? She wants to go to Cambridge University after the war, so Penrose gave her my name. We have corresponded since then. She is exceptionally erudite and appears to be very fond of him, although she is far too young.

Recently we had to nurse a severely injured Warrant Officer from Penrose's regiment. Recognising my name, he asked if we were related. He said that Penrose had dropped a bit of a brick; that his Colonel and men really liked him, but his fellow officers had got very cross with him as he keeps telling them how to do their jobs. Apparently, his course in Lydd was to get him out of the way for a little while, as his Colonel didn't want Penrose refusing an order he had given. The nice thing was how highly this man spoke of Penrose. He said, "He was a darn good officer, one of the best." It made me feel so proud.

Our men are so very brave. Honestly, there is not a man I have met who is not to be admired. In the worst of adversities, they find something to laugh about. If I had time, I would compose a joke book, for if all else fails, I could tell their jokes in music halls.

Your ever-loving daughter,

Juliette

Chapter 34

Célieux Ridge, France 30th May 1918

Note to reader: Those not interested in Penrose's active service in World War 1 may miss this chapter.

"SIR, COMMANDANT ÉTIENNE Guégan sends his best wishes and was wondering whether you would like to join him for dinner this evening?" asked Penrose's batman as he pored over a mountain of paperwork in his newly purchased wooden caravan.

When Penrose had returned from Lydd in March the previous year, he had taken to heart that this was going to be a long war and therefore he had to make himself as comfortable as possible. This was his way of doing it. His caravan, complete with bed, stove, desk, wash basin, oil lamps and windows, was his den on wheels. There were just three snags. It had taken nearly a year to arrive after it was first ordered. It was built with the quality of a first-class ship's cabin, making it so heavy it needed two horses every time it had to be moved, particularly when moving over a field. It was also far less use than Penrose had hoped because it was an immediate target vulnerable to shell attack. In recognition of the danger, its semi-permanent placement had become Cotta's Patch on Célieux Ridge, where it was hidden safely against the trees

Having made preparation for his own comfort, Penrose was spending much less time at Célieux Ridge. The demands on all his sections were never ending as his balloons were constantly moved up and down the front line following the incessant changes of instruction from Corp Command. He was therefore glad to have been ordered back to check on what had effectively become his reserve section stationed on Célieux Ridge and to spend a few days in his home on wheels.

Penrose looked up surprised to check on what he was being told. Only a few weeks before, the Germans had broken out from behind the Hindenburg Line[11] and launched a major attack between Soissons and Reims with Paris as their objective. The Spring Offensive had started. Further, for the last two months Paris had been fired upon daily by German long-range guns which were over 120 kilometres away and took over 200 seconds before each shell hit its target. So successful was the first day of the attack from three Krupp canons on Paris that the German Kaiser declared a national holiday. This shelling had resulted in a frenzied atmosphere in Paris, and the French government started to draw up plans to evacuate to Bordeaux. It made Penrose wonder what it was that brought Étienne to these parts. Surely, he had more pressing issues? More importantly, how does Commandant Guégan know where I am, he wondered.

"Please send my compliments to Commandant Guégan. Thank him for the invitation. Please tell him it would be my pleasure to join him at 7 pm this evening."

For a long time Penrose had thought that the installation of the telephone line between his command post on Célieux Ridge and the French Command post in de Foucy had proven to be a double-edged sword. While it meant that the two sides could communicate daily, and in far safer circumstances, the intelligence flow had almost stopped, for without the benefits of a glass or two of red wine, the discussions had become perfunctory and short. Yes, it would be a good thing to catch up.

The threat of snipers had long abated and so it was on horseback that Penrose travelled into de Foucy. It was the first time Penrose had been back since Flagstaff had been shot by a sniper. He thought of him as he rode past the spot and removed his cap in salute. He then resolved to write to his father about the trust fund for the men of his Balloon Sections which he had wanted him to start after Flagstaff's death. The casualties in recent months now made it even more important.

---

[11] The Hindenburg Line was a German defensive position built in the winter of 1916 – 1917 and then retreated behind in February and March 1917, laying waste to the land to the west as they left.

It was two older, wiser, perhaps bitter and certainly more cynical soldiers who sat down to eat in the same mess that they had done nearly three years before. Immediately Étienne and Penrose shook hands, there was a warmth between the two of them, only ever enjoyed by good friends reunited as though they had never been apart.

"Many thanks for your help at Verdun, and for so long," said Étienne as his opening remark, showing how long it was since the two men had spoken.

"Glad to help," said Penrose.

"Sorry we lost so many of your men," Étienne continued.

"Yeh, it was sad; caused a bit of bother, but it was the right thing to do."

"Holmes proved an excellent officer," continued Étienne.

"Yes, he's very good," agreed Penrose. He should have had a promotion long ago," at which point their attention turned to food, which was excellent as before. With the wine considerably improved, the two men talked freely about the war and in particular the political situation.

They both agreed that now US troops had arrived in Europe and with tanks on the battlefield, the war would surely be won. They both agreed that the question was whether this would be before exhaustion had set in, and with it an adverse turn of morale. Étienne was not sure, as the effects of the Russian Revolution weighed heavily on his thought processes. He wondered whether its influence would spread to the Western Front.

"Did you know that on 29th December last year the Bolsheviks abolished all ranks in the Russian army?" said Penrose, fairly certain he was imparting news.

"No," said Étienne looking both shocked and puzzled. "How do they expect to keep order?"

"My guess is that most of the officers will have left by now, gone home. They'll know that to stay will have meant almost certain death. Historically, that's what happens to officers in revolutions."

"What about the NCOs?" asked Étienne.

"They'll have nothing to do with such a ruling because they'll want to keep their extra pay. It will be the NCOs who are in charge now."

"Makes 'em damn lousy allies then," commented Étienne bitterly. "Do you think their revolution could spread to the Western Front?" he asked again, anxiously.

Penrose thought it would not, Étienne was not so sure.

"The Germans' Spring Offensive came as one hell of a shock," said Étienne, obliquely changing the subject. "I suppose we should have expected it given the situation in Russia, but of course you never do," he continued.

"For God's sake, I hope it's their last gasp," responded Penrose. "It was pretty damn devastating. Our intelligence estimates that the Germans fired, on the first day of their breakout from the Hindenburg Line, the same number of shells as we fired in the whole of the first week of the Battle of the Somme.

"The fog really helped them too," added Étienne, while mentally absorbing the shelling statistic.

"It certainly did. It added to the chaos on our side." Penrose paused, then continued: "The latest casualty estimates I saw suggest we've lost, dead, injured or captured, the same number of men as we lost in the first day of the Somme."

"What, over 50,000 men?" asked Étienne, looking quite shocked.

"That's what I'm told, probably a few thousand more," said Penrose. "Probably far more captured this time. They've also taken back almost all the land we won over the last two years," he added, being fairly sure he was not telling Étienne something he did not already know.

"Hell, I didn't know it was that bad," said Étienne truthfully.

"Yeh, well, it forced Lloyd-George to release about half a million men he had tucked safely away in the UK to go into the battle and with that, hopefully, the situation is now back under some kind of control.

"Will Haig send reinforcements to help us stop the German advance through Soissons and Reims?" asked Étienne.

Penrose didn't answer the question. He thought it was too loaded, too sudden. It was presented in such a way as to make Penrose think that it was this question that had given rise to their meeting, which is exactly what it was.

"I have to congratulate you on your promotion," said Penrose, changing the subject. "What are you doing now?"

"I am on Marshal Ferdinand Foch's staff, and between me and thee, if he or anyone else could tell me what my job actually is, that would be helpful."

"An ADC?"

"Yes, something like that, except he has five of those. In cricket, you have the position of Long Stop, the guy who catches the ball when the wicket keeper has missed it, don't you?"

"Yes," replied Penrose with a nod.

"Well, that's my job." Then, bringing the subject back to the current battle, Étienne continued his probing. "It's just now, with the Germans at the Marne River, Paris looks very exposed and the rumours are that the relationship between Pétain and Haig has all but broken down."

"Really?" said Penrose feigning surprise. He paused, then added, "I'm afraid it's become fairly well known that Pétain is looking terrible. Apparently, he said bitterly and out loud to Haig, so it was heard by his staff officers, that: *the Germans will beat the English in open country, then they'll beat us as well.* As you can imagine that didn't go down too well. The feeling is that this is something he shouldn't even be thinking, let alone saying."

"Oh dear," commented Étienne. "It's what Foch feared. Some are saying that the two men can't stand being in the same room."

"I don't know," said Penrose. "I would be surprised if Haig felt like that. He's too professional to let personalities get in the way."

"You only get to be a General by having the ego the size of a mountain," said Étienne. "Of course personalities are going to play a part. History has always shown it to be so."

Penrose thought for a moment. He knew Étienne was right and then smiled. "I've got it," he teased, "Foch wants to know whether Haig is going to send troops to support the French along the Marne River, or whether he's going to give Pétain a V-sign?"

"Ah, Agincourt," said Étienne, all seriously. "At least we are on the same side this time." He then added, "Why you rejoice in us cutting off your fellow countryman's fingers with a salute has always seemed strange to us."

"It's not a salute, Étienne," said Penrose, with a large grin on his face. "It's telling you to fuck off."

"Ah," said Étienne. "An English swearword I didn't know before the start of this war."

"Look, Étienne," said Penrose, seriously. "I don't understand the question. Foch was appointed Commander-in Chief of the Allied Armies only a few weeks ago, at the end of March, before that he was Commander-in-Chief of the Western Front with the title Généralissime. He's only got to order, and it will be done."

"Foch will not give Haig an order," said Étienne, firmly. "He knows it would be political dynamite. My bet is that the politicians have only given him the job in the expectation that he is there to referee between Haig and Pétain."

"I don't know what's in Haig's mind, but this is my guess: I don't think he's going to release troops to help on the Marne. It would weaken his forces in Flanders, risking a German breakthrough. My sense is that the German strategy is to divide, weaken, defeat and rule."

Étienne nodded in agreement.

"You can be sure that if an officer of my rank, with just three years' experience and no training in battle strategy, is thinking this, then it's fairly certain that Haig is hearing the same thing," said Penrose.

"Thank you," said Étienne. "Sincerely, thank you. It's what we thought, but it is useful to have it confirmed."

"There's another point, Étienne, which might help reinforce that thinking," said Penrose. "If Pétain did make his remarks about the English being beaten in the countryside, and the two men can't stand each other, then Haig is not going to give Pétain the satisfaction of being proven right by releasing troops to help out elsewhere."

"You're saying that this is just our fight."

"Well, not quite. I gather there are six British divisions in the sector which had been withdrawn from the front line for a rest but are now in the thick of fighting alongside you."

"Yes, there are, although none are at full strength. Please don't say I said this, but the problem is to some extent our own making. Our defences were not properly developed, even after all this time. Honestly Penrose, it's an embarrassment."

"And for us too," added Penrose. "The German Spring Offensive proved how badly we'd prepared our defences. Look, you've just got to hold on, along the Marne, for as long as you can. The Americans are now here. It will only be a matter of time before the tables are turned," he added encouragingly.

"What's happening locally?" asked Étienne changing the subject.

"Sniper activity has completely gone away, and for a long time everything has been noticeably quiet, until recently. For a while, it was the same story. One of us would send up a balloon so the other would too, our guns would fire a few shells at their guns or balloons and visa versa, then a couple of aeroplanes would come over and down came the balloons; all to be repeated the next day. It was almost as though there was a phoney war here. Suddenly, for no good reason, the Germans seem to have a couple more guns and these are aimed at our trenches along Célieux Ridge. For the last five days, from dawn until exactly 11.00 hours we get a constant barrage. We've taken a couple of direct hits which have made the men windy, but nothing serious. I gather the same is true for you?"

"Yes, we've lost some men too," said Étienne, "and as you know, we have no artillery at de Foucy, so we can't fire back so we're really dependent on your guns. But, for some reason which defeats me, we've two Renault FT tanks stationed there."

"You don't think the Germans are planning on attacking the Ridge, do you?" asked Penrose.

"Would you?" questioned Étienne, in a tone which suggested that he would not.

The two men then talked it through as though it were a military exercise and they were the Germans attacking the hill. Strangely, it was something they had never done before. Very quickly they dismissed an attack from the west, their rear, as it was too far to go around. They dismissed an attack from the north or south because the woods made it impossible for troops to move in to attack. No, the only way was from the east, over miles of fields, followed by a long steady climb and then a steep hill, and with balloon intelligence, it would be easy to see a build-up, and thus forecast its coming.

At the end of their discussion, Étienne and Penrose concluded that, even though the Germans might win the battle for the ridge, it would be at a huge cost of lives with little obvious benefit. They also decided that, with the village of Mivry still virtually deserted, and with no build-up of troops in Mincé, nothing was likely to happen soon. Nevertheless, Coeur de Foucy still remained a good place to station a reserve company.

At the end of the dinner, as they said their goodbyes, neither man could remember when they had last enjoyed such a frank and wide-ranging discussion on military and strategic matters, certainly not with their fellow officers. Perhaps it was because, whenever they dined in their messes or officers' clubs, there were always both senior and junior officers present. As a result, everyone was always judging and being judged. These two men weren't judging each other. They were just being good friends. Importantly, Étienne was going to tell Foch what he already knew. Marshal Pétain needed a rest.

As Étienne made his way back to his tent and bed, he stopped, turned around and went to find the Capitaine in charge of the Company residing in Coeur de Foucy. There was something niggling in his mind, and he couldn't place exactly what it was.

"I'm afraid he's asleep, sir," said the Corporel on guard duty at the entrance to the sleeping quarters.

"What's your name, Corporel?" asked Étienne.

"Bellanger, Mon Commandant. Corporel Georges Bellanger."

Étienne paused. He thought he recognised the name, so he looked hard into the face of the man in front of him until he was certain he did not know him.

"Corporel, I want to do an exercise first thing tomorrow morning. At the crack of dawn, at exactly 06.00 hours," said Étienne. "I want you to sound the alarm reporting Célieux Ridge is under attack, and then give the written instruction, I'm about to give you, to your Capitaine. I'm going to test your Company's responsiveness to see how quickly it can get its men into battle. There are to be no new orders or preparations tonight. You're to say nothing, nothing at all. Do I make myself clear? We'll just see how it goes."

The Corporel swallowed hard. They may have done this as a practice drill in Capitaine Guégan's day at Coeur de Foucy, but this was entirely new to him. He was truly anxious as to how his Capitaine and his Company were going to perform.

Penrose's horse ride to Cotta's Patch was accompanied by an uncomfortable niggle as to their defence readiness too. Immediately he arrived back at base, he gave instructions that the balloon would go up at exactly dawn, which would mean preparations were going to take place in the pre-dawn light. He was going to take his first balloon flight of 1918.

Chapter 35

Célieux Ridge, France 30ᵗʰ May 1918

BACK IN HIS caravan Penrose lay on the bed with his legs, still clad in his riding boots, dangling over the edge; his conversation with Étienne earlier that evening long forgotten. Very slowly he took out of his breast pocket the first ever letter he had received from Drew and unfolded it. He had read it many times, but he wanted to read it once again, just to make sure he had it right.

> *Lydd, Kent*
> *May 1917*
>
> *My Dear Penrose,*
> *Thank you for your delightful letter. Lydd has not been the same since you left. There is no one else to chum up with as we did. Everyone is either studying hard or being very school boyish.*
> *My father says he would be pleased to meet you. I mentioned your age formula to him. He thought it very odd that marriage should be so governed in polite society. His view, like mine, is that marriage is a matter for the heart and not some rule book.*
> *I know I could not marry a man who would not respect my need for learning; and therefore to wait until I finish at Cambridge, as you say, seems very sensible to me. Although with everything so fragile, it does seem rather silly to be planning our future. Who knows, you might find someone else over the years ahead, but I do hope not.*
> *Aviation sounds an interesting job, although somewhat dangerous. Is it something you can do from anywhere? Do you not want to go back to influencing how the country is run?*
> *Now women over 30 have the vote, I am wondering whether I*

shouldn't plan on being a Member of Parliament. Do you think it would be a hard thing to do? Would you mind terribly? Perhaps we could be the first husband and wife team in history to go into parliament. Wouldn't that be fun?

I have had a lovely letter from Juliette, suggesting a reading list. It's immensely helpful preparation for the entrance exam. I didn't know I would have to sit such a thing. It makes it all seem the more daunting.

Do take great care of yourself.

Fondly yours,

Drew

PS. What do you think of John Stuart Mills essay on the Subjection of Women? Its important to us that I know.

In all their letters, it was the only one in which she had written about them being a husband and wife team. She had also asked him, indirectly, whether he thought men and women should be treated equally. It seemed a most telling question. In his head, he wanted to make sure that he had interpreted her question correctly. He was being tested on the question of marriage; he was sure of it.

Chapter 36

France 30th May 1918

Note to reader: Those not interested in Penrose's active service in World War 1 may miss this chapter.

EXACTLY AT THE same moment Penrose and Étienne were taking their first sip of wine, Major Von Strader was standing six miles away, staring at Célieux Ridge. Ever since the German Army had fallen behind their Hindenburg Line defences, he had been in charge of three Stormtrooper[12] platoons occupying Mincé.

Almost every day he had studied the hill, with the British and French trenches at the top, and wondered how he might take it. The thing which amused Von Strader that evening was that he now knew exactly how he was going to do it, and when.

Unlike Penrose, Étienne, and their superiors, Von Strader had a different opinion of Célieux Ridge's strategic advantage. He was convinced, if the hill could be taken and held, then the four lanes between each of the five woods would provide a new direct route towards Paris; one lane would not be enough, but to take and hold the whole Ridge, would be very different. They would be able to

---

[12] Stormtroopers were specialist soldiers of the German Army trained to use surprise and infiltration tactics on Allied trenches. They were specially equipped for the task. For example, their uniforms were reinforced with leather patches on their knees and elbows to protect them when crawling, special bags were issued to carry grenades and their rifles were adapted to increase their close-range fire power. A feature of the Stormtroopers was the quality of its leadership where junior officers could use their initiative to change tactics in response to changes on the battlefield, and the way a second troop could quickly follow in support of a first troop if it had failed to take its objective.

march as the Roman Army, almost in a straight line. He had another reason, vanity. Slowly, he became obsessed with it as a prize. He had convinced himself that if the Ridge were taken with his plan then his name would go into German military history books and the ridge would be renamed, for all time, as Strader Ridge.

Like Penrose and Étienne, Von Strader had concluded that to attack from the north or south was not feasible. The planted forests made it impossible to move either way along the ridge. There was only one way. It was from the east and to do this would mean traversing about three miles over open fields and then attacking uphill; a huge tactical disadvantage.

Having decided the problem was insurmountable, Von Strader first decided to list his strategic advantages. Firstly, the British and French line was only one trench deep. If he could take that, then he could take the Ridge. Secondly, with trees behind them, it was impossible for the British to bring accurate artillery fire on any attacking troops unless they could get and keep a balloon in the air. The French had no artillery there. In fact, apart from a few guns to protect the balloon section, Von Strader concluded that the risk from British artillery was limited. Thirdly, over the eight-mile length of the Ridge, there were no more than two French Companies and two British Companies, about 450 soldiers in all, or one every 28 metres. For reasons of nature, these men automatically clustered with the woods at their rear. The French command post at Coeur de Foucy was the home of the one reserve company. Strader didn't know where the English reserve company was held, but he knew it was not close enough to affect the immediate battle.

With military odds of three attacking men to each one defending, Strader reckoned he would need 1,500 men to launch an attack. However, he was certain if he could bring in an element of surprise then he could capture the hill with far less than that. He knew that surprise was the key, and with a head-on assault, there would be no surprise. There had to be a solution to the problem. He just had to find it.

Inspiration comes from the most unusual places. The key is to carry the problem around in your subconsciousness and be open to ideas.

That is precisely what Von Strader had been doing for a few months when he went to the library in Mincé for his weekly French lesson. As he stood there waiting for his teacher, he was browsing the books on the shelves in the Histoire section, taking them out at random, flicking through the pages, and putting them back. As he turned the pages of one of the books, he saw a picture which caught his eye. It was of a painting dramatizing the death of Thomas 'Stonewall' Jackson following his attack at Chancellorsville. What particularly caught his attention was the fact that the scene was set around a forest. Without waiting, he impatiently took the book to his teacher and, interrupting her current lesson, demanded a translation.

Jackson, Von Strader learnt, had led 25,000 Confederate troops through more than 10 miles of wooded countryside, arriving on the flank of the Union line which he attacked in full force, and by surprise, sending the Yankees fleeing in an historic victory.

Throughout his following French lesson, Von Strader's mind was far away from what he was being taught. His thoughts were on how he could get enough men in to the woods behind the British and French lines and attack them by surprise from the rear. If he could do this, then he was certain that victory would be his.

Immediately he had conceived the idea of using the woods, he stopped the snipers going behind enemy lines on harrying missions. He did it in the expectation that the British and French would stop patrolling them. This way, these woods could become his wooden horse of Troy, hiding his men there until they were ready to attack.

The answer as to how to get his troops into the woods was so obvious, he could hardly believe his luck. The Tommies and Poilu[13] had left their front door open, for there was no trench between the French and British troops just a roll of barbed wire. All he had to do was wait until dark and walk through. Once in the woods in sufficient numbers, they would come out as a uniform raiding party and attack the British and French lines from the rear, allowing a full assault to take place from the front.

---

[13] Tommy was the German slang for a British soldier. Poilu was the German slang for a French soldier.

Night after night, with a small patrol as protection, Von Strader made his way unseen up to the barbed wire between the British and French forces. He studied the shallows in the ground and concluded that at certain spots, directly opposite his enemy, there was dead ground of about 150 to 200 metres from their lines in which he could hide troops under the cover of darkness, ready to attack. He was about to break one of the cardinal rules of battle. You don't bring your own forces to attack from the front and back at the same time, for this way, it is certain you will fire on your own side. But, Strader concluded, there must be an exception to this rule. It was, he decided, when there was no possibility of attacking from the flank.

Time and time again, Von Strader submitted his plans to his commanding officer, each time improving them. First, he wrote strategically. Then he wrote tactically. Then he wrote the orders each of the platoon commanders were to be given, and finally he calculated the logistical requirements. However, all these fell on deaf ears as Von Strader's commanding officer had been focusing on something different. He was working on General Erich Ludendorff's plan for 65 divisions to attack along a 60-mile front of the Somme. It was only when Ludendorff needed a decoy attack, after the German Spring Offensive had lost its impetus, that Von Strader's plans were retrieved from the files, dusted down, and examined. They were thought sufficiently plausible to at least cause confusion. As a result, Strader was promoted from Hauptleute to Major, told he could have an Abteilung (battalion) of just over 1,000 men, and he would have to succeed or fail with that. It was less than half of what he thought he needed to succeed, but now, with his orders received, he had to plan and execute his mission with just that number. He was optimistic that his name would go into the history books.

Four woods each capable of hiding three Zug (platoons) of 30 to 40 men in each would take just under half his force. His enemy, he decided, had given him the perfect access point to get the rest of his men into battle; the no man's land between the two trenches. His plan was that over several nights his men would quietly climb the hill, secretly cut their way through the barbed wire, replacing it afterwards so that it didn't look tampered with, and then hide in the woods.

Von Strader had concluded that hiding his troops on the French side would be easy, for once through the barbed wire they could hide quickly in the two woods to the south for there was nothing to stop them. On the British side, it was more difficult for two reasons. Firstly, the first wood to the north of his envisaged entrance had Cotta's Patch in the middle, full of Balloon equipment and artillery, so this could not be used to hide in. Secondly, Penrose had extended the British trench, so it now swept around the wood for a further 200 yards and to the south, such that this part faced the French woods into which the sniper had disappeared. It meant that Von Strader's troops were going to hide in the two woods further to the north. This meant going around and behind the first British wood before they could hide away in the other two. The chance of being detected, Von Strader concluded, was nearly four times as great.

Von Strader instructed his few remaining troops that were to attack through no man's land, where there were no trenches immediately in front of them, just barbed wire. They were then to wheel north and attack the 200 yards of new trenches ordered by Penrose. Once taken, they were to proceed into Cotta's Patch. In fact, it was in Cotta's Patch that Strader expected the biggest battle to be. Therefore, he ordered all troops, after they had achieved their objective of clearing out the British and French lines, to proceed to the battle on Cotta's Patch.

Von Strader was first instructed to attack on Saturday 6th April 1918. It was then delayed, almost daily, until now, when he was ordered to go at first light on Friday 31st May 1918 and so, over the previous week he had been secreting his soldiers into the woods; a task made much easier by the swirling mist which had captured the early mornings.

As Von Strader stood staring at Célieux Ridge, his body was wracked with a mixture of excitement and anxiety, for having spent months on his plans, his biggest doubt was whether he had enough troops to ensure victory. He could see himself in his dreams arriving on Cotta's Patch just at the moment the British and French surrendered, and his victory was won. Anticipation of the day ahead made it quite impossible for him to go to bed and sleep.

Chapter 37

France 31st May 1918

Note to reader: Those not interested in Penrose's active service in World War 1 may miss this chapter.

THERE WAS AN unusual swirling mist for the first 300 feet above Célieux Ridge which Penrose rode through on his first flight of 1918 until he came to clear blue sky. At about 1,000 feet, his balloon was caught by a slight westerly wind which took it towards the enemy lines where Penrose had focused his binoculars. It was when they were at 2,000 feet that the German guns opened fire on the British and French lines. At this point, Sgt. Langholme, the flight's pilot, and Penrose started to work together to estimate the range and bearing of the German guns which had moved up from behind Mincé, where they had previously been positioned, to being very clearly in view at Mivry. As they continued to rise to their planned height of 4,000 feet, Penrose shouted artillery instructions to his ground crew who had yet to open fire. Interestingly, not a salvo was fired in their direction. After fifteen minutes of constant firing there was a sudden change in the noise as the German guns in the distance started to fire smoke shells at the British and French lines. Then there was another change in sound, this time a series of very loud cracks.

It was on the sound of these cracks that Penrose and Langholme stopped looking outwards and looked directly below. Suddenly, all the way along the line, ant sized men were appearing out of the woods and attacking the British and French trenches.

"Where the hell did they come from?" shouted Penrose and Langholme together in a strange unison.

"Attack, attack, sound the alarm! This is not a drill," shouted

Penrose into the phone. The desperation in his voice conveyed everything that needed to be said.

It was then that Penrose and Langholme saw another set of menants appear out of the smoke. They watched through their binoculars as these men ran up the hill in the direction of the gap, between the separated British and French lines, and into no man's land between their woods. Penrose studied the land carefully looking for their rolls of barbed-wire defences, but these had been swept aside putting nothing in the Germans' way. He carefully examined the British trench to the east of Cotta's Patch wood and realised that, while it was manned, it was not under attack. Worse still, his new southern trench, dug specifically to deal with this eventuality, had not a single man in it.

At 4,000 feet the battle strategy was plain to see. What made matters worse, was that Penrose could see a trail of horse and carts leaving Mivry on the road which led directly towards the French lines bringing, what he was certain were, German reinforcements. If the French lines were knocked out by the attack from the rear, then those trucks would drop more men off at the entrance to no man's land and their position would be overwhelmed.

"Get Lt. Gray on the phone," yelled Penrose, demanding the attention of his most senior officer on the ground.

Once Gray was manning the telephone, Penrose slowed down and calmly gave his orders. "Gray, these are your orders. Start winching us down now, now do you hear! Take the two machine guns at Alpha and Beta and move them immediately to Charlie and Delta. Take every other man along the Cotta's Patch trench and move them into the new southern trench straightaway. There's not to be a man without a rifle, not a man, do you understand?"

Gray wrote down what he was told, confirmed in the affirmative and then immediately started to shout out the instructions.

"Gray, Gray," yelled Penrose into the phone.

"Yes sir."

"Please send Lieutenant Walker my compliments and tell him I am ordering him to rapid fire at will into no man's land. Bearing 175° to 185°, range ...," Penrose paused as he examined his map and scribbled a calculation, "... range 1,600 to 1,700 yards," he continued.

"What?" shouted Gray not understanding his orders.

The guns had always fired eastwards, toward the enemy lines in accordance with a calibrated firing plan which comprised a grid of 25 yards long and 100 yards wide. Then, with an observer using a clock code, with concentric rings of 25 yards, the firing of the guns could be adjusted to be brought accurately on the target. No work had been done on firing to the south. Why would it; it would mean firing towards an ally!

"Bearing 175° to 185°, range 1,600 to 1,700 yards," shouted Penrose again.

"But that's towards the French," protested Gray.

"For Christ sake Gray!" yelled Penrose. "We're under bleed'n attack. Get the guns firin' into no man's land. I repeat," he paused to check his numbers. "Bearing 175° to 185°, range 1,600 to 1,700 yards," he confirmed, "rapid fire at will."

"Bearing 175° to 185°, range 1,600 to 1,700, rapid fire at will," repeated Gray, the expression 'no man's land' confirming exactly what he needed to know.

"Confirmed," shouted Penrose and at that moment the winch jammed, and the phone went dead.

Penrose shouted his instructions again but to no avail. He looked down into the trenches. It was no longer ants moving about but men in armed hand to hand combat. German potato mashers were being thrown at short range. The start of the attack had done a huge amount of early damage along both the French and British lines. Penrose put his field glasses to his eyes and searched for alternative machine gun posts further down. There was one post on the French line. It was doing a lot of damage, but it didn't look as though it could hold out much longer under the pressure from the German attack.

The Corporal manning the Lewis machine gun at Beta was one of the first to be injured by a German hand grenade, with metal fragments slicing off his ear. Regardless, and on his own initiative, he took his team and his ammo and moved his post to Charlie where he had a 270° arc of fire east down over the hill and south over no man's land. Penrose was thrilled to see this gun open fire for it was having a devastating effect on the Germans. It was a post the Germans were going to have to take out if they were to win and Penrose knew it had to be held at all costs.

The most important thing now, concluded Penrose, was to get the French reserve company being held in Coeur de Foucy into the fight, and damn quickly. Penrose shouted into the phone again, but it was dead. He banged it and shouted further, but from the way Penrose threw it away in disgust, Langholme knew it was, once again, not working.

"I must jump," shouted Penrose.

"Let's just wait and see if they can fix it," said Langholme calmly. "This battle needs observation. You can command from here."

"Yes, you're right," conceded Penrose. "You stay at this height, but I can't command anything without comms."

Penrose was removing his greatcoat as he spoke, flinging it out of the basket to make way. He stuffed his map between his shirt and tunic and reached for the parachute harness which he strapped around his body. The harness was attached to the parachute, held in a cylindrical-acorn shaped container underneath the basket. He put one leg over and sat astride. Then he put the other over, clinging onto the sides, trying to keep his balance. It was then that Langholme moved to support him and, whether he wanted to go or not, Penrose lost his balance and was ejected into the air. His eyes widened. Bile was now in his throat and he could swear he felt his heart stop beating as he started to fall. Certainly, he was not breathing. The parachute snapped open, breaking Penrose's fall, the harness wacked into his shoulders and groin and his free fall was arrested.

Penrose floated in mid-air for a few seconds. The whistle of the wind in Penrose's ears meant he heard none of the shooting around him and, while he was looking at total carnage on the ground, he sensed a weird calmness he had never known before. Perhaps, he wondered, it was because he was about to die.

If Penrose had looked out, he would have seen the French Reserve company from de Foucy, ordered out by Étienne the night before as an exercise, now marching proudly on the French side of no man's land, breaking out from their order, and in sheer hatred and anger, running towards the Germans for what was to be an unholy battle.

Instead, he looked at the ground, bent his knees, and tucked in his elbows, as he had been taught. Still, nothing prepared him for the ground rush which came up and slapped him hard throughout his whole body. He was on the ground, rolling in agony. He fought for air, the wind having been knocked from his lungs. Penrose was sure every bone in his body had been broken.

Chapter 38

France July 1918

Note to reader: Those not interested in Penrose's active service in World War 1 may miss this chapter.

PENROSE WAS MARCHED through the door of the large wooden hut which had been established as a Court Martial in the grounds of a requisitioned farmhouse where he was being held under close arrest. He found it impossible to believe what was happening to him. Immediately after the Battle of Célieux Ridge, with the Germans defeated, he had been hailed a hero. Suddenly everyone saw what had been obvious to Von Strader and him; Célieux Ridge was on a direct route to Paris, and once captured, there would have been no stopping the German army until they got there.

"Left, right, left, right," shouted the sergeant to the right of him; he was escorted by a corporal on the other side.

"Halt," shouted the sergeant, just before the table at which three officers were sat; two majors and a full colonel, each bedecked with their medals. Penrose, and each of the men beside him, stopped, stood firmly to attention, and saluted. No salute was returned.

The colonel nodded to a lieutenant, seated at a table facing sideways to the court, who stood up. His chair made an embarrassing scraping noise on the unpolished wooden floor as he rose to speak.

"Name and rank?" shouted the Lieutenant. He was clearly addressing Dovingdon.

"Major David Victor Penrose Dovingdon," he responded, adding his army number for good measure.

"Were you the officer in command of 32 Kite Balloon Section on Friday, 31st May 1918?"

"Yes," said Penrose, deliberately omitting to say sir. "For the record I was also the commanding officer of 10 KBS, 36 KBS and 44 KBS," his tone reflected his attitude towards, what he considered to be, a total charade. This should damn well be a medal ceremony, he thought, not a sodding Court Martial.

"Say sir to an officer of the court," rebuked the Colonel.

Penrose stared at the Colonel, deliberately allowing his eyes to narrow as he did so. After a long, deliberate pause he said, "Yes, sir," in a manner which helped set the scene, for he was here to fight, not just for his life but against what he saw as a fundamental injustice.

"For the record," added the Lieutenant, his tone reflecting the same level of sarcasm as that adopted by Penrose, "Major Penrose was formerly the commanding officer of those balloon sections. He has been relieved of his command pending this Court Martial."

"Please read the charges," ordered the Colonel, at which point the Lieutenant started to read from a typed charge sheet.

"One: Major Dovingdon did on 31st May 1918, contrary to King's Regulations, desert his post, the basket of a Caquot balloon tethered and operated from a place known as Cotta's Patch on Célieux Ridge, being at a height of approximately 2,500 feet at the time of desertion.

Two: Major Dovingdon did at approximately 7.30am, on 31st May 1918, leave the flying balloon piloted by Sgt. Langholme, without the consent of its commanding officer, contrary to King's Regulations, and in doing so in the face of the enemy committed an act of cowardice as defined by Section 4 of the Army Action.

Three: Major Dovingdon failed to properly secure Célieux Ridge which enabled the German forces to penetrate his line and attack the British trenches from the rear leading to over 155 casualties.

Four: Major Dovingdon did on 31st May 1918 cause the death by murder of 46 French soldiers by giving instructions to artillery under his control to fire at will in a southerly bearing direction of between 175 and 185 degrees, and a range of 1,750 to 1,850 yards, directly into the path of the French soldiers coming into the battle."

It was the word murder, and the way it had been laboured, which threw Penrose from his stride. It was like a dagger to his heart and with it, while still standing to attention, he stopped listening. He heard a voice, droning on in the background, as other charges were read out.

Penrose was convinced he was on trial for his life for no other reason than the confusions of war. It was true; he had been responsible for friendly artillery fire on the French army as it marched onto Célieux Ridge and into the battle against the Germans on no man's land. A lot of French soldiers had lost their lives with many more badly injured. The scene of human destruction as the last German soldier alive, and uninjured, stood to surrender was one which Penrose would never be able to forget. In that moment of deafening silence, as one side knew they had won and the other lost, there was a single resounding shot from a pistol. Von Strader, who was badly injured, took his own life.

There was no doubt that it was British shelling which had abated the attack and it was the machine guns on the two French Renault FT tanks stationed at Coeur de Foucy which, when sent into the battle, gave the French and British their bloody victory.

Rather than celebrate the victory, as he believed both the French and British should have done, Penrose had found himself a pawn in a political game to keep the Allies united. Someone had to pay, to satisfy the French that justice was done for those whose lives were lost, and the person paying that price was Penrose. Not a word was being said about how the bravery of a very few French and English soldiers had defended a strategic routeway which, if lost, would have seen Paris at risk, and the death toll even higher.

Penrose's report on the Battle of Célieux Ridge was, as always, a frank and honest account of what had happened on that day. In his naivety, he admitted to the death of French soldiers by friendly British fire. Without anyone saying why, it was suggested to him that he withdrew his report and resubmit it. He did as he was asked; giving more detail, as that was what he thought was wanted. In his second report, he kept in the section on the French being killed under friendly fire. Why not? It was an accident and it was the truth.

Penrose was completely stunned when he was first arrested, but as there was no caution or immediate charge, he was not particularly worried. However, he found it strange to be questioned about his report, in extensive detail, by two officers from the Military Police.

An officer of equal rank, who was incredibly polite, went through it line by line. The result of the questioning was that Penrose was confined to barracks on his own surety as a 'gentleman'.

A few days later, another set of officers from the Military Police interviewed him. This time he was formally cautioned, and one officer asked a series of highly detailed and well-prepared questions, while the other took comprehensive notes. The interview was again very friendly and polite. The three men even found time to create a little jocularity out of the dreadful situation. It was then, right at the end, that the Senior Officer's attitude suddenly turned to stone. Everything before had been an act, to persuade cooperation. "I am arresting you for murder in that on the 31st May 1918 you did wilfully murder 46 French soldiers."

Penrose could not believe what was happening, and as he protested at the stupidity of it all, the two officers looked completely nonplussed. They were, after all, just doing their job.

In the days after that, he was lobbied to plead guilty and accept his punishment. All those who did the lobbying readily accepted that this would mean the death penalty. He was told it was his duty, and many times he was offered his pistol back on the understanding he would commit suicide.

Penrose declined to make this expected war sacrifice. One life, albeit his, for the loss of 46 French lives, would be proportionate, if this were his fault, but Penrose was sure it was not. It was one of those accidents of war for which no one person could be blamed. If there was any blame, it was with those that started this bloody war.

Penrose's refusal to plead guilty was immediately followed by him being arrested. It was the first time in memory that the regiment had to deal with the close arrest of an officer in wartime. It caused some immediate difficulties. In the end, his confines were a cleared out old horse stable attached to a large farm cottage with a complex of outbuildings which had been taken over by the British Army. It was known locally as 'Blag Cott'[14]. His room had been thoroughly

---

[14] The term Blag was the shortening of the French word 'blague' meaning joke or jest and Cott was the shortening of the English word 'cottage'.

whitewashed, every wall, floor, and roof truss. Apart from his bed, table and chair, there was not a spot that had not had at least two coats. Within the grounds of the farm, there were a series of sheds. Each had been erected to provide temporary accommodation to support the war effort, and one of these sheds had been commandeered, cleared out, and then set up as a courthouse.

"How do you plead to Charge One, in that on 31st May 1918 you did, contrary to King's Regulations, desert your post, being the basket of a Caquot balloon operated from Célieux Ridge?" Penrose was asked by the Lieutenant.

"Not guilty, and to all sixteen charges ... Sir," said Penrose, firmly.

"How do you plead to Count Two, in that on 31st May 1918, you exited a flying balloon without the consent of its commanding officer, contrary to King's Regulations?"

"Not guilty, and to all the sixteen charges ... Sir," said Penrose, again.

The list of all the charges was read out one by one, which included disobeying orders and numerous accounts of acting without authority. Penrose responded each time in exactly the same way. He was then given permission to sit at a table with his defence counsel, Sidney Caprang K.C. They had met the day before for the first time, and their one and only meeting had been for a total of just under three hours. This Court Martial was quite different from many of the others where soldiers faced the death penalty during the war; unusually Penrose had secured legal representation, very many others did not.

Caprang, a former soldier, had enjoyed a successful career at the Marine Bar before being called back to duty as defence counsel for many a hapless capital case which, to avoid embarrassment, the army wanted dead and buried; irrespective of the poor soul who inherited the body they wanted deep in the ground.

Caprang had enjoyed his former work as a shipping lawyer. It was well-paid but, most importantly, there was logic to the rules of the sea and the Marine Courts practised the law with fairness and an impartiality which had made it both internationally renowned and also the court of first choice for shipping litigants from all around the world. Now, Caprang was getting worried as to what, in this war, they were actually all fighting for. Whereas he knew it was vital to maintain discipline and morale, it was his 100% failure rate to win any case, even those which he thought he was certain to win, albeit they were small in number, which had destroyed his faith in British Justice. He now had very little heart for his job as he worried where his duty really lay.

Caprang rose to speak. He deliberately lifted his chair to avoid the scraping sound which had irritated him when anyone else had stood. He was the only one in the room not in uniform but in court dress of black jacket, striped trousers, crisp white wing-collared shirt and the most sober of ties.

"Gentlemen," Caprang began, which was an unusual start. "There are some immediate points of order for the Court to deal with. If I may, I would like to address them now."

The Colonel looked to the men at the side of him, then looked back at Caprang and nodded without saying anything.

"The law on desertion has a specific test. For a soldier to be found guilty of desertion it has to be proven that the soldier in question had no intention of returning to His Majesty's service at all or to escape some important part of the service. Further, the act of desertion requires the assumption of some kind of disguise, or involves concealment or some other suspicious action, for example, acting in a clandestine manner. It is clear from all of Major Dovingdon's actions that he did not leave the service. He did not even attempt to leave. In fact, as the prosecuting officer has to accept, on 31st May, Major Dovingdon stayed in the service all that day and every day thereafter. Accordingly, there can be no desertion charge to answer. It needs to be dismissed without wasting more of the court's time."

"Captain Carmichael?" said the Colonel looking in the direction of the prosecuting officer.

"As we take the court through the events of 31st May, I think we will be able to establish, to the court's satisfaction, that this charge is properly brought," said the Captain without attempting to rise from his chair. This small discourtesy irritated Caprang, who remained standing, as he had not yet finished his points of order. "In any case, as Counsel should know, desertion takes a number of forms including from the soldier's post to desertion from his unit."

"I beg the court," said Caprang determined to bring his authority to the proceeding, "but I should be most grateful if counsel, when addressing or referring to me, would afford me the common courtesies normally granted to all King's Counsel, namely the term 'learned counsel'. As to the wide range of possible forms of desertion referred to by counsel, this has no effect in law. Each case has to be judged on its facts, and not the facts of another case. I can assure the court that, since the war began, I have become quite an authority on Section 514 of King's Regulations, and the subsequent relevant sections under the heading of 'Desertion and Offences against the Establishment' and if it pleases the court, now is the appropriate time to discuss the law."

"We are grateful for your learned expertise," said the Colonel, laying emphasis on the word learned. "Is there anything else?"

"Yes Colonel, there is also the quite ludicrous charge of Major Dovingdon being absent without leave. This charge relates to the moment Major Dovingdon left the balloon until the moment the balloon was brought back down and was on the ground; a matter of some two to three hours. The argument being that, during that time, Major Dovingdon should have been under the command of the balloon's pilot but was not. The alternative construct is that the absence was less than a minute, being the time Major Dovingdon took to descend by parachute and resume his duties on the ground. King's Regulations Section 502 only deals with absence of one day or longer. It does not, I stress does not, deal with parts of a day amounting to hours or even less to minutes. Accordingly, this charge needs to be dismissed immediately too."

Again, the Colonel looked at Captain Carmichael for a response.

Still sitting, Carmichael gave the same answer as he did before. "It will become clear from the evidence as to why this charge remains appropriate."

"Sir," interjected Caprang. "A trial takes place within the confines of the law. A man cannot be guilty of breaking the law if there is no law to break. It is the duty of the court to understand the legal arguments before it proceeds to consider the evidence."

"I don't think we need to be reminded of the duties of this court, thank you," said the Colonel. "We will consider your points of order at a suitable time. I think we should get on with the trial."

"I have another six, no seven, further legal matters to argue, most of which relate to the charges of murder and inflicting grievous bodily harm," protested Caprang.

"I am sure you have," replied the Colonel sarcastically, "but I should be grateful if you would make them as we hear the evidence." He then paused, studied his court file for a little and said, "Captain Carmichael, from the court papers, we are aware of the main aspects of the case. We do not need you to summarise it for us, there is, after all, a war on. Perhaps you would like to call your first witness."

Interesting, thought Caprang, for once again the normal court procedures and formalities were being forsaken in the expediency of war. He was not going to yield for this reason, so he remained standing. "The Court is no doubt aware that the Court's failure to follow proper procedures will provide excellent grounds for my client to appeal any adverse decision," he said, knowing full well that there was no appeal against a decision of a Court Martial.

"Thank you," said the Colonel testily. "It would be helpful if learned counsel would appreciate that there is, as I say, a war on and we need to progress these matters as quickly as possible."

"Are we not fighting this war for the rule of law, justice and right?" Caprang asked and then paused. "I thought we were."

Chapter 39

France July 1918

Note to reader: Those not interested in Penrose's active service in World War 1 may miss this chapter.

"SGT. LANGHOLME, WERE you in charge of a balloon flight launched on 31st May 1918 at approximately 6.30 am?" asked Carmichael, still seated at his table.

Langholme was standing at ease in the middle of the court room. His mouth had gone dry as he had repeated the oath sworn on a Bible. He was feeling extremely uncomfortable. He knew Penrose was facing a death sentence and he didn't want to be involved in aiding or abetting that in any way. Like everyone in Penrose's units, Langholme thought the charges were dreadfully unfair, knowing that, if Penrose hadn't acted the way he did, Célieux Ridge would have been lost.

Langholme coughed to clear his throat. "Yes sir," he replied. Sunrise was at 06.06 hours that morning and Major Dovingdon wanted to be in the air at that time so we launched a few moments after 06:00 hours."

"Was Major Dovingdon a passenger with you on that balloon flight?"

"Yes sir, he was the observer."

"Is Major Dovingdon a qualified balloonist?"

"No sir, but he is highly experienced."

"Under King's Regulations, does this mean that you were the most senior person and in command of that flight?"

"Yes sir."

"Accordingly, although Major Dovingdon is of higher rank, he was to take instructions from you during the flight?"

"Yes sir."

"Was Major Dovingdon aware of these Regulations?"

"Yes sir, every time we flew together he reminded me of them, sir."

There was a pause as the prosecuting officer examined his notes.

"Sergeant Langholme, is it permissible for anything to be thrown out of a balloon?"

"No sir, not unless the balloon is in danger in which case things can be ejected. You have to remember there are always people below you."

"Did Major Dovingdon throw his greatcoat out of the balloon?"

"Yes sir."

"Did you give Major Dovingdon permission to throw his greatcoat out?"

"No sir."

"Did he seek your permission to throw out his greatcoat?"

"No sir."

"Was the Major aware that it was contrary to King's Regulations to eject anything from a balloon in flight?"

"Yes sir. It is part of the standing instructions that are told at the start of every flight to every unqualified balloonist."

"Even one as experienced as Major Dovingdon?"

"Particularly someone as experienced as the Major, sir, 'cause I wouldn't want to be put on jankers. The Major was extremely strict on this kind of thing." The mention of jankers caused a smile to go round the court and helped to gently relieve the palpable tension.

"Was the balloon in difficulties such that it would have been reasonable for you to give an order to Major Dovingdon to throw out his greatcoat?"

"No sir."

Again, there was a long pause as Carmichael examined his notes. This gave Langholme an opportunity to glance, with a look of curiosity, towards Penrose. He knew this was incriminating evidence against him, but what else could he say?

That morning, Langholme had been summoned in front of the Colonel who stressed how important it was that he told the truth and kept to his story, nothing more, nothing less. However, immediately after that, Prosecuting Counsel had approached him and, in a longer conversation, he felt they were trying to rehearse his answers, and the more they tried, the more nervous he had become.

Carmichael started his questioning again. "Major Dovingdon put on a parachute harness and jumped from the balloon that morning. Is that correct?"

"Yes sir," said Langholme, surprised by the question after such a long pause.

"Did you give permission to Major Dovingdon to leave the balloon by way of a parachute?"

"No sir."

"Did you tell Major Dovingdon not to make a parachute jump?"

"No sir."

"Let me be clear," said Carmichael. "You neither gave nor refused Major Dovingdon permission to jump from the balloon?"

"That's correct, sir"

"So he simply took command of the balloon, albeit that it was your responsibility to make all decisions?"

"It wasn't like that, sir," said Langholme. "It was obvious that there was a bad situation below and we 'ad no contact with the ground. We was working as a team, me and the Major. There was a lot going on. There was a lot of spotting to do 'cause a lot had changed."

"You were working as a team?" repeated Carmichael, allowing a cynicism to pervade his tone. "So had you relinquished command to Major Dovingdon?"

"No sir, under King's Regulations, I can only relinquish command if I am hurt and unable to perform my duties. I wasn't hurt, sir."

"So, Major Dovingdon just took over command from you. He assumed command as though it was his right as a Major to give you, a sergeant, instructions?"

"It weren't like that," protested Langholme. "We was just working together."

"When making a parachute jump from a balloon, are there certain rules and procedures to be followed?"

"Yes sir."

"Did Major Dovingdon comply with those rules and procedures?"

"No sir, not all of 'em, he was far too anxious to get on the ground.

But sir, he is an officer, he's 'ad the same training as me, sir. He knew what to do."

"How many hours have you had in the air, sergeant?"

"1,466 hours, another few hundred before I'm a qualified balloonist, but we don't have enough of those so it's a job I do 'cause I'm the most experienced."

"How many hours has Major Dovingdon accumulated as a balloonist?"

"I don't know, sir, you'll have to ask him that, but I would imagine it's a few hundred."

"So, are you saying that an officer with hundreds of hours of ballooning has the same level of experience as you, and is therefore qualified to take charge of the balloon?"

"Oh no sir, that's not possible. Hours in the air is particularly important in this job."

Carmichael paused again to prepare for his next set of questions. This gave Penrose an opportunity to look around the room. Everyone avoided his gaze.

"Sergeant, where was your post that morning?" asked Carmichael looking up, having gathered his train of thought for his next series of questions.

"My post was in the balloon, sir," answered Langholme in a quizzical tone.

"Where was the Major's post that morning?"

"In the balloon, sir."

"Could your post have been anywhere else?"

"No sir."

"Could Major Dovingdon's post have been anywhere else?"

"No sir, we have a log for each balloon flight and if your name is in the log then your post is in the basket."

"Was Major Dovingdon's name in the log for that morning?"

"Yes sir."

"Did the balloon come under attack that morning?"

"Yes sir"

"Was this before or after Major Dovingdon jumped from the balloon?"

"After."

"Did you and Major Dovingdon expect to come under attack in the balloon?"

"Oh yes, sir. At least I did. The wind was light and with all that going on below, I'm sure Jerry would have wanted us shot down. It would have been pretty dodgy for a few moments if we got attacked."

"Has Major Dovingdon been in a balloon when it's been under attack?"

"Not while he's been with me, sir, you'll have to ask him about when he 'as flown with others, but I'm fairly certain he 'as been."

"In your statement you say contact was lost with the ground at about 3,000 feet?"

"Yes sir."

"Was contact made between the balloon and the ground after Major Dovingdon jumped?"

"Yes sir, at about 2,000 feet, when the break in the telephone cable was fixed. Major Dovingdon ordered me to stay at my present height to provide observation for the battle below, so I stayed in the air spotting for another 90 minutes until the attack from two German Fokker planes caused a rapid descent. They got one or two shots off at us sir, puncturing the balloon a bit, but thankfully no fire."

"So you came under enemy fire. Was that a ground or air attack?"

"Air attack, sir," replied Langholme, thinking it a very stupid question given he had just said he'd been attacked by two aeroplanes. "We don't come down for shell fire but we do come down if we're attacked by planes. If they're in the air they're almost certain to hit the bag and if they do that it means no more flying."

"If I may, Sergeant, I would like to summarise your testimony," said Carmichael, seizing control. "Major Dovingdon's post was with you in the basket of the balloon. You did not give him permission to throw his coat out of the basket, but he did it anyway. You did not give him permission to make a parachute jump, but he did it anyway. Accordingly, he deserted you in the face of an expected enemy. Is that a fair summary?"

"It wasn't like that sir," protested Langholme. "I didn't say he could 'n I didn't say he couldn't. It's what Major Dovingdon decided to do 'cause of the situation on the ground. It was complex. I couldn't say whether it was right or wrong."

"But," interrupted Carmichael, "he didn't get your specific permission to jump, did he?"

"That's right sir, he didn't, but...."

Langholme was unable to continue as Carmichael interrupted, "And therefore without your specific permission he left his post without orders."

Carmichael turned away, not giving Langholme time to answer. Again he studied his text before continuing.

"When Major Dovingdon was in the balloon he gave instructions to Lieutenant Gray. What can you tell me about them?"

"Which ones, sir? There were several."

"Specifically, the instruction regarding the firing of the artillery guns," said Carmichael, with a sense of exasperation entering his voice.

"He gave Lieutenant Gray a bearing and a range and ordered the guns to free fire."

"What bearing and what range did he order?"

"The bearing was southerly so as to target the shells to land in no man's land."

"And the range?"

"I don't know, I can't remember."

"Did Major Dovingdon give his range instruction to Lieutenant Gray in yards or metres?"

This was the question Langholme was dreading. He wished he could remember but he couldn't. He racked his brain to try and remember but nothing was clear. If he remembered yards he was committing Gray to a murder charge. If he remembered metres then it was Dovingdon who would be making the 6.00 am walk to the firing post. He was in a dreadful dilemma. All the enlisted men were supporting Dovingdon. They knew he was a good and caring officer and Gray was useless. Yet it was the officer corps, was almost to a man, who appeared to be supporting Gray.

It was only the words of the Colonel the day before which gave Langholme comfort. "Tell the truth," he said, "and allow the sword to fall where it will. If you take sides and your false memory chooses one because that is what you want the result to be, then you will have wrongly influenced things and your conscience will bear the burden for a very long time." Langholme was grateful for that advice for the rest of his days.

"I can't say, sir," said Langholme confidently. "I am sorry, but I don't remember. What I do know is that we give all our range instructions in yards, 'cause we're the British Army, sir." With those two words, British Army, Langholme's pride resounded throughout the court room.

"I want to turn your attention to the firing of the British guns on the French troops. In your statement, you say that after Major Dovingdon had left the balloon, you saw French troops march into no man's land, break ranks and charge into battle with the Germans."

"Yes sir."

"You then say that it was when the French and German troops were in armed combat that the   British guns started to fire."

"Yes sir."

"Where did the shells land? On the English side or French side of no man's land or in the middle?"

"Definitely on the French side, sir. The direction was really good but some of the shells was over shoot'n and hittin' the French woods."

"You then say that, at some stage, the range was shortened, so that they landed in the middle of no man's land. Did you give these instructions?"

"No sir."

"If you didn't give them, who did?"

"I don't know."

Carmichael made a herrumping sound in an obvious sound of disbelief.

"The telephone wasn't connected by then," responded Langholme, in an unprompted defence.

"How much did the range come back?"

"About 250 to 350 yards."

"But it was you who gave instructions for the artillery to stop firing."

"In a manner of speaking, yes sir."

"Why?"

"Why," repeated Langholme, surprised by the question, given it had such an obvious answer. "It was bleeding obvious our guns was firing on the Frenchies and they had to be stopped. Both them and the Germans had taken cover in the shell holes. They had stopped fighting each other and gone to ground 'cause it was bloody carnage out there." Langholme's tone had now turned to one of constrained outrage as he remembered what he had seen.

"Carnage?" said Carmichael, testing the word as it seemed unlikely to him to have been one Langholme would have been familiar with.

"Yes, bleeding carnage," continued Langholme, reinforcing the word. "Also, the French tanks was coming onto the battlefield. Between them, the machine guns and the shelling, it was that which won it for us."

"Thank you," said Carmichael patronisingly. "So at some stage in your descent, the phone was reconnected and you could give orders again?"

"Yes sir. Only I ain't authorised to give orders. I can only tell and report what's 'appening."

"Nevertheless, you heard Major Dovingdon give instructions for the British Guns to fire into no man's land and you saw the shells from those guns kill French soldiers ... our allies in this war?"

Langholme paused. He didn't want to say yes in front of Dovingdon, for he knew if he did, he would be condemning him out loud. "It's all in my written statement, sir," he replied.

"That is not good enough," barked Carmichael. "You heard Major Dovingdon give the order to our guns and you saw them fire on the French soldiers."

"Yes sir, I heard and saw both those things, but I can't say one thing caused the other. D'ya get me? I 'ave no proof of a link so I won't say there is and I won't say there ain't."

Carmichael looked at his papers and then looked at the Colonel. He said nothing but simply nodded indicating that he had nothing more to ask.

Unlike Carmichael, who had remained seated, Caprang rose, at the invitation of the Colonel, to start his questioning.

"Sergeant Langholme," opened Caprang, getting the man's attention, but then he paused deliberately to give effect. "You said that Major Dovingdon and you had acted as a team. Do you always act as a team with your passengers?"

"No sir," said Langholme emphatically. "With regulars, well there's a team atmosphere amongst us. They know what we are doing and can help. The new boys, well thems that are not from a ballooning company, like the gunners, they have to do what they're bleedin' well told."

"So you had this team relationship with Major Dovingdon because he knew what he was doing?"

"Yes, he's been to Balloon School, sir. He was a good flyer. He knew the ropes. I didn't have to tell him anything."

"If you had been Major Dovingdon and seen the scene on the ground, would you have jumped using your parachute?"

"It was ever so complex. I remember Major Dovingdon saying he had predicted what was happening. He said he had told his higher-ups of the risk, but they had ignored him. He was pretty damn angry about it."

This was an unhelpful comment as an officer complaining to his men about failings of other officers was certainly in breach of King's Regulations. In fact, it was just about the only charge which the army had not laid against Dovingdon.

Caprang needed to move on, but suddenly there was an argument taking place outside the court doors, and the row pervaded into the room. This was then followed by them being forced open by a tall, overweight man wearing a battle dress top over civilian clothing. Very slowly he made his way to an area set aside for the public who should have been admitted but, on security grounds, seldom were.

"Who are you?" demanded the Colonel, in a very loud voice which reverberated around the room. "I will not have my court disturbed."

"Anthony Kerslake, the Times Newspaper, London."

"You have....," the Colonel stopped himself and started again, deciding to rephrase his question. "What rights do you have to attend this Court Martial?"

Kerslake had already taken his seat as he had not expected to be challenged further. The mere mention of The Times, London meant that most people acquiesced immediately.

"You need to show the Court your authority to be here," said the Colonel, pointing to the officer who had read out the original charges. The whole proceedings stopped as Kerslake stood and took a piece of paper, which had obviously been folded and re-folded many times, from his battledress pocket. He handed it to the clerk who opened the letter carefully. It was typed on Lord Kitchener's headed notepaper and under his hand. It was addressed 'To Whom it May Concern' and made it very clear that no one was to hinder or impede Kerslake, giving instruction for him to be afforded every assistance and courtesy he required. Secretly, Kerslake was pleased with the letter, for he had drafted the wording himself, taking extra time to ensure it covered almost every eventuality, particularly for moments like this. The officer clerk nodded to the Colonel to signify all was in order, and then asked Kerslake to resume his seat.

Caprang was highly irritated by the interruption. He had long appreciated that court proceedings had a natural flow about them which, when stopped, meant that the last impressions lingered the longest. The prosecuting officer, in the questioning of just one man, had done a sound job in making it clear to the court that Penrose had deserted his post without permission, contrary to King's Regulations, at a time when there was the expectation of an enemy attack, and it was Penrose who had given the instructions which had seen French soldiers killed at the hands of British guns. He knew he now had an uphill struggle.

"Sergeant Langholme," said Caprang, beginning his cross examination again. "In your written statement, you say that the telephone from the balloon to the ground stopped working and therefore it was not possible to let those on the ground know that a very dangerous situation was taking place."

"Yes sir."

"What was your assessment of what was taking place on the ground, sergeant?"

"Beg pardon sir, but I'm not conversant with making assessments." Getting more comfortable in his surroundings Langholme, was gradually returning to his usual style of speaking so he continued.

"However, it was bleeding obvious what Jerry was trying to do, and if he had succeeded it would have been a bleeding disaster. The Ridge would have been lost. Major Dovingdon's instructions meant the Germans were trapped in a pincer movement. They couldn't go forward because of the machine guns and they couldn't go back because of the shelling. Excuse the expression, but they were going to be a bit fucked, know what I mean."

"I think we know," said Caprang, "but please excuse me if I don't use that expression in my summing up. Now, if you had been Major Dovingdon, and seen the scene on the ground, would you have jumped?"

"I don't know sir. We have outages of the phone system all the time. Sometimes they get repaired, sometimes they don't. You can never tell."

"Did you ever say to Major Dovingdon that he was not to jump?"

"No sir. In fact, sir, if the truth was told, Major Dovingdon didn't exactly jump, he fell out. He was sitting on the edge, which makes the basket tip dreadfully, and it was me movin' which made the basket tip even more and caused the Major to fall."

The thought of a major falling from a balloon, once again lightened the mood in the courtroom which had become very tense following Kerslake's interjection.

"Major Dovingdon says, in his evidence, that by your actions in helping him into his harness, you tacitly gave him consent to jump."

"Yes sir, I did that, sir, 'cause I wasn't going to have an officer falling out of 'is parachute harness from a balloon I was commanding sir, otherwise it would be me what's 'ere sir and not him."

"Your actions implied consent for Major Dovingdon to jump, didn't they?"

"Don't know anything about any implied what's its, sir, but as I see it, if Major Dovingdon thought it best to jump then it was my job to help 'im."

Caprang listened to those last few words and thought they made an excellent point at which to stop his cross examination so he repeated, "So if Major Dovingdon thought it best to jump, you considered it your job to help him."

"Yes sir, that's what I said."

"If you had been giving instructions to the guns to fire in to no man's land, where would you have targeted them?"

"I didn't give no instructions," said Langholme, getting concerned.

"I know that, but where would you have targeted the shells, in the middle, the French side or British Side?" asked Caprang.

"In the middle and a bit either way."

"Do you know the range from where the British Guns were to the middle of no man's land?"

"I didn't then but I bleed'n well do now."

"And," prompted Caprang, "the range?"

"I can give it precise, sir, 'cause I've worked it out. The guns were in the middle of Cotta's Patch which means 250 metres to the edge of the wood. The wood is 500 metres wide all the way around, and no man's land is 1,500 metres wide, so its 750 metres to the middle. This is a total distance of 1,500 metres from the guns to the middle of no man's land."

"Why do you refer to metres?" asked Caprang hopefully.

"'cause the French maps we use are all scaled in metres but then overlaid with one thousand-yard grid lines."

"Do you know this distance in yards?" asked Caprang.

"Yes sir, I do now. It's 1,640 yards."

"Might this explain why Major Dovingdon says he gave the range at 1,600 to 1,700 yards, and not 1,500 metres, so that our shells would have landed in the middle of no man's land?

Carmichael shot to his feet for the first time in the proceedings, "It is not for the witness to explain the accused's actions," he protested.

Caprang looked at the Colonel and smiled a false smile, for he could only agree. "Just one last question," he said. "Does the British Army give its firing instructions in yards or metres?"

"Yards, sir," said Langholme with a look on his face which showed he was wondering why he had been asked the obvious!

Caprang then nodded to the Colonel indicating his questioning of Langholme was complete; a matter he confirmed by sitting down.

Carmichael had remained standing, and then without the permission of the Presiding Officer, he fired into Langholme. Caprang shot to his feet to protest but was waived aside.

"I would just like to check something which you said earlier. It was that Major Dovingdon's post was with you in the balloon. Is that correct?" asked Carmichael.

"Yes sir."

"Major Dovingdon left your balloon by parachute without your specific consent or instructions?"

"Yes sir."

Caprang knew it was exactly at this point the Prosecuting Counsel would want to end his questioning. One element of the case against Dovingdon was summarised in just those few words. It emphasised what Caprang already knew. The only way he was going to get Dovingdon off the desertion charge would be to win the argument that his post was not stranded high in the air in the balloon but on the ground where he could take charge of the battle.

It was just after 12 noon and everyone in the room was expecting a brief recess for lunch, so it was with some surprise that the Colonel adjourned the court until 10 am the following day. The bench rose, everyone stood and as soon as the judging officers had left, Penrose was marched, by his two original escorts, from the courtroom back to his cell, the former horse stables.

Kerslake stayed where he was. He was studying the body language of those in front of him. It appeared there was a genuine animosity between the prosecuting and defending counsel, which was unusual. Kerslake approached Caprang and simply asked, "How's it going?"

"If you want to see a miscarriage of justice, just stay around for a few days and watch this one. It's a classic," said Caprang. "You'll lose your faith in British fair play," he continued.

"What do you mean?" asked Kerslake.

"I can't say any more. Just stay around, watch, learn and report," said Caprang, as he stuffed his papers into his case, which he then closed with a force that came from a growing anger. He didn't just dislike the case he was defending, but he also found the bumptiousness of Carmichael insufferable. His case full, and with more papers stuffed under his arm, he moved away from Kerslake to indicate their conversation was over.

Chapter 40

France July 1918

Note to reader: Those not interested in Penrose's active service in World War 1 may miss this chapter.

LIEUTENANT GRAY WAS visibly shaking as he stood to attention while swearing on the Bible. With his weak frame and shrinking demeanour, he looked quite pathetic; far from being the leader of men he was supposed to be.

Immediately after Gray was sworn in, Caprang stood up to address the court. "Sir," he said. "It might help the Court to know that Major Dovingdon does not challenge Lieutenant Gray's witness statement, apart from one material fact, and that is whether Major Dovingdon's orders were for a range of 1,600 to 1,700 *yards* or a range of 1,600 to 1,700 *metres*. As the president of the Court Martial will appreciate, this is crucial, for it was the over-firing by the gun platoon which caused the death and injury of the French troop."

"Thank you," said the Colonel. "Does Major Dovingdon accept that Lieutenant Gray gave instructions to the artillery to fire at a range of 1,750 to 1,850 yards?"

"Yes, he does sir. We have the benefit of the log book maintained by the officer commanding the battery, giving the range and direction of each shell fired to support Lieutenant Gray's instructions."

"It seems to me the issue is incredibly simple," said the Colonel. "Dovingdon both in his witness statement and his battle report is very emphatic that he calculated the distance in metres and then converted this distance into yards, so as to give the range to the guns in yards. It is therefore in yards that Dovingdon says he gave the distance to Gray. Gray says that Dovingdon gave his instructions in metres so he converted the figures he had been given into yards before passing them on to the battery. Is this a fair summary?" The Colonel looked at Carmichael and Caprang for their agreement.

Carmichael nodded and stayed seated. Caprang rose to agree but was patted down in a hand signal from the bench.

"As a result of this cock-up, whose fault we still have to establish, the British guns overfired by some 150 yards hitting the French troop coming into the battle. Is that the nub of it?" asked the Colonel.

"It's part of it, sir," said Carmichael. "Not only was the range out by 150 yards, but as was reported by Sargent Langholme, the shells travelled as far as hitting the French woods and it was Major Dovingdon who gave those instructions to fire."

"Thank you," said the Colonel, exasperation seeping into his tone. "It is a point my colleagues and I have taken on board." He paused. "Perhaps you would like to question your witness."

"Mr. Gray, were you the officer in charge of 32 KBS on 31st May 1918 from approximately 6.00am?" asked Carmichael, still seated at his table.

"Yes sir."

"Did you receive instructions from Major Dovingdon on that morning?"

"Yes sir."

"What did he tell you about what was happening and what instruction did he give you?"

"He told me we were under attack from the Germans, and from the noise all around, that was fairly obvious; but I couldn't see any enemy. He told me to move two of the machine guns in the trenches defending our eastern perimeter to the new trench which defended our southern perimeter. He didn't say why."

"What else did he say?"

"He said that every rigger was to get a gun and get to the new trench straightaway. It was this instruction which made me think that this was where we were being attacked." Gray's voice took a different tone to the way he normally spoke. It now had a pretentiousness about it.

"And?" prompted Caprang.

"He said I was to give Mr. Walker my compliments and ask him to fire urgently at will into no man's land, bearing 175° to 185°, range 1,650 to 1,750 metres." Gray placed huge emphasis on the word metres.

"You then converted that number of metres into yards and gave these instructions to Lieutenant Walker?"

"Yes sir."

"Where was Major Dovingdon at this time?"

"I gather he was in the middle of Cotta's Patch, badly shaken up from his parachute jump."

"Now, Lieutenant Walker, in his statement, says that immediately Major Dovingdon arrived at the guns and found out they had been firing at a range of between 1,750 and 1,850 yards, he immediately instructed for the range to be reduced to 1,600 to 1,700 yards."

"So I understand, sir."

"In your statement, you say you first reduced the range to 1,600 to 1,700 yards and then back even further to between 1,500 and 1,600 yards.

"Yes sir"

"Lieutenant Walker is adamant that you were not responsible for the first reduction in the range. He is certain that instruction came from Major Dovingdon, but you were responsible for the second reduction in the range to between 1,500 and 1,600 yards."

"Can you explain the discrepancy between the two statements, yours and Lieutenant Walker's?"

"I cannot, sir," said Gray quickly, having been well prepared for the question.

Carmichael stopped and studied his papers. He then started again, but this time in a less aggressive, more conciliatory tone.

"Why did you reduce the range? Did you know our guns were overshooting?"

"No sir, but I did know that the new southern trench was under direct attack by the Germans, and by reducing the range I would be able to help relieve some of its pressure."

"Thank you," said Carmichael. "I have no more questions, sir," he said, addressing the Colonel.

At the nod, Caprang sprang to his feet. There was no contemplation

---

and no finesse. "You are a coward and a liar," he shouted at Gray, who positively recoiled from the ungentlemanly onslaught.

"The simple truth is that Major Dovingdon gave you instructions in yards and you wrongly assumed them to be metres. You then did the conversion again and passed on the converted numbers, and it was this which caused the guns to overshoot. That is what happened, isn't it?"

"No sir."

"Yes it is, otherwise when Dovingdon got to the guns, he wouldn't have changed the range instructions, which is what he did. He knew immediately the wrong instructions had been passed."

"I gave the instruction for the range to be brought back by 150 yards, sir; not Major Dovingdon."

"That is not Lieutenant Walker's evidence is it?"

"No sir. I assume we both gave instructions, at about the same time, Major Dovingdon and me. Lieutenant Walker remembers Major Dovingdon giving the instruction of 1,600 to 1,700 yards because he was physically present. It doesn't mean that I didn't give exactly the same instructions."

"Except there is no corroborative evidence, not one single piece of paper, is there?"

"No sir."

"No written note or message which accompanied your first set of instructions?"

"No sir."

"So what was it that made you reduce the range?"

"The telephone call I had from Sgt. Langholme. It was he who told me that we were overshooting into the French woods."

"And what was it which caused you to give instruction to stop the guns firing?"

"The arrival of the French tanks on the battle field sir. I didn't want to hit those."

"The fact is," said Caprang, his voice conveying disgust, "it would be you here on trial for your life if, as I contend, Major Dovingdon gave you instructions in yards, and it was you who made the mistake of assuming they were in metres, and so you did the conversion all over again. You're lying to protect your own skin. You pathetic little man!" With that Caprang dropped into his chair, in what would normally have been planned theatrics, except this time it signalled his true feelings of contempt.

"Except sir, I didn't give the instructions for the guns to open fire," said Gray defiantly. "That sole responsibility lies with Major Dovingdon. I did, however, give the instruction to stop them firing and with it, saved lives."

"If that matter assuages your conscience then you are even more contemptible, more deplorable than any other man fighting in this war," shouted Caprang angrily from his seat.

The Colonel, in the absence of a gavel, picked up his files and banged them hard down on the table. "Enough!" he shouted. "The court is adjourned."

Chapter 41

France July 1918

Note to reader: Those not interested in Penrose's active service in World War 1 may miss this chapter.

LIEUTENANT BENJAMIN WALKER'S rogue-like charm meant he was liked by everyone. He was the fourth generation of Walker's to take the King's shilling, except he was the first to join an artillery regiment. "No bloody point being in the cavalry charging at the guns," said his father. "Sure way to die. Better behind the guns, we learnt that at Balaclava."

By rights Walker should have outranked Penrose many times over, for he was a regular soldier first commissioned in 1910. However, the playboy spirit in him meant that anything but soldiering occupied his waking moments. In peace time he had developed the reputation of being the scourge of many a colleague away on manoeuvres for, without any forethought or conscience, he would seduce their wives through youthful comedic foreplay.

Walker's posting to Célieux Ridge in 1916 was in response to Penrose's demand that the guns there, needed to defend his balloons, should be able to shoot down any attacking German aeroplane; something they had singularly failed to do to that date. Out went the former battery commander and in came Walker to what everyone thought was a very cushy non-posting with no great expectation that he would do any better. It was why Walker kept his head down. In war, he had decided, the last thing anyone sensible should do is to be noticed. It could only lead to harm. Regretting his previous notoriety in the army he now made a point of being unobserved by those at HQ. Instead, he made his playground amongst the young French women of Coeur de Foucy.

The creditable thing about Walker was that he knew his guns; like a shepherd knows his flock. In 1914, when the war started, hitting an enemy target was a hit and miss affair with a few ranging shots being fired. These would be observed, and corrections made until the target was hit. It was all very inefficient. By 1918, Walker was an expert in target acquisition and predicted fire. This enabled him to hit his target first time, almost every time. There had been a huge improvement in the quality of shells, each now made to an accurate weight, but it was small things like the measurement of gun barrel wear, wind speed, air pressure and other meteorological factors, and taking these into account in calculating gun settings, which gave Walker his successes. But Walker was not alone; for it was the Artillery Officers who, as a cadre, arrogantly felt it was they who were winning the war[15].

It was after the lunchtime recess that Walker presented himself at court in his normal battle dress; quite different from all other witnesses who arrived very smartly turned out. This was deliberate. He wanted to give the impression that he had come from his field job and he had to get back there.

Once again Carmichael took the lead in questioning the witness. "Lieutenant Walker, were you the field gunnery officer on 31st May 1918 at Célieux Ridge at approximately 6.30am and in charge of three 18 pounder Mark IV guns?"

"Yes sir."

"Did you receive instructions from Major Dovingdon that day?"

"32 KBS also has attached to it one chassis mounted Mark III QF 13-pounder with a lined barrel so it can fire 13-pounder shrapnel shells for aerial artillery," continued Walker boastfully; not answering the question because he wanted the court to know the full extent of his responsibilities.

---

[15] By 1918 the British Artillery had developed their skills to such an extent that they were capable of firing a creeping barrage; a wall of shellfire, aimed just in front of the advancing British infantry which moved forward slowly, at a rate of about 100 yards every three to four minutes. This meant that shells were screaming a few feet over the heads of the advancing soldiers, in an incredibly dangerous and frightening tactic which was, nevertheless, very effective.

"Thank you for the clarification. Back to my question, did you receive any instructions from Major Dovingdon?"

"Yes, sir."

"What form did those instructions take?"

"They first came via Lieutenant Gray and not directly from Major Dovingdon."

"How did they come?"

"The first was handwritten, sir. It came from Lieutenant Gray via a runner. The second order and all others came directly from Major Dovingdon either orally or in writing."

"What were Lieutenant Gray's instructions?"

"To fire at will on a bearing of 175° to 185° with a range of 1,750 to 1,850 yards," replied Walker, confidently.

"Weren't you surprised?"

"Yes, not with the range, but with the direction. It was obvious we were under attack. It was when it was explained that the Germans were in no man's land that the direction made sense. In fact, it was good to have some precise instructions."

"How many rounds did you fire that morning?"

"I'm sorry sir, but I don't have that information to hand. It's in the log, but we were firing at around two to three shells a minute before I got new orders."

"So you knew where your shells were falling?"

"Yes sir, in Connard's Gap[16]."

"Where's Connard's Gap?" asked Carmichael, as it was not a place he had heard of before.

"The area between the French wood and the British one."

"What, no man's land? Why is it called the Connard's Gap?" asked the Court President. "It doesn't have that name on the map," he continued sternly.

"It was the nickname the troops gave no man's land," answered Carmichael sheepishly.

The major to the right of the Colonel whispered quietly in his ear, explaining exactly what the word connard meant, and the fact that it was none too complimentary of the French.

---

[16] Means 'shithead' in French.

"I think we will pass on that question," interrupted the President.

"You mentioned new orders. What were those and who gave them?" asked Carmichael.

"They reduced the range to 1,600 from 1,700 yards."

"How did you receive those orders?"

"They were given to me directly by Major Dovingdon."

"Are you certain that your first instructions set the range at 1,750 and 1,850 yards?"

"I am."

"You say that the instructions were written in Lieutenant Gray's hand. Where are those instructions now?"

"Lost sir, I cannot find them."

"That's inconvenient, isn't it! Where and when was the last time you saw those handwritten instructions?"

"I had them when I wrote my battle report, but not since then."

"Were you happy with the orders you got from Lieutenant Gray? Did they make sense to you?"

"Yes, they made sense, but as I said, only when I learnt from the runner that the Germans were in Connard's Gap."

For the next two hours Carmichael, as prosecuting counsel, asked more questions, each designed to prove the accuracy of the troop firing the shells into no man's land. Eventually, they stopped for the day, and for the first time since the trial began, Penrose was joined in his cell by his defence barrister. They broke bread together, although Penrose ate little as he had completely lost his appetite.

"How's it going?" asked Penrose.

"As well as might be expected," replied Caprang noncommittally.

"Doesn't look too healthy to me," continued Penrose.

Caprang nodded as he appreciated Penrose's little joke. "We haven't started the legal arguments yet. That's where all their weaknesses are."

"Yes, and you weren't allowed to." Penrose paused. "It doesn't seem as though it's been very fair so far."

"Indeed," agreed Caprang. "But the prosecution has to prove beyond reasonable doubt that you gave the wrong range, and so far all that has been established is doubt as to the instructions you gave.

If they cannot go further, then we are into the realms of reasonable doubt, and not beyond it. This means they have to find you not guilty. It's what the law requires."

Chapter 42

France July 1918

THE MARCH FROM the temporary courthouse to Penrose's jail cell was only a few hundred yards. He walked in the centre of the wooden walking boards, with his escorts walking either side of him; each had a hand gripped firmly on his arm, their feet splashing in the mud. Penrose had no thoughts. His mind was completely blank. Everything he was doing was automatic, for he simply could not believe what had happened. Penrose's time in court to hear he had been found guilty on all counts, and was to be shot by firing squad, had been no more than seven minutes at the most.

Immediately after he had been led back into his cell, Penrose stood completely stationary. The door was shut behind him. He distinctly heard the jangling of keys and the sliding of the bolts as the door was locked. His brain was not fully working, taken over by his bodily senses, which had never felt so sensitive, so alive. There was a tingling in every nerve in his body. His heart was suffering palpitations and there was a nauseous feeling in his stomach. Still he did not move. There was no anger or fight in him, just a resignation as to his fate. If he had been asked to describe how he felt, which no one ever did, it was as though he was in his own out-of-body experience, as if what was happening to him was happening to someone else, and he was looking on.

Still stationary Penrose looked around. It was only his eyes which moved. What an odd place to spend your last days on earth he thought. It was then that he noticed the smell. It was from the courtroom, where the sawdust from the shed's recent erection still lingered in his nostrils.

After some while he moved to the window and stepped onto

the concrete ledge, which went around the two outside walls of his cell, so he could look out over the tented fields and up into the sky beyond. Even though it was July the sky was full of dark grey clouds, hung heavily with impending rain. In usual times, Penrose would have observed how the ambience of the day suited the depressing situation before him, but these were not usual times, so he just stood there, staring out without thought.

The Colonel's words, 'shot at dawn, shot at dawn', constantly repeated themselves in his head to the point that he could think of nothing else.

Through the wall, Penrose heard the tapping sound of metal, so he moved to the other window, where again he stood on a concrete ledge to look out. There he saw dud shells being added to a stockpile along the outside of his cell wall. Even the accountants have their place in war, thought Penrose as he watched dud shells, which had failed to explode, being collected, counted, and verified for return to the manufacturer. His Majesty's government would get a credit note for every shell which did not explode and was returned to them.

The news of Penrose's death sentence went around Blag Cott like wildfire, causing the men working on stacking the dud shells to deliberately avoid looking up to see him standing at the window, and, if they did catch his gaze, then they very sheepishly turned away.

Chapter 43

France July 1918

THERE WAS MUCH about the war which made Anthony Kerslake angry, but rarely had he picked up his typewriter with such venom. He started to type. His fingers hit the keys as his thoughts turned into words. Three of four early drafts hit the ground, incomplete. His final draft, covered in ink scrawling's, was sufficient to read to a compositor. His work done, he now needed to find a phone urgently. He needed to get through to his Paris office who would then relay it to The Times in London. Time was very short, if his story was to make tomorrow's paper, and it was a story which had to be quickly told.

Standing in a phone booth in the Post Office, with the phone nestled into his ear, Kerslake started to dictate:

"Major David Victor Penrose Dovingdon has been found guilty of the murder of 46 French soldiers at a Court Martial in France. He has been cashiered out of the army and has been sentenced to be shot by firing squad. Unusually, his barrister, Mr. David Caprang K.C., told the court that he would be applying immediately to His Majesty, the King for clemency. It will, he told the court, "be the first application made to the King since the war began."

On a day in May 1918, a ridge in France came under surprise attack from the Germans. In the cover of darkness, a small German force of stormtroopers encircled the British forces and attacked from the rear, while their main force attacked from the east. A large German contingent managed to occupy land, just under a mile wide, between the French and English trenches, referred to as no man's land. It was from this position the German forces were then able to attack the English and French flanks to the north and south respectively.

Dovingdon gave instructions from the Balloon, in which he was the Observer, for the artillery to open fire into no man's land on the attacking German forces. Unknown to Dovingdon, a French platoon was marching into no man's land when he gave his order. Although significantly outnumbered, this French platoon was bravely engaging a much larger enemy when the British artillery opened fire. It was shelling from the British artillery which stopped the German attack. It was the rapid arrival of two French tanks into the battle which allowed the Allies to retain control of Célieux Ridge, an important strategic point as a potential gateway to Paris. Unfortunately, British shell fire resulted in the death and injury of several French troops. The British forces, positioned in a trench to the north of no man's land on the Ridge, also suffered a significant number of casualties in the fighting.

Dovingdon faced 16 charges in total, including the charges of desertion and cowardice, even though he was the senior officer in charge of the battle throughout. The charges came because technically his post was in the balloon and, without the express permission of the pilot, he parachuted out of the balloon to take direct command of the battle. Dovingdon decided to jump, a very brave act, because the balloon had lost telephonic communication with the ground.

Anyone who sat through the three days of the Court Martial, as I did, would not have come to the same conclusion as the Presiding Officers. Instead they would be recommending Dovingdon for both a medal and a promotion.

Immediately after he had been sentenced to death, Dovingdon addressed the court. Standing very smartly to attention, he spoke in a strong voice and without quiver or a moment of hesitation. He said: "My fate is the will of God. You, sirs, have been the instrument of that fate, in that you have corruptly colluded together for what you believe to be a good cause. Your actions need a name, an identity. I call it 'Good Cause Corruption'. It is the best I can find. The good cause being the unity of the Allied forces; for what is the life of one man if it keeps the Allies together to win a war which, to date, has required so much sacrifice from so very many people? The corruption is of the legal system. A true and just and fair legal system is the backbone of a civilised society. It is one of the things we have been fighting for these last four years. Regretfully, that legal system has been irrevocably damaged by your decision today. If you are fortunate enough to look back on a long life then, one day, as you reflect on this moment, you will realise that, just like Judas Iscariot, you too have accepted thirty pieces of silver and with it betrayed everything which runs through the soul of England and the English people."

It was one of the best speeches I have ever heard. The court was completely silent at the end. Slowly, the presiding Colonel rose to his feet, placed his cap on his head and, standing very firmly to attention, he gave Dovingdon the smartest of salutes. The two officers standing either side of the Colonel very quickly followed. It was the clearest sign that the three men felt they had done their duty by the army, but personally thought there had been a miscarriage of personal justice.

The report appeared on page four of The Times the next day. Not a word was altered. Instead the report gave rise to a small piece by the Editor asking whether the Allies' cause was not sufficient justification to keep them together; and did, for unity's sake, the French really expect the British Army to sacrifice one of their number for what was clearly a misfortune of war?

Chapter 44

France July 1918

IT WAS EARLY in the morning, on the day The Times report was published, that Caprang came to see his client, the condemned man. It was the first time since the verdict had been announced. Since the war began, Caprang had made too many of these visits and each time he had no idea what to say, except he knew that the odds were not on Penrose's side. However, this time there was a difference. He was certain there had been a miscarriage of justice, and it wasn't that he disliked what had happened, he abhorred it.

From the moment the Colonel pronounced Penrose guilty on all sixteen counts and sentenced him to death by firing squad, Caprang had worked through the night, like the devil, as he felt there was no time to spare. His first letter had already been dispatched to Field Marshal Haig. There was no appeal against a court martial verdict, so all Caprang could do was argue that the verdict was unsafe, and argue he did; two pages of an executive summary followed by thirty-five pages of typed argument in which he recommended that the death sentence be commuted to a term of imprisonment.

Penrose was seated at his small desk when the door opened and Caprang entered. He had a blank sheet of writing paper in front of him and a pen in hand. He had been like that for some time in an attempt to write to his mother, but he didn't know what to say. He looked up and said nothing.

"I'm really sorry," said Caprang. "It was not what I expected." His voice was calm and measured.

"Take a seat," said Penrose, unusually not standing up to greet his visitor. "It was not a good day, yesterday, was it? So much for the oath they all swore at the beginning of the trial promising to administer justice impartially, and without favour or affection," he added, sarcastically.

"It was a very bad day," confirmed Caprang.

"How long do you think I've got? Tomorrow morning, or the next day?"

"The sentence will first have to be confirmed by Haig, but before then he will have to have reports from your commanding officer, as well as from your Brigadier; all that takes time. However, I have already written to him. My letter will be with Haig by this evening at the latest."

"What did you say?"

"I argued that the verdict was unsafe."

"What do you mean unsafe? It's bloody well wrong!"

"If I say that, he will close his mind to what I'm saying. He needs to think that another court at another time would come to a different conclusion."

Penrose jerked his head slightly backwards. He understood the logic in Caprang's argument, albeit he didn't really like it.

"And if he doesn't accept that it's unsafe, then I've suggested the death penalty is commuted to a prison sentence."

"Oh thanks, how long?" responded Penrose, sarcastically.

"As long as he thinks fit, that's not for me to say."

There was a pause in the conversation.

"I also told him that you've appealed to the King for clemency. This will stop him doing anything...."

"Precipitately ...," said Penrose finishing off his sentence. "Have I?" he asked.

"I've drafted a letter to the King for you," said Caprang, as he produced a cardboard folder which he handed to Penrose, who placed it on the table without looking at its contents.

Penrose looked up, and without saying anything, he studied Caprang's face. His skin was thin and pale. He looked exhausted; except his eyes were steely bright. They showed the determination of a man who refused to accept defeat, ever. Those eyes gave Penrose back some hope which, only a few minutes earlier, had been totally lacking.

"I don't want to raise your hopes, but the British Army doesn't like to shoot its own men," said Caprang. "Time and time again, there are examples of men being sentenced to death, only to have that sentence commuted, and the man sent back to their regiment. The latest evidence is that only one in ten death sentences have actually been carried out. There's even a case of a soldier deserting twice, both times he was sentenced to death, and his sentence was commuted, with the man returned to his unit. I have been at this too long now to know that nothing is foreseeable when it comes to this war."

What Caprang didn't say was that, there had not been a single case of a soldier who, being charged and found guilty of murder, had not been shot.

"I bet none of those men were officers," said Penrose. "And none were caught up in an international incident which has become highly political, because that's what's happened to me.

In those few words, Penrose had summarised his situation. His judicial case was part of a much bigger story. There was a huge political issue at stake; keeping the Allies allied.

"Do you know, I think I could take all of this except the guilty verdict of cowardice," said Penrose, before he paused. "That's really going to upset my father."

Chapter 45

England July 1918

THERE WAS A dreadful tension in Col. Dovingdon's household by the time he came down to breakfast. His housekeeper had ironed The Times newspaper, just as the butler had done before he left to join the Colonel's regiment. She physically felt her spine chill, as with just a glance, she learnt that Penrose had been sentenced to be shot. Then, with her hand covering her mouth to stop herself blurting anything out, she read Kerslake's report on Dovingdon's Court Martial. She read every word slowly and carefully, and then did the same thing a second and then a third time, before she returned to ironing every page as though on auto-pilot, her brain completely suspended by the news.

The newspaper was placed, as it always was, on the breakfast table ready for the Colonel to read when he appeared in the dining room, which he did at exactly 8.30 am every morning. He helped himself to a cooked breakfast from hot dishes placed on the rich mahogany sideboard; dishes now filled to serve one person which, four or five years before, would have held enough food to serve seven or eight people, even though just one was eating.

Dovingdon placed his plate on the table, sat down, poured himself a cup of tea, picked up the ironed newspaper and folded back the front page, ignoring all the adverts it carried, so he could start reading from the inside page. It was a routine he had followed every day since he had left the army, whether at his country home or in London. He sipped gently at his tea in quiet contemplation as he studied the lead story, unaware that immediately he turned over to page four, his life was going to change inexorably.

It was the picture of his son which first caught Dovingdon's eye, and then the headline, "Shot for Murder." His heart stopped as his immediate reaction was that it was Penrose who had been murdered but then, as he read Kerslake's report, he learnt the story and of Penrose's true plight. The Colonel read each word in the column very carefully just once. He put the paper down, rested back on his chair and stared at the ceiling. He would never read the story again.

After some time of doing nothing, Dovingdon rose to go to his bedroom, where his wife was seated in her dressing gown at a table in her adjacent dressing room. The Colonel handed her the paper with the relevant page open without saying anything. At first, Lady Primrose started to smile as she saw her son's picture and then, as she read the headlines, her bright eyes popped wide open with shock. She looked at her husband. He clinched his teeth, sucked on his cheeks and nodded a nod of despair.

"You have to read it," was all Dovingdon said before he left and went downstairs. Despite Lady Primrose shouting, yelling even, for Stoddart to return, he completely ignored her. In his distress, he was completely unable to deal with her emotions too.

In his study, he sat at his desk wondering what he should do next. He was paralysed by a shame he had never felt before. The phone rang. Dovingdon ignored it, as he always did, allowing his housekeeper to answer and take messages. It rang again and again and again. Stoddart swivelled around in his chair, and with his desk behind him, he looked through the French doors, over the parkland, and into the hills and trees rising in the distance. Without thinking, Dovingdon rose, opened both doors and started to walk. The sun had just finished burning off the morning cloud. It was going to be a beautiful day, but Dovingdon was oblivious to all of that. His mind was only focused on one thing. The fate of his son.

Chapter 46

England July 1918

THE FIRST TIME both King George V and Field Marshal Douglas Haig knew of Major Penrose Dovingdon's Court Martial, and its decision, was when they read Kerslake's article in The Times. To say the report caused a disturbance in the upper echelons of society would be an understatement.

In the afternoon, at their almost daily audience, the Prime Minister, David Lloyd-George, advised the King to wait until Haig had read the court's papers before deciding what to do next.

"Something tells me that this decision will not sit well with the people of my Kingdom," said the King, accurately summarising popular opinion. "If the death penalty can befall an officer for doing his duty, as Kerslake suggests, then everyone is going to ask what chance is there for their son, brother, uncle or cousin?" It was a prescient observation, for it would be a remark made in many a public house on that day and for many days afterwards.

The matter was then raised at Prime Minister's question time which, by convention, was the last session of ministerial questions of the day. Lloyd-George calmly explained that, as the law required, Field Marshal Haig would review all the papers of the case, as he did with all death penalty cases, and come to a decision. "The House," he said, "should put its trust in one of England's finest soldiers to do the right thing by the convict, the army, the country and God."

By the time Lloyd-George was standing up to answer questions, there was mild panic in the Dovingdon household, for Col. Dovingdon had walked out immediately after telling his wife of their son's fate and had not been seen since. With his extended absence, Lady Primrose had gone from deep melancholy on learning of Penrose's conviction, through panic to near hysteria. It was only with the trusted Jack Morris, wounded and unable to fight, that the housekeeper dared share the news of Penrose, but he already knew. It was already all around the town. What he didn't know was that the Colonel was missing, and it was now Jack's job to go and find him.

Sitting in the Colonel's chair and staring out of the windows onto the same view as Col Dovingdon had done some few hours earlier, Jack was almost certain he knew where the Colonel had gone; so he started to walk too, instinct taking him along the same track.

Jack had been out for about two hours and it was getting towards late evening, with sunset only minutes away, when Jack saw the Colonel coming towards him. He wasn't walking with his usual crisp, firm purpose of pace. Jack waited.

"Have you seen a black and white collie on your walk, sir," asked Jack, making up a reasoned excuse as to why he might also be out. "She's a good dog what's gone miss'n."

"No, Morris, sorry I haven't."

"It's a bit late now, d'ya mind if I walk back with you, sir?" asked Jack. "I'll come out again tomorrow," he added, to give plausibility to his story.

"Of course."

"Really sorry about Major Dovingdon," said Jack, after the two men had been walking side by side for a little while, each adopting a more purposeful step, despite the grimacing pain Jack was suffering from the war wound in his leg.

"You know?" said Dovingdon, surprised.

"Yes sir. T'were in the morning papers so everyone in the town knows."

"Oh hell, yes," said Dovingdon realising the notoriety of their situation.

"Yeh, but they're all really supportive 'cause of what the journalist wrote."

"You've read the story?"

"Yeh, and this afternoon's paper from London, which said that the King and Mr. Lloyd-George had talked about it this afternoon, and he'll answer questions about it at Prime Minister's questions in Parliament later today."

"Oh God no, please no," said Dovingdon, his voice filling with distress.

"It looks good for Penrose; sorry, Major Dovingdon's appeal, doesn't it?"

The two men walked on, side by side in silence, each keeping a steady pace with the other.

"You don't have children, do you Morris?"

"No."

"But you've got lots of brothers and sisters?"

"Yes, eight of them."

"How old is the youngest?"

"Annie, she's seven."

"And I bet you feel the most responsibility for her, don't you?"

"Oh yes sir, even though she's growin' up, she's still the little baby of the family, gets her own way on everything."

"So Morris, let us say, God forbid, your house is on fire and you can save say four or five of your bigger, older brothers and sisters or you can save just little Annie, but you can't do both. Which do you save?"

"Why do you ask sir?

"Because Morris, that's my problem." They walked on some more in silence. "So which do you save?" Dovingdon prompted.

"Well, you save the biggest number first and then you save the baby," Jack replied.

"Not in this game Morris – it's one or the other."

"Or you save the baby, sir, in the hope that the bigger ones can save themselves," said Jack, as he wondered what the correct answer was.

The Colonel said nothing. Staring straight down on the path they were taking, he simply shook his head.

"I don't get it sir, I really don't," said Jack.

"It's like this. Penrose is your young Annie. The British Army and all its Allies are the rest of your brothers and sisters. It is vital that France and England stay united if we are to win this bloody war. The fact that the Russians have given up makes our task even harder. It means not a single solitary thing can get in the way of keeping the Allies together. The French army have already had one mutiny, possibly more. If we don't stay together then the war is lost. Irrespective of whether Major

Dovingdon is innocent or guilty, if the French expect reprisals for the killing of their soldiers, reprisals there have to be."

"What, are you gonna give up Penrose to save us losing this fucking war?" said Jack, his language turning blue in total disbelief at what he was hearing.

"Too many people have died already," said the Colonel firmly.

"Excuse me sir, but that ain't right. 'Cause of who yous are, yous 'ave access straight to the top. It's what yous lot do; yous look after yous selves."

"Just because I can do it, doesn't make it right that I should do it, does it?"

Jack didn't say anything.

"Before I ask, I have to put myself in the shoes of the people I am asking. Only this way will I know whether my request is reasonable," explained the Colonel.

"Hang on sir, this doesn't make sense. Don't you believe your family comes first in all things? In our 'ouse it was like a mantra of my father's, family comes first, he would say. It's the Morrises against the rest of the world."

"Of course, you're right, Jack." It was the first time the Colonel had used his Christian name so it jarred a little on Jack's ear. "Except when you're on the battlefield and your family is not around you; then you think about the man to the left and right of you, don't you? When you're a soldier, isn't it your mates who should come first?"

The words 'your mates' again jarred in Jack's ears. This was not the way the Colonel usually spoke. He was normally authoritarian, purposeful, and business-like. Instead, they were having an ordinary conversation with ordinary colloquial terms being used as though there was not a shred of difference between them.

"Suppose you're right there, sir," said Jack, not really knowing how else to argue.

"So you see my conflict is between the son in my arms and my brothers in arms and I have to choose one."

"Put like that, it seems one hell of a conflict to me," said Jack. "Are you sure it's like that?"

"I wish it wasn't."

"Aren't you gonna write to Haig and the King on Penrose's behalf to plead clemency?" There was something about the conversation which now made it comfortable for Jack to use the Major's Christian name too.

"No, Jack, I am not."

"Then, you're abandoning your own son?"

"I have to abandon one; it's either him or the army."

"Look sir, this is bleedin' nonsense. The army is big enough to look after its soddin' self. Yous 'ave to look after Penrose. It's your job. It's what a father does, for Christ sakes," cried Jack, getting very animated. "What yous goin' to say to Lady Primrose? She's worried sick and now she's gonna be bloody furious."

"I know Jack, its why command is such a lonely place." The quiet, calm reason in Dovingdon's voice was quite surreal. "It's the loneliest, most desolate, place in the world," he added, very gently.

"Pheeewr," Jack blew through his lips. "This ain't right sir. There must be something we can do?" It was as though, with the Colonel appearing to give up, Jack was preparing himself to take on Penrose's defence.

"I think we have to pray and trust in our God," said Dovingdon.

"Sorry sir, I ain't got no God. I lost 'im on the bleedin' battlefield. He makes no ruddy sense to me." He paused to allow the Colonel to voice some shock but nothing came. "If I did have a God, I promise you I'd pray for Penrose as you ask, but it seems to me we have to bleedin' well look after ourselves, 'cause no God ain't." There was a real conviction in Jack's speech for it was something he had thought a lot about since being wounded out of the army.

"Just think of the pressure Haig is under at the moment," responded Dovingdon. Do you really think it fair that I should put him under more pressure pleading for my son's life? He has a war to win."

"Yeh, I do, I bleedin' do. The papers say there's been a miscarriage of justice and that's what we're bleedin' fighting for, the proper rule of law," argued Jack, his agitation becoming really quite vocal.

"Then we have to have confidence that the army will come to the right decision when the case is reviewed."

"Well, they didn't come to the right decision first time, did they?"

"We don't know that, do we? We don't know what the relationship is like between the two armies. If a sacrifice has to be made to keep them together, then perhaps the law needs to turn a blind eye."

"Never sir, no. That just ain't right"

"Sometimes in a game of chess, you have to sacrifice a pawn or a castle to save your king and win the game."

The coolness of the Colonel's arguments worried Jack, for it was as though he had worked the problem all out and was now giving the answers. With pen and paper in hand, and time to sit and think undisturbed in the fields, that is exactly what he had done.

"But this ain't a bleedin game is it?" said Jack. Really sir, are you gonna do nothing?"

Jack abruptly stopped walking, for they had reached a point where two tracks crossed. The Colonel stopped just a couple of paces further on. His house was now visible in the close distance.

"I need to leave here," said Jack. "My route home is that way," and he pointed into the distance.

"Ah yes, of course, thank you Morris. You've been good company."

"Are you really gonna do nothing sir?" Jack asked pleadingly, but the Colonel walked off with renewed purposeful pace. He didn't answer. Instead, he just waved, without turning in acknowledgment.

It was past sunset, as Jack turned and set off towards home. It was getting quite dark as grey thunder clouds rolled over the skies. They were the perfect accompaniment for the way Jack was feeling. He contemplated the conversation they had just had. Christ, the Colonel was one hell of a tough bastard, he concluded. He wouldn't want him as a father, and then he remembered back to his own childhood. His father's permanent fear of upsetting the Colonel and the risk that any upset could result in him losing both his job and their home. This fear ruled the way Jack's father conducted his life, and that of his children; always subservient, a price paid with the welts on the hides of Jack, and of his brothers and sisters. The upper classes are a totally different race, Jack concluded. Bleedin' animals prepared to eat their first born to survive, he thought. Perhaps it was time for that revolution everyone was talking about.

Chapter 47

France July 1918

JULIETTE, ALONG WITH all her contemporaries, was too exhausted to read any of the newspapers. They measured the success of the war by the number of injured they were looking after, fewer patients and the war was going well, many patients and it was going badly. When each of them thought about it they knew this measure was illogical but it worked for them as a group, for it fairly reflected how hard they had to work to get the injured men well enough to go either back home or to the front. Their days were of constant high pressure with long shifts, at the end of which they collapsed into bed exhausted.

Juliette was thrilled to see a letter lying on her pillow when she returned after a long night shift and her heart gladdened when she saw Penrose's firm, slanted and flowery handwriting. However, her joy turned into a deep chill as she read:

> *Dear Juliette,*
> *You may have already read. I am in a spot of bother. There has been a bit of a brouhaha. The Times will be writing about it which means that it is all going to become frightfully well-known. I wanted to write to you about it so you are forewarned.*
> *These words are hard to write, for there is no easy way. I have been cashiered out of the army and have been sentenced to be shot for desertion and murder. By the time you get this letter the sentence may well have been carried out.*
> *I want to explain to you their coming. I did not desert as I have been accused, and found guilty. I merely changed my posting on the battlefield which, as a senior officer, I am allowed to do. There is no question - I did order our guns to fire towards the French, and*

this resulted in many French soldiers being killed, but there was no *mens rea* on my part and therefore no act of murder. My sentence is a political ablation to French sensibilities. A lamb slaughtered on the altar of war.

I think I am quite fortunate in knowing the manner of my death. The fact that it will be quick and painless. It has never been dying which worried me, merely its means, so while the timing is not of my choosing, I do not think to be shot by firing squad is too bad an end. There will be a lot of brandy beforehand, so I will be drinking many a toast.

Ma and Pa are going to be desperately upset. Particularly Pa who will be horrified by the fact that I have tarnished and damaged the Dovingdon name, something which he holds very precious. Please look after them. It will be too hard for me to write. They just need to know I am truly sorry I have let them down and that I love them terribly.

Would you be so kind as to write to Drew and explain the circumstances? I do not have the heart to write. I simply do not know what to say. Please help her get into university because she so wants it to happen. Do tell her I love her.

A long time ago, I urged Pa to establish a fund to help the families of the soldiers under my command. Many have lost their breadwinners and many others were so very badly hurt that it will be impossible for them to work again. They will be in immense hardship. As soldiers, Pa and I have a responsibility to do everything we can to help them. Please make it your job to assist Pa so that it does happen. Even a little will help a lot.

My last written words are to you, my most wonderful sister. Even though you are younger, your intelligence, energy, tenacity and caring has always been an inspiration. There have been many occasions when I have been so proud of you, but never more so than when you became a nurse. You have always been the engine driver in your life, whereas I have always been the passenger in mine.

When this war is over, go back to university and campaign for better things; for greater fairness and equality; for I now know that there is no difference of rank between men who stand side by side at the barricades ready to charge, and the women into whose hands they fall when injured.

After the war, for I am sure it is nearly won, our world is bound to change. You are one of those rare people who have the ability to make change happen for the good. I charge you, dear sister, to go about that task with haste.

You are a very special person, and I am so proud to have had you as my sister. I am so sorry that I have let you down.

Please do not think badly of me.

Forever and always, my love,

Penrose

Juliette read the letter two or three times, taking in no more than she did the first time. She rose from the bed where she had been sitting. Without a moment's thought she walked from her tent, on the wet greasy footboards, into the tent which sufficed as Matron's office. There, without saying a word, she handed Penrose's letter to Matron to read. Matron took the letter and read it carefully, in silence. She looked up at Juliette without saying a word and read the letter again.

"Oh, I am sorry," said Matron, genuinely surprised. "I read the papers, but I didn't connect."

"It's in the papers already?" asked Juliette.

"Yes, yesterday morning's I think."

"Can I see it?"

"Yes, of course."

"I need compassionate leave, immediately," said Juliette.

"Certainly."

"I need to go now!"

"Of course. How long for? One week?"

"I don't know, probably longer. I have accumulated a lot of untaken leave. Could it be two weeks?"

"Yes, two weeks, and if you telegram me because you need a third week then that will be fine, but no longer."

"Yes, Matron. Thank you, Matron," said Juliette.

"Come back as soon as you can; we need you."

It was just as Juliette was making a rapid exit, that she heard Matron calling her back.

"What are you going to do?"

"See my brother's commanding officer, see Penrose if I can, and then see my parents."

"His commanding officer won't see you."

"Yes, he will," replied Juliette, her voice a tone of steel.

"Given it's you, he probably will," said Matron, admiration falling into her voice. "Do you ever not get your own way?"

Juliette said nothing. She just smiled weakly and then added, "We're about to find out."

"Go and pack, and by the time you've done that I will have your passes organised and have found the newspaper."

"Thank you Matron."

Juliette was just leaving for the second time when Matron called after her. "Sister Dovingdon, do read that letter from your brother again. It is beautifully written."

Juliette heard her words but took no notice. Her mind was focused on her mission. It was only years later she would ordain this letter from her brother as one of the most precious items in her life.

Chapter 48

France July 1918

COMMANDANT ÉTIENNE GUÉGAN learnt of Penrose's plight from Le Figaro the same morning as the readers of the Times, for the story had been syndicated to them from its Paris office. Interestingly, Le Figaro had also included a short editorial commenting on the story. It argued that the death of 46 Frenchmen, at the negligent hand of their Allies was not a matter which should be of concern to French sensibilities. If the English court had decided that the crime of murder had been committed, then the appropriate penalty must follow. The article determined that France's only interest was in a fair trial. It concluded by saying that: the sadness for the people of France was that The Times thought that the trial had not been so.

The French deaths at the Battle of Célieux Ridge had been a matter of some interest, but it did not gain the cause célèbre status in France which the English were now ascribing to it. Guégan had been interviewed twice by the British Military Police but, as he had only instructed the company stationed at Coeur de Foucy to carry out a relief exercise on their front line the night before, and he had left at first light, just as the troops were setting off, his evidence wasn't given much weight.

Why had he given the order, he was asked repeatedly, but he had no answer.

The fact that his order had directly resulted in men's deaths was not something Étienne was prepared to contemplate. He would have taken exactly the same noncommittal attitude to Penrose's plight, except for three things. He knew the man to be shot. That man had helped them win the Battle of Verdun, but most importantly, he knew the French soldiers' deaths at the Battle of Célieux were an accident.

It was why, on reading Le Figaro, Étienne immediately walked down the corridor to the offices of Marshal Foch, Commander-in-Chief of the Allied Armies.

Chapter 49

France June 1918

JULIETTE AND ÉTIENNE arrived at Montreuil-sur-Mer at almost the same time. Juliette came by taxi and Étienne by train from Paris. It was a town which Étienne knew well. It had been the base for a French military academy until General Haig took over the town as his headquarters for the British Army. The suffix sur-Mer amused almost every Englishman there for, although the town was on the Canche River, the sea was some distance away.

If Juliette's matron thought that seeing Penrose's commanding officer meant seeing the Colonel of his regiment, then she did not know the Sister in her charge. As far as Juliette was concerned, there was only one person who could change events, that was General Haig, and that was her destination.

Étienne's destination was the same, but he was coming as the emissary of the French army. Without any mention of his involvement in the battle, or his motives, Étienne had persuaded Marshal Foch that it would be good for allied politics and French morale if they were seen to be both magnanimous and generous, and that he should write to Haig requesting that Major Dovingdon's sentence be commuted to a long term of imprisonment. Foch, sensitive to the politics of the two national armies, thought that Pétain, who was Commander-in-Chief of the French army, should write such a letter. Pétain, recognising Foch's seniority, agreed, but on one condition; his signature would not be on any letter which made any request to Haig for anything.

It was a long journey to Montreuil, which Juliette started by sitting in silence, deep in dread. It was when the taxi driver discovered she could speak French that he started a conversation, and very quickly she rediscovered the fluency which she had once enjoyed, while taking particular care with her pronunciation. It was the taxi driver who negotiated their way past the sentries stationed at the entrance to the ramparts and battlements of the old town. He also helped find her lodgings, not in a hotel but in a small family home of distant relatives. The town was packed with British soldiers, so finding somewhere to sleep was a problem which she had not anticipated.

Juliette joined the family for dinner. It was here that her hosts said how delighted they were that she was staying, given that it was forbidden for women of the Women's Army Auxiliary Corps to enter private houses, hotels, restaurants, or cafés. "I am a QAIMNS Nurse," said Juliette, by way of hasty explanation, for she genuinely did not know the rules that applied to her when she was away from her hospital. She had holidayed many times at Guillaume's Hotel at Berck Plage, and no one had ever said anything about what she could and couldn't do.

Over dinner, Juliette learnt of the strict curfew and the difficulties this placed on the lives of those living in the town. She was told of the problems, caused by the plight of the refugees, who had swarmed into the town seeking work, and the tented settlements which had resulted around the edge. They talked of the German night bombing air raids on the town which had started at the beginning of the summer. She was told how all the soldiers and officers of the garrison had been ordered to sleep either in the woods or deep in the tunnels of the town. Alarmed, Juliette enquired of her own safety, but her concerns were dismissed with a shrug. 'Aucun Français a peur de son lit par des lâches allemands'[17], she was told. It was a phrase which had obviously been used many times in disdain at the British orders, for it tripped too easily off the tongue.

Of bigger concern to the residents of Montreuil, and to Juliette's hosts, was whether, with so many sleeping in the woods, the British Army would honour the rental treaty made with the Mayor, Edmond Dupont, in which they had agreed to pay FFr 4.50 per month for every British soldier who stayed within the town's boundary.

Juliette was quizzed in great detail about the nature of her visit, but

---

[17] No Frenchman is made afraid of his bed by German cowards

she said nothing, for she knew any mention of Penrose would bring her out in tears. All she said was she was here to see General Haig. It was in response to this remark she learnt Haig was not stationed in Montreuil, as she had been led to believe, but just over two miles away at Château de Beaurepaire, a country house tailored to his every need.

Étienne quickly found lodgings in the officers' mess where he dined that night. He was able to testify that the rumours of the excellence of the wines were true. However, very much to his chagrin, not a bottle from his family's vineyard, Château de Gressier, could be found; a matter he was determined to fix the next day with a telegram to his mother. Over dinner, he was quizzed heavily on the French attitude to the war. With a paucity of insight to French thinking, the British officers drank every word in their thirst for knowledge. Étienne made it clear that he was not speaking for France, but for the men under his command, who were tired to the point of exhaustion. He explained what everyone already knew but, coming from a foreign voice, it reinforced the point.

"It was clear," Étienne said, "that the Germans had spent a fortune trying to subvert and foment disorder in Russia with huge success, as evidenced by the subsequent revolution."

He went on to talk, almost without interruption, as to how he saw things. Russia had been in a civil war, and revolutionary chaos, since 1917, and with it, the Eastern Front had collapsed. The signing of the Treaty of Brest-Litovsk by Russia and Germany in March 1918 had resulted in Russia's formal withdrawal from the war.

"With the benefit of Germany's very efficient railway system, all of their forces have now been brought to bear against us," said Étienne. "Their huge attack against us on 21st March was much sooner than I, or anyone else, expected. Having won on the Eastern Front," he continued "they now have the confidence and high morale which travels with all winners, so they took the opportunity to attack early, and quite frankly gentlemen, neither of our defences were up to the task, were they?"

"Do you think the war is lost?" asked one officer, dejected at Étienne's analysis.

"Good God no," he retorted, concerned that anyone could think this. The fighting is going to be sustained right through the summer into the winter, as last year," he predicted, but with the Americans now in the war, with their troops landing in such huge numbers, and with our tanks on the battlefield, the whole strategy is changing once again. I think we are bound to win. It will just take time, a lot of time, but maybe it's time we don't have."

Later that night, in the officers' club in the École Martrell, perhaps because his tongue had been loosened with wine, or perhaps because he had such an attentive audience, Étienne explained he was seeing Field Marshal Haig to discuss the "Dovingdon Affair."

"But we all thought you wanted it," said the first person who spoke. "Is this not what France wanted?" he was asked, by an accompanied chorus of others. Étienne did not answer.

"But he killed your own," added a voice.

"Yes, but it is clear it was an accident, a regrettable accident. Our investigations show as much."

The men all around him nodded.

"The thing is, we would not want to shoot one of our officers if the tables were turned," said Étienne.

There was a general measure of sympathy to that notion.

"What my soldiers hate, in fact, I might even say all soldiers hate, more than anything else is injustice, and from our perspective, it appears there may have been an injustice."

"It's the same for us," said one of those in the group listening around him. "If Dovingdon gets shot then our soldiers' reaction is likely to be the same."

"Then don't you see that a death sentence on Major Dovingdon plays straight into the hands of injustice and those wishing to undermine our society?"

Étienne's message was clear. If the British army shot Dovingdon, and did not commute his sentence, then they would be adding to the flames of discontent in the Allied armies, and perhaps in the British and French populations.

"We are going to win," he said, "but we need to think of the France we want," he paused, "and you need to think of the England you want, when this war is over. I can tell you what we don't want; its revolution,

Russian style, and we have to start working to make sure that doesn't happen right now. It's why I am here."

There was an instantaneous round of applause as Étienne closed his small speech.

Chapter 50

France July 1918

BY COINCIDENCE, ÉTIENNE and Juliette arrived at the sentry box guarding the entrance to Château de Beaurepaire at exactly the same time. Juliette's taxi was just in front of Étienne's British-provided staff car. Neither of them had an appointment, simply expecting to be seen, so both pretended that they did. The guards, desperate not to foul up and be sent to the front, had an officiousness about them which would have made any regimental sergeant major proud. Eventually, in the fight to gain access, both Étienne and Juliette got out of their vehicles to remonstrate with the sergeant on duty.

"If your name is not on the list, then you cannot come in. Those are my instructions," said the soldier, leaning through the gate house window as he leered at the woman in her nurse's uniform, standing bolt upright in front of him.

Juliette remained very calm. One thing nursing had taught her was how to deal with men of all types, including the jobsworths.

"Sergeant," she said sweetly, deliberately promoting him above his rank of corporal, "I'm Miss Juliette Dovingdon. Lord Robert Cecil has written to Field Marshal Haig asking him to see me," she lied. "He arranged for me to see Field Marshal French at Saint Omer, and now I am here to see Sir Douglas. Will you please let me through?"

The crispness, clarity and presence of Juliette made everything she said sound extremely plausible, which, in the process, worried the corporal. He'd never had to turn away a woman before.

"Did you say, Dovingdon?" asked Étienne.

"Oui, Monsieur," replied Juliette, speaking French in recognition of his uniform and accent.

"Any relationship to Major Dovingdon?" he asked impatiently.

"Parlez en français, s'il vous plaît," said Juliette, not wanting that name to be any reason for her not to be given access, as she finished off very quietly with the words, "Mais oui, c'est mon frère."

At this point, Étienne decided that he was no longer prepared to wait. He quickly concluded that her request was probably a disastrous one, but then again, he knew he did not understand the English class system as, from her behaviour, this seemed to be the card which Juliette was playing.

"Sergeant," said Étienne firmly, "this is my identity." He handed over his identity card. "As you can see, I'm a Commandant with the French army on the staff of Marshal Foch. I have an important letter from Field Marshal Pétain of the French army. I must deliver it either in person to Field Marshal Haig or to his military secretary. I suggest you phone Field Marshal Haig's ADC immediately and get me access."

Instinct told the sergeant that Commandant Étienne Guégan was a man whose refusal would cause him problems and so, after a phone call, Étienne's staff car was authorised through. His car passed around Juliette's taxi and just as it was under the opened barrier, it stopped. "Mademoiselle is coming with me," said Étienne. The corporal said nothing. Juliette abandoned her confused taxi driver with the words: "don't go away, I'll be back," and she ran swiftly to climb into the back of Étienne's staff car.

The journey to the house was quick; however, by the time they arrived at the front door of the château, there was an orderly ready to greet them. They were shown into an antechamber where they waited. Little was said as they studied each other. They found the other's accent incredibly sexy. It was the first point of notice in their magnetic attraction. They would say that the other was typically French or English, except that Étienne was much taller than Juliette's view of the stereotypical Frenchman. In Étienne's view, Juliette was much slimmer, with far more style, than the stereotype he had in his mind of a typical Englishwoman.

Eventually, one of Haig's ADCs came to see them. "Please, I will speak for both of us," said Étienne, continuing to speak in French, as they had established at the outset. "I can assure you that my message is more important and will be more effective than yours," he continued.

Juliette started to protest.

"Mademoiselle," said Étienne, continuing in French, "I invited you to come in with me. If you do not do as I ask, I will simply instruct the orderly to throw you out. Do we understand each other?"

The look of sternness in Étienne's eyes meant that he was being serious and would take no truck. Juliette backed off.

"How can I help you?" said the ADC.

"I've come to see General Haig, or, if he's not available, his military secretary."

"The Field Marshal is not here, Commandant," said the ADC, recognising Étienne's proper rank, "and Major Templeford is very busy."

"Please be assured, my army," he then paused for effect, "and my government would not have sent me unless it was of vital importance. Here is a letter from Marshal Pétain addressed to Field Marshal Haig, requesting that the death sentence for Major Dovingdon be commuted to a prison term."

"Thank you. Is that all?"

"No, it is not," said Étienne, upset by the dismissive way he was being dealt with. "The French army does not send a Commandant to deliver a letter which is capable of coming by courier. It comes with a message which is so politically sensitive that it cannot be written down. It is why I have come as an emissary-in-person."

Twenty-four hours ago, there had been no message, but Étienne's conversation in the English mess the night before had enabled him to develop one. "To give this message, I either have to see Field Marshal Haig or an officer of very senior rank who will be able to talk to him straightaway."

The ADC took the letter, opened it, and read its contents.

"How is your French?" asked Étienne.

"Quite adequate," said the ADC tartly. "I would not be on Haig's staff if it was not," he explained, arrogance pouring through his lips. "Please wait here."

Étienne and Juliette waited. Neither said anything to the other, both worried that they might be overheard. They stood, they paced, and they sat, in no one position for too long, as their impatience could not keep them still. They waited for well over an hour until an orderly escorted them to a large room with a grand desk at one end and a round table at the other. There was a fire burning in the grate. Even in early summer, Château de Beaurepaire had a permanent dampness about it which created a chill in the rooms if not warmed. As they entered the room, it was clear there was a deputation to meet them.

The ADC who quizzed them on their arrival introduced the two men standing in the middle of the room. "Major-General Sir Harold Ruggles-Brise," said the ADC, introducing him first. Étienne saluted while Juliette curtsied. She thought it was the appropriate thing to do. Ruggles-Brise returned the salute and offered his hand, which Étienne took and firmly shook. There was no similar offer of a handshake made to Juliette. The ADC then introduced "General Sir Richard Hakin," a man known to the French army by his English nickname of Thruster, given to him by the Australian army. He was not held in high regard. He had a reputation for organising pointless stunts which cost lives. Étienne and Hakin saluted. They both shook hands as Juliette curtsied once again. Hakin's eyes were cold and heartless. Étienne wondered how his men served under him.

"I have a message from Marshal Pétain," said Étienne. "It's not written because if any word of it were to appear anywhere else, the message would be formally denied. Further, it is not a conversation he feels he can have, even if it were to be in private."

"Then why is Nurse Dovingdon here?" asked Hakin.

"I invited her because, above only Major Dovingdon, she has a vested interest in what I say, and," he stressed the word and, "in keeping it confidential."

"Please go on," said Ruggles-Brise, smiling sweetly at Juliette as he spoke. He was clearly seeking to take charge of the discussion.

"I believe you are aware of our difficulties after the Battle of Aisne in the spring of last year," said Étienne.

"The second battle," Hakin corrected him.

"Ah, yes, the second battle," agreed Ruggles-Brise.

"As you can imagine, it's a matter of great sensitivity, particularly to Marshal Pétain, who had to sort it out," said Étienne.

"General Duchêne had ordered that every tenth man in the 32nd and 65th Infantry Regiments be shot for mutineering," added Hakin, looking directly at Étienne. He was deliberately rubbing salt into what he knew would be a French army wound.

"Yes, I know that. I understand they were two reserve battalions who refused to relieve those on the front line," replied Ruggles-Brise, not wanting to be outdone in the knowledge stakes.

Étienne smarted at the way the English seemed to gloat at the French disciplinary issues. "Yes, of course you had your own difficulties in Étaples last September, didn't you," he interjected "And, oh yes, also the year before that." Then he added, by way of reinforcement to show he knew what had happened: "On both occasions one man was selected and shot for mutiny, is that not so?"

"Quite so," said Ruggles-Brise realising that perhaps their spelling out of the French army's misfortunes had been neither the wisest nor politest of behaviour.

"You will also be aware of the problems last year with the Russian army leading to their withdrawal from the war," continued Étienne.

"Some ally," said Hakin, snorting in disgust.

"As you are no doubt aware, the Russian Revolution, the People's Revolution, started in the Petrograd[18] garrison," said Étienne.

No more was needed to be said between intelligent men; the message was clear. Shoot Major Dovingdon and the soldiers, whether British or French, might mutiny and a public revolution might then quickly follow.

"Just before the war, a poet called Rudyard Kipling wrote a poem," said Étienne. "It might be helpful if I quoted from part of it." He then changed his tone, deliberately allowing his voice to mellow, as he started to speak from memory, and in rhyme:

"The Saxon is not like us Normans.
His manners are not so polite.
But he never means anything serious

---

[18] St Petersburg name was changed to Petrograd in 1914 because it sounded less German. Its name was changed to Leningrad in 1924, and back to St Petersburg in 1991 following the collapse of the Soviet Union.

Till he talks about justice and right.
When he stands like an ox in the furrow
With his sullen set eyes on your own,
And grumbles, 'this isn't fair dealing,'
My son, leave the Saxon alone."

"What are you telling me?" said Ruggles-Brise, a little annoyed by
the suggestion that the English were not as polite as the French,
then becoming visibly cross at the seemingly hidden message that, if
Dovingdon was shot, the British army, as a bunch of Saxon peasants,
would revolt.

Juliette was impressed with Étienne's recitation but like
Ruggles-Brise and Hakin, she was instantly shocked by its possible
misinterpretation. She could see immediately that the verse had not
been well-received.

"I think the Commandant is saying that the British are known
for their sense of justice and fair play," interjected Juliette quickly,
"and that fair play would be best served by commuting Dovingdon's
sentence from one of capital punishment to something less."

"Exactement," said Étienne, pleased that Juliette had made his
message clear.

"We will make sure that Field Marshal Haig is apprised of your
message," said Ruggles-Brise with a wry smile, amused at the way
Étienne's strange choice of poem had very nearly back-fired.

"One other thing," said Étienne. "The French army will not be
issuing any notice or making any official comment to the papers, but
it will, in confidence and without attribution, be briefing Le Figaro
that France does not want Dovingdon shot on its behalf. Marshal
Pétain thought it best that I should see you before our soldiers are
made aware of our view."

Ruggles-Brise looked at the wording of Pétain's letter and noticed
it wasn't actually signed by him. Haig's loathing of Pétain was widely
known. He wondered whether this was the reason that Pétain had not
signed the letter.

"The letter's from Pétain but not signed by him. Why is that?"
asked Ruggles-Brise.

"The letter has been signed by Marshal Foch," answered Étienne.

"But the letter is from Pétain?"

"Yes, indeed."

"Then why did he not sign it?"

"Time and logistics, sir, only that," answered Étienne, wishing it had only been that.

"Time and logistics," repeated Hakin sarcastically, as he turned away, signifying for him, this meeting had just ended.

Chapter 51

France July 1918

PENROSE WAS LYING on his bed, his hands clasped behind his head, staring at the ceiling. He was doing his very best to empty his mind. If he thought about what he was facing, his lack of a future, the wife and children he will not have and the things he will not have done, he found his brain felt as though it would explode. His trance was broken by the rustle of keys in the lock. Gently, he turned to look towards the opening door.

"Your batman has brought you this, sir," said the guarding corporal, offering up an opened envelope which had been read by the censors. It was obvious from the soldier's demeanour that he knew its contents. Penrose took the letter which he half expected to be from Juliette, replying to his missive of doom, or perhaps Drew. He had not written to her because he worried about how she would react to his predicament.

Penrose did not recognise the writing. He opened the letter and started to read.

> *Billingshurst*
> *Sussex*
>
> *Dear Major Dovingdon,*
> *It is with great regret and deep sadness that I must inform you that Miss Drew Stubman and her father were killed in a car accident on Friday 31ˢᵗ May.*
> *I am Drew's aunt on her mother's side and am having to deal with their affairs as they have no other relatives.*
> *In this regard, I have come across the sweet and charming letters*

you have written to Drew. These suggest that you and she were terribly fond of each other. For this reason, I need to share with you this tragic news.

Mercifully, Drew was killed instantly, while her father was unconscious for several days before passing away. At least he did not have to bear the agony of knowing of Drew's death.

Drew is buried between her mother and father in Welborough Green churchyard for it is where Stanley Stubman (her father) had chosen for his retirement. They both loved the village so. It is a wonderfully peaceful spot. I know that she will be contented there.

I am sure, like all of us, you are seeing much pain and sadness, but I would ask that you take just a little while to pity and pray for this one small soul who has now been lost to us. She was so beautiful, intelligent and strong; it made her quite unique. I cannot help but think that mankind is poorer for her leaving us to be taken by God. He must have had great desideratum for her, for our need was beyond measure.

I send you my sincerest condolences.

After he had scanned the letter and taken in its message, Penrose sat on the edge of his bed, and with his elbows on his knees, he leaned forward and allowed his head to collapse into his hands. He was in total despair.

He picked up the letter again and started to read it, this time more slowly, evaluating each word to get a true sense of its meaning. He looked for a date on the letter; there was none. He looked at the envelope, but the postmark was smudged over the stamp. He then turned to the date she had died. It was the same day as the Battle of Célieux Ridge. Could that day have been any worse, he cussed. His anger was followed by an immediate relief, for she had died without knowing what had happened to him. He knew she would have worried so. He also knew that, if you ever needed to choose a person to be in your lifeboat, Drew and his sister would be the first he would call. He was devastated as he realised, in Drew's case, he could not now make that call.

Penrose returned to his bed and his previous position of lying on his back. His sense of hopelessness had been renewed, but this time it was coupled with an overwhelming sense of morbidity. Without Drew, he concluded, there was no purpose in living. He contemplated death and dying. Why should he live when so many were dying around him? It made no sense. It was, he decided, the act of a selfish man to try and stay alive when so many others had died. Perhaps, to die by firing squad was not such a bad option. It would be very quick. Should he consider himself lucky to die this way? Perhaps he should. Was this the way he was going to meet Drew again, in the afterlife? Was this their destiny? Had this been pre-ordained by God he wondered?

Penrose's thoughts were broken as one of his guards brought in his lunch tray with a glass of water. Penrose hardly acknowledged him for his depression was so deep that he could barely move.

Time drifted on, for there was no sense of it in Penrose's cell. He thought about being dead and the sense of lying cold in his coffin. To simulate the effect, he rolled onto the floor and lying on his back pulled the heavy horsehair mattress on top of him. Then he shuffled under the metal frame of the bed until he came up parallel to the concrete foundations of the wall. Lying still, he allowed the cold of the flagstones to penetrate his body and the heavy weight of the horsehair mattress to slowly suffocate him in the claustrophobia of his self-made coffin.

At that moment, as Penrose was contemplating the nothingness of death, a lorry containing injured servicemen swept into the farmyard. As the driver turned, he didn't yank hard enough on the steering wheel, and as a result, his front wing clipped the detonator of one of the dud shells which had been stored outside of Penrose's prison cell. He had watched them being placed there time after time without a thought. There was immediate oblivion. For hundreds of yards around nothing was left standing. The dump of unexploded shells had done exactly what they hadn't done when they should have, exploded!

Chapter 52

France July 1918

ÉTIENNE AND JULIETTE re-grouped at Montreuil-sur-Mer railway station at 3pm as they had agreed, both with a small amount of luggage in hand. Their journey to Paris was complicated, involving three changes of train, and was going to take well over five hours. Neither of them had eaten, so they sat down at the little café, which the stationmaster's wife ran as a profitable sideline, and each supped at a bowl of vegetable soup and crusty bread. Slowly the station filled up with expectant passengers wanting to make the most of their short furloughs.

As they ate and chatted about their plans for saving Penrose, there was a huge explosion. It was big enough to rock the building, but not so large that your first instinct was to duck.

"That's an arms store going up," said Étienne, by way of an aside comment.

"How do you know?" asked Juliette.

"It's way behind our lines and there was more than one explosion," said Étienne nonchalantly, but with the train arriving in the station, neither of them thought anymore about it.

On the first of their train journeys, Étienne and Juliette sat opposite each other. They did not speak, for a general melancholy had overtaken them both. But then this sense of depression sat over everybody who had to make decisions in this most dreadful of wars.

Being responsible, and taking tough decisions involving other people's lives, changes you. It had changed both Étienne and Juliette. Étienne, for knowingly commanding men to a painful death; and Juliette, from the nursing of such men, knowing that there was little she could do except help relieve the pain until they died. As a result, neither was as gregarious or as joyful as they had been in their youth. Further, when something happens which gives your body a deep sense of shock, it is usual to go either into a deep, silent shell or become very excited, almost hysterical, with the need to talk. Juliette had already discovered she needed silence, and this explained why, during their journey to Paris, she said very little to Étienne.

On the next train they sat next to each other in a formal manner but still not talking. Finally, on the long train journey into Paris, because the train was so crowded, they sat with their bodies squeezed together, each feeling the warmth and comfort of the other. At first, Juliette dozed on Étienne's shoulder, and then he on hers. Finally, she lay across his chest as his arms enveloped her in a protective shell. It was only as they approached Paris did they start to discuss where they might stay. Juliette suggested the George V Hotel, the Hôtel de Crillon or the Ritz, as these were places she had stayed with her mother and father in her youth.

"You must be joking?" retorted Étienne. "On a commandant's salary, I could just about afford the bar bill," he said, teasingly. It wasn't that he couldn't afford it, as on his salary he could; he just thought they were unnecessarily expensive. They had a grandeur and haughtiness which was not to his taste. He could do expensive, but not now, not with what they were doing.

"There is a little hotel on Rue Greffulhe or if we can't get in there, we can walk around the corner to Rue Castellane," he suggested.

Juliette allowed Étienne to take charge. He was certain to know better than her. "All I need are clean sheets, a clean bath and hot water," she replied.

That night, in the hotel of Étienne's choice, after she'd had a repast of tomato soup and bread, Juliette slept for the first time without a knot in her stomach. She was sure she was on her way to saving her brother's life.

While Juliette slept, Étienne tossed restlessly from one side to another. Two opposing thoughts kept oscillating throughout his mind: how he wanted to make love to the English woman next door, and how he dreaded tomorrow dealing with the newspapers, for he didn't trust them. As far as Étienne was concerned, they were venal; only ever promoting policies or products that were in the best interests of their owners.

As they lay in their beds, little did either of them know of the events taking place in a hospital just outside Montreuil-sur-Mer.

Juliette and Étienne met early in the morning for petit déjeuner. Étienne's remaining job was to confidentially brief Le Figaro, but Juliette's charm suckered him into agreeing that they should work as a team, so their jobs list comprised two things: to speak with Alfred Capus from Le Figaro, and Anthony Kerslake from The Times. Their campaign was a simple one. They would travel between the offices of Le Figaro and The Times until they got the audiences they sought.

At Le Figaro, it was easy to see Capus. He was its editor-in-chief and a man who couldn't abide the economics or operations of producing a daily paper. His only interest was the story and when this was being told by a pretty English girl, its veracity supported by a senior French officer, and involved the incompetence of the English and a rescue of one of their number by the French, then he was in seventh heaven. Juliette left the meeting knowing that they would get a supportive editorial. As Capus explained, they had already covered the story based upon the Times report, but now the French army had an interest, it gained, for Capus, a new lease of life.

Étienne and Juliette lunched together and for the first time they started to talk as friends talk, one to another, without any agenda. In the afternoon, they learnt that Kerslake would not be able to see them, so Étienne went to see friends at the Ministry of the Armies, while Juliette walked the streets of Paris trying to do some shopping. She bought nothing. Instead she stared in amazement when she saw some of the damage caused by German shells fired from over fifty miles way. It would be a special treat to enjoy an afternoon sleep which is what she chose to do.

That night, Étienne and Juliette dined together in a little bistro which, despite being nearly full, had a very cosy ambience. Two very elderly piano and guitar musicians played gently in the corner. By the time they left that night, each subconsciously knew that they would be friends for the rest of their lives. It wasn't a breathless heart-wrenching love, although both were physically attracted to the other.

It was, to use that old cliché, the finding of a soulmate, someone with common experiences, opinions and intellect. It was simply that they each liked the qualities of the other, and this gave them a bond which they both knew would not be broken. Étienne had one other motive. He wanted to take her to his bed, but as they stood in the hallway saying their goodnights, Étienne didn't have the confidence to press home his unknown advantage, for had he done so, Juliette knew, she would have yielded.

The next morning, Juliette and Étienne invaded the offices of The Times where they were pointed in the direction of a little café. There they found Kerslake drinking coffee accompanied by a small jug of high-proof anise, which it was illegal to sell, and a large jug of water. It was true to say that he was as exhausted as any man from the war. Kerslake had reported from the front line in secret until he became embedded with the army as a journalist. His constant battle was not just with the shells and the task of staying alive, but with the censors who fought him every step of the way to stop him telling his story. At the start of the war, he had been threatened with being shot for treason as he reported to the nation stories which the army did not want told. Now, embedded in the army, with only five other journalists, and with such a large war to cover, the pressure on him had become almost intolerable.

Kerslake listened carefully as Étienne gave an off-the-record, no names briefing.

"The French army has made representation to the British army to lessen Major Dovingdon's sentence. They don't want him shot," Étienne said, quite emphatically.

Kerslake was fascinated. He was aware of the editorials in Le Figaro which said that under no circumstances was Major Dovingdon to be shot on the assumption that this was what the French wanted. He also remembered the closing sentence of the article, for he thought it well-written: *French civility requires that the decision to impose the death penalty has to be based upon the facts and the law, nothing more and nothing less.* But learning that the French army had sent an emissary to Haig, was a new story.

"Do you know if Major Dovingdon has pleaded to the King to commute his sentence?" asked Kerslake.

"No," answered Juliette very softly.

"I was in Court when your brother's barrister said he would be appealing to the King, so I imagine it has happened. I certainly reported that he was appealing."

There was silence as the coffee, which Juliette and Étienne had ordered at the outset, was delivered.

"I will cover the French request for clemency in the same story as your brother's injury from the Montreuil explosion," said Kerslake

"Injury, explosion?" said Juliette. "What injury? What explosion?" The blood emptied from her brain and she began to feel quite faint.

"You haven't heard?"

"Heard what?" replied Juliette, her voice falling as she felt quite queasy.

"There's been a huge explosion at the farm where Major Dovingdon was tried and held in prison. Fourteen have been killed, about the same number injured. Your brother's one of them, badly injured I'm told, probably fatally." He paused. "I'm very sorry."

"How? Where?"

"A dump of dud ammunition wasn't so dud. It blew up and he was in the way. As I say, I'm really sorry."

Juliette couldn't speak. Her hand automatically clasped her chin and lips in response as her mouth immediately fell dry. She desperately wanted to cry but was too choked up inside. She first felt nauseous and then completely numb as every one of her conscious faculties left her body.

Kerslake didn't want to be in their company any more. He felt uncomfortable watching her grief. In any case, there was nothing more for him to learn or do. So, using the typical excuse of the journalist, that he had a deadline to meet, he apologised once again and left.

As they walked back to the hotel, Étienne asked Juliette what she planned to do now.

"I have five days leave left. I need to see Penrose and then get home to my parents. I'm not sure I will be able to do it all in time."

"They won't let you see him," said Étienne, confidently.

"Why not?"

"He's sentenced to death."

"He's dying."

"That makes it doubly certain that they won't let you see him," said Étienne strongly.

Juliette was usually up for any fight but, strangely, not this time. She wasn't sure Étienne was right, but she didn't want to be humiliated so she took his advice.

"I have a friend, Judith Parfett, she's a nurse," she said. "They'll let her see him, or at least she'll be able to find out how he really is. She's good at that kind of thing. I must send her a telegram. I need to do it now, straight away." There was an urgency in her voice and a renewed energy in her body.

"Good idea, and then ...?

"I'll go and see my parents. I've only seen them once since I came out in August 1915 and that was Easter last year. I don't know why, I've had leave, but....it all seems very long ago."

"That's a good idea. They will need some support in getting an appeal organised. Much of winning this kind of thing is to get public opinion behind you, and I think we have started that here. It should be followed up and quickly."

"Do you think I should go and see Penrose's barrister?"

"Yes, definitely. In fact, he's the first person you should go and see."

"Why?" asked Juliette, for even though it was her suggestion she was puzzled. "You know there is no appeal?"

"Yes, but there is clemency, and if there is any chance there has been a miscarriage of justice, then clemency is a more likely outcome."

Juliette didn't know why she had suggested it, but now Étienne had articulated a reason she was more comfortable with the idea.

"What are you going to do?" asked Juliette.

"I have to go back to work," said Étienne. "I ought to leave now. When are you going to leave?"

"Now, at least as soon as I have sent my telegram. I have no reason to stay," she said.

"Shall we travel together, at least as far as we can?"

"Yes, please," replied Juliette. "I would like that."

As they travelled out of Paris from La Gare du Nord, Étienne on his way back to the Front and Juliette to England, they sat side by side in a cosy, familiar warmth. Again, they travelled in silence, but this time it was with the contentment of each other's company.

As they travelled, Étienne tried to work out who this Juliette girl really was. A woman from Cambridge University, who spoke excellent French, yet was serving as an ordinary nurse. A woman who could secure an audience with a Field Marshal yet bathes the wounds of the ordinary soldier. A woman who thought nothing of staying in the very best hotels in Paris, and yet her appearance was so natural, as though personal vanity was furthest from her mind. She was, he concluded, a complex mix of black and white, dark and shade, blended with compassion, common sense, and quick wit. He had to admit that she made an excellent companion. Should he marry her he wondered? There was no doubt she was incredibly good looking, even sexy in a funny English way. Would she marry him? He really wasn't sure. As a former farm boy and now as a soldier, he wondered what he had to offer her. Very little, he decided, depressing himself. Certainly, she would have plenty of suitors. He promised himself he would think about it again when the war was over, but it was a promise which was broken within twenty-four hours, and every twenty-four hours thereafter as Juliette kept coming into Étienne's mind.

Chapter 53

France July 1918

TRUE TO THEIR words, Alfred Capus and Anthony Kerslake wrote their stories for Le Figaro and The Times respectively. Both reported that the French army had sent an emissary to Haig requesting that Major Dovingdon was not to be shot on account of French sensibilities, just on the facts of the case. They each ended with the news of Penrose's life-threatening injuries. In addition, The Times covered the fact that Penrose had pleaded for clemency to the King. This made it a newsworthy story, soon picked up by all the other newspapers.

It was the presentation of various newspaper reports to the Medical Officer responsible for Dovingdon's care that prompted action. Until that moment, the M.O.[19] had assiduously avoided anything to do with Penrose for he saw little point in saving him from his injuries for him to be subsequently tied to a stake and shot. He had, therefore, been left, along with other triaged patients, to die. However, Penrose would not die, and from the newspaper articles it became obvious to the M.O. that Penrose had powerful friends. It was for this reason only, and with matron in tow, that he went to examine Mr Dovingdon.

At a nod from the M.O., a nurse, summoned by Matron to Dovingdon's bedside, pulled back his bedclothes. The stench of Penrose's filth hit their nostrils. The M.O. put his stethoscope to Penrose's chest and listened to his breathing. It was incredibly shallow, but his heartbeat remained strong and regular.

"Clean this patient up will you, please nurse," instructed the doctor. "He needs to be treated as an MMN for the purpose of nursing care.

---

[19] Medical Officer

I'll write a prescription for morphine to be injected if he regains consciousness."

"Yes sir," said the nurse, knowing that MMN was the medical code for Might or Might Not live.

"He was at the Montreuil explosion," said Matron, as they walked back to her tent. "He was the closest to the shells, yet miraculously came out alive. There's not a cut or graze on his body."

"My guess is the shockwave of the explosion caused a huge air pressure change and that has torn his guts apart inside. One of his lungs is not working and the other is barely coping; probably about 30% capacity. How he avoided any shrapnel defeats me," said the M.O.

"I am told he was found on the floor under a mattress, a bedstead and a pile of rubble. It appears the shrapnel flew directly over him; quite miraculous."

"Well, he should have bloody died. It would have saved us all a lot of bother," said the M.O. gruffly.

Matron nodded in agreement. "We'll keep him clean, smart and presentable in case any of the brass turns up to see him, and that will be it," she said.

Chapter 54

England July 1918

TO SAY THAT they quarrelled would be an understatement. Juliette had argued with her father many times, but it was always courteous, respectful even, but not this time. Learning that her father had done nothing towards saving Penrose's life caused Juliette to rage at him in a fury and anger which was so profound in its frustration that she could have easily struck him.

The fact was that Colonel Dovingdon didn't recognise the woman in front of him. How could he? She was no longer the young, innocent girl who would play in the nursery, ride a pony, disappear off to school and do as she was told, compliant to his command; for the war had changed things.

Every nurse, whether they were a VAD or a QAIMNS, who served at or near the front, was changed by the experience of war, particularly in their relationship and understanding of men. They saw first-hand the vulnerability of men in pain from their wounds, many dying in appalling agony. In their nakedness, their mystery was gone and with it came a sense of equality. Gone was the deference to men of her mother's era. Juliette, having seen the mess the men had made of war, was no longer prepared to be a second-class citizen and certainly not where her father was concerned.

Juliette did as Étienne suggested and went to see Sidney Caprang in his barrister's chambers in the Inner Temple in London. She arrived in London late afternoon the day before and took a room in the Savoy Hotel so she was ready to present herself at nine o'clock.

Although she had no appointment to see him, Caprang received her graciously. He immediately explained that, as it was a Court Martial, there was no appeal. A fact she already knew. The matter would be decided by General Haig, and if he confirmed the sentence, then there was a final appeal to the King. He assured her that Haig was very unlikely to make a decision without speaking to the Palace first, which is why the petition to the King was so important. He explained that he had already sent his appeal to Haig seeking that the sentence be commuted, and Penrose had signed the petition to the King which he had drafted. Again, it had been sent. Caprang showed his delight with the newspaper coverage but stressed it was important for there to be a public petition to No. 10 Downing Street. He was concerned that nothing seemed to be happening.

Caprang then spoke about the specifics of the case in the minutest of detail. Juliette was impressed that he could remember such things. As he spoke, his temperament changed, from one of resignation at another defeat, to one of sheer anger at the decision.

"Do you know I was involved in the defence of the Étaples 1917 mutineers? Do you know, a thousand men mutinied, about one hundred were arrested, found guilty and sentenced, but only one, Corporal Jesse Short, was shot?"

Juliette shook her head.

"In Étaples, they chose one. It could have been anyone but on this occasion it was poor old Jesse Short whose luck ran out. They did the same the year before and chose some poor sod then. It's all designed *pour décourager les autres*."

Juliette looked perplexed, for she was not sure what she was being told, and Caprang sensed it.

"Look," he said, with a brusqueness he had not shown before. "The army doesn't like shooting its own soldiers. They tend to do it sparingly."

Juliette nodded for she now understood.

"The army now has a problem. In sentencing Major Dovingdon they thought they were doing the French a favour. It appears it's not a favour the French want. So there is now a very fine line to be played. We have to give the army a reason to commute the sentence, while not boxing it into a corner so it becomes bloody-minded and decides that shooting him is the quickest way of getting out of its difficulties."

"Can you help us?" asked Juliette.

"I have done all I can," replied Caprang. "If your brother gives his consent, then I will be happy to share with you copies of the pleadings and petitions I made to General Haig and His Majesty."

"Penrose is severely injured in hospital. He can't give his consent."

"Then I'm...."

Juliette interjected. "I have a Power of Attorney over all my brother's affairs. Will that work?"

Depending on the precise wording, Caprang agreed it would, and once the logistics of sending and receiving documents had been worked out, the Power of Attorney was quickly retrieved from the safe at Child's Bank, just around the corner on Fleet Street. In a familiarity rarely shown in the Inner Temple, Juliette kissed him on the cheek by way of a thank you and she left with copies of the pleadings and petitions in her hand. She was heading for Impice House and home.

On the train, Judith read the petition to Haig. It was over half a centimetre thick of closely typed pages. It explained in minute detail the numerous reasons the decision of the court was unsafe. Not once did Caprang use the word wrong. His plea to the King was much shorter, just three pages, but this time the typing was spread out. It was the most precise of executive summaries.

To the contrary, Colonel Stoddart Dovingdon's argument was a simple one. The army knows best and if Penrose being shot keeps the Allies together, then it was a life worth sacrificing. Dovingdon didn't say this to Juliette but he was reflecting a true fear amongst the political and ruling classes that the revolution, which had started in Russia, and was moving inexorably through Eastern Europe towards Germany, would arrive on the shores of England. If Penrose's life could, in some small part, stop this from happening, so as to keep the existing order, then to Colonel Dovingdon it was as good a sacrifice of a life as any man who had died on the Somme. It was exactly the opposite argument to the one Étienne had made to Field Marshal Haig.

Juliette took her father through Caprang's letters in great detail, for he refused to read them himself. Then she pointed to Kerslake's articles in The Times; firstly, criticising the decision of the Court Martial, and then to the fact that the French did not want Penrose shot. Still, the Colonel was not moved.

"If the King had decided not to offer sanctuary to his Russian cousins for fear of creating revolution, and as a result they've been shot, then who am I to write to the King and plead for my son's life?" he asked, almost shouting. He then added, from the top of his booming voice, "I've never pleaded for anything, and I'm not going to start now."

Juliette remonstrated with her mother who responded meekly by saying she was sure her husband was doing the right thing. The fact that her mother supported her father's position irritated Juliette beyond measure. It was this response which, for the very first time, made Juliette realise why she had never enjoyed a close rapport with her mother, as mothers and daughters should. In fact, it was coming close to the point where Juliette was beginning to despise her mother for being so pathetic; for it was clear that, any confidence Lady Primrose might once have enjoyed had evaporated over her years of marriage.

"Why can't you see the difference?" Juliette pleaded with her mother. "A man who dies on the battlefield dies a hero's death, whereas the shooting of Penrose is forever going to label him as a coward and murderer?"

Juliette then used the one weapon which she knew might have some effect. "You don't think, do you, that you'll be invited anywhere after this. There are those who are saying he should get a medal, but if he's shot, you, me, we'll all be shunned for ever, even in the butcher's!"

It was Jack Morris who helped explain the Colonel's dilemma. "He has to choose between two loyalties," he said to Juliette, when they met in the garden of Imptice House; a place which Jack had started to call 'Empty House' after his walk with the Colonel.

"One of his loyalties is to his family. The other is to the military, which he has served all his life," said Jack as, reverting to the standards before the war, he started to put his shirt back on over his tanned body, glistening in perspiration. "The trouble is the Colonel thinks the army's infallible, when they're not," he said angrily. "He doesn't think they could've made a mistake. Well, look at this damn war. Isn't that proof enough!"

Juliette looked into Jack's face and then deeply into his eyes. He was her one true friend, she thought; the one person in her life who would do anything for her. It had always been like that, for neither could remember when the other hadn't been there. Sometimes in the day, when they were growing up, they acted like brother and sister, other times as mistress and servant. Unknown to Juliette, Jack was genuinely in love with her. To him she was the perfect woman, but it was his father's wrath that killed any thoughts that she might be his, and so his love for her remained unrequited; his secret, like the pain in his leg, was a hurt which never went away.

"They've made a mistake this time," said Juliette, weakly, but unconsciously, playing the hapless maiden, in the expectation that Jack would ride to her aid as he had always done.

"Even if they've made a mistake, the army couldn't admit it," said Jack bitterly. "That's 'cause it could cause distrust in the men who they 'ave to lead. The army has one abiding motto: it has to be right in all matters, even when it's bleedin' obviously wrong."

"I thought it was 'Be the Best,'" said Juliette, not in tune with Jack's sarcasm.

"Look," said Jack sharply, "your father thinks that if a miscarriage of justice has fallen on Major Dovingdon then he's suffered no worse fate than any soldier injured or killed in the course of their duty. 'e told me that 'imself."

Juliette took hold of Jack's arm and squeezed it tightly. It was her way of saying thank you to him before she turned in silence and walked away.

"Be the best, be the fuckin' best," said Jack out loud to himself. "What a fuckin' joke!"

It was at breakfast the morning before Juliette was leaving to return to her hospital that she and her father had their final showdown. A telegram had arrived from Judith:

PENROSE UNCONSCIOUS BUT STABLE. NO BREAKS OR EXTERNAL INJURIES. GOOD NURSING. OFF MMN.

"Look," said Juliette, reading the cable out loud. "He's going to live. He can't be got well again for the ruddy army to shoot him. You have to help!" There then followed a tempestuous argument with neither conceding anything. It was very loud, heard throughout the house and well into the gardens, for Juliette had never screamed at anyone before in the way she was yelling at her father.

Finally, in a calm, soft voice, Juliette gave her ultimatum.

"Either you work, and you work hard, to defend Penrose," she said, "or you will never see me again, ever."

Colonel Dovingdon said nothing.

"Papa, do you understand?" she asked. "You will never see me again."

There was a stillness in the room as they both contemplated the statement. There was nothing further to be said between them. As far as the Colonel Dovingdon was concerned, his son had died during the war, bringing the family name into disgrace. It was not a matter for further debate.

When Juliette left, she didn't say good-bye. She was now, she decided, entirely on her own!

Chapter 55

France November 1918

THERE IS A moment between all-out war and peace when one side knows it has won and the other side knows it has lost. This was the case during the whole of October 1918. It was a time when those who had served at the front began to think that they might survive and go home alive. It was a time when everyone stopped taking risks in the expectation that there might be a tomorrow.

Before boarding the boat train to England to see her parents, Juliette had written a long thank you letter to Étienne expressing her gratitude and saying she was sure that his efforts to stop Penrose from being executed had been the most influential. She chose her words carefully as she did not want to tempt fate. This started an exchange of letters between them; some long, some short, and with each page written, there became a mutual longing to meet again. The closeness which they had felt, on their train journeys to and from Paris, was missing from their lives. Eventually, they were able to get leave at the same time and so it was on 9th November 1918 they arranged to meet in Lille for lunch.

Unknown to the other, both Étienne and Juliette arrived the day before and had arranged to leave the day after, so important was this lunch date to each of them. Lille had been liberated from the Germans in May earlier that year. A large element of the town had been destroyed but the need of the locals to make money had meant that the hotels, hostels, cafes, and bars were open again, albeit that the city was heavily guarded and fortified. Not knowing how badly Lille had been damaged, Étienne and Juliette had agreed to meet on the steps of Église Saint-Maurice as it was a place they had both visited before the war. They weren't sure that it would still be there, but if not, the rubble would be a landmark around which they could find each other.

They both arrived at the church slightly early, neither wanting to risk being late. When their eyes met, they both stood still. Then they started to run and then broke back into a walk again, until neither could contain themselves anymore, and so it was that they ran into each other's arms. There was an immediacy about their embrace which caused them both to break off quickly in embarrassment. They recoupled, holding each other in their arms in a long, body swaying hug which neither wanted to end.

"Have you heard?" said Étienne excitedly, still holding her close.

"Heard what?"

"The Kaiser has abdicated, he's gone. He is in exile."

Juliette broke away to inspect Étienne's face to test what she was being told.

"What? Wilhelm's gone? The war's won?" asked Juliette, her voice puzzled from the news.

"Any day now."

"You mean it's over?" asked Juliette, tears filling her eyes and her lips starting to tremble with emotion.

"Yes, it's over."

"How?" she asked perplexed. "We might have started winning but they still have a damn big army to defeat and it's a long way to Berlin."

"It's the war we haven't seen," said Étienne. "The Germans are starving. Throughout the war they have never controlled the seas and therefore haven't been able to import the food they need."

"Really? I've been so involved in my little bit, I haven't paid much attention elsewhere," and then she repeated the word, "Really?" looking at him just to make sure she had heard correctly. "But they had Poland for their food?" she added slightly confused, but none of that mattered anymore.

"Let's go inside," he said, after nodding with a broad grin across his face.

The church was badly battered by German shelling, but it was not destroyed. Holding hands, they climbed the steps. Inside, Étienne purchased six candles, three each, which they lit in front of an ancient picture of the Virgin Mary cradling baby Jesus. Both simply stood there staring at the flames, nothing was in their minds. There was something very calming about the flicker of the flames. Quietly, they moved to the pews where in silence they both started to thank God for their survival.

Very slowly, without saying anything to the other, Étienne and Juliette each concluded that any God who creates such destruction and misery was not a God who should be thanked. But this logic was immediately at odds with the deep spiritual feeling which was overwhelming each of them and enveloping their senses.

On leaving the church, they found a little café to eat in. It was warm and good to be out of the November chill. They sat down at a table undisturbed by any kind of service.

"What are you going to do now?" asked Étienne.

"I don't know. I know I don't have a home to go back to. I might go back to Cambridge. I might stay in nursing. I will probably stay here until Penrose is better," she replied.

"Have you seen him?"

"Yes, he's in hospital, still very poorly and weak. His lungs are badly damaged, and he finds it hard to eat."

"What about his sentence?"

"Nothing, it appears no one is going to consider that until he's out of hospital. I have a sense it's something nobody wants to deal with."

"I can understand that," said Étienne sympathetically.

"Also, it's not a sportsmanlike thing to shoot an injured man, you know," she said in a posh male accent. "It's not good sport if the fox can't run free from the hounds, what ho," she continued mockingly. "And you?" she continued, returning to her normal voice.

"I'm going home; I'm giving up the army as soon as I can. I couldn't take this....," he paused and restarted. "I couldn't take this carnage all over again."

Étienne looked around the room for some service but there was none.

Instead, he looked at the English lady with the thick dark auburn hair, hazel eyes and a mouth so wide it couldn't help but smile. Under his gaze, he noticed she was becoming flustered as her face and chest had both gone a little redder. For it was true, Juliette was feeling an overwhelming desire of lust for the officer in front of her. It was as simple as that.

"I don't think I told you," said Étienne turning his eyes from her gaze to the table cloth. "I didn't say before, because ... well." He paused. "I don't think you know ... but it was me who ... I gave the order for the garrison to go on to Célieux Ridge. I did it the night before, just after I'd had dinner with Penrose. It was supposed to be a training exercise, a rehearsal ...." Etienne stopped speaking, as he closed his eyes. He didn't want to say any more.

Juliette's eyes widened as she looked in to his strained face, not believing what she was hearing.

Why?" she asked, her whisper screaming with its intensity.

Etienne stayed silent for a long time. Once again, he found he didn't know how to answer. "It was a whim, a sense, a feeling," he replied.

"A whim, a feeling," repeated Juliette. There was a trace of disbelief in her voice.

"Why was Penrose in his balloon so early that morning? It's not where he should have been. He must have had the same kind of premonition," said Étienne, seeking to rationalise the irrational. "Things had changed on the ground, small things, but they're things you can't point to," he continued. Penrose and I both knew it. Soldiers get an instinct for these things. The longer you live in a war the better that instinct becomes. You learn to trust it. That's what we both did that day."

"Did he know you were sending your soldiers on to the Ridge?" asked Juliette, before adding quickly, "did he know of your rehearsal?" Her voice strained as she fought to keep the volume under control.

"No," said Étienne. "He can't have known."

"You know, if you hadn't ordered your soldiers out, then Penrose wouldn't be where he is now! Would he?" The ardour that Juliette had felt just a few minutes ago was rapidly evaporating from her veins.

Étienne nodded his head woefully.

"If only the Germans hadn't attacked. If only I hadn't given the order. If only ... My war is made up of ten thousand if onlys. Penrose will be the same. It's a blight every officer has to live with." There was deep melancholy in Étienne's voice. "If I hadn't done what I did, then there would have been no tank support on the battlefield. The British shelling might not have been enough. The battle could so easily have been lost." He was now speaking as an officer reporting, not as a man seeking to woo the woman opposite him. "If I hadn't done, if Penrose hadn't done, what we did, then the story today could have been very different. The Germans could've been sitting in Paris right now."

"I am sorry," said Juliette. "I am really sorry, I didn't mean to blame. It's so easy to look for someone to ..., isn't it. We all do it. We try and make sense of the things that don't make sense to us. We try and rationalise things which defy logic, defy our expected order of things. I'm sorry. I am really sorry," she repeated, as she shook her head slowly from side to side.

"May I ask one question?" said Juliette after a pause in their conversation. She didn't wait for Étienne's consent. "Why didn't you tell the British this?" she asked.

"I did, many, many times. It's in the statement I gave them. The British military police interviewed me twice. I said the same thing every time. It was a bloody accident."

"You didn't say that at Beaurepaire, did you?"

"No, of course not. They already knew. By Beaurepaire the game had changed. It was no longer about saving an innocent man. It was about the politics of war. It had to be about that, nothing more nothing less."

"Your statement wasn't in the court papers. I know because I've read Étienne's barrister's file," said Juliette.

"Of course not. Why are you surprised? The British wanted him found guilty. They are hardly going to give my statement to Penrose to help his defence, are they?"

"But they have to, it's only fair," protested Juliette.

Étienne gave a long and heavy sigh, designed to let her know she was being naïve.

"I didn't know there'd been a trial. I didn't even know he'd been charged. If I'd have done, I'd have made sure Penrose knew, but I didn't. The first I knew was when I read about it in the papers. You British, you have an expression: 'fuck up', don't you?"

"Yes, but it's not one used in polite society."

"Well, the British fucked-up this one good and proper."

Juliette smiled and then she laughed. She found there was something incredibly charming about a soft French accent delivering this most used Anglo-Saxon swear word. She reached out to touch his arm, and on his touch Étienne laughed too.

"Are things no better with your father?" asked Étienne after their laughter had stopped. He needed to change the subject.

"No, it's why I can't go home," she replied.

"It's a generational thing, you have to understand that."

"Well, I don't," she said emphatically. "In any case, with the war over, whatever reason he had before has now gone."

Étienne noticed a hardening in Juliette's tone and he, once again, rapidly changed the subject. So it was, in the intensity of the conversation which followed, that they sat in the restaurant for nearly two hours without noticing that no one had come to serve them.

Eventually, they abandoned where they had been sitting and walked around Lille for a while until they found a little restaurant which was open for business. This time they ate while they sat and talked. It was the maître d' who told them about the curfew, and with the bill paid, Étienne walked Juliette back to the small hotel she was staying. They had both stopped talking. Juliette was enjoying being on his arm and in his company; but unknown to her, Étienne was becoming anxious. He couldn't imagine not having her in his life and this was putting his mind in turmoil. More importantly, he was certain, that now the war was over, there would be hundreds of English officers wanting to marry her, for she was so darn pretty. It was worse than that; she was truly beautiful, and practical, and clever. Mentally, he ran a score card and, in every measure, he was sure she was better than him. She was, he thought, out of his league. And yet she had come to see him, but even in this, he decided in self-deprecation, it was only for her to say thank you for helping her brother.

By the time they reached the steps of Juliette's hotel, Étienne had decided he had no option but to ask Juliette to marry him, and yet, as they stood there saying their goodnights, he could not find the words. They kissed each other gently on the cheeks, held hands, and when

Étienne broke away, Juliette felt her heart sink as she didn't want the moment to end.

It was just as she was turning to go inside that Étienne said, "I don't suppose....," he stopped.

Juliette assumed he was going to suggest that they meet tomorrow, which is what she desperately wanted him to ask.

"I don't suppose....," he stopped again. "Do you think....?" He was finding it impossibly hard. "Please," he said at last, "will you marry me?"

Étienne repeated what he had said, more firmly, so he could make sure he had spoken the words he had intended. As he said them for a second time, his heart fell because of the look of puzzlement on Juliette's face. For her part, she did not believe what she was hearing. Étienne stood stunned as he took her shocked expression as a rejection.

Marriage was not a thing Juliette had thought about since she had arrived in France; before yes, but not now. Her thoughts had always been on today, tomorrow and survival. But there was no question. She knew she had to say yes. So very slowly, gently, and in the most perfect French, she replied very formally, "Yes please, thank you, that would be very nice."

They looked at each other and in their embarrassment they both smiled. Neither knew what to do next. It was the sound of a whistle blowing, warning of the curfew, which caused their tryst to end. They kissed very briefly on the lips. "See you tomorrow," said Étienne as he turned, and with that she stood there and watched him walk into the night. It was only then that she realised she knew nothing of the man she had agreed to marry, except that he was a good man; a man who made her happy. It was, she decided, all she needed to know.

It was the cold which woke Juliette at four in the morning. The eiderdown had fallen from her bed onto the floor leaving her body exposed to the freezing air. With her bedclothes reorganised and warmth creeping back into her body, Juliette thought of Étienne and marriage.

She tried to remember all the men she knew and compared them one-by-one to Etienne. She was surprised how many eligible men she knew. In her mind she paraded them as though they were horses in a ring before a race. Not one compared to Étienne. No one made her feel the same way. No one made her feel as important, but above all, no one made her feel like a woman as Étienne did.

There was only one other possible person. It was Dr Barclay. She knew she loved him, but he was married and too old, but he made her feel exactly the same way as Étienne did. She was always that little bit more excited when he was near. Her life was so much better when he was close by. Above all, Dr Barclay was a friend, a true friend and that is what she knew she had found in Etienne.

In any case, she owed it to Etienne to marry him now he had asked. She would have gone to his bed without a wedding ring if that is what he had wanted. She owed him for helping save her brother's life, and if marriage was his price, then it was a price she would gladly pay.

As Juliette's thoughts swapped between her choice of wedding dress, and bridesmaid, and what it would be like to make love to a man, a reality dawned on her.

Etienne's evidence of ordering the French troops on to Célieux Ridge was vital to Penrose's defence. Evidence the British Army had deliberately buried. It would never reappear. She knew that. Étienne had that evening offered to write a new statement, but if they were married it would immediately be challenged. She could hear the arguments now as they set out to discredit Étienne and his new report. They would claim it was only written to save the life of his wife's brother. They would say the new statement was nothing more than a dowry payment for her to marry him.

"I can't marry him, I can't marry him!" exclaimed Juliette out loud. If I do, I risk the chance of saving Penrose, she thought.

Juliette jumped out of bed and, with her bare feet on cold wooden boards and the eiderdown wrapped around her shoulders, she paced the floor in panic. I can't marry him, I can't marry him, yelled more loudly into her brain. Then it dawned on her. If she didn't marry Étienne then perhaps, he might not write his statement at all!

She would get Étienne to write it and then break off their marriage, she thought. It was the only thing to do. But then she realised, that didn't solve the problem. It didn't extinguish the challenge to Étienne's motive.

Juliette slept not another wink that night. She had a conundrum and there had to be a solution. She knew she had to find it.

Chapter 56

France December 1918

Dear Mama,

I have some news which I would like to share. I am getting married to Commandant Étienne Guégan. We will be making our home in Bordeaux. Sadly, because of Papa's decision not to help Penrose, I will not be coming home.

Étienne is a very good man. It was he who appealed to F.M. Haig on behalf of the French army to commute Penrose's sentence. I met him then. He has also written to F.M. Haig to explain that the troops ordered into no man's land were sent there as part of an exercise in reinforcing the front-line, ordered only the night before. There was no way that Penrose could have known French troops were going to be there. I am sure this will help F.M. Haig to do something different, but who knows? Months have gone on and nothing gets decided.

Penrose will not be coming for he is still in hospital. I saw him about a month ago but only for a few minutes. He remains under arrest and so visitors are very tightly controlled. I simply pretended to be a nurse on duty, and no one said anything. He is much better but still very weak. He is a long way from walking the 100 paces which he has to be able to do before he is discharged back to the military police, but then this hardly gives him an incentive to try. Everyone is rushing to close things down, so very soon his hospital will be packed up and he will be sent home.

Penrose showed me a letter he had telling him that Drew had been killed in a car accident. He was very melancholy about it for I am sure he imagined they would be together.

My wedding will be at the Église Saint-Maurice in Lille. Judith will be my bridesmaid and Dr Barclay will be giving me away. It is the last thing he will do before he goes home. I will miss him terribly. We will be a small wedding party.

Judith is to be married too, but back in England to a wonderful artillery officer. He won the MM when in the ranks and is now a TG[20]. He sold printing equipment before the war but now wants to become a vicar. Judith will be a brilliant vicar's wife. We have promised faithfully we will never lose touch.

I always dreamed that I would walk down the aisle on Papa's arm, but his denial of Penrose and subsequent excommunication makes that impossible. I do not understand his stubbornness even now when the war is won. I cry just from the thought of it. Perhaps it is even sadder that you will not be there to help me dress. You have done so much for me and this is your right. I know you won't defy Papa which is sad when he is so wrong.

The dress I have bought is made of beautiful white silk and lace. It is old and therefore very delicate. There are no new dresses to buy here and I have no time to go to Paris. The Belgian woman I bought it from was married in it. She says it brought her good omens all her married life, so I am hoping it's the same for me. She wept as she parted with it, which made me quite sad, except she was so happy for me that it did not seem so bad after all.

I cannot believe how quiet it is now. First thing in the morning, with the snow and fog, it is eerily so. Sometimes it seems so like England.

You will always be most welcome to visit when we have a home and I can invite you.

With lots of love and affection,
Juliette

---

[20] Temporary Gentleman, or the term TG, refers to an officer who held a war duration commissions and who came from a social class outside of the traditional officers' class.

Chapter 57

France March 1919

ÉTIENNE AND JULIETTE sat close together in the railway carriage holding each other's hand. As they stared ahead, each was in their own thoughts and daydreams. There was the same calm contentment between them as they had when they sat side by side at the end of their first journey together to Paris.

As other people boarded the train, or walked down the corridor past their first class compartment, they looked in and saw an immaculately dressed French Commandant and, on his arm, a beautifully dressed lady, both looking as though they were leaving for their honeymoon. To some extent they were, for at this very moment Étienne and Juliette were saying goodbye to their old life and starting afresh together.

Étienne sat very still, taking pride in the fact that he was married and taking home the most beautiful girl in the world. He could feel his body physically relax as his mind was no longer filled with thoughts about the next campaign, or battle, or even manoeuvre. He was exhausted by war and glad to be leaving it behind. He never signed up expecting to be responsible for the lives of others, but that is what happens to some in war, and that is what had happened to him. It caused him pain, not a conscious pain, which comes from a physical hurt, but the kind that creates a pressure in the brain which manifests itself by never being at peace.

Juliette was exhausted too, but for a different reason. Springing Penrose from hospital, where he was still under military arrest, had put her under enormous strain too, and even now, with him safely placed in the hospital carriage in the same train, she was still not sure they had got away with it.

As soon as it was clear that Étienne was going to be released from the army, Juliette had told him that she was not leaving to go to Bordeaux without Penrose. Étienne was going home and, as his wife, she had to come too. The war was over, and it was her duty to be at his side. Each recognising the determination of the other, there was only one course of action; Penrose had to come too.

There is one thing that war teaches its survivors and that is how to blag. Étienne had become a past master, aided significantly by his rank. His plan was an easy one. It was to present written orders instructing the hospital to release Major Penrose Dovingdon into his custody for further questioning by the French military police as to his conduct in the Battle of Célieux Ridge.

With a simple schoolboy printing set, Étienne produced a copy of General Haig's headed paper, typed on the instructions and signed it, not with Haig's name as that would be a crime, but with the name of a fictitious adjutant signing on behalf of Haig. The next stage was easy, with an ambulance commandeered under his instructions, a driver and two soldiers in tow and with Juliette in a borrowed French nurse's uniform, they presented themselves unannounced at General Hospital No 3 at Le Tréport where Penrose had been recently moved. He had been moved there as part of the process of getting him back to England, but his onward journey had been deliberately delayed. There was real concern that there would be public protests if he was shot by firing squad in the Tower of London, as was the required custom; France, well that was another place, another matter.

Penrose was the hospital where Juliette had started her army nursing career all those years ago, and she found it strange going back. In fear of being recognised, she deliberately changed her hairstyle. With a wave of forged instructions, and with lots of stamping of the feet and shouting in French, Étienne and Juliette got the British to discharge Penrose into the alleged care of the French military. Penrose said nothing for, despite it being nine months since he had been blown up, pneumonia had caused a sudden and unexpected relapse. It meant he was now semi-oblivious to his fate.

The ambulance journey from Le Tréport to Paris Montparnasse railway station was completely exhausting for both Étienne and Juliette. Now they sat completely still on the train trying to empty their minds of worry. Juliette was enjoying an inner warmth which came from her deep love of Étienne. Although she had not known him long, she knew that Étienne was strong, honourable, and above all, kind. Now she loved him even more because unquestioningly he had risked everything to protect her brother and get him to safety, if only temporarily.

Juliette looked sidewards and slowly studied Étienne's face. He is handsome, she thought, and then reassured herself, but not too handsome. He's just perfect, she said to herself.

But unlike Étienne, who was going home, Juliette was going somewhere new. It was the realisation of this unknown which suddenly overloaded her brain with a mixture of excitement and anxiety, with fear being the dominant feeling, as she worried that they still might be caught for springing Penrose from hospital. She might relax once the train started, she told herself, for then the chances of them finding him and his accomplices would be far less.

Juliette's thoughts turned to her father. Now she had banished him, she missed him more than ever. Through the war years, he was the crutch she felt she could always rely on, but now he was gone. As she thought further, she felt an overwhelming sense of anger, just as a loved one has to a deceased relative. The day she became Madame Étienne Guégan should have been one of the happiest days of her life, but it had been saddened by the fact that her father hadn't been at her wedding to give her away.

She puzzled as to why he had disowned Penrose from the moment he was found guilty. Could he not see it was a travesty of justice which, as a father and a soldier, he had a duty to put right? Well, now he no longer had either a son or a daughter, she thought. Did he understand why? He didn't, of course. Her father simply thought it ridiculous, and selfish, that a professional soldier should take a bride at such a time, conveniently forgetting the time of his own wedding. The war might have been won but, to him, there was no certainty of peace. For Juliette it was the lack of true peace which made her marriage to Étienne an imperative, for she knew she would hate herself forever if Étienne were to die and they had not been married even for one minute.

In the quiet and stillness of the carriage, Juliette considered her plea to her father to support Penrose and his absence of help. She thought of the letter Étienne had written to Haig just before they were married saying that, as the man who had ordered the French troops into no man's land, he would happily swear on the bible that his soldiers' deaths were an accident.

Once again, she wondered whether marrying Étienne had sealed Penrose's fate for the worse. Étienne's evidence would be seen as tainted. It would be dismissed as being given by a fiancé doing his absolute best to stop his wife's brother being executed. She was certain of it. You cannot be the daughter of a colonel without learning the army's skills of machination. She closed her eyes, tipped her head right back and started to breathe heavily through her open mouth to help control her panicking. She turned to tell Étienne, for she had not shared her concerns with him before, and then, seeing the look on his face, she said nothing, for he looked entirely different from even just a few moments ago.

Something had changed in him. The strain of war, and his responsibility for the lives of others, had meant that, all the time she had known him, even in their intimate moments, his face muscles had been constantly tight. In front of her eyes, they were now visibly relaxing. She had seen that same peaceful look on their honeymoon and with that thought, as those few idyllic days at Guillaume's Hotel came flooding back into her memory, she unconsciously smiled. The future would have to deal with itself she thought.

Étienne and Juliette had giggled many times during their first night together, for not knowing it was their honeymoon, M. Guillaume had dismissed Juliette to bed, insisting that Étienne stay with him for a nightcap. If a secret was to be shared, Juliette was quite pleased, for she was anxious about undressing in front of her husband for the first time, but she was distinctly less pleased at the time it had taken Étienne to extract himself from Guillaume's liquor bottle.

As Juliette remembered and relived their honeymoon lovemaking, Étienne was still staring straight ahead. His thoughts were on his father. He had died unexpectedly but peacefully, sitting in a chair while dozing. It was in the middle of the second Battle of the Somme and Étienne was not able to get away for his funeral. The thought of not being able to say goodbye had saddened him then, as it did now. He knew the first thing he would do would be to visit his grave. He hoped his father would have been proud of him. He was not sure.

Like all surviving men, who had the responsibility of leading others who had died, it was not the glories Étienne remembered, for there had been some, but they didn't seem so at the time, nor now. Rather, it was the mistakes and wrong decisions taken, the guilt for which never passes. It was the constant self-questioning of whether better decisions could have been made so that his men need not have died which wore him down. "It was the orders, it was the orders," he would say to himself relentlessly, but it never helped assuage the dreadful guilt he felt.

Étienne thought about his mother and how, as the war dragged on, their letters became less frequent, to the point where they were virtually non-existent. When his father was alive, there was a stream of letters, but as the conditions at the front got worse it was hard to write, pretending everything was all right, when it wasn't. It was also the fact that after writing so many pointless reports and vetting the letters home of his soldiers, even penning a few for those who could not write, he had no energy to report on his own affairs; even to the point that he had not told his mother he was married and bringing his bride home.

The corridor was jam-packed as the train moved off, but they remained alone in their compartment. Those travelling with first class tickets chose other compartments not wishing to interfere with, what was obviously, a special moment for two loving people. As the carriage jerked into movement, they squeezed each other's hands. Étienne reached across and, with his free arm, he squeezed Juliette's closest arm, pulling her into him. They looked at each other and smiled, a deep loving smile, and slowly, very gently they touched lips in the briefest of kisses. They then both turned to look out of the window to watch the ever-changing scenery as the train gathered pace and they went back to their own thoughts.

They did little for the next hour. They did not read, nor did they talk much. They just sat there watching the world go by, both just thankful they were alive. Eventually Étienne announced that he was going to change, after which Juliette said that she would then go and check on Penrose in the hospital carriage. Étienne assured her that he would be all right but understood why she wanted to go.

Étienne took his only civilian suit, shirt and tie from his suitcase and fought his way down the crowded corridor to the lavatory, where he quickly changed. As he placed his uniform on the coat hanger, he swore that he would never wear it again. It was a chapter of his life which, like millions of others, he was determined to close. But like all those who made the same promise, he did not realise that once a soldier, always a soldier. It was a part of your life which would always remain with you, for good or ill, for always.

Back in the compartment, Juliette said, "So, it's au revoir Commandant Guégan and bonjour Monsieur Guégan!"

Étienne nodded in amusement and then added teasingly, "Lieutenant-Colonel, s'il vous plaît," reminding her of his promotion just weeks before he had resigned.

"Ah, oui," she said, "Mon Colonel," and with a smile on her face, she raised her hand in a formal salute.

Étienne removed his medals from his uniform and carefully folded it into his suitcase. He wrapped his medals in old tissue and laid them on the top. Normally, he would not wear his medals but that morning, to be formerly discharged, he had to present himself in full military uniform to his Commanding Officer. The fact that he was in a Commandant's uniform, and not that of a Lieutenant-Colonel, was noticed by all but discretely not mentioned, for the war had caused considerable shortages. After that, there was the mad dash back to the ambulance in which Juliette and Penrose were waiting and on to the station to catch the train before it departed.

Étienne took out a vacuum flask from his case and Juliette produced some sandwiches, at which point the habit of war was too much for both of them. Étienne opened the door and invited those standing in the corridor to come and sit with them. He did it without consulting her for if she were the kind of woman who would object, she would not be wearing his ring. For Juliette, it was an obvious decision and proved once again what a wise choice she had made in the man she had married.

Over the next four hours there was a general sharing of what they had between them. As they quickly found out, each had been discharged from the army and was travelling home on a warrant. There was no discussion of their experiences. It was something to be left behind. But there was a common prayer; they would never see anything like it again.

On their arrival at Gare Saint-Jean in Bordeaux, Penrose was again semi-conscious. He had drifted in and out of consciousness throughout the long journey from Le Tréport Hospital. For the most part he had lain completely still, on his back, corpse-like, doing nothing but breathing a heavy laboured breath.

Penrose's transfer to the hospital in Bordeaux went smoothly. The military telegrams sent by Étienne, with his new rank, demanding a hospital place, ambulance and taxi, meant everything was ready. He was surprised that his authority had worked to the extent it had in a place where, just four years before, no one would have taken much notice of him.

Étienne and Juliette went by taxi with the ambulance to the hospital to make sure Penrose was settled in, and then late in the evening they set off to their new home.

"Château de Gressier," said Étienne to the driver. It was the first time Juliette heard the name.

Chapter 58

France March 1919

THE MARCH NIGHT air bit into the taxi even though the heating was on. Juliette snuggled up to Étienne and slept on his shoulder. He had tried to persuade her to remove her hat, as he was sure she would be more comfortable with if off, but for Juliette there were certain standards, one of which was not to appear for the first time in front of her mother-in-law hatless. This meant that for both Étienne and Juliette the journey was less comfortable than it should have been for the pins in her hat dragged at her hair and the rim incessantly rubbed and dug into his face as the car hit each bump in the road.

The night was completely still as the taxi drove through the village of Latoire, past the church where Étienne's father and the Guégan family had, over the centuries, been buried. They turned off the main road towards Château de Gressier. There was not a cloud in the sky and the frost on the vines sparkled in the light of the full moon. The Château sat lonely and imposing in the fields.

The Estate was the construct of Étienne's grandfather, of whom the stories were legendary. He built the first part of the house, so it was told, next door to a large cottage which had been his home since birth. He told everyone, including his wife, he was building cellars to store the Estate's wine and so, with a huge footprint, he dug down deep into the chalky soil. The task took an age, for just as everyone else thought the cellar must be big enough, his grandfather would decide it was not and kept digging, making it longer and wider. He supervised the laying of almost every brick, making sure that the arches, which would hold up the floor and walls above, were of craftsman standard, saying confidently that they "had to last a thousand years." When these were done, he started to build a house of magnificent proportions above, albeit one which was obviously out of balance, for there was no imposing front door which would have been in keeping with the style and character of houses at the time. Instead, there were two simple double doors, at either end of the house, made of heavy oak. These side doors went into identical large halls at each end of the house, with identical imposing polished oak staircases. Symmetry was one of its strongest features, with the windows exactly the same at the front, back and side and equidistant apart. There was no doubt in everyone else's mind, it all looked very odd. To Étienne's grandfather, his building was precious and magnificent and would, one day, rival the palace in Versailles or, at least, that is what he said.

Just as the building was nearing completion, with the downstairs panelling of locally grown and matured oak just needing to be polished, Étienne's grandfather appears to have had a change of mind, for he rapidly re-engineered the building into a home, introducing a kitchen, bathrooms and even central heating. Some say the turning point came on the night that Étienne's grandmother chose to lock him out of his home as a punishment for flirting too romantically with one of the village girls. While all this fitting out was going on, his grandfather started to store wine from his own estate in his own cellars, confident that he would get a greater price for his wine tomorrow than today.

Then came the day that went into village folklore, for nearly every man in Latoire was involved because, as they later explained to their disapproving wives, they knew that their job would be at stake if they were not. Without telling his wife, Étienne's grandfather called all his vineyard labourers together, and as his grandmother yelled profanities, and threw missile after missile at him, his grandfather's labourers moved them lock, stock and barrel into the new house which was by then, and would be forever more, known as The Cellars.

The day after the move, Étienne's grandfather set about knocking down their old Cottage. Once the land was clear, he started to build a new cellar, adjacent to the house he had just built with a gap of about twenty-five metres. It was identical in almost every respect to its neighbour, even to the number of bricks and half bricks in each row. They were twins, side by side. This time, Étienne's grandfather incorporated the kitchen and bathrooms as he went, but apart from that, you could not tell The Cottage, as the new house became known, from The Cellars.

Once it was built, Étienne's grandfather moved into The Cottage while his grandmother stayed exactly where she was in The Cellars; now, they rarely met let alone spoke. Once again, Étienne's grandfather slowly filled the cellars of The Cottage with his wine, having now established, beyond doubt, that there was a premium price for his vintage wines. "It's better than having money in the bank," he would say, as every franc he had went into his vineyard and his home.

Needing more cellar space, Étienne's grandfather started to build an underground cavern between The Cottage and The Cellars eventually joining the two buildings together underground.

His last task was to connect the two upstairs by way of a magnificent gallery built between the two houses and over a decorated arch. This room had large double windows at the front and rear, giving a vista over the whole Estate, and thus his grandfather's name for it: The Gallery. Étienne loved this room for he remembered standing there, with his grandfather's hands resting gently on his shoulders, looking out over the Estate, as he shared his future plans. It was a place of calm against the bustle of business. These moments were always quiet and considered, where secrets were shared and enjoyed. Étienne thought these moments were his alone, but if each of his brothers had been asked, they would have said that those moments were special to them too. To each, their grandfather was an incredibly special man.

Étienne's grandfather's last act was to re-roof both houses, with a vista of dormer windows, to make them appear as one building, and then he rendered it white. These last changes made it a beast of a building, in stark contrast to the other great houses of the region, built in blocks of limestone. For his grandmother this was the last straw. She complained bitterly that it made her home look like a debauched English coaching inn, and her anger at him mounted with each stroke of the paint brush.

While working gently in the field, just as the last crop of grapes were being gathered, probably with his wife's scolding ringing in his ears, Étienne's grandfather stopped, sat down on one of the stone whitewashed perches that he had placed at the end of every row of vines, and looked up the hill at the house he had built. He then cast his eyes over the land he had cultivated since he was a boy, just as his father had done before him, and then, with his head tipping forward such that his chin rested peacefully on his chest, he very slowly drifted into unconsciousness and died.

It was only a few months later that Étienne's grandmother died. It was said, kindly, of a broken heart, for although she couldn't live with her husband, she no doubt loved him. She certainly admired him for he was so many things that she was not, but wished to be. She was his life's companion and without him she seemed to have lost her purpose and did not want to live anymore.

Étienne's father took over running the Estate, slightly coming out from under the shadow of his father. The buccaneering and chaotic ways, which had dominated the estate during his grandfather's lifetime, came to an end. Étienne missed the excitement as a more sober and careful modus operandi took hold.

Étienne's father introduced systems, order and structure, where there had been none before. It was as though his grandfather's demand for symmetry had been replaced with his father's compulsion for order. In the process, it gave Étienne an overwhelming feeling that his life was slowly but surely being smothered out.

Étienne volunteered for the army in late 1910 to escape the cabin fever created by his father. He didn't know war was on its way. Politics and world affairs were of no interest to him and killing was the furthest thing from his mind. He joined because he expected the army to give him the excitement he hadn't felt since his grandfather died, and for which he was yearning. Others expressed the fear that the discipline of army life would not give Étienne the freedoms he expected, but he cast them aside, quoting his grandfather who would say that "life without discipline is a life without purpose." In any case, what else was he going to do? With his two elder brothers the Estate had its heir and the spare.

In fact, the freedoms Étienne discovered were those that every man enjoys when he breaks from the reins of his childhood. Illogically, those freedoms were even greater when carried by an officer and, thus an alleged, gentleman. This rank gave access to places denied to others, and permitted behaviour which, if carried out by anyone else, would have been considered reprehensible. In other words, Étienne found that soldiering gave him the time of his life, ... until the war started.

It was just after 1.00am when the taxi turned right onto the drive of Château de Gressier, with the white monolith of the building silhouetted in the distance. It had been Étienne's home all his life and now he was returning; except with the house in sight, Étienne started to panic. He sensed the same feeling of claustrophobia which had started just after his grandfather died, and only left him on the day he joined the army. But this time it was worse. Étienne had known fear before, each time it was rational, he could understand it, but not now; not when this was his home, where he expected to be safe.

Étienne's fear had good reason, for running the de Gressier Estate was never supposed to be his destiny. This was to be the job of his elder brothers, but with his eldest brother, Jean, now laying at rest in a graveyard in Flanders, which he shamefully had never visited, and his middle brother Frank without a grave because there was nothing of his remains after the shell burst, the duties of running de Gressier now fell on him.

Chapter 59

France March 1919

THE GRAVEL CRUNCHED under the tyres as the taxi turned left off the drive, swung right around an ornamental roundabout and pulled up to a stop, underneath the Gallery between The Cottage and The Cellars, and outside the side doors of both houses. Each was shut up for the night.

"We are here," said Étienne, waking Juliette from her slumbers.

He was reluctant to move, then steeling himself, he opened the car door and climbed out into the darkness, the lights from two flickering nightlights danced around an apparent cave.

Étienne walked around the car and tried the door to The Cellars. It was the way he'd always gone into the house, even in his grandfather's day. He was surprised to find it locked. The house was never locked. It was always open. He suddenly felt resentment at being locked out of his own home. It had never been like that. He was just about to bang on the front door and wake the household when suddenly, out of the shadows, he was challenged by a large man, thickset and threatening, wielding a shotgun which Étienne saw was pointing directly at him.

"Who are you? What you want?" shouted the man, aggressively.

"I'm Étienne Guégan. Who the hell are you?"

Swearing was rife in the army but the use of strong language, which had rolled off his tongue in wartime, no longer seemed appropriate, even at the point of a gun.

The man moved closer, ever threatening as he moved into Étienne's personal space, with the barrel of the shotgun millimetres away from his chest, the man's bulk bearing down on Étienne's slim frame.

Very quickly, and with a speed which caught the man unawares, Étienne snatched the barrel of the shotgun so that it no longer pointed at his chest but at the ceiling. In doing so the man's fingers slid onto the trigger and two shots blasted into the timbers of the Gallery floor above, with the pellets burning Étienne's skin as they went and leaving a deafening ring in his ears.

Étienne, not realising the firing was an accident, rather than an attempt to kill him, pulled the shotgun towards him, and then, with the man tugging on it, he rammed it straight into his stomach using the man's own energy to increase the power of the blow, such that he collapsed, releasing the shotgun as he went. Étienne held it firmly as the man groaned in agony, curled up in a ball on the ground.

The Château was now truly awake with lights appearing in every room as its inhabitants, in various forms of night attire, rushed to find out what was happening. Juliette hastened to be at Étienne's side. She was shaking but relieved to find that Étienne was safe.

Using the butt of the gun, Étienne banged on The Cellar's door demanding to be let in. It was then that he could see his mother coming towards him. With the hallway now in light, she could not see out. The glass in the windows on either side of the doors being mirrors of reflected darkness.

Étienne's mother opened the door only slightly and then, seeing Étienne, she stood absolutely still. She saw nothing else. Indeed, it took time for her to comprehend what she saw. She had received no warning he was coming. Further, she was used to seeing him dressed as an officer. Now he was in civilian clothes. This was not her son and yet unmistakably it was.

Étienne climbed a couple of steps, and gently pushed the door further open so he could move into the hall, at which point his mother threw her arms around his neck, and as she did so her knees buckled under the weight of her emotion. Étienne held her close as she tried to catch her breath between wails of despair and the joy of her son being home, safe. Four years ago, she had had four men in her life; now she had just the one. The pain and the agony of those three deaths poured from her body as she held him. All her aims and aspirations, nay her whole future, now relied upon Étienne, her youngest son, on whose support she was, at that moment, physically dependent too.

Étienne did not notice Juliette climb the steps into the hall of The Cellars where she was now standing perfectly still. In the darkness, she had attended to her hair, smoothed down her clothes and was now feeling reasonably presentable to meet her new mother-in-law.

"Mother," said Étienne breaking away, "I want you to meet my wife, Juliette."

"Your wife?" said his mother. Her voice rose slightly in shock.

"Your wife," she repeated. "You're married?"

Juliette had the same feeling of surprise. How could he not have told his mother about her?

This time, Étienne's mother did not buckle. She moved forward and pounded the sides of her fists into his chest.

"How could you not tell me? How could you not tell me?" she yelled, and with each pounding of each fist there was the release of an anger which had built up over all of the war years.

Étienne smothered his mother's fists in his own hands and held them, and her arms, tight against his chest. With this she sensed a power, a determination and safety. She realised Étienne was no longer the boy she had last seen. He was now a man, strong and protective.

Juliette was feeling extremely uncomfortable for she, a stranger, was prying on a very personal moment. The witness to a breakdown of emotion which, looking at Étienne's mother, she was sure was a rare occurrence, possibly never seen in the past or ever to be seen again. She was also embarrassed for she had, very reasonably assumed, that his mother would have known of her existence, and there would be a welcome befitting her status as a daughter-in-law.

Étienne's mother stared at Juliette. They both then looked at Étienne, who intuitively knew he was in trouble for not having said anything, but then he had not said a lot of things. Juliette's first reaction was one of disappointment; was their marriage so unimportant to him that he had not even mentioned it to his mother, or perhaps, she wondered, was his mother unimportant to him? It was a conundrum she was finding hard to fathom. Juliette and his mother each looked at the other, beginning to work out the order that they were now to play in Étienne's life.

The silence was broken by Étienne coming to attention, and

formally saying, "Mother, meet Juliette, Madame Juliette Guégan. Juliette, please meet my mother, Madame Guégan, Madame Magdelena Guégan."

Étienne was slightly amused at the comedy of introducing one Madame Guégan to another Madame Guégan but his mother was not.

"Madame Étienne Guégan and Madame Lionel Guégan," said his mother formally, correcting his form of address.

Juliette stepped forward to shake Magdelena's hand, turning her own slightly to show off her engagement and wedding rings, and saying, in perfect French, "It is a pleasure to meet you, Madame."

"You're English," said Magdelena in a start, at which point she took Juliette's hand and looked at Étienne, disappointment imprinted across her face. Her expression questioned why he had chosen not to marry a good French girl.

"Oui, Madame. I am English," said Juliette.

The man who had confronted Étienne was standing ruefully on the doorstep, neither coming in nor going out, for it was now clear to him that his challenge was not just unfortunate, but that his failure to have the safety switch on the shotgun would not be taken kindly by the new master of the de Gressier Estate.

"Hugo, you can go," said Magdelena. "You can meet Capitaine Guégan properly in the morning." Did Étienne's mother not know of his real rank? Had he not told her he'd been promoted, twice, wondered Juliette.

Étienne and Hugo looked at each other. The challenge that Hugo had in his eyes when the two men first met was now steelier, more threatening

And you are?" asked Étienne.

"Hugo Coudace, the Estate Manager," he replied proudly.

Étienne nodded to signify his agreement with Hugo's dismissal.

"I'm sorry, sir" said Hugo, "but I didn't know who you were. I thought you might be a burglar, an intruder...."

"And how many intruders do you think arrive by taxi?" said Étienne gruffly, dismissing the apology. Years of dealing with the silly and unacceptable excuses of his men had taught him that they had to be challenged immediately rather than left lying and gathering plausibility beyond their value.

"We will meet in the morning," said Étienne, closing the door and dismissing him. He made sure that the shotgun remained his side of the door. In all of the killings Étienne had seen, it was the deaths of children, and those from accidents, he found the hardest to deal with; for it seemed so unfair and without purpose.

The taxi driver banged on the door. In Étienne's anxiety to remove Hugo from the scene, he had forgotten about the taxi driver or their luggage. Their cases quickly appeared and the taxi driver, paid with a hefty tip, left with an exciting story of how the de Gressier Estate's manager had nearly shot his newly arrived master. The news would be in Latoire Village by lunchtime the next day.

Étienne and Juliette were served with warm milk in the kitchen. Magdelena gave instructions to a posse of servants for the lighting of fires in The Cottage and the making up of beds. With their cases carried upstairs, Étienne and Juliette undressed in front of the fire and climbed into bed. There was a chill and dampness in their room, which had not been aired for a very long time. Lying side by side on their backs, their arms by their sides outside of the blankets and their heads propped gently upwards against the pillows, each was lost in their own thoughts.

Juliette was quite mournful. Somehow the journey here had seemed as though it was all part of her honeymoon, but now it was over. How many marriages, she wondered, born in the bright burst of the star shells of war faded as quickly as they do? She knew tomorrow would bring a new reality.

Juliette was also deep in wonder as to why Étienne hadn't told his mother he was married. Was the fact that she was English cause for disapproval?

Suddenly Étienne announced, "I had two brothers."

Juliette didn't move. At first the statement bounced off her, as though it had never been said, and then very slowly it entered deep into her thoughts.

"They died in the war," he continued.

In her shock, Juliette struggled to find the right words.

"It was never the plan that I should run de Gressier," he said. "Even as I came back here, it was my intention to move on." The singularity of his intention did not go unnoticed by Juliette.

"I don't know why I never told you," he said. "Perhaps it was all just so far away," he offered lamely. "Perhaps I never expected to come here. For this was never my destiny. It was my brothers' and now they're gone it's been made mine."

There was a pause. Juliette instinctively knew there was more. "I have to make a decision," he paused again. "We have to choose," he said in a reflective tone, which was half questioning, half matter of fact. "What do we do? It's not easy."

Juliette turned on her side to face him. Still they didn't touch. Étienne stared straight ahead. The muscles on his face were taut again; just as they were when she had initially met him.

"I didn't say about us, because I didn't write much." Étienne exhaled, air streaming forcefully from his nostrils. "I did at first but.... it all got too difficult. The war got harder." He paused again. "It just got harder to write, and then, when Jean was killed ... and Frank ... and then Papa died ..."

To Étienne, those few words were enough explanation. He reached across to his side table and switched off the light. The room was now lit by the flames from the hearth but there still remained a chill and dampness in the air.

Juliette desperately wanted to know about his brothers, but she instinctively knew not to ask. Nursing had taught her that he would say as soon as he was ready, but that might be a long, long time away. They both fell asleep and, for the first time since they'd been married, they did so without touching each other. The complexity of the situation they were now in made it impossible for them to share the intimacies which had become part of every earlier bedtime.

Chapter 60

France March 1919

ÉTIENNE'S BODY CLOCK, drilled by years of army life, woke him at 5.30 am and with military discipline he was immediately out of bed. He dressed quietly, and with Juliette still deep in her slumbers, he left the house. It was still dark. He walked down the drive, past The Cellars, to the Estate's perimeter road. There he turned left and walked down the hill towards the river, which was on the southern boundary of their land. The only sound was of gravel crunching under each footstep. Étienne examined the vines in their winter sleep as he went. They were looking in good condition. He noticed the paucity of crunched clam, oyster, and scallop shells on the soil, at the base of the vines, used to provide protection against the leaching effect of the rain while at the same time adding nutrients.

Étienne stopped at the river and looked into the water. It was clean, clear, and appeared hardly to be moving; odd given the amount of winter rain. He studied its darkness and noticed thin layers of ice, floating like little islands, which he knew would disappear as soon as the sun rose.

After pausing at the river, Étienne turned right and walked along the river edge onto the road where he turned right again. Ignoring Latoire village, which meandered around the main road on his left, he climbed back up the hill where he turned right into the churchyard. He tried the door to the church. It was locked. The cemetery, where Étienne's father was buried, was surrounded by a stone wall with just a small entrance from the churchyard. He walked through the entrance turning left to the east wall where he found the burial row reserved for members of the Guégan family. It was the quid pro quo for them donating the land for the building of the church. There was a simple engraved cross to mark the spot where Étienne's father lay. No ceremonial stone had yet been organised, but, thought Étienne, perhaps it was still too soon, as the soil still had to settle. Étienne thought of his brothers and wished that he could bring them home to lie where generations of Guégans had been laid to rest before them. He wandered from his father's grave to his grandfather's grave, where he stood a little while, and then he went over to a wooden bench where he sat down and contemplated the scene before him and the lives of those that rested there.

There was complete silence. No singing of birds, no sound of mankind and his machinery and no movement of air. The sun was just rising and, being low in the sky, it pierced Étienne's eyes which he closed to allow what little heat there was to fall on his face. With his eyes shut, he immediately heard, ringing in his ears, the sound of machine guns and shells bursting. He opened his eyes and the sound was gone. He shut them again expecting to hear the same sounds but as he listened intently all he heard was the sound of silence. Étienne sat in puzzlement, for he was certain it was the machinery of war he had heard loudly in his skull, so he opened and closed his eyes several times but there was still only silence. The fear, pain and suffering, which had been indelibly carved deep into his soul, were, for this moment, at peace within him.

If Étienne was in any doubt about his future before, there was none after the hour or so he sat in the graveyard, for were not his duties and responsibilities here? Duties and responsibilities which had been borne by generations before him, and which through fate were now his. With a new resolve and a very clear purpose, he retraced his steps back to Château de Gressier.

At the Château, Étienne wandered through the basement of The Cellars and The Cottage, known as the cave, uninterrupted, for it was still early and no one was at work. Gradually he noticed a change. It was not obvious to him at first, but now it stared him plainly in the face. No longer were there bottles and bottles of wine stacked neatly, accruing in value. Instead, the cellar was denuded. Étienne's heart sank for it was in this cave where the wealth of the Guégan family had, for two generations, been stored.

Setting off at a pace, Étienne strode to the large barn which sat at the end of the Château's drive on the other side of the Estate's perimeter road. It was built by his father as the Estate office and winery using the timbers and roof slates from three old disused barns; one from the Estate and two he had bought, all in an effort to save money. This huge purpose-built barn contained the presses, and the oak fermentation tanks and storage barrels needed to make the wine of which the Estate was so proud.

Long ago, Étienne's grandfather had decided not to be part of the region's cooperative for pressing and fermenting his grapes, being very precious about their origin. He would only be involved with the cooperative at the bottling stage, when he would supervise every aspect with a temerity which added to his legend amongst the villagers.

Étienne was shocked to see the barn completely stacked with barrels from floor to ceiling. As he walked, he tapped each of them within his reach, listening to hear whether they were full or hollow. Just as he was making his appraisal he was disturbed.

"Good morning, Étienne," said Hugo Coudace, in a tone which Étienne noticed implied the question; what are you doing in here and why?

"Good morning, Monsieur Coudace," said Étienne, and intending to deal with the impertinence immediately, he added, "and, please, it is Monsieur Guégan in future."

"Ah, good morning, Capitaine Guégan," said Hugo barely able to disguise the sarcasm as he spoke.

"It was Colonel," said Étienne politely, "but now I am simply Monsieur," he paused, "just Monsieur Guégan, please."

In an attempt to control events, Coudace moved deliberately inside Étienne's personal space, at which point most people would have automatically taken a step back, but Étienne stayed exactly where he was.

"Do you have my gun?" asked Coudace, changing the subject but coming to a matter which was closest to his mind after last night's events.

"Yes, it's in the house. You can collect it any time but," and Étienne paused for effect, "in the army it is a disciplinary event for anyone to carry a gun without the safety switch being on. From now on it is the same here. Anyone carrying a gun without the safety catch switched on will lose their job, and they will not come back. Do I make myself clear?"

"Oui monsieur," said Coudace.

"What regiment did you serve with?" asked Étienne.

"I didn't, monsieur," said Coudace, backing off from a subject which was clearly sensitive.

Étienne waited for an explanation, as might be usual, but none was forthcoming so after a few seconds he turned sharply to his left and continued his inspection of the barn.

"Can I help you?" shouted Coudace, in a tone which indicated worry or concern, rather than an attempt to be helpful.

"No thank you," said Étienne, who now spent more time poking into machinery and cupboards than he might otherwise have done if Coudace hadn't continued with the same confrontational approach he had adopted the previous night.

Étienne returned to The Cottage to find Juliette awake, dressed and making fires so as to warm the house through. It was obvious from the damp and dust that The Cottage had not been lived in for some time. She had already thought it odd how, just five short years ago, she would not have dreamt of doing such chores, leaving it to one of the maids to do. And yet, here, after years of nursing, it was now natural for her to get stuck into any job which had to be done, and getting heat into the house was one of the important ones.

"Where have you been?" she asked, looking up from the hearth of the room which was obviously the library.

Étienne didn't immediately answer. Instead he asked, "Have you seen Mother?" Juliette shook her head.

Étienne told of his morning and of his decision to stay and manage the Estate of Château de Gressier, but he did it in such a way as to lead Juliette to think the idea was partly her own. He spoke of a wonderful place to bring up children, of having a home to settle in, and in the process, without Étienne saying, Juliette recognised that it was just what Étienne's mother would have wanted. He spoke of her father and mother joining them but, even as he mentioned it, Juliette knew that would never happen.

Étienne spoke for the first time about the ownership structure of the Estate and how through a series of trusts it was his and then held for his children. He told how he could walk away from it all, sell up and do something else, but he sensed it would be wrong. It would be throwing away his past, his heritage and his children's future.

"It's la territoire; it's in here," he said, tapping his chest. "It's in my blood. I can't leave. I am really sorry, but I can't leave. Please understand we need to make our lives here."

Juliette said nothing. She just nodded her agreement.

She had always assumed, as a result of her trusts and the generosity of her father, and from the way Étienne behaved, that she was far wealthier than him. She couldn't think of one occasion when they had discussed money, other than when they were going to get paid which was a common subject of all men and women in the war. In all their dealings, they each had just enough money to do most of the things they wanted, for neither of them was extravagant in their tastes. Their upbringing had taught them both to be frugal and then, in the fields of war, the amount of money you had seemed completely irrelevant. Gas, bullets and shrapnel didn't choose their targets on the basis of who had the most or least money.

Étienne talked of the terms by which Juliette and he would live in The Cottage. His mother would live in The Cellars, each a separate home. Each was not to go into the other's home unless invited. The Gallery over the drive between The Cottage and The Cellars, would be Étienne's office, his sanctuary. Étienne was quite passionate about this. It was one of two conditions which were not up for negotiation. It had been his grandfather's room and it had to be his. The second condition: Étienne was to run the Estate on his own; his mother was to have no further involvement.

They talked of Penrose and his needs. They had successfully sprung him from military hospital, but it was going to be a long time before he was well and he certainly couldn't go back to England. The Estate would be a good place for him to be as soon as he was well enough to be moved.

As he spoke, Étienne sat, strode, stood, and then paced as he became more agitated. Juliette had not seen him like this before, so she continued to kneel at the hearth, listening, quietly allowing him to arrange his thoughts, only acting with the occasional gentle prompt.

Étienne sat down in one of the high-back winged chairs close to the fire and stared at the flames which were starting to bring warmth into the room. Juliette turned away from looking at Étienne's face and into the fire too. They said nothing as they each moved into deep contemplative thoughts; Étienne on how he was going to tackle his mother and Juliette on how she had always imagined going home to England to be with her father, going back to Cambridge to continue with her studies, going back to a time which had obviously passed.

After a little while, and as the silence got louder, Juliette got up, walked across to her handbag and took out several pieces of paper.

"I think my Father would expect me to give these to you," she said, uncomfortably handing him her bank statements before sitting in the chair the other side of the hearth.

Juliette was deliberate in the use of the words 'I think' for if Étienne had been an Englishman, she would have been certain of her father's attitude. Although the Married Women's Property Act allowed Juliette to own property in her own right, she knew her Father did not approve of her managing her own money and would expect her husband to take over from him in supervising her financial affairs. However, being married to a Frenchman, she was neither certain of her father's wishes nor of her rights to have such money under French law.

Étienne looked at the statements and the balance involved. The sums were incredible.

"There is more," she said, uncertain as to his earlier reaction.

Étienne stood up and to attention. His face took on a seriousness which immediately worried Juliette for she had not seen it before.

"Madame," it was the first time he had addressed her so formally. "Thank you, but no! This is yours. It is never to be mine. What is mine is yours but never," he paused to give emphasis "never is yours to be mine." With this he folded the bank statements neatly and returned them to her. "I hope we are understood on this." It was the first time in their relationship he had given her a specific instruction.

"I am sorry, Étienne," said Juliette. "I didn't mean to offend you, but I couldn't keep it a secret."

"You didn't," said Étienne, leaning down to kiss her gently. "It's just, well, there are certain rules and a husband having his wife's money is not one of them." Juliette smiled for she knew she was right to love him.

Étienne nodded, but for him the subject was not closed. "Except," he added, "there might be two things you could buy?"

Juliette looked at him, waiting for his announcement.

"Some new clothes; I think the days of the nurses' uniform are over," he said, looking at what she was wearing. It was true, her wardrobe was very limited indeed.

"And a car," he added. "This place is miles from anywhere and you will find it impossible to do anything without a car. I am not sure what the Estate has got which you could use."

"It is done, sir," she said mockingly, pausing before adding, "but you will have to help me buy the car." On this they both smiled.

Étienne and Juliette knocked on the door of The Cellars and walked in. Their approach was as a delegation. They found Magdelena sitting at a desk in her sitting room, a shawl around her shoulders and a blanket across her knee. It was cold in the room as the fire was giving off little heat. Étienne touched the radiators. They were stone cold. He moved to the hearth and raked the fire to give out more heat.

"Don't do that!" his mother instructed fiercely.

Étienne ignored her and continued to make up the fire putting on new logs to build it up. Magdelena continued to ignore them, focussing on her writing. Étienne pointed Juliette to a chair by the fire. She could not help but notice the atmosphere between Étienne and his mother. The welcoming of the long-lost son was now replaced by a chill as cold as the temperature in the room.

"Mother," said Étienne. There was no response. He waited. "Mother," he said again.

Magdelena slowly placed the cap on her fountain pen and carefully laid it to the side of the paper she was writing on. Juliette felt intimidated. It was as though she was back at the London Nursing School sitting in front of Matron at the time of her first interview.

Magdelena got up slowly and placed the blanket on a chair at the side of her desk. For the first time, Juliette got to look at her. She was much smaller than she appeared in the gloom of last night's lights. She now looked like a little round ball, which surprised Juliette, for Étienne was so tall and thin, and yet there was a similarity. They had the same brightness of eye and thickness of hair; albeit hers was almost pure white, while Étienne's was a dark auburn, now peppered with grey to make it seem lighter. Juliette studied what she was wearing, for while there was no doubting the quality of her clothes, they had seen better days. In fact, there was a similarity to the heavy woollen cloth of her father's favourite suit, a bit grubby and crumpled, but nevertheless a favourite.

Magdelena moved slowly and stiffly to a hard chair at the side of the hearth, and leaning heavily on the polished wooden arms, she sat down with a sigh. Juliette wondered how her father and Magdelena would get on. Not well, she concluded, remembering that the French and English had been fighting each other for over 900 years.

Étienne stood and stretched slowly to his full height.

"Mother," said Étienne.

"Oui," said Magdelena, and in the process, she gave her consent for him to start.

"I need to plan my future, our future," said Étienne, looking towards Juliette, "and this depends on you and this conversation." He spoke crisply just as though he were commanding his troops.

"I have taken legal advice," he said, knowing it was untrue, but nevertheless believing what he would now say would be true, although years later he would discover it was not. He paused.

"Mother," said Étienne, restarting the conservation. "I have decided to sell Château de Gressier. Following the death of Papa, Frank and Jean, I have the power to make this decision." He spoke these words quickly so there was no interruption. He then paused to allow his Mother to digest the importance of what she was being told.

"You can't," said Magdelena, sitting bolt upright to reinforce her message.

"I can and I will," said Étienne urgently. "Unless...."

"Unless what?" spat out Magdelena, knowing she was being set up for an ultimatum.

Étienne set out his terms. He paced a few paces left and then right as he did so. They were issued one by one, each given a descending number and set out with precision. Juliette was impressed, for he spoke with clarity and detail beyond that which they had shared together. It was as though he was reading from a scripted legal document. It was similar to the presentations her father's solicitor had given him in the meetings she had observed. The facts calmly and carefully presented without emotion or bias. She took comfort for it confirmed what she already knew. If Magdelena rejected their proposal then Étienne would be able to make an alternative career, any career.

"Oui," said Magdelena.

"Oui, what?" said Étienne.

"Oui, I agree," said Magdelena.

"I will have control and you will not interfere, not once, not at all?" he continued.

"Oui, it is time I retired," she said.

"Château de Gressier will be sold one day," she said bitterly, "but the further away that day is, the better it is for me."

"Why will it be sold one day?" asked Étienne, completely puzzled by her remarks.

"Because it will fail; everything you do fails. If it had been Frank or Jean here, I would have been safe, but with you ... non!"

Juliette was shocked by this exchange. Was she saying she wanted one of her other sons alive instead of Étienne? Did she not see the man in front of her? Did she not know her son was a highly decorated officer? Was she still seeing him as a schoolboy? Questions which Juliette would never ask, but which perhaps might help explain why he had not written and told his mother about her.

Étienne did not look crest-fallen or depressed by this last exchange. He was clearly used to being treated as the unwanted and failed third son. He was now past being damaged by such insults.

"I will write this up tonight as an agreement for you to sign tomorrow." Étienne looked at Juliette, signalling it was time to leave.

"By the way, what can you tell me about Monsieur Coudace," asked Étienne.

"Ah, he's a good man, a very good man," said Magdelena. "He's the one person who has kept de Gressier alive since you three left and your father died."

"Where did he come from? Why did he not serve in the war?"

"I don't know. Your father would have been able to tell you all that."

"Do you know there are no bottles left in the cave, hardly any? All the wine appears to be stored in caskets. Why is that?"

"Leave Hugo alone," Magdelena said defiantly. "He's a good man," she said, purposely repeating herself. "He's kept the place alive." It was a strange, edgy response which immediately rankled Étienne.

"Mother, we have agreed I am in charge now," he replied, adopting a similarly recalcitrant tone. "I will decide who is a good man or not. Not you."

"I did not agree that I could not offer advice. I am giving advice. He's a good man," she responded firmly.

Étienne knew there was little point in arguing. He moved forward and did something which was, to Juliette, very odd given the exchange he and his mother had just had. He leaned down and kissed her on the cheek, just as he had always done, before leaving her and making an exit.

Étienne strode off back to The Cottage, making it clear that the interview was over. This left Juliette to stand up, nod, smile sweetly at Magdelena and scurry to catch up. Étienne was waiting for her just outside the door of The Cellars. He reached to hold her hand and they walked under the Gallery back to The Cottage hand in hand.

"Its nearly lunch time and we need food," said Juliette as she walked in to the kitchen. She was very conscious that they had not eaten and there was nothing in the house to eat. "We need to go to the village."

"I need to go to the bank. I am completely without any cash," added Étienne.

"I have some cash," said Juliette, "enough for food for a couple of days but not enough to stock up."

"Let's go into Bordeaux and when we get back I'll speak with Coudace again. There are so many things I don't understand."

"Speak to Coudace tomorrow," said Juliette. Let's take today to buy what we need and get settled into our new home." The words, 'our new home', were said with a comfort and warmth which gave her a feeling of happiness. At last, after five years of living out of a suitcase, they both had a place to settle down.

"And, tonight I must write the agreement with Mother," Étienne said, placing the emphasis on the word 'and'.

"And, tonight I must write to my mother," said Juliette, copying his style.

Chapter 61

Château de Gressier March 1919

ÉTIENNE WAS AGAIN up early, and with the written agreement with his mother folded neatly into his jacket pocket, he made his way into the winery barn. After much hunting and searching, he found the old stock books which his father, and his grandfather before him, had used to record the Estate's annual production of wine; the barrels and then bottles produced, stored, and sold. He noticed the last entry was over three years ago and so, in the expectation of there being a replacement, he searched, opening drawer after drawer, but these just revealed pile upon pile of old and dirty papers, each pile without apparent order or purpose. Newspaper cuttings were mixed in with bank statements, invoices, receipts, and payslips.

As Étienne lifted each pile of paper, so the dust penetrated his lungs and the grime attached itself to his fingers. After spending a little time in sorting through the chaos, Étienne realised there had to be a methodology to his task and so, opening two trestle tables in the middle of the barn, he went around every one of the desks and cupboards taking out its contents and settling them in piles on the table tops. He opened the solid oak filing cabinets and immediately saw that they too, were stuffed to the gunwales with papers. They would have to wait until later.

Slowly the Estate workers drifted into the barn, surprised to find Étienne there. His mere presence made them uncomfortable and the fact that he had been rummaging around made them doubly so. Étienne acknowledged each as they arrived but said nothing else, simply turning over page after page from the piles in front of him.

"Merde, what's going on in here?" shouted Coudace, and at this each of the Estate workers became more sheepish, for he had not seen Étienne.

"Bonjour Monsieur Coudace and Bonjour Gentlemen," said Étienne, in an upbeat voice.

"I wish to inform you that, from this moment, I have taken over running Château de Gressier, in all its forms. My Mother will no longer have any control over the Estate. She has agreed that she is not to give instructions to any of you, none whatsoever. She will have one maid and a cook whom she'll instruct and no one else. This has been agreed in writing between us," he continued, waving the unsigned agreement in the air. "You cannot be dismissed if you refuse to obey her instructions, but you can and will be dismissed if you carry out her instructions without my actual consent. I stress, you are not to take any instructions from Madame Guégan. Do I make myself clear?"

Those in the room nodded. Those who knew Étienne from long ago, recognised the man, but not the person within the man. He was no longer the schoolboy they teased and played with but a man, comfortable in himself and his authority, taking the lead and giving commands. Commands which they instinctively knew had to be obeyed.

"The first thing we are doing today is to count stock. A stock take has not been done for a very long time. We used to do it monthly and we will go back to doing it monthly. How many people do we employ on the Estate and are they all here?" Étienne asked, directing his question towards Coudace.

"Nine monsieur, plus me but excluding the women who work for your mother in The Cellars," said Coudace. "But they are not all here. Some start in the fields straightaway."

Étienne counted the people in the room; there were six plus the two of them. Quickly he divided them into three teams and, issuing them with pen and paper and explicit instructions, he set them to their stock-taking task. The instructions were ones he had heard his grandfather and father give before him. The older ones, who had been in the Estate a long time, were pleased to be doing a job they had previously done because it was through the stocktakes that they got a sense of how the vineyard was doing.

Once everyone was at their task, Coudace tackled Étienne. "Monsieur, you had no right to touch my things," he said, pointing to the pile of papers on the table.

"Monsieur, you had no right to bring your private things and keep them in my winery," said Étienne.

"Madame allowed me," he retorted.

"Monsieur Coudace, Madame Guégan did not give you permission because she did not know. Let me be precise," said Étienne pausing, "from this moment any permissions or consents or authorities Madame Guégan gave are rescinded. They are all at an end. Do I make myself clear?"

"You have made yourself very clear on many aspects this morning, monsieur," said Coudace, realising that former Lieutenant-Colonel Guégan was not a man to pick a fight with unless it was on your terms and at your timing. Deciding he had much to lose, Coudace thought that now was not the time to fight. He had to make a tactical withdrawal to protect his position. His time would come, but it was not now.

"What are my duties, responsibilities and authorities, monsieur?" asked Coudace, changing the subject fast.

"I intend to look after the business side. You will be responsible for the maintenance of the Estate. The men will continue to report to you. The Estate looks to be in reasonable shape," said Étienne. "Naturally I want to supervise the harvesting, pressing and winemaking. It is something I understand. I have sat at my father and grandfather's knee and been taught by the best."

"Naturally," repeated Coudace, in a conciliatory tone.

"How is it that you are here monsieur?" asked Étienne. He changed his tone too in response to one which was friendlier, less formal.

"It's a long story monsieur. The telling is for another time, but I have been here for nearly five years; long enough to know what's going on."

With the stock taking finished, and not finding all the bank statements in the barn, Étienne went to find his mother in The Cellars.

"Mother, here is our agreement," he said, passing the folded paper to his mother who was sitting at the same table as he found her yesterday.

Magdelena flicked her head upwards in acknowledgement.

"Mother, do you know where the bank statements are for the last couple of years? I would like to get the accounts prepared."

"Ah, the accounts," said Madame Guégan. "Monsieur...." she paused as she searched for the name, "Monsieur...." she stopped again, his name forgotten, "used to do the accounts for us." She paused again, then added "And the tax, but after Papa fell poorly, well, they just stopped happening. I don't know why."

"Monsieur Delmas?" enquired Étienne.

"Oui, Monsieur Delmas," said Madame Guégan, pointing to a cupboard under the staircase.

After sitting on the floor for half an hour, sorting through all the different papers, Étienne gathered what he needed and made his way to the Gallery.

Oh, how he loved this room, he thought as he entered. It had not been used since his grandfather had died. It had become almost a shrine to his memory. He would be happy here he told himself.

Étienne placed the papers he had gathered on his grandfather's table and then lit the fires either side of the room to try and give it some heat. He turned on the radiators, more in hope than expectation that they would provide any warmth.

Walking to the Gallery windows, Étienne could see that Coudace was in the fields talking privately to each of the winery workers in turn. He wondered what they were talking about.

If he had been able to hear he would have quickly noticed how each conversation went exactly the same way. Each worker commented on how nice it was to have Étienne back. Quite the commanding officer was the general consensus. In turn, Coudace told them how Monsieur Guégan had just confirmed that he remained in charge of them. He then asked how much each owed him, for Hugo Coudace was the moneylender to all those who worked in the vineyard, winery and on the small farm. They were all in debt. In the winter months, when the work was less and their wages with it, they were pleased with the easy way in which Coudace enabled them to borrow. Any money borrowed was paid back with summer overtime, which he organised in lots of ninety minutes with each hour of overtime worked paying back the loan and the extra half an hour being his return on his investment. They had not realised that by borrowing from him they had effectively made themselves his servants. It was through his monopolistic control of their work that he ruthlessly exploited his control. It meant that the word "kind" was always omitted from any conversation about him.

Each worker gave him an estimated amount. Coudace would reply with a precise amount and then stepping forward in a manner designed to intimidate he would say: "And to any question Monsieur Guégan asks you, any question at all about the Estate since he left, the answer is you don't know. You know nothing of what has happened here since Monsieur Lionel fell poorly, and you certainly make no comment about the way I run the Estate. Do I make myself clear? Any problems for me will be doubly bad for you," he threatened. "It would be a shame to have no work, a loan to repay and certainly no chance of taking another loan," he said, staring intimidatingly into the eyes of each worker. "Do I make myself clear?" He repeated the phrase taken from Étienne. He felt it gave him a new air of authority.

In each case, Coudace walked away and then returned to ask a simple question. "Who owns the house you live in, monsieur?"

"Monsieur Étienne," each worker would reply.

"I thought so," said Coudace. "It would be such a shame....," he continued, allowing these few words to hang in the air as he walked away.

The conversation worried each man as it was intended to do, as were the words which were unsaid. They only wanted to come to work and earn their money. They didn't want to get involved in any battle between Coudace and Étienne which they now feared was on its way.

Étienne worked hard at his papers and was shocked at what he found. It was as though the Estate had produced no wine for the last three years. Nothing reconciled and certainly nothing added up. He looked up and saw that the day was about to come to an end. He suddenly felt hungry. He had not eaten all day.

Taking the stairs which took him down to The Cottage, Étienne immediately noticed a difference. There was a warmth and sweetness of smell which had not been there yesterday. The dust had gone and been replaced with hospital cleanliness.

Étienne found Juliette on her knees washing the wooden floor in the library making her way out through the door backwards. It was her last job before closing the door on a room which had taken her most of the afternoon to clean. She had chosen this as the second room, after the kitchen, which needed cleaning, as with the fire burning, she felt it was the one in which she and Étienne would spend their evenings.

Étienne helped her up and, with him carrying the pail and the cleaning equipment, they returned to the Kitchen.

"I need you for ten minutes," he said, "and you will need your coat."

"Afterwards, can we eat?" asked Juliette.

Taking her hand, Étienne led Juliette on a walk through the roads and pathways of the Estate. The moon was very low and, albeit very dim, it appeared very close to the earth. It was a glorious evening and so started a practice where, irrespective of the weather, each day at sundown, they would walk and talk about their day. This would be their moment.

That evening as they ate in the kitchen, Juliette started the conversation by reporting that Magdelena had sent a cook and two of the maids from The Cellars to work in The Cottage. Étienne told of the unfortunate attitude he found Coudace held towards him. "It was as if he thought I was a fraudulent interloper," he complained.

"All the maids like him," said Juliette.

"You were gossiping with the maids?" questioned Étienne.

"I wouldn't call it gossiping," Juliette complained mildly, "but I asked all three of them about the Estate and they all talked about him quite a lot."

"What did you learn?"

"It was funny really. They said that those who didn't know Coudace would describe him as simple, but then they also said he had an innate sensibility and learning. He was a man with a knowing who, as a result, was of very few words."

"He was not short of words with me or with the Estate workers this morning," commented Étienne.

"Yvette, one of the maids, said a strange thing," said Juliette. "She said that despite being the most ruthless man she knew, he had a gentleness which allowed him to walk with God."

"Walk with God?" questioned Étienne.

"Those were the exact words," said Juliette. "He could walk with God."

Étienne and Juliette sat in silence for a little while as they each contemplated this remark.

"Do you know that Hugo works on our vineyard and manages two others, including one which he apparently owns?" said Juliette after a little while.

"How does he do that?" asked Étienne surprised.

"I was told the names of the vineyards, but I can't remember them now," said Juliette. "They said how he always seemed to be in the right place when anything important happened."

"Is that why he walks with God?" questioned Étienne, sarcastically. "Do we know where he came from? I am sure he's not from around here."

"Not really," replied Juliette. "The maids said he arrived penniless but then suddenly he appeared to have money. Apparently, it came from his compensation, but from what they don't know. He said he had a reserve job, got hurt doing this and so received a pay-out."

"No soldier gets compensation from being hurt in their job so why should a reservist get a pay-out?" questioned Étienne, affronted at Coudace's apparent source of new wealth. "It doesn't make sense."

Juliette nodded her head in agreement. "All I can say," she continued, "is that everyone likes him. He seems very popular. Perhaps we've got off to a bad start, with him trying to shoot you."

"Perhaps," said Étienne, closing his knife and fork together. The conversation was at an end and so was the dinner.

That night, as the cold wind blew down the valley, those that worked on the Estate had little sleep. Étienne worried about Coudace, Coudace worried about Étienne, and all the workers were concerned about the battle that they knew was coming. However, the talk that evening between the husbands and wives of the Estate was about the beauty of Juliette, how nice she was, how perfect her French was, even though she was English, and how much Étienne had changed.

Chapter 62

Bordeaux March 1919

EARLY THE NEXT morning, Étienne was outside the door of the offices of Monsieur Delmas, Expert Comptable. There was no one there when he arrived so he sat in his mother's car and waited. Eventually a smartly dressed middle-aged man appeared and opened up.

"Monsieur Delmas?" said Étienne as he approached him.

"Oui."

"I am Étienne Guégan from Château de Gressier."

"You want my father, monsieur," said Delmas abruptly, "but I don't think he will want to talk to you."

"Why?" questioned Étienne.

"It is in the past monsieur. I do not wish to talk of it, nor will my father."

"Why not?"

"I think you know why, monsieur."

"I am sorry but I don't. I have had nothing to do with the Estate for many years. I have only come back now because I am the only son left."

"From what I hear monsieur, I suspect you have come back to very little. Good day," and with that Monsieur Delmas went in and shut the door.

Étienne returned to his car, puzzled, and wondered what to do next. He went to the phone box and phoned Monsieur Delmas. In a very short conversation he was reminded of the name of Monsieur Liard, the family lawyer. The conversation did not end well though, as in his closing remarks, Monsieur Delmas suggested that Monsieur Liard would not wish to deal with him either. Something had gone terribly wrong, for when Étienne left, the Estate of Château de Gressier was held in the highest of esteem. Now it appeared they were blacklisted by the professions of Bordeaux.

Étienne drove to his bank, and at the counter, he asked to see the manager. He immediately feared the usual rigmarole of any perceived lesser person trying to see one perceived to be more important, and in this instance, Étienne was not prepared to be treated as the lesser person. He decided it was time to use his rank.

"Monsieur," said Étienne, to the clerk at the counter. "I am Colonel Guégan. I have just returned to Château de Gressier having been away for several years for reasons which I hope are obvious." He decided to lay it on thick. "In that time, my father has died and my two brothers have been killed. My family have held an account here for over 100 years and I have had an account here since I was a boy. Would you please extend my compliments to the Manager and let him know that I should be grateful if he would see me before the end of the day. It is a matter of some importance. I will be at Le Grand Hôtel opposite the Theatre this morning and can be contacted there." With that, Étienne stood to attention and left.

Étienne settled himself into the lounge of the hotel and ordered a coffee. He was being ostracised and could not understand it. He was wondering what to do next when the bank messenger arrived. Spotting Étienne, he went up to him.

"Colonel Guégan?" asked the messenger.

"Oui," said Étienne.

"Monsieur Colbert sends his compliments and asks that you join him for luncheon at Restaurant de Rachel at 1pm today."

"Thank you," replied Étienne, assuming that Monsieur Colbert was the bank manager as the insignia on the messenger uniform made it clear he worked for the bank. "I will be there."

Monsieur Robert Colbert could not have been a more generous and courteous host. As he asked questions of his mother, Étienne sensed Colbert was relieved that there was a new member of the family to deal with, and so regularise their affairs with the bank. "We still have accounts open for Messieurs Lionel, Frank and Jean as we have had no instructions on how they are to be dealt with," he said apologetically. Monsieur Colbert agreed to change the banking instructions on all the Estate accounts, provide Étienne with copies of all bank statements over the last three years and, most importantly, he promised to phone Delmas and Liard and use his good offices to arrange a meeting for Étienne to see them later that day.

Monsieur Colbert was as good as his word, for at 4.00pm that afternoon, Étienne was welcomed into the meeting room in the offices of Messieurs Delmas Senior and Junior. There was a clear change of attitude.

"Messieurs," said Étienne, "I would like to begin by offering you both a sincere apology; a very sincere apology." Since it had worked so well with Monsieur Colbert, Étienne decided to use the same phrases as had prompted the bank into action. "As I believe you are now aware, I have not been involved in the affairs of the family or Château de Gressier for over seven years, for reasons which I am sure are obvious. In that time, my father has died, and my two brothers killed," he repeated. "My mother has tried to manage the Estate, but I fear, in these circumstances, it has been too much for her. I returned two days ago, having relinquished my commission, to run the Estate. You were the very first people I called upon as you have a long relationship with us, and I need your help."

"We had served the de Gressier Estate for over 100 years, and then we were dismissed without reason or even a thank you," said Monsieur Delmas Senior bitterly. "To add insult to injury, our last invoice, which is over two years old, has still not been paid."

"Why?" Étienne asked, confused.

"We thought you were here to tell us, Colonel," said Monsieur Delmas Junior, his voice trying to lighten the atmosphere in the room which had become very tense as a result of the hurt expressed by his father.

"I have returned to find that the caves at Château de Gressier are almost empty. Most of the wine in bottles has gone, with maybe 20 percent left, and the wine produced over the last couple of years is stored in barrels. It looks as though the Estate has sold two or three years of stock but there is no evidence of this money coming into our bank account. When I learnt we had produced no accounts for three years, then I knew something was wrong, for this is not how my family behaves."

"Colonel Guégan," said Monsieur Delmas Junior.

"Please, Monsieur Guégan," said Étienne. "I prefer this title as I would like to leave the war behind us." There was a murmur of approval. "Of course, monsieur," said Monsieur Delmas Junior. "My father recognised there was a problem at de Gressier over two years ago."

"Monsieur," said Monsieur Delmas Senior, "I was most anxious for Madame Guégan. It was clear that she was becoming very frail and far less able to deal with her affairs. I did try to help by insisting on systems and even making more effort to audit and check things but...."

"My father's attempts to help resulted in us being summarily dismissed, monsieur," interrupted Monsieur Delmas Junior. At this, he took a letter from his files and handed it to Étienne. It was typed on Château de Gressier notepaper, signed by Magdelena Guégan and, as he had just been told, it was a summary and perfunctory sacking.

"I am sorry, but this is not right," said Étienne.

"We agree monsieur."

By using all his charm, agreeing that he would pay their outstanding invoice, and make a hefty payment on account of future work first thing the following morning, Étienne achieved his purpose; a full investigation into the financial affairs of Château de Gressier, the production of up-to-date accounts, and completion of all outstanding tax returns.

As the meeting was ending, Monsieur Delmas Senior was handed a note which he studied for some moments. "Monsieur Liard will meet you at 6.00pm at the Tabac d' Hectoire," he said. "It is good you are seeing him too. I know he has been worried about your mother for some considerable time."

Étienne left with Monsieur Delmas Senior telling him how he had changed since he last saw him as a little boy working the fields with his grandfather. "They were good times," he said with a sigh, which recognised he was getting much older and those times were not coming back.

The Tabac d' Hectoire was a scruffy establishment, with oily washed-down table-cloths and seats which had seen far better days.

Monsieur Liard was already at his usual table. A small earthenware jug of locally produced anise spirit was on the table with a much larger jug of water at its side. There were two glasses and Monsieur Liard was already drinking from one as he quietly contemplated the crossword. Of course, he never filled it in for this would enable others to see his work. Like a teacher, he had long learnt that you leave nothing on the blackboard which might allow another to critique your work.

There was only one customer in the Tabac allowing Étienne to assume that it was Monsieur Liard, so he went up and made his introductions. There were the same apologies, the same heart-tugging reasons for absence, the same 'Monsieur' not 'Colonel' conversation and Étienne's concern about three years' missed production of wine. Monsieur Liard was more sanguine, less hurt than the Delmas. He also offered his condolences at the loss of his father and brothers; something which was missing from his earlier meeting with the accountants.

"Over recent years I have not acted on your mother's many instructions with the speed I otherwise might have," said Monsieur Liard, "because I did not feel that those were her true instructions."

"Please explain?" said Étienne puzzled.

"Monsieur, I have known your mother and father for over thirty-five years. Not well admittedly, but well enough to know what I believe they would wish, irrespective of my counsel."

"Go on," beckoned Étienne.

"Two years ago, I received written instructions from your mother to sell three parcels of land belonging to the Estate to a Parisian company whose details appeared anonymous and for a sum which was below what I estimated to be the fair value of the land. I went to see Madame Guégan and she appeared to know nothing of the instructions but, on being told of them, she confirmed that these were her wishes. She was both concerned and confused. I showed her the letter she'd written to make sure it was her signature. She said it was but in a manner which indicated that she knew she had made a mistake but didn't want to admit to it. Monsieur how is your mother?"

"Why do you ask?" said Étienne

"It is over two years since I saw your mother and..." Liard paused.

"Excuse me, I don't know how best to say this, but when I saw her last she appeared to be mentally quite frail."

Étienne's expression changed for Liard had said explicitly what both the Delmas and Colbert had very carefully implied.

"Thank you, monsieur, but I was negotiating with my mother only two days ago about taking over the running of the Estate. We had a very forthright set of negotiations on the terms of my returning home and we reached an agreement which needs notarising." Étienne handed over the signed agreement which had both his and his mother's signature appended. "I can assure you that in those negotiations she showed no signs of mental fragility. In fact, far from it." But as Étienne said these words he knew that the negotiations had been all one-sided, a fait accompli.

"What happened on the land sale?" asked Étienne.

"These things take time to have everything ready for the notary public, monsieur," said Liard, "Particularly so in war and when the buyer is uncertain." Liard smiled the smile of an experienced solicitor who, when in doubt, knew how to prolong matters if he thought it was in his client's best interests for him to do so. "I assume you wish me to cancel the sale of these lands?"

"Most definitely," said Étienne. "Do you think the buyer could have been a Monsieur Hugo Coudace?" he continued.

"Ah, the man who it is said 'walks with God'."

"You've heard that said of him too? Is it how you see him?" asked Étienne, seeking to draw a response.

"I cannot say, monsieur. I have only met him once. It could be. What I can say is that no one in Bordeaux advised your mother on the sale. I would have known if they had. Coudace apparently has a good reputation as a farm manager, but one wonders whether that is not influenced by all the loans he makes to all the vineyard workers and farmhands."

"Loans to farmhands?" enquired Étienne.

"Why monsieur, you appear to have a lot to learn about what is going on at the Estate de Gressier." As soon as it was out of his mouth, Liard regretted saying it, for it smacked of criticism of Étienne which he didn't intend.

"Étienne," said Liard, addressing him by his Christian name for the first time, just as an old friend of the family might address one of his friends' children. "I have learnt in this life never to trust anyone on the recommendation of another. I make my own judgment. It is counsel I now offer to you."

"I tend to trust people until they let me down," said Étienne.

"I can only reinforce my suggestion. In respect of the Estate de Gressier, it would be wise for you to act differently in the future," said Liard, to which Étienne nodded wisely.

The matter then turned to the winding up of Lionel, Frank and Jean's estates. "Do Frank and Jean have any children?" asked Liard. Étienne shook his head silently.

"They all had wills," said Liard "so the matter will be straightforward as these give very clear instructions. After some small specific gifts, you are the resultant beneficiary, but I need your instruction to start work."

Étienne signalled agreement.

"I don't have a will on my file for you," said Liard. Do you have one, Étienne?" he asked.

"I had a standard army will," he answered, "but I'm married now, I suppose I need one." Liard nodded but said nothing more. He wisely sensed that this was not a subject for now.

The meeting ended naturally with the two men at ease in each other's company. They agreed that Liard would come out to Château de Gressier the following Monday to deal with an agenda which seemed ever-increasing.

Liard got up. "The Estate of Château de Gressier survived the Great Wine Blight fifty odd years ago, I am sure it will survive the effects of this war," said Liard, trying to cheer Étienne up. They shook hands and in an instant Liard was gone.

Étienne started to leave, but a cough from the Maitre d' indicated there was the matter of the bill to pay. He took the earthenware jug to the bar. A sum of money was demanded and Étienne handed over what appeared to be the right amount of cash; his attention a long way away.

Étienne arrived home to find Juliette worried, not just because he was very late but because she had just cooked her very first dinner for her husband; a simple English dish of cottage pie, cooked beyond the point of ruin, which would now not get the approval of his delicate French palette.

Juliette served the scrapings as dinner while Étienne told her of his day, and then with their first shared bottle of Château de Gressier claret, they dined and discussed their plans for the future. Coudace, Magdelena and Penrose were foremost in their thoughts.

Just as agreed with Juliette the night before, Étienne started the next day by retrieving a typewriter from The Cellars and placing a sheet of paper in it. He very slowly tapped out a notice to his staff. It forbade the lending of money by anyone who worked on the Estate to anyone else who worked on the Estate, with dismissal as the penalty.

Étienne thumped the final full stop with force which reflected his determination on this matter. As he removed the sheet from the typewriter, he wondered whether his instructions would have an adverse effect on morale. It was the test of every officer who ever gave an instruction. Étienne decided that, at that moment, he needed to buy loyalty. He put the sheet back in the typewriter and added that he would make a loan of up to 10% of each worker's salary in the event that they had a financial emergency. The loan would be repaid by agreement and there would be no interest charged.

Not one member of staff spoke to him about the notice. There was a strange, unnatural silence.

Chapter 63

Château de Gressier March 1919

BOTH MONSIEUR DELMAS and Monsieur Liard arrived with their respective entourage of junior accountants and lawyers. They each took positions around the Gallery boardroom table with their acolytes coalescing around their bosses. Étienne and Juliette sat at either end of the table, each privately wondering what all this was costing them.

Étienne brought the meeting to order, turned to Monsieur Delmas and, with a nod, invited him to start the proceedings. He had a series of reports neatly bound and stacked up in front of him.

"Monsieur, Madame," said Delmas, "I would like to start by thanking Monsieur et Madame for the prompt payment of all our invoices." He looked at them each in turn as he addressed them. Juliette thought this an interesting way to start a meeting, for amongst gentlemen, the discussion of money was always a matter left to the end, as though it was an incidental which had to be agreed.

"And," continued Delmas, over-emphasising the word; "my father has asked me to extend his sincere apologies for his absence. He is none too well at the moment and sadly the journey to Château de Gressier and this meeting would be have been too much for his poor health." In truth, this was only part of the reason. The reality was that on hearing of Madame Guégan's dementia, and the huge losses to the Estate which were about to be revealed to its owners, he felt very guilty at having let her down. His sense of guilt, coupled with a feeling of sadness as to her health, would not allow him to continue an involvement in the Estate's affairs.

In silence, one of Delmas' assistants handed out the documents, one by one, to Étienne and to Juliette and then, seeking their permission, he gave a copy to Monsieur Liard and each person in the room.

"I come with very grave news," said Delmas, deepening his voice as he elongated the word grave. "Catastrophic might be a better word, for it would appear that since we last carried out an audit, the Château has lost just over two hundred thousand francs. In fact, it would be wrong to categorise it as a loss because, so far as our work can reveal, the Estate has been profitable over each of those years. The problem is that these profits and much more have gone in cash payments to Madame Magdelena Guégan. To be precise, in the last four years Château de Gressier has made a total profit before tax of some two hundred and eighty thousand francs on which there is a substantial unpaid tax liability." Delmas paused as he allowed this news to sink in. "Madame Magdelena signed for receiving cash on the sale of wine amounting to nearly three hundred and fifty thousand francs, but we cannot discover how or on what this money has been spent because it is no longer on your balance sheet."

"What?" said Étienne, "I beg your pardon, but I really don't understand. Are you saying my mother has taken and spent over three hundred and fifty thousand francs in cash over the last three years? On what? It's impossible?" The pitch of his voice became higher, giving away his anxiety.

"Monsieur Guégan, here is one of the slips which Madame Magdelena signed," said Delmas as he handed over a purchase order and invoice clipped together. "Over three years, Monsieur Marian Genet of Genet, Bechard & Toit has purchased literally thousands of bottles of wine. Monsieur Genet tells me he paid your mother cash for the wine. As you will see from the invoice, which is stamped 'paid in cash' it has been signed as received by your mother. We have been in touch with Genet and he confirms that each one of the transactions with him is genuine. He says the price he was offered for the wines was very low, but the condition was that he paid in cash when he collected it." Delmas paused, "I consider Genet to be an honest man, monsieur."

"But we never dealt with him before," said Étienne.

"I know Monsieur," said Delmas "but Genet assumed that the Estate was in some kind of financial trouble and needed the cash, which is why the wine was so cheap. He is a clever businessman, monsieur. He knew the value of the product, so rather than swamping the market, he sold it slowly, getting the best price for himself and maintaining the value for you."

"Coudace," said Étienne, "Coudace. What has he to do with this?"

"Both Madame Magdelena Guégan and Monsieur Genet say that Coudace was never present when the wine was sold. Coudace admits introducing Genet to Madame Magdelena," he continued, "but he says that followed Genet calling in on the Estate to see if he could buy some wine at wholesale prices. There is nothing to suggest that these losses are of his making."

Étienne lifted his eyes and looked at Juliette. She looked back, with a gentle consoling smile indicating it would all be all right.

"Monsieur, Madame, the situation is grave because you owe one hundred and twenty thousand francs in taxes which must be paid immediately, but it appears there are only a few thousand francs in the bank account."

"The Government must understand that there has been a war," said Étienne defensively.

"If there had been no war, you would have been chased for this money long ago. I'm afraid the government is so short of money it has stopped being sympathetic to people in tax arrears."

Étienne clenched his teeth and nodded.

"Further, you need to bottle your wine in the casks if it is to be sold, but that takes an investment in bottles and working capital, and each month you still have the wages to pay."

"I am sure the bank will lend us the money against the value of the Estate," said Étienne, immediately relieved at an idea which would get him out of his immediate problem.

"They will lend something Monsieur, but nothing like the amount you need."

"How much?"

"My estimate is about half your requirements. We have produced a cash flow which shows money in and money out for the next twelve months. We should study that."

The room went silent as everyone searched for and then examined the cash flow documents that Delmas had produced. As he looked at his own copy, Delmas gave a commentary on key aspects, the assumptions they had used and what they meant. With the number in minus at the bottom of the pages getting bigger and bigger month after month, the situation was, as Delmas had said, very grave.

"Monsieur," said Juliette breaking the silence. "I think my husband and I need a break. We have been sitting here for over two hours and there is a lot to digest. I will arrange for some refreshments to be brought up." She looked at Étienne who was grateful she had taken the lead. He had an overwhelming sense of being ground down in information overload. It had happened in battle, and it was happening here now. He had never before contemplated the issues before him, let alone seen a cash flow. While its principles were easy to understand, the complexities of its structure meant it was something which would need much greater study.

"There is one other very important matter which has to be discussed before you go," interrupted Liard, who had said little up to this moment. "Monsieur Delmas has spoken about the outstanding taxes payable on the profits of the vineyard, but there are also the outstanding wealth taxes not paid for four years, and the legacy and estate succession taxes, all of which are payable on Monsieur Lionel's death."

"How much are we talking about?" asked Étienne, despair beginning to sink into his voice.

"About the same again," said Delmas.

"How can it be the same again?" yelled Étienne. "Our bloody wealth has gone. We can't be taxed on wealth we don't have."

"Monsieur, I appreciate this is shocking news, but I am only the messenger. I am giving you the best estimate I can. It may go down. It may go up. But until Monsieur Delmas has finished his work it can only be that, an estimate."

"Yes, you are right, I apologise. I am sorry. I think Madame Guégan is right. I think it is appropriate for us to have a short recess."

There was an unpleasant dampness in the air as Étienne and Juliette stepped outside of The Cottage. They walked their usual course and, as always, their first few hundred paces were taken in silence.

"The money in my father's, Frank's and Jean's bank accounts will just about pay the Estate's tax liability on our mythical profits." He laid emphasis on the word mythical. "We might be about thirty thousand francs short," said Étienne, revealing a fact of which Juliette had been unaware. "We will just have to pay that off over time. My bet is that if we pay a little every week then the tax officials will not take us to court."

"That's good, it's probably the biggest immediate problem partially solved."

"Did you hear Delmas say he had a legal duty to advise the tax authorities of our liability now he knew of it?"

"I thought he worked for us. Is he not supposed to be on our side?"

"Apparently not when it comes to taxes."

"It makes you wonder what we've been fighting for," added Juliette, totally perplexed, for the principle was one completely alien to those born north of the English Channel.

"And I've got enough for us to live on," Étienne added, in case Juliette was anxious. She squeezed his hand in a fond response.

"I am sure the bank will lend us money against the value of the Estate, so we can bottle the wine and keep the Estate in place," said Étienne more confidently than he actually felt.

They walked on a little further in silence.

"But it still leaves the wealth and inheritance taxes," added Étienne after a little while. "I'm sure we can pay the inheritance tax in instalments but the wealth taxes, I just don't know."

Juliette suddenly stopped walking. Étienne stopped too, a couple of paces further on; their linked arms now broken apart. He turned and looked at her. He had seen that look once before when she refused to leave Penrose behind.

"Étienne," she said. "This is my home now. This is my problem too. We have the means not to borrow from the bank."

"You do, but I don't. There may be a time when we have a problem, but it is not today. This is my problem, not your problem, and I don't want to make my problem our problem."

"But it is our problem."

In five years' time, when we have been running the Château together, then those problems will be our problems. But this problem has been created by my family, not us, and therefore it is one I have to solve by myself." He kissed her gently on the cheek. "Thank you, but not now; maybe later, but not now."

They linked arms and slowly walked back to the meeting in silence. The window had been opened to let in some much-needed fresh air and a petit repas was being served with a glass of Estate wine to all their guests. Juliette and Étienne both asked some further questions. Juliette drilled down into the detail more thoroughly than Étienne, apologising each time for her poor French, which was not an issue for she was communicating perfectly; it was only in the French ways that she had much to learn.

The meeting closed, each with an agenda of tasks which was going to keep them extremely busy.

Chapter 64

Château de Gressier March 1919

IT WAS LATE evening when Juliette joined Étienne in the Gallery. He was doing nothing, just sitting contemplatively in his grandfather's chair with piles of paper neatly stacked in front of him. Juliette guessed, from his look, that he was measuring the task in front of him, but if the truth were known, Étienne's mind was a complete blank. Only the blackness of the Gallery windows, looking out over the fields, had any fascination for him.

"Is this our boardroom table?" asked Juliette, as she made her way to it.

Étienne shrugged in disdainful acknowledgement as only Frenchmen know how.

"And this is my end?" she said, pointing to the place at the end of the long table where she had sat earlier.

Étienne nodded a silent, I suppose so.

"And this is your end?" she continued, pointing to the other end.

Again, Étienne shrugged his shoulders dismissively.

"Is this end the head of the table?" she asked, pointing to where Étienne had sat earlier.

"Sometimes, sometimes not. It was wherever Grandpa sat and he sat anywhere."

"Good," said Juliette. "Come and sit opposite me, there," she said, pointing to the two chairs opposite each other in the middle of the table.

Étienne did as he was told, looking at Juliette as he did so. A little earlier, she had been in a housecoat, cooking and cleaning in the kitchen, so he was perplexed to see her dressed as though she were ready to dine in the very best of households.

"Étienne, I would like to talk, please" said Juliette.

"Have we not always been able to talk?" answered Étienne, a little affronted by the contrary suggestion.

"Yes, as Frenchman and Englishwoman, as lovers and friends, but I don't think always as husband and wife."

"We talk as husband and wife on our evening walks, don't we?"

"We talk as business managers reviewing the day." She paused and then with tears dampening her eyes she said, "Étienne, please. This is different."

Étienne reached across the table and took each of her hands in his; instinctively knowing that he should say nothing more.

"I have nowhere else to go," she whimpered.

Étienne was tempted to say something but decided to stay quiet, for why would she need to go anywhere else?

"And I don't want to go anywhere else. I want to stay here."

Étienne gently nodded.

"I want to stay here with you. I want this to be our home."

"It is our home," Étienne added, both very quietly and encouragingly.

"But it isn't, Étienne. I sense you feel that you are just a lodger here. This house is so full of ghosts for you."

Étienne knew what she was saying was true, and from the look on his face she knew he had understood her.

"Étienne, I want children. We both agreed before we got married we wanted children, but since we arrived here we have not made love, not once."

Étienne was shocked, almost affronted at the accusation, but he knew it was also true, for somehow the oppression of Château de Gressier, and everything he had come home to, had killed his libido.

Again, Juliette acted on the expression on Étienne's face. "I'm not blaming you," she said, in his defence. "I am blaming here. It is making us not us." Never had Juliette spoken a truer word.

Étienne started to rub the back of each of Juliette's hands with his thumb as a small sign of support for he knew she was right.

"We can't move forward until we ...," she paused "... you have sorted out the financial mess here. Yet it's an impossible task, and if not impossible, certainly one which will blight our marriage for the next ten years, and we don't have that time. I don't have that time ... if we are to have children." It was on the word children that Juliette started to weep; a little tear gathering in the corner of her eyes.

Étienne got up and walked around the table to where she was sitting. Helping her up, he took her tightly in his arms giving her the support and comfort she had been missing since stepping across the threshold of Château de Gressier only a few weeks ago.

They moved away from the fire, which was burning them both, to the large window overlooking the front of the Estate. Their eyes set on the drive, the small lawn, the vines and the trees beyond.

"I want to have children here too," he said. "But I want it to be better for them than it was for me. I want it to be like it was in my grandfather's time when we were all equal, him and me and my brothers. After Grandpère, my father was in charge, always the boss, always demanding, always insisting everything was better. My grandfather just made it so, but by never being the boss. He was always ... the leader of equals."

"Are you and I equal's?" asked Juliette.

"Of course, why not?" It was said so quickly and easily, for there was never any doubt in his mind. Then he added, "Of course, I'm more equal in some things and you in others."

"Like?" said Juliette, now puzzled.

"I'm more equal in physical strength and you are more equal because you can have babies. It's that kind of more equal."

"Étienne," said Juliette, as she moved back to her seat at the table. "I want to do something." She waited while he resumed his seat. "I want to buy 50% of Château de Gressier. This way our lives here will be equal."

Étienne said nothing at first for the idea came as a complete surprise. The thought of using her money had not crossed his mind since they spoke on their walk and he had rejected the idea.

"I promise to leave my 50% to our children, so it stays in your family," she said, urgently trying to sell the idea.

"But you own half of it now. I can't sell you something you already own half of."

"No, I don't," she responded firmly. "It is all tied up in your family's trusts. You might be the beneficiary, but you are not the legal owner, the family trust is. This way you and I become the legal owners of half."

Étienne knew he was defeated on the argument.

"Please Étienne," said Juliette, her voice almost begging in tone. "It's the best solution, honestly."

Étienne didn't say yes, and he didn't say no. Instead they went through the numbers again, totting up how much they owed, how much they had and what they needed to keep the Estate trading. He then took off the amount which he thought he could borrow from the bank.

"No bank borrowing. Étienne, we will have no bank borrowings," said Juliette.

"Why?"

"We are in strange times and I don't trust the banks. My trust will act as the bank and lend us the money we need. It will take security over the land just as a bank would."

"I would have to repay it all, everything, every franc and with interest," insisted Étienne.

"We would have to repay," corrected Juliette. "Yes, if you wish. When my father invested in companies, he made it his speciality to pay a small amount for the shares he was buying and would lend them the rest of the money they needed, which had to be repaid. We can do the same thing."

Very slowly Étienne came to accept Juliette's idea as the obvious solution, and without him ever saying yes, the discussion moved from one of principle to the practicalities of getting it done.

That night, Juliette and Étienne made love for the first time under the timbers of Château de Gressier with Juliette holding him tight into her, in her desire to get pregnant. But, unlike before, rather than be submissive to his lovemaking, she rode him to a frenzy of pleasure. It was the most positive statement of the equality in their marriage that Juliette could make. She knew from the joy on Étienne's face that he was seeing it in the same way.

Chapter 65

Château de Gressier May 1919

THE NEGOTIATIONS BETWEEN the trustees of Juliette's Trust and Monsieur Liard for an investment in Château de Gressier took far longer than either expected, for Juliette's trustees insisted on structuring the transaction in exactly the same way as her father had done with all his private equity investments. This was something entirely new to Liard who only worked at one pace, slow, methodically slow. The difficulties of language translation, coupled with the complexities of two different legal systems, would have tested Liard to the extreme, but with Étienne and Juliette being of a like mind, and both anxious to avoid conflict, their instructions to their respective lawyers were always clear and concise.

Immediately after the notary public had put his seal on the necessary legal documents, Étienne, with Juliette at his side, called together everyone who worked on the Estate. He told how he discovered that over two hundred and fifty thousand francs had gone missing since the start of the war, and how there were huge unpaid tax bills, made worse by additional taxes payable on his father's death. It meant, he told them, that the Estate was bankrupt. He paused as he allowed this fact to penetrate their consciousness. He went on. The situation was so dire that there was a real risk the Estate would have to be sold and each of them would lose their jobs.

The room looked in union at Coudace, each person feeling that he was responsible for the demise of Château de Gressier. The great Château de Gressier. Coudace showed no reaction. It was as though none of this mattered to him. Coudace did not observe them looking at him. Instead, his whole focus was on Juliette and how lovely she looked.

Étienne explained how Juliette's family had come to the rescue by investing in the Château. "I am telling you," he said, "if it were not for Madame Juliette, we would all be out of work." There was a small round of applause directed at Juliette which she acknowledged with a small nod.

Étienne ended his little speech by adding: "as in our marriage, so it is now in our business, Madame Guégan and I are equal partners."

Étienne took no questions. He simply took Juliette by the hand, and with another small round of applause accompanying their footsteps, they returned to The Cottage.

Juliette's investment started a period of immense action over which Étienne exercised zealous supervision. The wine in the casks was bottled. The cellars under The Cottage and The Cellars were cleared out until there were just bare walls which were whitewashed several times over. The wine racks were put back just in time for the bottled wine to be laid down. Étienne then went through the barn clearing and tidying. Everything had to have a military order about it which made the workers reminisce about Étienne's father, and the time he was in charge, for the structure and discipline were very similar.

Juliette was tackling just as big a task, making The Cottage habitable, but with one tenth of the staff. This part of the château had not been lived in for years, each room in its own time warp, unchanged apart from a cursory clean once a week. Even the magazines, laid out on the tables for the guests who never came, had yellowed with age.

Each week, sometimes twice a week, Juliette travelled into Bordeaux to see Penrose. She wanted him out of the hospital and with her at de Gressier, where she would be able to nurse him properly, for his progress in getting better was desperately slow. Secretly, she was worried he would be recognised, for his picture had been in every paper, whereas with her, he would be one stage further away from being detected. She emptied out the dining room and adjacent games room of The Cottage, which she made into a bedroom and study for him, and planned for his release a second time.

It was exactly eleven months after Penrose was first blown up that Juliette collected Penrose from Bordeaux Hospital and took him back to Château de Gressier. His freedom was like turning on a switch, for immediately Penrose started to improve. It was as though his mind had decided there was something to live for, and in response his body started to repair itself.

In a series of letters from his batman, while Penrose had been in hospital, Juliette learnt that all of Penrose's wartime possessions had been packed up in his caravan and left locked in a field belonging to the mayor of Coeur de Foucy. Juliette could never say why she thought it important that Penrose's caravan be returned to him. Perhaps it was her yearning to go back to the front to see if anything had changed, or the need to see the place which was the cause of all Penrose's troubles. Whatever it was, she had convinced herself that Penrose would get better sooner if he had his caravan at de Gressier. It would be his den; a private space which would be exclusively his. For this reason alone, she knew she had to go and get it.

Leaving Penrose in the care of a local nurse, Juliette set off for Célieux Ridge accompanied by two very elderly Estate workers, both skilled horsemen who had never travelled outside of Bordeaux before. The three of them travelled by train, firstly to Paris, then on to Arras, where she skilfully bought three horses before travelling into the village of Coeur de Foucy and presenting herself to the mayor.

After proving her bona fides with the keys to the caravan, there proceeded to be an unexpected negotiation as to the appropriate storage fee. You don't travel all this way for an old caravan unless it is important, thought the mayor. And, if it was that important, then what was a fee of two francs a day in the scheme of things?

As her men set to work harnessing two of the horses to the caravan, Juliette rode the third horse out of Coeur de Foucy. On leaving the village, she instinctively turned left to travel along the road where Jim Flagstaff had been shot by sniper fire, but she knew neither his name nor of the event. Just past where he had died, she stopped and looked up toward Célieux Ridge and what, at the top, was no mans' land, a place of total carnage. She could go no further. To travel on would be to walk on the graves of dead souls, she thought. With the sun lightening the view, and with peace and holy quiet all around, Juliette decided to capture that moment, but only in her memory.

With two horses harnessed to the caravan, and the third tied to the rear, Juliette took hold of the reins, and with a heavy shake, the three of them set off back to Bordeaux. Her experiences as a nurse on horse-drawn ambulances during the war gave her a skill which quickly won her travelling companions over; but it was when she insisted, wherever they ate or stayed there should be equality of treatment, that the eccentricity of the Englishwoman was first established, for this was not the ways of Latoire villagers.

Juliette left her posse at Achiet-le Grand. The two farm hands would travel onwards by road, with the three horses and the caravan, back to de Gressier, while she caught the train to Paris and then Bordeaux. With Penrose poorly, she wanted to get back to him and Étienne as soon as possible.

There was something about the way Étienne was standing at Gare Saint-Jean in Bordeaux, looking forlorn and crestfallen, which made Juliette feel guilty for being away. But suddenly, on seeing her, he popped back to life and with that simple reaction she knew, as if she ever needed it re-confirming, that he really loved her.

Penrose's very first few steps out of the Château were to greet the arrival of his caravan which looked magnificent. After it had left Coeur de Foucy, the two men had taken great pains to wash and polish the caravan each time they stopped for the night on their travels, so that the original greens, yellows, reds and golds now shone in the sunlight. Even the chimney had been blackened to make it look like new.

 Penrose climbed the steps, and, with the keys to the padlocks shaking in his hands, he opened the door. He struggled to sort out the cupboard door and draw keys sent to him by his batman, so it took time to unlock and open them up. One by one their contents were revealed. With each revelation, the most painful of memories came flooding back. The full set of cups, saucers, bowls, and plates which Lord Finton had brought out with him were there, wrapped and completely unbroken. What a cruel justice that his crockery makes it through the war unscathed, but the man did not, thought Penrose. He then rediscovered both Captain Trowton's and his own Webley revolvers, wrapped together in an oiled cloth in the bottom drawer. Without thinking, he checked the guns to make sure they weren't loaded. As he put them back so his hand stroked a Luger pistol jammed between an ammunition box still full of bullets and the sides of the drawer. He took it out and stared at it. Other than remembering it had been confiscated, he had no idea why it was still in his possession.

Penrose checked the cupboard where he hung his clothes. They were there, just as he had left them when he had been arrested. As he moved them along the rail, so he found, hanging from a hook, the Lee Enfield rifle which had been issued to Jim Flagstaff. Ever since his death it had stayed at Penrose's side. As Penrose stroked the now rusty bayonet, he thought of Flagstaff and realised it was the only gun he had fired in anger throughout the whole war.

Juliette watched Penrose carefully, deliberately leaving him alone before climbing the steps to see properly what was inside. Sitting on his bunk bed she was genuinely surprised for, from the outside, it appeared no more than a shed on wheels. However, the inside was built with the craftsmanship only found in a ship's first-class cabin. It was skilfully built and the mahogany polished to a deep red shine. Everything was perfect even down to the stove and inbuilt wash basin.

Sitting in his old wooden sea captain's chair, Penrose pulled open the wide drawer which hung under the desk just where he sat. At the front of the drawer was the camera he had purchased in Harrods just before he joined his regiment. The cases of film he had bought at the same time were still in their packaging, unopened. In all the war years he had never taken a photograph. It wasn't neglect and he wasn't always too busy. It was just that, every time he thought he might take a picture, he realised there was nothing about the war of which he wanted to be reminded.

As Penrose looked further inside the drawer, laying diagonally from one side to the other, he found his father's officer's swagger stick, with the silver topped emblem of the Hampshire Regiment. Underneath the stick, but unnoticed, was Penrose's map of the land at Célieux Ridge which he had abandoned in the basket when he parachuted into Cotta's Patch at the start of the battle.

Juliette and Penrose looked at the swagger stick and then at each other. In this most English of settings, they were immediately reminded of home and an overwhelming feeling of homesickness hit them both. There was nothing either could say for each knew the story only too well. Instead, standing up, they took each other in their arms and hugged. Never, in the whole of their childhood, had they held each other like this before. They might have survived the war, but it had broken their family, and nothing was going to be able to put it back together.

Chapter 66

Château de Gressier Summer to Christmas 1919

THE ARRIVAL OF Penrose's caravan encouraged him to start a fitness routine designed to garner his strength. He would walk first thing in the morning for exactly ninety minutes. At first, he only covered a few yards, but soon his objective was to cover more ground than he had done on the previous day. He would then have coffee with Magdelena, after which he would work on his defence against his death sentence. Juliette had given him her copies of all of Caprang's papers relating to his Court Martial and he was surprised at the extensive notes Caprang had made both before, during and after cross examination. He had been incredibly thorough. There was no transcript.

Penrose would join Étienne and Juliette for lunch. In the afternoon, until late, he would work in the fields tending the vines along with the other workers. He moved very slowly and cautiously at first, but day after day Penrose's strength grew.

In the evening, Penrose would work in the nursery tending the new vines, and then after a light supper, which he deliberately took on his own so as to leave Juliette and Étienne alone, he would retire to his study to read; slowly he worked his way through the extensive range of French novels which adorned the Cottage library walls. Living each day as it came, he started to give himself permission to have hope; a hope that he would have a future. Without responsibility, other than to himself, Penrose found his time recuperating at de Gressier a truly wonderful experience. When you are made to believe that you won't see tomorrow's sun, there is something truly invigorating when you do. Each day brings its own renewal that only a reprieved man can know.

The 1919 harvest was good but not exceptional. With Étienne

supervising the grape-picking and winemaking with the same thoroughness as his grandfather, it was the view of the sommeliers of Bordeaux that the wines of Château de Gressier could, for that year, sit alongside the best wines of the region, to be compared to a Château Margot or Château Mouton Rothschild. It was greater praise than either Étienne or Juliette expected.

For the first time they began to admit to themselves they knew exactly how the wine business worked. It was no more than simple arithmetic where the pluses had to exceed the minuses. At the end of the harvest, they could work out their income and estimate what their costs would be for the forthcoming year, and with this they learnt that cost control was vital to their future success. Just a few cents on the cost of a cork or a label made a big difference when so many bottles were involved. The secret to their business was in paying attention to the detail, and if the war years had taught Étienne and Juliette anything it was how to do that. As the last bottle went into the storage racks, Étienne and Juliette were confident in Château de Gressier's future. But then it hit: Spanish flu came to Latoire village.

The flu, which had raged throughout Europe in 1918 and killed over 45 million people worldwide, seemed to have abated but by late autumn 1919 it was back as virulent as before with half the villagers and Estate workers catching the virus, the very young and very old suffering the worst.

It was impossible to say who precisely brought the virus onto the Estate, but Magdelena's maid and cook were the first to fall poorly, followed quickly by Magdelena, then Hugo Coudace, with Étienne being the last to fall ill.

Juliette turned the upstairs of The Cellars into a small hospital where she barrier-nursed each of her patients to make sure the virus spread no further. She feared for Penrose as his frail lungs would not have been strong enough to fight the disease should he have caught it, but Juliette's nursing skills made sure he escaped. Each bedroom smelled of soap and disinfectant, and downstairs there was a permanent dampness in the air as sheets and pillowcases were boil-washed. Flu might have come to Château de Gressier, but Juliette was damn certain it was not staying.

After about five or six days of the illness, each of Juliette's patients started to recover, and while it appeared that Magdelena was getting better too, very suddenly she relapsed becoming delirious from her temperature which was too high and beyond control. Slowly, she drifted into unconsciousness. Having seen death's door many times, Juliette called Étienne from his sick bed to sit with his mother. She thought it would be a kindness to them both that they shared her last moments.

Étienne dutifully held his mother's hand until she took her last breath. He said not a word nor did he shed a single tear. With her soul gone, he simply placed her hands by her side and got up. Very deliberately he poured some water from the jug into the bowl on the tabletop and slowly washed his hands, taking time to do the job properly. Juliette lifted the sheet to cover Magdelena's face, but Étienne didn't look back, and with the drying towel still in his hands, he left his mother's bedroom never to return until her possessions were long gone.

"Are you all right?" Juliette asked in a loud whisper as she followed him down the corridor.

Étienne turned around and looked at her. "Yes, I'm fine, thank you," he said. There was not a drop of emotion showing on his face.

She followed him as he climbed the few extra steps into the Gallery. "Étienne," she said, perplexed at his lack of emotion. "What are you going to do?"

"I'm going to do what Penrose told me to do."

"What's that?"

"Make a list and have a cup of tea."

This small phrase caught Juliette short, for these were her father's words. It was exactly his expression, said very many times, but coming forth in a French accent, it was all so weird.

"Is there a crisis?" Juliette asked.

"No, why?"

"Because that's the condition; it's only in a crisis that you...." She stopped for it was obvious that he was not listening. He moved to his desk where he sat down, opened a drawer, took out a clean sheet of paper and placed it on the top. He took his pen in hand and wrote nothing. After a long pause, he wrote: move from The Cottage to The Cellars; for it was from the Cellars that history dictated that the de Gressier Estate was run.

Juliette sat opposite watching Étienne's every move, but her thoughts were not with him but with her mother and father. Suddenly she realised that they must be getting vulnerable with age too, and without Penrose or her, who was going to look after them through to their deaths?

When Étienne came back into Juliette's focus, there was something different about him, but she could not say what it was. It was as though a coil, which had been holding him tight, had suddenly sprung free and with it his whole demeanour had been re-inflated. He had arrived back after the war as a man, and then slowly, he had acquiesced, shrinking in rank to one of an oppressed adolescent. Now, with his mother dead, he was starting the slow re-transformation process of returning to the man she once knew.

All his life Étienne had sought his mother's approval. However hard he tried, and he did try hard, his efforts were never good enough for her. Now, with her death, she was no longer his judge and jury. With his new found freedom, Étienne was, for the first time in his life at de Gressier, giving himself permission to be his own person.

Chapter 67

London and Bordeaux January to October 1920

ON NEW YEAR'S Eve, Étienne and Juliette danced all evening to the gramophone player and a selection of records which they bought as their joint Christmas present. One moment they were dancing cheek to cheek. A few minutes later they were jigging in laughter to jazz and ragtime. Arm in arm, they were genuinely happy, and everything was right with their world. At midnight, they were joined by Penrose and together the three of them raised a glass of champagne to toast in the New Year and celebrate the beginning of the new decade. Each was feeling as optimistic for their future as they had ever done.

That optimism lasted until precisely noon on Friday 2nd January, when with telegram cable in hand, Étienne cursed and swore, for he knew he should have seen it coming. There were enough warning signs but like most of France's vineyard owners, while he knew of the prohibition laws passed in the United States one year earlier, he was lulled into doing nothing because his peer group were supremely confident that these laws would be repealed before they came into force. However, this confidence was misplaced for prohibition was coming into force on 19th January 1920 and the telegram was from their US distributor cancelling their wine order for the forthcoming year, and for the foreseeable future. They took five thousand cases of wine each year, one quarter of their production, and now they were taking none. Their largest customer and a ten-year relationship ended on the signature of a President's pen.

Étienne's immediate thoughts turned to Canada as an alternative market, but he soon discovered that they were into the same craziness. For the first time in Château de Gressier's history, it was going to have to seek out customers rather than customers coming to them.

England had always been a good market for their wine and Penrose and Juliette were confident it could be made better. Given their predicament, it had to be made so.

Under the guidance of Penrose, and with Juliette writing the formal letters, considerable effort was made to ensure Étienne was properly introduced into English society. They debated long and hard where he should stay when he visited London. Étienne wanted something small, cosy, and inexpensive, just as he had chosen for them in Paris; whereas Juliette and Penrose knew that, to be properly received, he had to stay at Claridges. However, with no room available, the booking was made at Penrose's second choice, the Savoy Hotel, simply because "it was such fun having breakfast overlooking the River Thames."

Juliette and Penrose schooled Étienne intensively in the rigours of English etiquette, insisting that his rank be included on his business card. "It would be terribly bad form to include your rank just because you served in the war, but since you were a professional soldier before the war started, then this would be both proper and expected," explained Penrose.

There was further debate about including military decorations and once again, after much wrangling, with Étienne wishing to be as inconspicuous as possible, it was agreed that only the abbreviations for his Legion of Honour and Croix de Guerre would be added.

With a stock of five cases of wine duly delivered to his room at the Savoy Hotel, Étienne started his work as a travelling salesman visiting the wine merchants of London. In the process, he discovered how much he loathed the experience of selling wines. Orders were politely placed, one or two cases to try, but nothing in the volume Étienne needed. However, there was something strange about London which he loved. It gave him a sense of freedom which he did not have at home. An oppression, which he carried everywhere with him at de Gressier, was cast off, just as it had been when he joined the army for the very first time.

In the evenings, Étienne dined at the very best of London's private members' clubs as the guest of those to whom Juliette had written. On every occasion, the conversation turned to what had happened to Penrose. When Étienne told that they had been together immediately before the Battle of Célieux Ridge and explained his involvement in 'the Penrose story' he found there was a mysterious and unexpected opening of doors. Suddenly orders were arriving from people he had never met or presented to. The Royal Household, the Foreign Office and Downing Street all ordered one hundred cases of both his red and white wines. The Treasury, the Dominion Office and the Indian Office all ordered smaller quantities, but it was clear that the word was travelling. It was as though the establishment was coming out in force to say thank you for supporting one of their own.

The Sommelier at the Savoy Hotel at first refused to meet with Étienne which made him very anti the place. However, it was the observation by the receptionist of the arrival of large amounts of high-ranking correspondence which bought Étienne to the attention of the General Manager. So it was that, on Étienne's penultimate afternoon in London, he was in the American Bar pouring glasses of red and white wine for a tasting. Étienne did as he always did when there were other people around, he offered them drinks too. On this occasion, he took a glass of both red and white wine to a gentleman sitting by himself.

"It's always good to have a second opinion," said Étienne, as he placed the glasses on the tabletop in front of the man with the Financial Times and spectacles on his lap who was, nevertheless, looking on.

"Is it true that you are supplying wine to the King?" asked the General Manager as Étienne returned to their table. The man with the newspaper, on hearing the word King, listened more intently.

"I'm sorry but I am told it is bad form to discuss one's relationship with the Royal family."

"But you are now on the wine lists of Whites, Boodles, Athenaeum ... Brookes?" continued the General Manager seeking some verification of what his receptionist had been saying.

"I am really sorry, but I am sure you would not want me discussing any business we might do with your competitors," said Étienne, not really trusting the man asking the questions.

The General Manager nodded, taking the refusal to answer as the confirmation he needed.

"I simply allow my wines to speak for themselves," said Étienne, bringing that line of enquiry firmly to an end.

The price for different quantities was discussed, and it being virtually his last day, and for no reason other than the cursedness he felt towards the hotel for its earlier slight, Étienne added a further 25% to the prices he had quoted elsewhere.

The man sitting at the next table, who was more interested in Étienne's affairs than in his own, was the youngest ever chairman of a US bank. He was now a partner in a successful New York stockbroking firm with a highly tuned rumour mill, which supported a share pump and dump operation. Together with his insider trading skills, it was delivering to him a large fortune each week. In addition to having an eye for a deal, he had an instinct as to when to get into and out of the market, and that was exactly what Joseph Kennedy was doing in London, getting out.

The US Government had persuaded Kennedy to invest in a plantation to produce latex to ensure that the US had a sufficient supply during the war. It was now obvious to Kennedy that, with no war, the plantation would never be profitable. He needed to sell it fast on the expectation of its future profitability, and Queen Wilhelmina of the Netherlands, through her advisors, was his chosen quarry. He was in London to sell her his stake in Continental Farms, giving her an investment in the *future* of latex production in the United States.

After the General Manager left Étienne with a promise to place a substantial order, Kennedy beckoned to Étienne, asking if he could join him. The two men made their introductions and exchanged business cards. Kennedy studied Étienne's card carefully and then asked, "Did you fight?"

It was an interesting question because most people asked if he had served, but there was something more direct, more personal, and more intrusive in the way Kennedy had phrased the question.

"It's what those initials at the end indicate," replied Étienne, once again using a tone intended to shut down that line of discussion.

"Why are you now selling wine?"

"It's my family's vineyard."

"Did you sell into the States?" asked Kennedy, leaning forward to hear the answer.

"Yes, we had a good distributor there, but he's shut up shop now there's prohibition."

"How much did you sell there?"

"About five thousand cases a year."

"Jesus, that's one hell of a lot of wine to shift."

"We've never marketed before," responded Étienne defensively. "People always came to us. This is my first trip and I've already sold about 50% of the shortfall so I think we're going to be okay."

"Would you like to sell some three thousand cases to me?" asked Kennedy.

"Where?" Étienne asked.

"Probably into either Bermuda or Canada."

"You're aware of Canada...."

"Yeh, yeh, yeh," said Kennedy cutting him short. "Sure, Canada's got prohibition but it's on a province by province basis, and as the Quebec vote in the prohibition referendum showed, no Frenchman is going to allow an American to tell him he can't drink French wine. Once the wines landed in Québec well ..." Kennedy said no more.

Very quickly the basis of the deal was agreed. Kennedy wanted a twenty-five percent discount to the price Étienne was charging to the Savoy because he was buying in bulk. They eventually agreed a twenty percent discount. Étienne had to take payment in dollars and fifty percent of the price would be paid immediately the wine was on-board ship in France, with the balance paid immediately it landed in Bermuda or Canada unseized.

"You have to take some of the importation risk," insisted Kennedy. "I'm not gonna take it all otherwise you might get careless and I end up getting screwed."

The two men then started to chatter quite freely, and a genuine friendship started with Kennedy's easy-going Irish charm blending well with Étienne's newly found relaxed nature. It was a relationship which was to serve Château de Gressier well for the next twenty years.

On Étienne's return to Château de Gressier, Juliette and Penrose listened with great interest as Étienne reported on his trip, and then, in a somewhat circumspect manner, he told of his conversation with Kennedy and the deal he had done.

"He told me his company, Somerset Importers Inc., has the distribution rights to Haig and Dewar's whisky and Gordon's gin," said Étienne, in support of his argument that he had done the right thing.

"But why's he buying when everyone else is selling?" queried Juliette. "It doesn't make sense to me."

The three of them discussed long into the night the proposed deal with Mr Kennedy. Étienne argued that if they only got half the money it would be better than nothing. They only went to bed after they had agreed that Juliette's lawyers would check the status of Mr Kennedy and if he were found to be bona fide then they would continue.

The message they got back not only confirmed Mr Kennedy's bona fides but also gave an explanation. He was sure that prohibition would end, at which time he expected demand would exceed supply, and at that moment he expected to make a killing. Perhaps killing was not the right word, for in the spring of 1920, Somerset Importers Inc. was in the process of becoming one of the main suppliers of alcohol to Frank Costello and Samuel Bronfman, stalwarts of the New York mafia. Together they were going to ensure that the very best of the Bordeaux wines would remain available to the customers of the very best of the nation's hotels. After all, prohibition was for the masses, not those who were used to enjoying the finer things in life.

Étienne's return to Château de Gressier also returned him to his secret torture from which he had been free when in London - mud! Since he had returned from the war, it had very slowly, but surely, become an obsession with him. It had grown as a problem and it sat heavily on his very being, controlling everything he did.

Everyone was aware of the huge efforts Étienne had made to banish puddles from the vineyard, as every spare franc was spent on tarmacking the roads, cobbling the paths and most importantly digging drains, ditches and soakaways, but no one knew why, for Étienne did not know himself. Only neatly tilled soil, growing crops, and grass was allowed. So obsessive had he become that he would not go out if it had been raining unless he absolutely had to. It was only when he went on his evening walks with Juliette that, irrespective of the weather, the sight of mud didn't bring back memories of the sweet acidic smell of the decaying bodies which lay unburied for weeks on end, and which, in the ferocity of the fighting, each man ignored as they crawled over them in their desperate attempts to stay alive.

Other men returned from Verdun with shakes and sweats from memories of the shelling, the trenches, and the sights they had seen. For Étienne, every puddle or swamping pool of brown liquid triggered memories of stepping on, through and over rotting, decomposing, smelly, slimy bodies. It was a sight which, for his sanity, he needed to keep buried. Now Étienne had been released from the emotional toxicity of his parents, Château de Gressier had found another way to take away his happiness, but neither he, nor anyone else, knew exactly why.

Chapter 68

Château de Gressier October 1920

PENROSE LOOKED AT his new identity document and the name David Victor Daunier. He wondered whether he had done the right thing in wanting to leave a trace of his past in case he needed to go back, but not one so obvious that, if anyone started to pry, they would be able to look back into his history. Given the consequences if they did, he felt he could not be too careful. He abandoned the name which everyone used because it was so unusual but kept his other two Christian Names. He originally chose Downing as his surname after his Cambridge College, but a discussion with Étienne and Juliette had persuaded him that it would be easier to get him a new French identity if his name were not so English. Penrose chose Daunier as his surname, simply because it was the nearest French sounding name to his first choice.

Étienne and Juliette were equally as anxious to get Penrose his new identity as quickly as possible. They felt certain that it would not be too long before someone from the British military police came looking for him. They were not only willing but active participants in getting him a new identity. Letters from Lieutenant-Colonel Étienne Guégan and Nursing Sister Juliette Dovingdon confirmed his identity, and with a trip to the notary public, and an interview with the mayor, the formalities were done. The registrar issued Penrose's new identity papers recording David Victor Daunier a citizen in France born on the same day as his real birthday but in the town of Ypres, where everyone knew the records had been destroyed in the war.

In the British Army, there was a deliberate policy of derogation in the matter of Major Penrose Dovingdon. There was an unsaid acknowledgement by everyone who touched the file dealing with his appeal against the death penalty that it was a political nightmare, not to be re-opened willingly, particularly while he was dying somewhere in a French hospital. The unspoken consensus was that was the best place to leave him.

Anthony Kerslake, Penrose's lawyer, occasionally wrote to the War Office making the odd enquiry as to whether Haig had decided to commute Penrose's death sentence, and to the Palace asking if the King has granted clemency; but each time he asked he was told there had been no new developments. His attempts at finding Penrose in France yielded nothing, not even if he was dead or alive. It was as though Penrose had never existed.

The simple fact was that, after the war, everyone wanted to get home, and no one wanted to make a decision. So it was that Penrose continued in the army with his whereabouts unknown. No one had even told the Pay and Rations Department that he had been cashiered out of the army and they should stop paying him. Why should they? He was going to be shot in a few days. His pay continued at the rate of a major, until his company was merged into another. It was at this point that his new commanding officer decided he was not prepared to pay for a man who wasn't on active duty, and so someone somewhere made the decision to stop Penrose's army salary.

Some things are best left lost, never rediscovered, and so it was with the case of Major Penrose Dovingdon.

With his new identity, Penrose opened a bank account in Bordeaux. Using the Reform Club as his address, he wrote to Child & Co. under his old name giving instructions that they should transfer all the funds in his bank account, less £100.00, to his new account in Bordeaux. He wrote a letter to the Trustees of his Trust, which he had witnessed by a notary public, gifting all the monies and assets in his trust fund to Juliette and instructing them that they were to advise her accordingly. He said nothing about this to her.

And so it was that with his new identity, twenty-four cuttings of the vines from Estate de Gressier which he had cultivated during his period of convalescence, the silver topped officer's cane which had been his father's, a small suitcase and the clothes he stood up in, Penrose left Château de Gressier. He had money in his pocket and money in his bank account. What more did he need, but to live?

He said no farewell. Instead, he left a letter:

My Darling Juliette and My Dear Étienne,

It is time for me to leave. I know I have not outstayed my welcome, but it is important to me that you should be free to enjoy and expand your married lives without my burdens.

We do not know of the actions being taken by others to find me. While I stay here, I put everything that you two have, and are now working for, at risk. It is time, for your safety and mine, that I move on.

My Sweet Juliette – you have been the most perfect sister. I admire and love you more than words can express, or you can ever properly know. Because of your efforts and your love for me, I am re-born and given a future which is now mine to make.

I have left two suitcases. In one I have left behind all the papers I have prepared for my appeal, if it ever comes to be made. Unquestionably, I made fateful decisions that day. They caused the Kaleidoscope to twist and the pieces to fall in a dreadful accident which badly affected the lives of hundreds of people, and for that I am truly sorry. I hope and believe these papers incontrovertibly prove that I committed no crimes at Célieux Ridge and should be pardoned.

I do hope that, one day soon, you can find it in your heart to seek a rapprochement with Papa. Perhaps, as a soldier, I can understand his decision easier than you. I am uncomfortable with the fact that, because of me, you are estranged from Mama and Papa. You were so close to them once, and so it needs to be again.

Dear Étienne – my comrade-in-arms. In our times we both saw incredible acts of bravery. It was all around us. It inspired us and, as a band of brothers, it brought us closer together, but in this we were all going the same way – towards the enemy. In defending me, you went against the perceived wisdom, against the flow of thought, against the crowd and against our side. To do such a thing is rare. It was a unique act of moral bravery for which I am, and will be, eternally grateful – thank you.

Please look after Juliette for me. She is, as I think you know, the

*most precious person in the world. I am only comfortable in leaving
in the knowledge that you will look after her.*

*I am now going to make a new life in a land of dreams and
opportunities. I will not be coming back, and that is my vow. It is
not fair that you should live your lives wondering if, hoping that, I
will turn up. I will not. Instead on those special days, look up at the
moon, remember our poem and think of me, for I promise I will be
thinking of you, and through those moonbeams I will be sending you
my love and prayers.*

My Love Always,
Penrose

Penrose's departure struck Juliette to her core. She sobbed the cries
of the broken-hearted, for that was exactly how she felt. It wasn't just
that he was gone but it was also that he was her only English ally in
these strange fields of Frenchness. He was the bedrock which helped
her to make sense of the French culture. As together, and in great
secret, they mocked some of its structural peculiarities. It was this
which made it possible for her to begin to feel at home in this strange
but wonderful land.

In her quieter moments, when the crying stopped and she wasn't
feeling so betrayed, Juliette understood why Penrose had gone; and so
whenever anyone asked about him, which was very seldom, Étienne
and Juliette would both say that he had emigrated to America, and
whenever there was a full moon, without fail, Juliette would look at
the sky and think of him.

Chapter 69

Château de Gressier November 1920

ÉTIENNE AND JULIETTE walked together towards the river. In a week or two's time winter would start in earnest but it was still mild enough for them to wear summer coats and ordinary shoes. Usually they found something to talk about on their evening walks but not today. Both were silent, pensive; their thoughts were on the same subject, their first shipment of wine to Québec, but what worried them were entirely different matters.

"You know we're breaking the law?" said Juliette, as they stepped off the gravel drive and onto the grass.

"What law?" asked Étienne quizzically.

"The United States prohibition laws."

"But we're not shipping to the United States, we're shipping to Canada, to Québec."

"Which is also introducing prohibition laws," responded Juliette quickly.

Étienne had already picked up a few sticks, as he usually did on their walks, and at the river's edge he mindlessly threw them into the water and watched as they sailed away, speeding up as they funnelled through the bridge and into the distance.

"It means we will never be able to go to America," said Juliette, seeking to reinforce her point.

"Why?" asked Étienne, as he turned towards her shocked.

"Because we'll be arrested for aiding and abetting a felon. If the FBI …"

Who? asked Étienne, not having heard the expression before.

"The FBI, the Federal Bureau of Investigation. It was set up about ten years ago to deal with breaches of US federal law and across-state crimes such as bootlegging and alcohol smuggling. If they find our wines, they'll know we supplied them because our labels are on every bottle, and then we'll get done, certainly implicated."

"Don't be ridiculous. They could have come from anyone, via any route," retorted Étienne. "They could've come into the country long before prohibition started."

"But they didn't. They came directly from us and if the FBI get to see our telexes then they have all the evidence they need that we were involved in smuggling wine into the United States."

Étienne's face froze as Juliette's analysis sunk in. We've not broken any French laws," he said defensively.

Juliette nodded, "but that doesn't stop the US government from seeking our extradition because we broke one of theirs."

Étienne shrugged his shoulders and grunted as only a Frenchman can. "It is impossible. Could you see a French magistrate extraditing a Frenchman for selling French wine?" he asked. "No, I don't think so!"

"Yes, I can, certainly when politics demands it. Have you not noticed how little the individual counts when intra-country politics are involved? It's how the last war started; with no politician giving a fig for you or I."

Étienne grunted again, but this time dismissively.

"Just after the war started my father hosted a dinner where some very senior people from the Foreign Office were present; you know, ambassador level," said Juliette pressing on with her point. "I remember it well because an English professor living in Persia was caught having an affair with the unmarried daughter of a regional governor. To make an example of her, and because of her seniority in their society, she had been sentenced to death by stoning. He was sentenced to receive 200 lashes. The only reason he wasn't sentenced to death was because he was an Englishman. It was a strange decision given the Qur'an's instruction to kill all infidels, of which the professor was clearly one. When the gentlemen from the Foreign Office were asked what they were going to do about this, I remember his answer very clearly. The eldest spoke for all of them. He said in all seriousness: 'Nothing, sometimes there are more important things than a young man's hide'. He never said what was more important. We all knew what he was talking about. It was to make sure that nothing was done which might stop Persia from remaining neutral. I remember blurting out: 'Not if you're the young man, there aren't'. My father gave me such an angry look, I said nothing more all dinner."

Once again, and for more times than he could remember, Étienne felt quite in awe. In response, he locked her arm lovingly into his as they started their journey up hill and back to the Cellars.

"Never think any government's going to protect you," said Juliette. "It doesn't work like that. They protect only themselves, ... even in France."

"You know we have no alternative, don't you?" said Étienne, accepting the wisdom of her words.

Juliette didn't respond.

"Unless we supply Joseph we'll go bust!" he said.

"No, Étienne, we won't!" rebuked Juliette. "de Gressier may go bust," and she waived her arms in the direction of the fields of vines, "but not us. There's still plenty of money in my trust."

"Yes, but what about everyone else. Without Joseph's order, how are we going to pay those who work here. You can't keep subsidising de Gressier year on year. It's too big a business. The money will soon be gone."

"So you're saying you have to break the law to keep everyone here in work, is that it?"

Étienne paused. He didn't like the accusatory way she had spoken. "No Juliette," he said very firmly but softly. "It's not like that. It's us, it's not me, it's not you, it's we. We must make the decision, not for us, but the whole village. Are we to put people out of work because of a bad US law?" he asked.

"But it's the law," said Juliette.

"But it's a bad law and we have a moral duty to ignore or disobey bad laws."

"Who says it's a bad law? Alcoholism is a dreadful curse," argued Juliette.

"Every full-blooded Frenchman," said Étienne as he broke off linking arms and held her hand instead. "For five thousand years wine has been made and sold. A few zealots will not see the business ended, I can promise you that."

Juliette looked at him and, although her face did not change shape, her eyes brightened signifying her approval. "Not just married, not just business partners, but partners in crime too," she teased, almost laughingly.

But Étienne was not ready to laugh for he knew Juliette had made an important point. "You're right," he said. "We need to be extra careful. We can't do anything about the label because it's our wines Joseph wants, but you can be sure prohibition is going to allow a lot of villains to make a lot of money. I think Joseph's probably okay. He's got too much to lose reputationally. But I suspect further down the line there will be some very nasty people involved. We're going to have to take extra care. I think we're going to have to put something, or someone, between us and Joseph, don't you?"

"Who, what?" asked Juliette.

"I don't know," said Étienne shaking his head. "I really don't know, but I think we should do something."

Chapter 70

Bordeaux November 1920

DOMINIQUE BELLANGER WAS no churchgoer. She had no need of faith, finding it all too complicated to think about. More importantly, she felt deeply let down by an alleged loving God who had allowed such a horrible war, leaving her a widow and her son without a father. However, this Sunday it was going to be different.

She dressed her son in his best clothes, made sure his hair was neatly cut, his shoes polished and his face and hands spotlessly clean. She tied back her hair, put on her best coat, and proudly pinned Georges Bellanger's medals onto his son's jacket. With Stephen smartly by her side, they went to church. Other children had other days to be proud of their fathers, but since Stephen didn't know his father, she felt it was the one day in the year when he could, and should, be ostentatiously proud of his. For this reason, above all others, it was important for her to be there on this, and every other, Remembrance Sunday.

After the service, the congregation gathered outside the church by the war memorial where, under the words '*Quand vous rentrerez chez vous, dites-leur de nous et dites: Pour vos lendemains, nous avons donné notre aujourd'hui*',[21] Cpl. Georges Bellanger's name was inscribed.

As Dominique and Étienne stood in the area reserved for the families of the bereaved, a voice read out the names of all those who died in the Great War, and she felt an overwhelming sense of pride as she heard the name of Cpl. Georges Bellanger in the roll call of the dead.

By the way that they looked and carried themselves at the Remembrance Parade, Dominique and Stephen were making a

---

[21] *When you go home, tell them of us and say: For your tomorrows we gave our today.*

defiant statement to the rest of the world: They were doing just fine on their own. More importantly to Dominique, no one was going to criticise the way she was managing as a single parent and in bringing up her son.

It was the voice which first struck her. It was familiar but she couldn't place it. It was a French voice, very strangely reading a British poem:

They shall grow not old, as we that are left grow old:
Age shall not weary them, nor the years condemn.
At the going down of the sun and in the morning,
We will remember them.

Just as the congregation were repeating the last line in French, as it was written in the service sheet: *"Nous nous rappellerons d'eu,"* Dominique looked up from the ground and she saw him. Étienne Guégan was looking straight into her eyes. She would not have known but his heart was leaping uncontrollably too. They both looked immediately down again and then up; each embarrassed at spotting the other.

To Étienne Guégan she looked as she did over ten years ago. She had not changed. She had the same delicate beauty with an exquisite face mounted on a long slender neck. The black coat she was wearing emphasised her waistline, just as the dress she had been wearing, when they first met, had done.

He smiled at her, but her face didn't change expression. She did not move, other than to hold more tightly to her son's hand. The only thing she could see was that Étienne Guégan was wearing the uniform of a Lieutenant-Colonel of her husband's Regiment. They must have known each other, she concluded with a certain amount of agony.

She started to stare at him. Her focus was on the whole man standing very tall and erect. She recognised the same brightness of his eyes and his captivating smile but before he was a boy; now in front of her was a man, with a fuller body, who appeared very confident in himself and yet there was a weariness etched upon his face. Still she didn't smile back.

Étienne and Dominique first met at his cousin's 21st birthday party. Dominique was the best friend of one of their other female cousins who asked whether Dominique could come to the party too as, having no boyfriend, she didn't want to come alone.

Immediately Étienne saw Dominique, he was captivated, as was every man. Her slim figure, bright eyes, wide smile, and long shiny hair set her apart from the crowd. Clearly Dominique made an impact, for even to this day he could describe the silky white dress with a delicate floral pattern which accentuated her bust, narrowed at her waist and then fell down the A frame dress as though she were carrying a posy. Dominique loved what she was wearing at the party. It gave her a confidence which normally eluded her at such events.

Étienne thought she was quite lovely, and without a girlfriend of his own, he devoted much of his attention to her. He danced with her on every occasion he could without making it look too obvious. They laughed, they teased, they joked and, of course, he showed off. In the gardens, away from the chaperones, they kissed, gently at first and then more passionately, for this was the first real kiss for both.

That night when the house was quiet, Étienne left his bedroom and went down the corridor into the room where Dominique was sleeping with her cousin. Silently he knelt by her bed, wiped her hair from her face and very gently kissed her. In her sub-consciousness, she placed her hands behind his neck and firmly kissed him back. With this encouragement, his hand went under the sheets and lifting her long nightgown he started to caress her tummy, her thighs and very gently stroked her breasts. Without a word passing between them, Étienne took her hand and led her from her bed and down the corridor into his own bedroom. Closing the door, as they kissed, he gently slid the straps of her nightdress to the side of her shoulders, allowing it to fall to the ground. Slowly, he encouraged her into his single bed. There they lay, naked, kissing and exploring each other's bodies, but every time he came to enter her, she moved away. She was not going to be his that night. Instead they exhausted themselves in an unconsummated passion until she fell asleep in his arms. In the morning when he woke, she was gone.

In that final summer, before Étienne went to Saint-Cyr Special Military Academy, and before life was to become serious for him, they took every opportunity to be with each other. They would sneak

away to laugh, joke, play, and caress each other's bodies without a
care in the world, and while they spent many hours naked together,
Étienne kept to the boundaries which Dominique had firmly set on
that first night. They promised each other that they would write,
meet up and forever be friends. As all lovers, forced to separate by the
circumstances of the time, they cried as they parted.

The pressures of Military Academy meant that Étienne did not
keep his promise. Each thought of the other often, but as each day
ended, the summer of 1910 went further into the distance of time.
When she heard of Étienne's posting to North Africa, and without a
word from him, she assumed their relationship was over and it really
hurt; made only a little bit more bearable by the thought that she had
not been so foolish as to give herself to him completely.

Dominique met Georges Bellanger in her first year at university,
where she was studying French history and he was reading
mathematics and physics. He had his heart set on becoming, what
would later become known as, an aeronautical engineer. He was a
studious man, very tall and thin with his hair receding. He was quite
different from Étienne, not least, he was three years older. Georges
was fascinated by powered flight. He didn't want to fly. It was all far
too exciting and unpredictable for him. What he wanted to do above
all else was design and build aeroplanes. Dominique loved Georges'
dependability. He was honest and caring, and having many similar
traits to those of her father, they developed a friendship which drifted
into a romance. Georges worked incredibly hard and enjoyed two
early promotions for his efforts. This meant that, now financially
sound, their engagement was a natural and obvious step. They were
married in the June, just weeks after Dominique had obtained her
degree. Years later, Dominique would admit to herself that, as she
waited in bed on her wedding night for Georges to join her, she
thought about Étienne and wondered why it was not his ring she was
wearing and why she was not sharing this moment with him.

As Dominique and Georges settled into married life, they felt their
world had everything on offer. Dominique went to teach in the local
school. They joined the local orchestra, played tennis, and went for
long walks along the edge of the river or the sea. They established a

routine and found true happiness in their companionship and pleasure in each other's arms, and so it would have remained, except in August 1914 Germany invaded Belgium and France was at war. Their family life, together with millions of other families, was instantly thrown into chaos.

Georges would speak excitedly about how his flying machines would change the war, and with them France would easily win. As others volunteered, Georges stayed where he was doing his designs and working on complex mathematical models, for he was convinced that this was where he could help the war effort the most. It wasn't that Georges was cowardly. As a mathematician, used to working on his own, he had become introverted in nature and putting himself forward was not something which ever crossed his mind.

Two years after they were married, Dominique and Georges had a son. It made their union complete. At her insistence, they named him Stephen, for it was the English equivalent of Étienne. Dominique questioned herself as to whether it would be a betrayal if she chose such a name. Why not the name of her grandfather whom she loved, she asked herself, but every time she cuddled her small bundle of joy, she knew he was an Étienne too. Although there was a war, Bordeaux was a long way from any action, and with their new son, life for the Bellanger's was as happy and contented as it could possibly be.

All this was to end when there was an unexpected change in the reserve occupation rules and Georges received his call-up papers. He was conscripted into the army like millions of others before him. One morning, he kissed his baby son, who was only a few months old, while he slept peacefully in his cot. Slowly, Georges descended the stairs and at the bottom he cradled his wife in his arms, as they rocked gently. Then holding both her arms tight to her side he kissed her, not on the lips but on the forehead, and then he was gone. He didn't look back. If he looked back, he knew he would never be able to leave.

From that moment Dominique's world became dominated by just two things: bringing up her son and letters from her husband. Each letter talked about possible leave and seeing each other shortly, and then one day a telegram came. Dominique was convinced it was a telegram informing her of Georges' leave. She had no premonition that it was the same telegram that millions were to receive over the course of this war. It told her Georges was dead. He died in battle on 31ˢᵗ May 1918 having fought gallantly for his country. It was signed, without Étienne's knowledge, by Commandant Guégan, as were thousands of others. In her distress, Dominique did not connect the name with Étienne.

As with such telegrams, although they were supposed to be confidential, everyone knew of the bad news long before the recipient and so very quickly Dominique's house was surrounded by friends and neighbours giving support. She could not bear the attention. Quietly, she took the telegram, climbed the stairs to their bedroom, opened the Bible by the side of their bed and placed it in the inside cover. Later on she would write a few words on a separate sheet of paper which were appropriate to Georges and which she would place alongside the telegram; but for now she sat on the bed, the Bible in one hand resting on her lap and the other hand propping her up. She stared at the floor. There were no tears. The tears would come later she told herself, when she buried his body, but not now. Now she had to plan and work out what was best for Stephen. She had to make sure that he was a credit to Georges and his memory.

The days drifted as Dominique did no housework. She simply cared for her son. It was all that mattered. She cuddled him as he slept, often sitting for hours in a rocking chair gently swinging backwards and forwards. She spent hours in her own thoughts, making a plan. It only took one thing to bring it about and that was finding somewhere new to live. Dominique had convinced herself that she had to move. She was sure she would get sucked into the past if she stayed where she was.

It was only a few days after making her decision that she read that the owner of the fisherman's cottage, set on the edge of the Garonne River, had been killed at sea. It was now up for sale. Immediately she saw the photograph, Dominique knew it had to be hers and once a plan had been formulated in her mind, the execution was easy. She quickly sold the house which she and Georges had bought with a hefty bank loan and money gifted by both their parents. She sold Georges' car, his bicycle, everything down to the smallest of his possessions, keeping just a set of cufflinks which were his father's so that these could be passed on to Stephen. With everything, other than the bare essentials, turned into cash, Dominique bought the fisherman's cottage, paying much less for it than she expected. However, what she did not know, while every local did, was that the cottage was prone to flooding. Not badly, maybe one or two feet of water would spill over the bank at high tide, once every ten years or so, staying for a few hours, then sweeping out to sea as the tide went out.

The cheapness of the cottage meant she had the money to put in some simple flood defences and make it uniquely for her and her son. It was in the fisherman's cottage that Dominique found solace, forgetting about the past, and only thinking about the future. She started work again, teaching part-time at the local school in Saint-Louis-de Montferrand, joined the local orchestra in Lormont and focused all her attention on bringing up her son. When she thought about it, she was lonely for adult company, but otherwise quite contented.

Étienne made his way to Dominique's side as quickly as possible. He took her left hand in his right-hand and went to kiss her on the cheek as old friends of equal standing might do, but instead she shied away.

"Dominique?" he said puzzled, wondering from her reaction whether he had got the wrong person.

"Madame Georges Bellanger," said Dominique quite sternly. She was conscious that eyes were watching this highly decorated senior army officer.

"Georges Bellanger, Cpl. Georges Bellanger," said Étienne, turning from her to check the name in the Roll of Honour.

"Oui monsieur," Dominique replied. She need say no more.

Étienne reached down and again took her left hand in his right. This time he lifted it to his lips. In doing so he noticed her wedding ring, and as he looked back into her eyes, he found he was becoming emotional and starting to well up. Étienne clenched his back teeth and forced his lips together so as not to cry, but it was all too much. He turned away as a tear began to fall down his cheeks to be wiped away by a leathery glove.

"You knew Georges, you knew my husband?" she asked to the back of his head.

"Yes, he was a very brave and exceptional man," he replied, looking deeply into her eyes.

"You have a son," he said, more as a statement than a question.

"Yes, he's called Stephen," she said, introducing the child by her side.

"I think I knew that," he lied, "but I didn't connect you two ... I am so sorry. I must circulate. There are people I must see, or to be precise people who expect to see me. Can we meet, please? We have so much to say."

"Do you know how Georges died?" she asked.

"I do," he replied. "Can we talk about it another time?"

"Yes," she said emphatically. "Yes, I would like that."

"When could we meet?" he asked.

"Thursday, next Thursday," she said. "Le Café on Rue de Créon, three o'clock. It's near the cathedral Saint-André," and with that she was gone. No smile, no goodbye. She just turned and left.

Chapter 71

Bordeaux November 1920

ON THURSDAYS, DOMINIQUE would always finish school at 12 noon. She would not collect her son from his childminder until five o'clock. These five precious hours were ones which she saved for herself. She normally treasured her moments of solitude, but on this Thursday afternoon she had an important meeting which she had not stopped thinking about from the moment she proposed the time and place.

Dominique washed herself all over with a warm flannel and then put on her best underwear, worn only on her wedding day and then reserved for the day her husband would come home; only now he wasn't; his grave was with his brothers-in-arms, at the steps of Célieux Ridge. She chose a white blouse and then decided everything else should be black. She rarely wore black. It was a colour which depressed her. It didn't give her the gaiety of life which she so wanted, but today would be a formal meeting. As a widow, she owed it to her husband to be respectful to his memory. Except, as she looked in the mirror at the last minute before going out of the door, she thought she looked too dowdy so wrapped herself in a delicate turquoise scarf to add colour.

Dominique arrived at the café early and was sitting down when Étienne arrived exactly on time. He parked his motorbike outside, removed his goggles and re-shaped his hair with his fingers. The adrenalin of riding his bike was still coursing through his veins. This meant his body exuded energy and excitement which clashed with the quietness of the café. He sat himself down on the chair and without acknowledging Dominique, asked the waitress for a wet towel or serviette.

"I shouldn't have come by goddamn bike," he announced,

addressing Dominique for the first time. "You always end up so damn filthy. I forgot how darn cold it is." With this, the waitress brought him a wet serviette and a dry towel and he proceeded to wash his face and hands on them before leaving them scrunched up on the side of the table.

"Oh, that's so much better," he said, "I feel like a human being again."

Dominique was appalled at his behaviour. It was not the proper thing to do to wash oneself in public like that. The barbarisms of war should not find their way into the dining room, she thought. This is not the Étienne she knew. He was kinder, gentler, and softer; not brash and egotistical like this. His behaviour re-affirmed why she had been wise to marry Georges.

And they started to talk. As they chatted, Étienne calmed down and very slowly he became almost the person she once knew; for as was obvious to all those around, no one came back from the war unchanged.

Dominique told of the death of both her parents. She talked of Georges' death, the effect this had on his parents, and how they now devoted all their attention on their only grandson. This in turn enabled her to talk about Stephen.

"I named him after you," she said, her face looking serious. Étienne smiled, not knowing what to say in response. "Stephen is the English equivalent of your name, did you know that?"

Étienne shook his head. He was still absorbing the compliment of Dominique naming her son after him.

"Are you married?" she asked. Dominique raised her eyebrows in surprise when he said he was.

"She's English," he said, by way of defence. "A nurse I met during the war. She was nursing in England and came over to tell General French that he had to do a deal with the Germans to free Nurse Cavell."

Étienne puffed out mock laughter showing what a silly idea he thought it was, and then, remembering Juliette's pluck, added, "Damn well saw him too. Mind you, it didn't make a difference. The Germans shot the poor woman."

Dominique grimaced.

"General French told her she couldn't go home because nurses were needed in his hospitals, and that's what she did for nearly four years."

"Were you hurt?" asked Dominique.

"No," said Étienne. "Got through the whole darn thing without a scratch. Makes me feel quite guilty really."

"How did you meet her?"

It was the question Étienne dreaded for the truth might be too painful to be told.

"Her brother was court martialled by the British for ..., in fact a whole host of things," Étienne replied. "It was very complicated, but because some of our soldiers lost their lives, the British thought they would do the right thing by us, so they sentenced him to be shot. It was a political thing really, because militarily he did the right thing." Étienne hesitated for he was fearful of the rest of the conversation. "I knew him very well," he continued, "because we were liaison officers for our respective armies operating in the same sector. He spoke French. I spoke English. We came together simply because of that."

"What was his name?" asked Dominique.

"Penrose Dovingdon, he was a major."

"Did he outrank you?"

It was a strange question. Étienne thought back. "Yes, technically, he did then." He then changed his mind, adding emphatically, "No, the British were always damn silly in that sort of thing."

Dominique studied Étienne for she wondered whether he protested too much.

"I really liked the guy," he continued. "I knew it was no one's fault that our men had been killed. It was just one of those bloody stupid things which happen in battle. I persuaded Pétain it would not be good for Anglo-French relations if he were shot. Also, after what happened at the Aisne, it wasn't going to help our soldiers' morale. I was given the job as emissary to stop his execution."

"So, she married you to say thank you," teased Dominique.

"Something like that," said Étienne.

"Juliette, that's my wife's name, and I arrived at Field Marshal Haig's HQ to plead her brother's case and that's when we met. We then spent the next couple of days together telling the story to the French and British newspapers."

"Yes, I remember reading about it and wondering whether it had anything to do with Georges being killed. Wasn't her brother blown up or something?"

"Yes, his prison cell was blown up by accident and he was badly hurt. The British then spent months getting him well again, just so, when he was well enough, they could shoot him. Hell, the war was over for God's sake," said Étienne, despair sinking into his voice. "What was the bloody point!"

Dominique then asked the question Étienne was dreading. "How did Georges die?"

Étienne sighed; he hated anything and everything which took him back to those days. It was all so long ago and yet so close in time. He paused to gather his thoughts.

"The Germans attacked through a gap in the British and French lines. It was a strategically stupid gap, but the damn British insisted on it because they didn't want our soldiers damaging their troops' morale; or so they said amongst themselves. Once in the gap, the Germans split in two, one half turning right to attack the British flank and the other half wheeling left to attack our flanks. It was a brilliant move as these were our weakest points, and if they had won, they would have opened a direct route to Paris. They stormed our trenches by surprise causing total carnage. Georges' company was sent to counter-attack. There were no defences. We hadn't built them. He was leading his squad out into the battlefield when they were hit by a shell. They all died, all together, instantly. He would have known nothing. I am sorry," he paused. "I am really sorry."

Étienne closed his eyes for there was more to tell, but he just couldn't say. How could he say that it was his order which sent Georges into the attack? How could he say that it was his brother-in-law's shell which had killed her husband and widowed her? Dominique watched, as with his eyes closed, Étienne slowly shook his head from side to side.

"How do you know this?" she asked, very softly responding to Étienne's obvious distress.

"I knew the outline of what had happened, and because I was seeing you, I phoned the regimental adjutant to get all the facts," he lied. He already knew exactly what had happened. Each decision made, each order given, just milliseconds in the making, now lived endlessly in his memory, as did all those decisions which had resulted in men dying. Each and every order Étienne gave, which resulted in death, caused him to hate himself more; and even now he found it almost impossibly hard not to feel an overwhelming sense of shame, particularly when he was asked to re-live any event. Like everyone else who was there, Étienne had decided it was something best not talked about.

"Thank you, Étienne," said Dominique, after a long pause. "I can see how much this all hurts, but it is a relief to have the whole story." Those few words, 'the whole story', dug right into his chest as if they were a knife.

In all their storytelling, they had leaned forward to talk to each other intimately. Now Étienne slumped back into his chair. He was quite exhausted; completely and emotionally drained.

"I think I must go," said Dominique looking at the clock on the wall. "My son will be home soon."

"I must too," said Étienne, "But can we do this again soon, please?"

Dominique smiled, for secretly she was hoping he would ask. Deep down she knew, as she had always known, that in Étienne she had a good and true friend.

They agreed to meet the next Thursday, not at 3 o'clock, but much earlier so they could have some lunch together.

"Come by car," insisted Dominique. "I don't want you to behave in a manner fit for the coal pit washhouse."

The rebuke was well taken!

Chapter 73

Bordeaux December 1920

DOMINIQUE HAD TRIED hard not to think about Étienne since they last met. Every time a thought of him came to mind, she shook her head vigorously, casting it aside to think about something else. But at night, in the darkness of her bedroom, at that gap between being awake and asleep, she did think of him and how they used to lie naked together. Into her imagination came the sight of him shaking his head slowly from side to side and saying, "I married an English girl," in a way which suggested, he was admitting he had made a mistake.

For his part, Étienne had thought about Dominique constantly and was anxiously excited about their next meeting. He had taken extra care about his dress and had been to the barber's especially for a haircut and wet shave. He felt so much cleaner and fresher after the steaming hot towels had worked their magic on his beard. He just wanted to be perfect for her.

Dominique took extra care as she dressed for school that day. Her thoughts were in conflict for, while she was determined not to encourage him, she dressed with bra, panties, and stockings as a mistress might and yet at the same time was planning her defence in the event that Étienne tried to seduce her. "I'm a widow with a son to take care of," she practised to herself out loud.

They arrived at the front door of the café at the same time. "Let's not go in," said Étienne. "Let's go somewhere else." With that, he took her hand and led her to his car just a few metres away. She said nothing as he opened the car door.

"Where are we going?" she asked, after a little while of Étienne driving in complete silence.

"Let's just get out of the city," he replied.

As they drove, he reached for her hand and held it, gently playing with the end of her fingertips. After turning off the main road at Saint-Michel-de-Fronsac, they climbed the hill and stopped at a château with a restaurant renowned for its Michelin star food. There were just the two of them in the dining room, famous for its panoramic views of the Dordogne River as it curved toward Bordeaux. So intense was their attention on each other that they noticed nothing else. After they had eaten, and in the glow of a bottle of red wine, Étienne paid the bill. As before, he led her, not out through the front door where his car was parked, but through the back door into the stable courtyard.

"Come with me," he said, taking her hand, just as he had all those years ago. He took a key from his pocket and opened the door to a small bedroom with its own bathroom beautifully renovated from an old stable block. It was one of the first motels in France.

Dominique went in first, her mind not catching up with his intentions. Once inside Étienne bounced onto the bed still in his overcoat. He encouraged her to come too, kicking off his shoes as he did so.

There they lay, on the bed, facing each other as they had done years before. The only difference was that, rather than being naked, each was in their winter coat which they were wrapping around the other. Then they started to kiss. Gently, slowly, and attentively at first, until their embrace was as full, passionate, and consuming as it had been all those years before.

"You planned this," said Dominique, accusingly after they had stopped kissing.

Étienne smiled.

She looked for the words of defiance which she had practised over the many nights before, but they wouldn't come from her mouth. She wanted him just as she had when they were young teenagers and she knew he wanted her.

Étienne stood up and took off his overcoat, jacket, and tie. He checked the heating as he kicked off his shoes. The room was already comfortably warm.

"Wait there," said Dominique disappearing into the bathroom. Étienne lay back down on the bed, his hands behind his head. He didn't care what happened next. He was just thrilled to have her next to him. Alone, just in the moment.

Dominique reappeared after a little while wrapped in a warm white bath towel. Wearing a camisole, french-knickers, stockings, and suspenders, she climbed between the sheets. Étienne stood up, quickly stripped himself naked and climbed in beside her. He took her into his arms, and they kissed passionately pulling their bodies, one into the other. Slowly, Étienne gently unwrapped the towel, as though he were unwrapping a birthday present. Lifting her camisole, he slid his hands across her breasts. These were less firm than before, but as he kissed and teased her nipples, they rose in the excitement of his touch. He kissed her flat tummy where a few small stretch marks reminded him of her motherhood and, as his hands fell between her thighs, he found she was ready for him. Gently, he removed her stockings, caressing each leg as he did so. Then she turned round so that he could undo the back of her suspender belt, displaying her buttocks which were firm and round. Slowly, she lifted her buttocks so he could slide down her blue silk french-knickers. Lifting off her camisole, she lay back on the bed, completely naked apart from her engagement and wedding rings. Étienne studied her picture of loveliness as he covered her with the top sheet. Slowly, she placed her engagement ring on the side table. She thought about taking off her wedding ring but decided against it. She was her husband's wife, and even though he was dead, it would be a betrayal of the love she still had for him if she were to take it off.

This time they made love properly, without any of the restraint of the past. Étienne came far too soon to satisfy Dominique. Oh, how he loved her. Oh, how foolish he had been not to make her his, he thought, in an exhausted afterglow.

As he lay still, Dominique explored Étienne's body. He was all muscle. There was no fat on him anywhere and while his stomach, buttocks and chest muscles were tight, powerful, and immensely sexy; it was his smell which was the aphrodisiac. It was a smell of confidence. It was a smell which said, "I will make sure you are kept safe."

She wanted him again, properly this time, and Étienne, conscious that he had failed to please her, responded by becoming the most attentive lover. Once more they made love, each focusing their attention on pleasing the other rather than themselves. Étienne wondered, as Dominique threw her head frantically from one side of the pillow to the other, whether, in shaking her head, she wanted him to stop. But the vigorous movement of her hips, and the groans as she sucked for air, showed how much she was enjoying what they were doing. Suddenly, she stopped shaking her head and involuntarily threw it backwards, her mouth wide open and her eyes disappearing upwards into her head, as an orgasm pulsated uncontrollably throughout her body. Étienne exploded once again inside her. Neither could move.

They lay side by side in exhaustion, still coupled, staring at each other, saying nothing as neither wanted to break the moment. Their breathing was in the most perfect of unions.

"Did we ......" she whispered, her face quizzical. Perhaps she was talking to herself, but it was just enough words for Ètienne to understand what she was thinking.

"We did," he said very gently. His voice was deliberately mellowed to convey the comfort Dominique was seeking.

Dominique slowly got out of bed and, completely naked, walked towards the drawn curtains and a pink flowering heather growing in a ceramic pot placed in the centre of a small chest of drawers. She lifted the pot and studied the plant carefully. Its vibrant colour said everything about the way she felt. Flushed in the joys of love making, embarrassed to have fallen so easily, while consoled by the fact that both the heather and her were capable of thriving in the winters of life.

Ètienne studied the back of Dominique's' body from her head to her heels. He was mesmerised as he wanted her shape, her form, her beauty, frozen in time, sculptured in marble, for he was certain that, of all the great sculptures of women, none had been as beautiful as the view before his eyes. He panged with a strange sense of jealousy for he wanted to own her, to possess her, to have her for his, untouched and unchanging.

Dominique, unaware of the intensity of Étienne's gaze, pinched off three of the longest stems of heather to create a little posy of flowers. She too wanted to remember this place, this time, this moment and so they would be taken home as a keepsake to be dried, pressed, and treasured forever.

"I am sorry, we need to go," said Dominique after a long silence. "I cannot be late for Stephen," she added turning towards him. "He gets in at 5 o'clock."

Étienne turned to the bedside table where he had placed his watch and looked at it. They would have to hurry.

They travelled back into Bordeaux in silence, each enjoying the memory of what had just happened. It was only when Étienne was parked outside her house that he asked: "Can I see you next week?"

"If you come here at 12.30," she replied. "I'll cook something."

Nothing else was said. They didn't kiss. The only visible sign of their renewed relationship was the way that they held hands, just a millisecond longer than they otherwise might.

Chapter 74

Bordeaux 1920 - 1924

THURSDAYS BECAME INCREDIBLY special for Étienne. It was the day he would travel into Bordeaux to be with Dominique. It was the one day in the week when he could be himself, for it was the one day when he escaped from his never-ending fear of mud; a silent phobia which held him in a constant state of anxiety, only to dissipate when he was in a city or by the sea.

At the vineyard, every time he saw mud, his mind was absorbed by the thought of drowning in the liquid ooze as the sights, sounds and smell of decaying bodies and battle came back to haunt him. Like millions of others, he had to bury what he had seen, and his time with Dominique enabled him to do just that for a little while each week. She dispossessed him of his demons of war, and Étienne truly loved her for, in her company, he was genuinely relaxed and happy.

His first port of call on arriving in Bordeaux was always to the bank to pay in the cheques which had arrived during the week. He would also hand over a list of wages which had to be made up into wage packets for him to collect later. Then, as usual, he went into the city, doing the jobs which everyone, irrespective of rank, must attend to. Most times he would visit the library returning the books of the previous week, in his case mostly unread, and selecting others in a random fashion, based more upon their title than any other criteria. His priority was Juliette's reading list, not out of guilt as some might assume but, simply out of a desire to please her, for he genuinely loved her too. No later than 12 noon, Étienne would return to the bank, sign for the wage packets, put them in his satchel and leave. There was always one extra envelop made up for Stephen with an amount equal to a man's weekly wage. Instead of putting it in his satchel with all the others, he would place it inside his jacket pocket.

Étienne then travelled, as he always did, out of the city to Dominique's old fisherman's cottage on the river bank where, depending upon the weather, he would park either his car or motorbike in front of her three large wooden double doors, painted a light blue, which stretched across the whole width of the cottage and faced the river. Behind the doors there was a very large room taking up the whole ground floor. In times gone by, this room would have stored fishing equipment, tables and baskets. It was where the catch of the day was gutted and sorted before the fish made their way to market. Now, this downstairs area had a woman's touch. The walls, not plastered as the cottage was prone to flooding, were immaculately whitewashed. After suffering her first flood, Dominique had the floor laid to oak, with each plank screwed to the crossbeam, so that after a flood it could be lifted up, dried out and re-laid. The application of polish since the last flood in 1919 meant that the floor now shone. About this room were the peripherals of her son's childhood, some sports equipment and chairs and tables for sitting outside under the summer sun, all hung from the ceiling in the expectation of the next flood. To most people it would have been just a garage, but to the owner it was an extension of her home and as such it needed to be treated with love and respect. Equally as important if the doors were open for a stranger's gaze and they looked in, it had to look neat and tidy, so no criticism could be levelled at her.

The stairs to the first floor were by the side of the cottage, and as Étienne climbed the wooden steps he would breathe deeply and enjoy the smell of the wet, salty air. At the top, he would stare out over the river and study the scene. Summer, winter, tide in, tide out, cold, rain or sunshine, he just loved the views before him. He would wait happily, sometimes for minutes, until the door was opened. The house was always spotlessly clean. Whatever the time of year, there were always flowers making the whole scene as pretty as a picture. This was Dominique's home and he loved being there.

If he was early, Étienne would drive a little way along the riverbank to the end of the road and wait. He would stare contemplatively over the estuary, deep in thought, until it came to 12.30pm. It was the only time in the week when he was punctilious in his behaviour. At exactly the appointed time, he would knock upon Dominique's front door which she would then open. He would take her hand, as two friends might, kiss her softly on both cheeks and she would invite him in.

The upstairs of Dominique's home was completely open plan, apart from two bedrooms and a bathroom at the back. This gave an enormous area which acted as an all-in-one kitchen, dining and living room. There was a huge window running the width of the house which opened on to a veranda. It meant that not only were the views spectacular, but when the sun shone, it soaked a warmth deep into her home where the light accentuated Dominique's artistic nature; for she was blessed with style and an ability to blend colours in a strange oxymoron of conservative bohemianism.

They would always eat something very light and easily made, as Dominique was a carefree cook in keeping with her artistic temperament. Sometimes, if the weather was nice, they would go for a walk along the shoreline. Sometimes, when it was cold or wet, they would go into her bedroom where, after Dominique had removed her engagement ring, they would make love. Gentle, soft, tender and passionate lovemaking which saw their bodies melt, one into the other, such that they felt as though their hearts were physically touching. Sometimes, they just sat on her veranda and talked and other times they would sit in silence, bathed in the knowledge that the other was there.

Étienne loved this woman. She was in his thoughts when he woke in the morning and when he went to sleep at night. He wanted her so much, but they both knew it could never be, and so they accepted what they had and with it these moments became very special.

Dominique loved this man too, but she felt truly guilty in their relationship, for she needed him. It wasn't a possessionary need, for she didn't need to own him. It was the spirituality they had between them which she needed. It was a feeling which could not be defined; expressed only in the way they held hands, looked into each other's eyes and felt in their souls. From these small signals, Dominique knew that she gave Étienne something he needed too, and somehow this made it all right

Chapter 75

Bordeaux June 1924

WHILE THE SEASONS came and went, and with them the vines of de Gressier gave up their fruits for wine in a mode which reflected the different summer weather, there existed three consistent but very different obsessions at the Château.

Juliette was obsessed by her failure to get pregnant. Baby after baby was being born in the village and, as she held each of them after their christening, the yearning for motherhood had become a pain which would not go away. Saying nothing to Étienne, Juliette practised every known quackery in the hope that it would work and one day she would have a child.

Étienne had grown ever more in love with Dominique; his need to be with her became obsessive. At the same time each week, he was released, for just a few hours, from his otherwise ever-present aqua-mysophobia[22]. It created an addiction to his visits to see her, which had a grip on him equal to that suffered by an addict for heroin.

The third obsession was held by Coudace who, each Thursday, woke, bathed for a long time, washed his hair and neatly trimmed his beard. Then, wearing his very best work clothes, he would find some excuse to call upon Juliette, who, unlike Étienne, permitted him to use just her Christian name when he was not present.

Carrying an infatuation worthy of a schoolboy, Coudace would arrive at about noon with some minor issue. Sitting around the kitchen table, with the cook and Juliette working the stove, they would gossip. Hugo would give Juliette his views on how the Estate should be run. With every idea she acknowledged, she fed his insatiable

---

[22] Fear of mud and muddy water

desire to make her his own. It was a desire which had started as she gently nursed him through the flu. As she mopped his febrile brow with a cold damp cloth, his brain subconsciously absorbed the smell of her perfume. As he focused on Juliette's face, he thought it was the most beautiful thing he had ever seen. Now recovered, he found the mixture of her beauty and the fragrance of her scent so potent, it was almost impossible for him to control his feelings towards her; a matter not unnoticed by everyone on the Estate of Château de Gressier, except Étienne and her.

On this Thursday, Juliette had felt the best she had ever been. It was as though the universe was directing all its power at her as she emanated happiness and joy in everything she was doing. The reason: she was pregnant. She skipped around the kitchen, engaging Hugo in joyful banter and teasing his seriousness, as she readied the kitchen for lunch.

Just as Hugo was swinging his feet under the kitchen table for the soup which Juliette was serving, Étienne was removing his coat, gloves and scarf as he always did when the front door of the Fisherman's Cottage was closed. There, he would take Dominique in his arms and kiss her with a very soft, passionate kiss on her mouth, instantly creating a sexual tingling throughout both of their bodies. It was the way they had greeted each other for the last five years. Whatever care they might have had, it instantly disappeared at the moment of their first touch.

"I have some news," said Étienne breaking away. "Juliette is going to have a baby." It was said perfunctorily, without any emotion, as though one might announce an ordinary bit of news.

"Oh, Étienne, that's lovely," replied Dominique responding without any emotion too, as there was a simplicity with which Étienne made his announcement which Dominique felt she had to imitate.

"It's going to be twins," he added, and with those few words she felt as though her stomach had been cut in two.

"Oh, how lovely, when?" she continued, trying hard to control her voice against the emotions welling up inside her.

"Juliette's not quite sure. She thinks the middle of December."

"You've known for some time?" she asked, with an accusing tone.

"No, I was only told on Sunday."

"Juliette must have known before, surely?

"Perhaps. She didn't say."

As they spoke, Dominique found her mind and body were in a different time and space. She was hurting beyond all hurt, for she knew exactly what this meant. She would never see him again. She would not allow it.

They moved to the balcony, where they sat side by side and held hands as they always did. Very slowly, each sipped from their wine glass as they stared over the estuary and made small intermittent comments on what they saw. There was no talk of the twins. The sky was dark grey with low storm clouds racing, and the wind whipped white foam spray from the wave tops of the dark green sea. It was a scene which was as figurative to Dominique's feelings as had ever been seen.

Leaving Étienne where he was, Dominique went to the kitchen to serve the stew which had been cooking in the pan since early that morning. As she stirred the pot slowly, she tried to think about how she should make these their last minutes together perfect, but she was hurting too much; everything she did was on autopilot. Étienne came to join her, and standing behind her, he took her in his arms and squeezed her into him as he kissed her gently on her neck. "It will be OK," he said, instinctively knowing what she was thinking. "Nothing will ever, ever separate us."

Dominique said nothing. She didn't know what to say, but in his arms, she became determined that she would make this his last visit. One which they both would remember for the rest of their lives. It was therefore her, and not Étienne, who led them to her bedroom where they made love with an energy and passion which only true lovers know. In their nakedness, there was a happiness which excluded from their thoughts anything other than the two of them.

As Étienne stood on the doorstep saying goodbye, he could sense the fear in Dominique. He assured her time and time again that he would see her next week. She didn't have the strength to disagree or say that they were ended. She didn't want to fight on their last time of being together. Instead, as she closed the door behind him, she crumpled to the floor in pain. Her legs would simply no longer hold her up. She was hurting beyond hurt, and nothing else mattered. Her chest was crushing her so tightly that she could hardly breathe, as her stomach stabbed convulsively into her heart. It was only when she heard the sound of her son's footstep on the stairs did she steal herself, for their life had to go on.

The next Thursday, Dominique's cottage was empty when Étienne called. Instead of her presence, there was an envelope pinned to the door with his name on the outside. Her letter to him had taken all week to compose. She said how much she loved him; always had and always would. She thanked him for being there for Stephen and her. She told him that his first duty was to his children, as was hers to Stephen, and he would be betraying that duty if he invested any more time in their relationship and not with his children. Your family is to be the most important thing in your life, she commanded. It cannot be shared. For this reason, we must never see each other again.

Étienne popped an envelope for Stephen through the letter box, and very slowly descended the wooden steps. Sitting in his car he re-read her letter time and time again. He was totally crushed by the words on the paper. How could she forsake him? Did she not realise how much he needed her? He started his car and drove, not knowing where he was going to. His mind was in a daze. It couldn't end. He would not allow it.

The following week, she was again not at home. He delivered his envelope for Stephen and then drove to her school to see if she was there. She was not, so he toured the vicinity to see if he could find any sight of her. Week after week, he followed the same routine not knowing that Dominique was hiding from him downstairs, behind the blue doors to the old fisherman workshop. She would sit there quietly as she heard his car arrive, listen to him climb the steps, wait patiently for her to answer, and then leave. It was obvious from the heaviness of his steps that he was in pain. Both were truly hurting, but Dominique was determined to be strong enough for them both. She knew she had to be, for there was one thing she was certain, Étienne would not give her up voluntarily.

Weeks later, a second letter, pinned to her front door pleaded for

Étienne to stop calling. She told him it was the only way they could start to rebuild their lives. She had loved no one like she loved him, and always would, but for the sake of his children she had to let him go, and he her.

Étienne ignored her pleadings for a little while longer, but immediately after his twins, Victor and Victoria, were born, he stopped calling. With those two little bundles of helplessness in his arms he knew exactly what Dominique had meant.

Chapter 76

Château de Gressier February 1925

JULIETTE WAS SITTING quietly at her writing desk in the library overlooking the drive, the front lawn, and the vines and then the trees in the distance. The lawn was lifeless and everywhere was still in its wooden form of winter rest. Every time she looked out, she was pleased with her decision to remove some of the vines, which originally went all the way along to the edge of the drive, and replaced them with grass, such that there was now lawn which receded into a curve ending by the front gate. It meant it gave the château a semi-English garden feel, although she would never tell Étienne that.

Juliette was taking a few moments to write her diary while her twins had their morning sleep. But her thoughts were mainly elsewhere. She was wondering about Étienne and what he was really doing all day. She knew on Thursdays he did the banking and went to collect everyone's wages but surely that couldn't take until early evening, which was when he always got home. He said it was the time the bank took to count all the wage packets. Why then didn't he phone through what was required the day before? But he always refused, saying it wasn't safe. Instead, she concluded that perhaps he deserved some time in peace and quiet, away from the constant pressures of the vineyard, for everywhere you looked there were always jobs to be done.

In fact, Étienne couldn't come home, for although he was no longer seeing Dominique, he took that time, when they used to be together, to be on his own and away from the risk of seeing mud. Travelling in his car to some spot, he would stop and just watch the rest of the day go by, doing nothing but think and daydream; but mostly, thinking about Juliette and Dominique and his love for these two women.

Juliette was musing on what to write in her diary when she saw, in the distance, the shape of a man walking up the drive. This was most odd, as nearly everyone drove to the house. As he got closer, she could see the man was carrying a suitcase. It was obviously heavy as he passed it from hand to hand. She discarded any further thoughts, presuming him to be a travelling salesman. Nevertheless, without a car or a bicycle, it was still very odd. As the man walked towards the house, he did something which he wouldn't have dared do if he were a traveller looking to make a sale. He left the drive and started to walk across the lawn, directly towards the house. As he got closer, Juliette knew she knew him. She couldn't say why. It was just some sense that she had seen that figure somewhere before.

Juliette left her chair, went to the side door and walked out into the drive. She shivered as her body recognised the change in temperature, from the warmth of the house to the chill outside. Juliette moved towards him, and he to her. They were attracted like two magnets. She walked slowly but Jack, recognising her, started to walk more quickly and then he started to run, breaking between a walk and a run, his case banging clumsily against his legs.

Juliette stood still. "Jack, Jack Morris," she said, as he stopped so close to her that he was invading her personal space, but this was the last thing on her mind as, completely unexpectedly, she wrapped herself around him, breaking into tears and then sobs. She was thrilled to see him.

Other than her brother, he was the first Englishman she had seen in over seven years. Was it a recollection for the fondness of their childhood? She didn't know. All she knew was that she was overwhelmed with joy.

"Come in, come in," said Juliette, struggling to take the heavy suitcase from Jack and hold his hand with the other.

"What are you doing here?" she asked.

"All in good time," said Jack.

"Is Papa all right?" she asked, anxiously.

"Yes, he's fine."

"But, why are you here?"

"I have come to see you, see how you are," replied Jack, "and to see your babies."

"Did Papa send you?"

"Yes, Colonel Dovingdon sent me."

"Oh," said Juliette, the expression in her voice immediately expressing disapproval.

A few minutes later, sitting around the kitchen table, Juliette served tea with warm buttered tea cakes. She chatted away nervously about Étienne, their meeting and the vineyard. Jack found it strange that not once did she ask about his journey. It was only when she heard her babies crying, did she break away from her excited monologue to look after them. With her gone, Jack prepared himself by placing on the kitchen table the two packages which Colonel Dovingdon had given him for his grandchildren, and the envelope addressed to Juliette.

It was about half an hour later when Juliette returned with two very tiny babies, only a couple of months old, one on each hip. One baby was dressed in white and the other in blue.

"Are they identical?" he asked foolishly.

"One's a boy, the other's a girl, hardly!" she mocked.

The boy, Victor, was put on Jack's lap as Juliette sat down and stared at the packages.

"From your father," he said, as their eyes touched fondly.

"And the letter?" she enquired.

"That, too."

Slowly, with Victoria balanced over her shoulder, and with one hand, she undid her father's presents to his grandchildren. With the lids open, she studied them for some time without moving. She then took each out of its box in turn and slid them through her fingers. The gold pocket watches were identical, apart from one had 'ia' added, after the name Victor in the engraving, to make it Victoria. It seems a strange present to give a girl, she thought as she continued to stroke them. Each had a tactility about them as the smooth watch glass radiated warmth back into her fingers.

"Lovely," was her only word to Jack as she put them back in the boxes and closed the lids. The letter remained untouched.

Jack stayed for a few days and they chatted as equals, for that was how they had played when they were young; then one day for some reason which still baffled her, he suddenly stopped coming. However, right now, it was as though they had never been apart; the years in between fading, as is the sign of any true friendship.

"When we were young, I remember thinking I was going to marry you," she said. "And then you were gone. Was it my father who disapproved?" she asked. It was a question it had taken her over sixteen years to ask.

"Nah, give over," replied Jack, dismissively. "Marry below stairs, you'd never have been allowed."

"You didn't know me very well," said Juliette.

Jack nodded in agreement. "I think my dad was scared that if anything happened, well, he'd lose his job, his house, everything." There was a long pause. "I remember it clear," he said. "I was aged about ten or eleven. I was given the thrashing of my lifetime by my father for being too friendly with you. He rarely hit us kids, but by God he did on that day. 'e really hurt me."

"What?" exclaimed Juliette, truly shocked at what she was being told. "Is that why you stopped coming?"

Jack nodded, silently confirming it was true.

"I am so sorry. It was so different then," said Juliette sympathetically, touching and then holding onto his arm.

Jack smiled forgivingly as their conversation stopped to meet the demands of the twins.

Over dinner the first evening, Étienne, Juliette and Jack talked about where they'd served in the war, how Jack got hurt, they spoke briefly of the unfairness of Penrose's court martial and swapped guesses as to his whereabouts, but mostly they talked about the social changes the war had brought on both sides of the Channel.

It was at breakfast on his second day, when Juliette had organised specially for Jack a cooked full English breakfast, that the issue of Penrose's Court Martial was raised for a second time.

"He was definitely not guilty," said Juliette, when Jack quizzed her about his trial. "I have his defence papers upstairs; they prove it beyond all doubt."

"How did you get them?" Jack asked.

Juliette said nothing.

"Did he come here after the war?"

Again, Juliette said nothing, and then with a winning smile added, "Étienne and I saw him in hospital just after the war ended. I don't know what happened to him after that. He just disappeared."

That afternoon, as Étienne went to work, Juliette and Jack pored over Penrose's papers. On the top, there were around 50 or 60 pages of neat script in Penrose's hand. It was just as one writes an essay or a business report. It annotated minute by minute what happened on that fateful day in May 1918 when the Germans attacked Célieux Ridge. It specified exactly who did what, where and when.

"This is the important bit," said Juliette thumbing to a page about one quarter of the way through the report. "The question for the court was whether Penrose gave his orders in yards or metres. He always maintained he wanted his guns to fire a distance of 1,500 metres. He knew this was the distance of the guns in the middle of Cotta's Patch to the middle of no man's land which was his target. He said he gave instructions for his guns to fire at a range of 1,600 to 1,700 yards; translating this backwards, it means 1,450 to 1,550 metres, i.e. fifty metres either side of his target. Another officer, in giving his evidence, swore that Penrose gave his instructions to him in metres, so he converted them into yards yet again, before he passed the instructions on to the guns. In effect, he took the 1,600 to 1,700 figure Penrose had given him as metres and converted them into between 1,750 and 1,850 yards. The effect of all this was that, rather than firing at a target 1,600 to 1,700 yards away, as they should have done, they actually fired a distance of 1,750 to 1,850 yards. They overshot by about 150 yards and straight into the French forces which had been brought up to defend the area."

"How does Penrose prove he gave his instructions in yards?" asked Jack.

"Because it's here on the map he used, look," said Juliette, turning over each pack of evidence until they came to the map.

"This is the French map of the area. They were standard issue to the British Army. You will see that their scale is in kilometres, but they've been overlaid with grid lines which are to a scale of 1,000 yards," said Juliette. "This map was found in Penrose's caravan after I'd collected it from the Somme."

"One thousand metres to a kilometre," said Jack, just to reassure himself.

"You will see here in pencil the sum 1,500 divided by 36 and then multiplied by 39.3 and the answer he got of 1,637. You see its Penrose's handwriting." Juliette's voice was becoming shrill in her excitement.

Jack looked.

"And here, you will see the sum 1,600 again divided by 36 and then multiplied by 39.3 to give 1,746, but he has crossed it through. He says it proves he thought that distance was too far."

"Why point three?" asked Jack. "Isn't it strange to take it to that degree of accuracy in the middle of a battle?"

"Penrose was a pedant when it came to arithmetic," said Juliette. "Multiplying by a decimal point would have made no difference to the speed he worked and knowing him he would've wanted it to be accurate."

"So, what you're saying is that these workings prove that Penrose wanted to fire at a range of 1,600 to 1,700 yards, which would have meant the shells would have landed on the Germans and not on the French."

"Yes, precisely," said Juliette, excitedly.

"And then the gunnery officer, thinking that the instructions were still in metres, took the figures and converted them into yards so they overshot."

"Yes, yes," said Juliette impatiently, but it wasn't a gunnery officer. It was an officer in his Balloon Section.

"Was this evidence given at the trial? Did they see this map?"

"No," said Juliette. "His personal effects disappeared almost immediately after he was arrested. This map, his field sack and all his other things were packed away safely in his caravan by his batman. It was good luck that I decided to go and get it after the war had ended. I only did it because I thought it would help him get better."

"Hang on," said Jack. "How come, in his report, Penrose has referred to his calculations on the map? He must have been...."

Juliette smiled a sheepish smile, knowing she had just been caught out.

"Where is he now?" Jack asked.

"I genuinely don't know. He was here convalescing, working on his defence, and then one day he was just gone. Everything was neatly packed up." There was real sadness in Juliette's voice, as she remembered how much she missed him.

"Why didn't he appeal?"

"There is no appeal. He was waiting to hear whether Haig would confirm his sentence or whether the King would grant him clemency when he was blown up."

"Colonel Dovingdon took it all very badly," said Jack.

"And so he damn well should," said Juliette emphatically. "He refused to help. I begged him to write and plead for Penrose's life, but he wouldn't. He wouldn't go against his precious army."

Jack was shocked at the vehemence of Juliette's attack.

"He chose his precious army against his son. How could he? How dare he?" she spat out in anger.

"Perhaps he thought it was better to keep the French as our allies."

"Don't be ridiculous. We went into that damn war to help the French. It was on their soil we were fighting, not ours," she retorted. "They had a duty to be on our side!"

"Have you two not spoken since?"

"No and we won't," said Juliette animatedly.

"Did you know I had to go and look for the Colonel on the day the newspaper came out saying Penrose was to be shot?"

Juliette shook her head.

"He went out in the morning, immediately after he'd heard the news. When he wasn't home by late afternoon, I was sent to find him. He'd been walking and thinking about the problem all day."

"It's a good job some of us did something more than just think," added Juliette, sarcastically.

By the nature of Juliette's responses, Jack knew the subject was closed. There was no point in sharing with her the Colonel's thinking. Instead, he neatly put back together Penrose's bundle of evidence as though it had never been opened.

"The chap from the Times was very supportive of Penrose," commented Jack.

"Yes, he wrote a couple of very good articles defending him."

"I also gather that the French came out in support too."

"Yes, that's how I met Étienne," said Juliette. "In fact, both those make my father's behaviour even worse. How come the French army can come and help an English soldier? How come the Times can report a miscarriage of justice, and yet my father can't fight for his son?"

"You met Étienne defending Penrose?" asked Jack quizzically, seeking to clarify Juliette's earlier remark.

"Yes," she replied, before breaking into a detailed description of their meeting and then working together.

"Do you want me to tell Colonel Dovingdon about the evidence I've seen?" asked Jack once Juliette had stopped telling her story.

"If you want to," replied Juliette. But as she answered, Jack knew he wouldn't say anything. It would only make the old man feel worse than he already did. There was not a day in the seven years since the war had ended that Colonel Stoddart Dovingdon had not thought about both his son and daughter, and how they had become estranged from him.

Chapter 77

Bordeaux November 1927

ÉTIENNE KNEW DOMINIQUE would be there but, after such a long period, he was hopeful that he would be able to see her again without bringing back the grief he felt at the loss of her friendship. Each Remembrance Sunday for the previous two years, he had deliberately been to other services so as not to see her. This Sunday, with Juliette and his two children by his side, duty brought him back to the war memorial which recorded, amongst others', the sacrifice of Dominique's husband, Cpl. Georges Bellanger.

The priest took a passage from the Book of Matthew for his sermon theme: "*You have heard people say, love your neighbours and hate your enemies. But I tell you to love your enemies and pray for anyone who mistreats you*", he read before continuing: "*Then you will be acting like your Father in heaven. He makes the sun rise on both good and bad people. And he sends rain for the ones who do right and for the ones who do wrong. If you love only those people who love you, will God reward you for that? Even tax collectors love their friends*".

Étienne saw her as he moved to the pulpit to read from St Paul's letter to the Corinthians. Dominique looked exactly the same as she had when they had rekindled their friendship here eight years ago. Stephen was by her side, wearing his father's medals as he had done then, but now they fitted his chest rather than swamp his little body. She had already seen Étienne. He was thinner, greyer. Their time apart had not served him well. Deliberately, she did not look at him. Instead, she stared at the floor, as he moved down the aisle.

"*Love is patient, love is kind*," he read. "*It does not envy, it does not boast, it is not proud. It does not dishonour others, it is not self-seeking, it is not easily angered, it keeps no record of wrongs. Love does not delight in evil but rejoices in truth.*"

Étienne looked up from his reading, and Dominique looked up from her lap. Their eyes met just as Étienne spoke the final words which he knew by heart. "*It always protects, always trusts, always hopes, always perseveres.*" He paused, and then speaking directly to her, with his voice very slightly quivering, he read the last words: *"Love never fails."* Dominique's mouth went dry and her tummy churned for, as those words reverberated around the church, she would swear that everyone knew he was talking directly to her.

After the service, Étienne introduced Juliette to Dominique and Stephen and he pointed to Georges' name carved on the memorial as their two children ran around the churchyard, "He was one of our heroes," said Étienne. "We were in the same regiment."

"I am so sorry," said Juliette, her few words conveying a profundity which, at that moment, was lost on Dominique, who was studying Juliette enviously. What was it that made Étienne speak words of love directly to her when his wife was so beautiful, charming, and graceful, she wondered. In those few minutes of their meeting, she really liked her. They could, Dominique realised, be good friends, for Juliette was natural, down to earth, and perfectly ordinary.

After a little while Étienne broke away to introduce Juliette to all the families of the bereaved. In each meeting, there was a kinsmanship which, in an exchange of very few words, acknowledged that Étienne was their informal leader. The one they could turn to. The war might be at an end, but these families were his brothers-in-arms too, and never to be forgotten.

Through those few introductions, Juliette renewed her pride in her husband for, in the bustle of the day, she had forgotten about his heroic past and had stopped seeing him as others did. He was a man who ran towards you when you were in difficulty, not a man who ran away. A man who stood on sentry duty, and in doing so pronounced, "I will keep you safe!"

Out of the corner of his eye, Étienne saw that Dominique and Stephen were leaving. He rushed to be with them, just to say good-bye.

"I think God planned that," said Étienne.

"Planned what?" asked Dominique.

"My reading."

"I thought that was your choosing?"

Étienne shook his head, unable to speak as water filled his eyes and the emotion of being close to her took control.

"It's never been the same...," he said. "Every day the war is with me. At every turn I am reminded of it all. It's only when I'm with you...." his voice started to break, "I don't think about it. I....," he paused. "I really miss you." His words were said with such pleading that they were impossible to ignore.

Dominique put her fingers to his lips to stop him talking. Then she swiftly kissed him, very gently on the cheek and walked off, deliberately leaving him behind. This was not the time or the place.

From a distance, Juliette watched them carefully, telling herself that their speaking related to regimental business which, in a small part, it did.

The next Thursday, Étienne climbed the steps to her fisherman's cottage, as Dominique knew he would. Rather than being out, she was in, and ready for him, as she had always wanted to be.

Chapter 78

Chateau de Gressier May 1928

"JOE, JOSEPH WANTS me to go to Québec," said Étienne walking into the library in the Cellars.

"Joe, Joe Kennedy?" asked Juliette quizzically as she looked up from writing in her diary. Why? when?

Étienne didn't answer. Instead he handed over a long letter, which he had rolled tightly, and sat in the chair by the side of her desk. They sat in silence as Juliette read carefully through the scroll. She had never learnt to skim read and always thought she was better off for that fact.

Étienne studied Juliette's face as he always did in these moments trying to read her mind. In his thoughts, he wished he could paint the scene before him. He wanted to capture each moment. She looked more beautiful, more enigmatic than he could ever remember as her face made tiny changes to reflect the narrative as it unfolded before her.

"Will you go? asked Juliette, looking up for the first time since she started to read.

"I don't know. What do you think?"

"He seems very keen. He's even got your travel arrangements worked out, the boats, the dates, everything."

"Will you come too?" asked Étienne wistfully. "We could make it a holiday, a family holiday."

Juliette didn't answer. "Will you go first class or steerage," she asked instead.

"Steerage," he answered without thinking. "Why waste money."

Juliette smiled weakly as she remembered how parsimonious Étienne had been when it came to choosing hotels on their first trip to Paris together. It seemed such a long time ago and he had not changed in these attitudes one bit.

"Why such a rush? Why not go after the harvest?"

"Because the St Laurence Seaway freezes up in winter. Its only in summer that there's a direct route between Cherbourg and Québec"

"I don't understand. Why does he want you to go?"

"He says he wants my help in building up a stock of wine in Québec ahead of the end of prohibition. He's certain Al Smith is going to win the presidential election, and with-it prohibition will come to an end. He said he was putting a lot of money into Smith's campaign to make sure he wins."

"Joe's a Democrat? I don't believe it," retorted Juliette, almost mockingly. "If there ever was a stereotype Republican its Joseph Kennedy!"

Étienne nodded his agreement. "My bet is that it's a Boston Irish Catholic thing."

"Still doesn't make sense. It was Woodrow Wilson who introduced prohibition, wasn't it, and he was a democrat. Do you remember, Joe said his father ran a saloon in East Boston? Why would you support a party which puts your father out of business?"

Étienne shook his head.

"I don't understand what extra is added by you going there?" said Juliette, before returning to study the letter.

"He says he wants us to help stock a warehouse in Québec, so I imagine its warehouses he wants me to see."

"I get all of that, but I don't see what's in it for us?"

"Extra volume, extra sales," said Étienne uncertainly.

"So we pay for a warehouse, we stock it with our wine in a country where it is illegal to sell alcohol so Joseph can only pay for it when he buys it from us. It doesn't seem a great deal to me."

"I thought I might make a new blended wine from the second presses from the vineyards around here, a mix of Merlot and Cabernet Sauvignon, and ship that across in barrels. They'd do the bottling and labelling in Québec."

It was Juliette's turn to nod appreciatively. "We could source that wine quite cheaply, couldn't we? So, what, you'd find the bottlers and packers while you are there?" she asked.

"I don't know what I'd do exactly. All I know is that Joseph wants me to come."

They sat in silence each considering the risk of being in a country where, at any moment, Étienne could be arrested. Their comfort was derived solely from the fact that the proposed meeting was in French Québec. Any other place and it would have to be no; but Joseph Kennedy knew this.

"You know you have to go, don't you?" said Juliette.

"Why?"

"Because he won't trust us if you don't. He'll assume you'll be working on his plan with someone else and so he'll start working to find someone to replace us. He'll want an alternative to us and when he has that, he'll dump us. No compunction."

"Jesus, that's devious."

"Yes, and he's clever, and Irish and a survivor. He's been taught to trust no one."

"Is that the wisdom of years of Anglo-Irish politics?" asked Étienne.

"Be sure, be sure," mimicked Juliette in a soft southern Irish accent. "You need to remember, in Ireland, when they sell farmland the two farmers mark out the boundary with stones and then every night each goes out to kick the stones a few feet in the direction of the others land. They don't do it to gain an advantage. They do it in the certain belief that the other guy has already cheated them. They genuinely believe they are returning to what was already agreed."

"And they'll all go to confession afterwards, I suppose," grunted Étienne at the hypocrisy of it all.

"How long will you be gone?" asked Juliette.

"It would mean nearly four weeks away, and I can't afford the time. In any case if I go, we should all go. We could make it a bit of a holiday."

"No, not after Titanic. I am not going to risk Victor and Victoria's life on a boat to Canada. No, we'll stay here," she decreed, not wholly discounting the risk of Étienne being arrested.

"Titanic sank over 15 years ago. It's all much safer now," protested Étienne, but to no avail.

Juliette looked down and scrolled through the letter once again.

She was checking the dates of sailing. "You'll be back well before the harvest. That's the important time and, with that declaration, the decision was made.

Whether he liked it or not Étienne was going to Québec.

Chapter 79

Québec August - September 1928

AT CHERBOURG HARBOUR Étienne climbed the first-class gangplank with a spring in his step to board Canadian Pacific SS Empress of France bound for Québec. The reason he changed his mind from steerage to first class was two paces in front of him.

As Dominique stepped on board the ship, she turned to look at Étienne and smiled. He beamed back. They shared the same nervous excitement that pulsated throughout the whole ship, for this was, for most of its passengers, the journey of a lifetime.

Étienne and Dominique's cabins were next to each other. He had insisted upon it. But their first moments on board were not together as they might have hoped. Each was taken over by a stream of porters, valets and maids asking questions and giving instructions. It was sometime before they were able to meet up again in the first-class lounge for afternoon tea. Here they addressed each other as Madame Bellanger and Monsieur Guégan in a formality which they both found faintly ridiculous and thus amusing. After tea they toured the boat and watched the lights of Cherbourg harbour fade into the distance. As the boat headed out into the evening sky, ominous dark grey clouds started to roll in from the Atlantic, but neither took any notice.

Later, as Dominique walked with Étienne by her side into the dining room, she felt a mix of contentment and pride. The fact that etiquette dictated that she should not take his arm did not worry her one bit. She loved the pink silk dress she had chosen to wear and from the look on Étienne's face she knew he liked what he saw too. Its highly fashionable plunging front and back, was of the time. It was revealing and very risqué. It was only the double material of the collar roll and lapel falling into a small Tudor rose in front of her tummy button which stopped Dominique exposing herself, and the dress being declared obscene. It was not the kind of dress which could be worn in Bordeaux on any occasion, but on-board ship, who cares.

"My maid said it will be a bit rough tonight, at least until we're through the Celtic Sea and out into the Atlantic," said Dominique as Étienne made some hasty place name changes to make sure they sat next to each other. It was an understatement. During dinner the boat rose and fell and rocked from side to side until Étienne first turned green and then felt seasick. Leaving Dominique at the table, he returned to his cabin where he was violently ill. He stayed there for the next four days hugging the lavatory bowl and wishing he were anywhere else. It didn't matter where. Just anywhere which stood still. When the time came for the mandatory lifeboat drill Étienne didn't move. There was no point in going somewhere else to die when he was certain he was dying where he was.

Dominique tried to be attentive, but she was dismissed without grace as Étienne's temper reflected that of an innocent man on his way to the gallows. In truth, he wanted Juliette to look after him and he cursed the fact that she wouldn't come.

It was only when the boat was in the relative calm of the Gulf of St Lawrence did a pale and emaciated Étienne leave his cabin for a slow walk around the deck. The last time he felt so ill was when he'd had Spanish flu and his mother had died. It was an event which had a strange mix of seeming to be both yesterday and a very long time ago.

The boat docked overnight at Québec's port and, for the first time since they had left Cherbourg, Étienne joined Dominique for breakfast. With each morsel of food and sip of coffee, Étienne rose into bloom, like a wilting flower recovering from the rain after a long drought.

"I am sorry I was such a poor companion," he said apologetically.

"You poor thing," responded Dominique. "You missed meeting some nice people. Captain Griffiths was a good host. Did you know our new Chargé d'Affaire to Canada was on board with his wife?"

Étienne shook his head.

"He'd been working with Aristide Briand on the Kellogg-Briand

Peace Pact. Now it is all agreed, and ready to be signed, he's been promoted and rewarded with a holiday in Quebec before he starts work."

"What, the non-aggression pact between France and the US?" asked Étienne dismissively. Deep down he resented the fact that a diplomat was having a holiday paid for by his taxes.

"Yes."

"Pure political vanity, ridiculous hyperbole."

"That's exactly what he said. In fact, he was very indiscreet about Briand, and well, about the whole Government."

"He must be the only sensible chap amongst them," grunted Étienne sarcastically.

"But he was hopeless at everything," said Dominique shaking her head. "I beat him at chess, easily and he lost a fortune in cards which, thankfully for him, his wife won back."

"I didn't know you played?"

"I didn't before, I learnt on board. But I won every game of chess I played, well after the first one," she announced boastfully, "and I leave a little richer than I started, not much, but enough.

"Cards?"

"Yes, Poker, after Bridge, when most had retired."

"You play Bridge?"

"Yes now, but not before."

"Who did you partner? asked Étienne, as he felt pangs of jealousy sink into his chest. He didn't like sharing her one little bit and the thought of other men enjoying her company truly hurt.

"Oh, anyone who would have me," she answered innocently.

Chapter 80

Québec August - September 1928

A PONY AND trap took Étienne and Dominique from the boat up to the towering Chateau Frontenac Hotel with its green roof. There it sat majestically on the cliff heights overlooking the river. This time there was no pretence with separate rooms as Étienne booked them in as Mr and Mrs Guégan.

They had been lovers for a long time, but secure in their hotel room, it felt different. Before there was always something pressing. Their moments together snatched between the daily tasks of living. Now there was nothing to impose. They had only each other to excite and tease, to play with and enjoy until they fell into a contented sleep.

If there was any doubt about the love the other had for them, it was expelled in that room for there was nothing mechanical or perfunctory about their love making. In a love so profound, they each sought to be generous, energetic, and fulfilling. To give the other more than they would ever receive, and, in a confusion of overwhelming joy, Dominique's eyes filled with tears causing Étienne to hold her even tighter. In turn, it intensified the emotion which pulsated throughout their bodies and flooded their brains until exhaustion overtook them.

"You look like you've won the Prix de L'Arc de Triomphe" said Dominique as they lay peacefully side by side after waking.

"Oh, I have, and so much more," admitted Étienne as he rolled on top of her. Each sparkled with happiness as their mouths grinned widely. They looked searchingly into each other's eyes and once again their souls touched, for they shared a common thought. There never was a more perfect moment than this.

Dominique's hair fell in waves around the white pillow, framing her face. As the light struck, her soft flowing fibres shimmered between shades of light and dark with all the colours of the rainbow sprinkled between them. Étienne wanted to stop and hold that moment for her face had never looked so beautiful. He thought about taking a photograph but, with her breasts laying bare, he knew she would not like it. He didn't want to spoil the moment, so instead, he burned the picture deep into his memory before he kissed her, and they started to make love once more.

Sustained by champagne, orange juice and room service it was not until mid-morning the following day before Étienne and Dominique ventured outside to walk The Plains of Abraham and see the Citadel de Québec.

"Aren't you glad you're here with me and not Juliette," said Dominique as they watched the garrison soldiers fire the noon day gun. It was the first reference to Étienne's wife made by either of them for a long time.

"Why?" asked Étienne surprised.

"Just think how superior she'd feel right now learning how a handful of English soldiers defeated us to steal Canada."

"She already knows. She boasted about it before we left. Apparently General Wolfe's climb up the cliffs here is taught in every English school. It seems Wolfe, Joan of Arc and the Battle of Agincourt is all the history they seem to learn. Oh, and our revolution. It helps them feel better about themselves after their defeat by William the Conqueror." Étienne's tone was a mixture of serious and mocking.

"But Joan of Arc defeated the English!" protested Dominique, noting he'd said nothing about Waterloo or Trafalgar.

"Yeh, but they burned her at the stake, so for them, that makes it a victory."

"But she was a woman."

Étienne shrugged his shoulders. There was nothing more he could say.

Chapter 81

Québec August - September 1928

DOMINIQUE DIDN'T JOIN Étienne, Joe Kennedy, and his small entourage, for dinner in a private room in the hotel. As could be expected, Joe had booked into the Presidential Suite which explained why it wasn't available when Étienne enquired, but then he would never have paid that price.

Étienne was shocked when he saw his dinner companions. Joe and one other were modestly suited as though they were New York bankers. The others, with their wide lapels and bright ties, looked as though they would have been more at home in the nearest speakeasy. However, it was the thoughtful way that, on the sideboard, ready to be served with their meal, were several bottles of Château de Gressier 1921, which put Ètienne at ease. It was an acknowledged vintage because that summer had been the hottest for over 35 years.

Most of the dinner was spent with Joe Kennedy complaining about his mistress, Gloria Swanson. She was in Europe filming 'Queen Kelly'. It was one of the last silent movies ever to be made. It had the infamy of never being shown in theatre. Joe was its producer and, along with Swanson herself, was a major financier. Joe used an awful lot of Anglo-Saxon swear words as he concluded that, whatever he had done to her sexually, she was now doing to him financially, but ten times over.

At the end of the dinner, Joe summarised, for those sitting around the table, the exchange of letters between them. It was when George Ramus spoke did everything become much clearer to Étienne. Ramus was a lawyer and the only other person professionally dressed. He was an expert in the prohibition laws. As a result, he had acquired a string of distilleries and was now one of the biggest, if not the biggest, bootlegger in the US. He was so wealthy he had no reason to be there other than as a favour to Joe Kennedy.

Ramus was there at Joe's invitation for one purpose. To persuade Étienne he wasn't doing anything illegal. Ramus carefully explained that the 18th Amendment to the US Constitution didn't prohibit the drinking of alcohol, but it was the Volstead Act which set out the Federal Rules enforcing the ban. This made it illegal to produce, import or sell alcoholic beverages. On top of that each State had its own prohibition legislation. All this made it a legal minefield and a lawyers' paradise. However, there was a huge loophole. There was an exemption for alcohol used for medical purposes and thus there was a large industry in providing medical gins, whiskey, wines, and certificates.

"By labelling your wine as being "for medical purposes only" said Ramus confidently. "It would be perfectly legal for you to import it into the US and sell it there."

Joe Kennedy nodded to Ramus appreciatively. His job had been done. It was then that the evening descended into a schoolboy farce as the mobsters, as Étienne was later to describe them, partook of far too much brandy and whiskey which had mysteriously appeared, as did the women who were now surrounding them.

Étienne didn't want to be there anymore. He felt decidedly uncomfortable, as though he was being set up for a trap. He made his excuses and left, promising to see them all in the morning, only to find that Kennedy and Ramus quickly followed him out of the room.

"We're leaving straight away after breakfast," said Kennedy immediately he and Ramus were standing outside the elevator. The others will show you around tomorrow and the warehouses they think will work for us.

I thought you were staying here with us for a few days," said Étienne, not disguising his shock and annoyance. He then quickly regrouped. "Are any of those properties I'm seeing tomorrow owned by you Joe?" asked Ètienne with a grimace which was half threatening, half teasing.

"Not yet" he replied, "but if they have a good tenant ......" He didn't finish his sentence. He didn't need to.

"I'm not doing it," announced Étienne to Dominique immediately he was back in their bedroom. "I travel five thousand kilometres to see Kennedy and he gives me one evening, that's it. I can't believe it," he continued angrily. "He's a narcissistic little shit!

Étienne threw off his jacket and kicked off his shoes. "I'll go with them tomorrow as I agreed. I'll see what they want me to see, but that's it. No more." There was a determination in his voice which had become rarer with his ageing.

Dominique shared a few words of sympathy which Étienne hardly noticed.

"He had an impressive lawyer there called George Ramus. He's probably as good and as an untrustworthy a lawyer as you can possibly find,"| he continued. "And the rest, they were all straight from central casting. If they were French, they'd all be from the port side of Toulouse. Do you know, they all had strange nicknames like, Bugsy and Lucky," announced Étienne. "It's not for me. None of it. I have this horrible feeling that they see me as the goose they're ready to pluck.

Étienne paced the room as he did his thinking out loud. As always, when he spoke about de Gressier and its wine business, Dominique listened patiently. She didn't comment or make any observation other than to make sure she understood what was being said. The outside world had come crashing into their room with stark reality.

Étienne had breakfast with Bugsy and Lucky. He was still none the wiser as to their real names. It was why he took extra effort to study their room keys and remember their room numbers. He would get their names from reception later and check them out. They were joined by a small team of real estate agents whose sales pitch was as hard and as driven as anything you might find in central New York. It was the antithesis of Bordeaux. As the agents continued through their presentation introducing property after property, their tone aggravated every one of Étienne's nerves to the point where he would have easily turned down the bargain of the century. It was when he commented that, with so much warehouse space available the rents seemed incredibly high, did the selling stop. Like rank amateurs, they had oversold themselves.

It was with some relief that they eventually left the breakfast table and started to drive Étienne around the empty warehouses of Quebec. They also toured the warehouse where Kennedy's de Gressier wines were stored. Étienne was appalled as it was no more than a dry shed where his wines would bake in summer and freeze in winter. However, it was the fact that his wines were sitting alongside a large stock of some of the finest whiskies from Scotland and best gins from England which determined Étienne's response. They were labelled 'Somerset Importers'. They belonged to Joseph Kennedy!

Dominique's day was far more refined. She pampered herself in the morning with a facial, a massage, manicure, and pedicure. She followed that by having her hair trimmed and blow dried. The first four of these were a new experience for, as a single mother and teacher, they were not items which could adorn her budget. Afterwards, she went shopping for she wanted to buy Étienne a memento of these days.

Having refused the invitation to lunch, Étienne got back to the hotel room early in the afternoon. Dominique had not returned. He was as determined on his course of action as he ever would be. He knew Joseph wouldn't like it, but his intuition was grasping his stomach with fear. With great certainty he went to the armchair and, with hotel paper and pen balanced on a magazine on his lap, he started to draft a letter to Kennedy. It would be sent as soon as he was back at Château de Gressier.

His message was simple. The arrangements under which he shipped de Gressier wines from Cherbourg to Québec would end on 31st December. He would be pleased to continue to sell Kennedy the same number of cases from the beginning of next year as he had been for the last seven years and at the same price as he had charged the previous year. He also offered to supply forty barrels of 'Château Auberre', the name Dominique had invented for his new Merlot and Cabernet Sauvignon blend. After 'the angels share[23]', it would be enough wine for over ten thousand bottles. There was one major difference. He would not ship to Québec anymore. He would only deliver to a port in the United Kingdom; any port of Joseph's choosing but he would

[23] Evaporation

get paid immediately his wine was on board ship in Cherbourg. He would no longer take the 50% import risk he had been taking. As he explained in his letter, Kennedy had gone to great pains to show him there was none.

Étienne shared his work with Dominique immediately she returned to the room. So focused was he on his efforts that he failed to notice the small but important changes she had made to her style. Feeling bruised, Dominique read Étienne's missive. "Very good, very sensible," she said sternly, as though she were a teacher commenting on his work.

"Do you think so?" he asked, seeking her added assurance.

"Yes." It was a simple retort which summed up Dominique's growing resentment at not being noticed.

"To lose Joseph as a customer would be very bad for our business," stated Étienne nervously.

"For Joseph to lose you as a supplier would be very bad for his," replied Dominique confidently.

With that, Étienne neatly folded his work in half, placed it on the table and looked up. "You look lovely," he said gently. "Different, but lovely."

One compartment of his mind had closed, and another had opened. "I don't know what you've done but its suits you. It really does."

With those few words, the outside world, which had previously crowded into their bedroom, left, allowing the two lovers to resume doing what lovers like doing best.

"I have a present for you," said Dominique, as the cool of the evening started to stream through their bedroom window. She climbed naked from their bed and searched through her handbag.

Étienne always thought there was something very sensuous in the way Dominique moved when she had no clothes on. It was as though, knowing she was being watched, she deliberately sought to move with greater grace and poise.

"I want you to have something to remind you of here, of us, now," she said as she handed a parcel of tissue paper.

Étienne unwrapped his gift carefully to reveal three small silver maple leaves each etched with its veins, identical in shape but slightly different in size. Each of the silver stalks was set in a base of polished maple so they could stand together or apart. They were an exquisite, breath taking work of art.

"I thought of only buying either one or two of the bigger pieces, the mummy and the daddy, but it didn't seem right. It needed to be kept whole. I then realised what the small leaf represented to us," said Dominique.

Étienne's mind raced nervously ahead as it seemed obvious to him that the smaller piece might be a reference to a baby or child they did not have.

"It represents how little we have of each other, but how ..." Dominique stopped, got off the bed again, and took the three leaves to the table. "Look," she said. "With the smallest placed in the middle, how important it becomes. That's us. It shows how the little bits of time we share together count towards our whole lives. It makes the whole picture. It's a picture of who we are."

It was an observation which left Étienne truly humbled.

Chapter 82

Québec August - September 1928

ÉTIENNE AND DOMINIQUE stood at the stern of the SS Empress of Scotland and studied the meandering path of green and white phosphorus created by the turn of the ship's propeller. They watched the shoreline as Quebec disappeared into the background. The river was still. Hardly a ripple appeared on the surface.

"It's a beautiful city," said Dominique wistfully. "I think I could live there."

"They say it's the Paris of the Americas. It's a city for lovers," said Étienne, as he leaned closer and took hold of her hand. "Perhaps we should go there next?"

Dominique didn't answer and a heavy silence fell between them. Each was drawn deep in to their own thoughts. Not least, Étienne who was not only dreading the journey home but had a bigger unvoiced fear.

He had placed the draft of his letter in a compartment of his brief case for safe keeping. He was certain it had been there. For he had checked it several times. Now, the day before they sailed for home, it had gone missing. Étienne was certain it had been taken, not least because the three silver maple leaves, which he had placed on top of his case before going to dinner the night before, had been moved to the side. He asked Dominique about it just the once, but her denial of any knowledge confirmed his worst fears. It had been deliberately stolen. Why, he did not know.

"Do you know the English have a much nicer name for voyage de noces?" asked Dominique breaking into Étienne's thoughts. It was a question which reflected her thinking. "They call it a honeymoon, le lune de miel."

"We call it that too," interrupted Étienne, still not engaging fully with Dominique's train of thought.

"Honey, le miel, because in ancient times it represented fertility. Apparently, the father of the bride would give the groom honey beer for a whole month to restore him, hence the word moon, lune," she said.

Étienne looked at Dominique puzzled. He found it very strange that any father would want to assist a man to have sex with his daughter.

"I think we should call these few days in Québec our jours de miel" said Dominique, "for they have been just like honey ... sweet, natural, lovely.

Étienne squeezed her hand. "Les jours de miel," he said. "It's perfect."

"You know it can't get better than these last few days, don't you?" said Dominique seriously.

Étienne puffed out in response, not really understanding what she meant.

"We can't be together. You know that, don't you," she said. "You can't leave Juliette and your children for me. I know you think about it, but you can't do it. I won't let you. I can't and I won't." There was as steeliness in her voice.

"And if we have children?"

Dominique paused for the question shocked her. Did he think about these things too she wondered?

"Because I'd like that," he added.

"Étienne," said Dominique formally and then she paused as she thought. "To have your baby would be wonderful. I couldn't think of anything nicer, but it can't be, it won't be. We have this far and no further." She gesticulated with her hands to emphasise the boundaries she was setting.

"You know just before I go to sleep at night, I think of you," said Étienne. "When I wake up in the morning, I think of you again."

"How do you think that makes Juliette feel?" said Dominique, her tone reflecting her disapproval.

Étienne thought for a long while. "I don't know" he said. "It's strange. At the same time, maybe a bit before, maybe a bit afterwards, I'm thinking of her too, but she's there to touch and to hold and you're not. I suppose it's that which makes the difference. She has me with her and you do not."

"Do you think we would have become lovers if Georges hadn't been killed?" asked Dominique. It was a question she could never answer for herself.

"Oh yes," said Étienne confidently. "You and I are written in the stars. It's meant to be. You know that don't you. Whatever happens, I will never, ever stop loving you."

Chapter 83

Bordeaux November 1930

AN AIR OF gloom set over Étienne as he travelled back to Château de Gressier from London. His pre-Christmas sales visits had not gone well. The stock market crash, some twelve months earlier, had taken its toll leaving many of his customers without money, and those that had it were not spending, otherwise than at much lower prices compared to the year before. Over the last few years, inflation had increased his costs out of all proportion, and as Étienne had already discovered, business was not much fun when the outgoings exceeded the incomings. He also knew he was about to have a difficult conversation with Juliette, because he had done something which he didn't think she would approve.

In the quiet of his empty first-class carriage Étienne thanked his lucky stars for the new contract he had signed with Kennedy. It was over double the volume of their original contract and the US Dollar price he was being paid had remained the same. The devaluation of the franc against the dollar meant that Étienne was now getting almost four times the amount in francs per bottle than he had when their deal was first done. It was this one contract which was keeping the de Gressier business alive.

It was unlike Kennedy to accept Étienne's Québec proposal without a fight, but he did. There was only one change to Étienne's proposal and that was the idea of a new Château Auberre blended wine was abandoned "for another day," wrote Kennedy.

The reason for the change of heart, Joe Kennedy was in a different fight. As a result of his impeccable understanding of markets, he had foreseen what was coming. While he was still telling everyone to buy, he was in a race to sell everything he possibly could and turn it into cash.

There was another reason Étienne and Juliette had to thank Joe Kennedy. It was a throwaway remark, made by him during his Québec trip, which had caught Étienne's attention and started him thinking.

"This can't go on," said Kennedy melancholy. He was referring to the perpetual increase in stock market prices. "When the bellboy is giving stock tips, then disaster is guaranteed. In any case," he continued, with an unusual flatness in his voice, "there will be a time when the infrastructure is built, and everyone has all the electric lights, cookers, irons, and vacuum cleaners that they need. Consumer demand can't keep pumping the electrification economy forever. Someday it will end, and when it does, so the whole darn thing will come crashing down." He then added, "it will make the Dutch tulip bulb market bubble look like a teddy bears' picnic."

Kennedy's talk of a tulip bulb bubble played on Étienne's mind. On his next visit to the library he learnt the apocryphal story of how, over a few days in 1637, the rarest of tulip bulbs had traded for as much as ten times the average person's salary, and then the price fell to be worth just a small fraction of the original purchase price. Allegedly, it left many people in ruin, particularly those who had borrowed to join in the speculation. It was a story which captured Étienne's interest. He had taught himself about business, and his knowledge of international trade and exchange rates had come by accident, but there was a whole world of finance out there which he now knew he didn't understand.

It was this lack of knowledge which prompted Étienne to start withdrawing books on economics from the library on his Thursday visits. He absorbed himself in them as though they were the latest novel. After he had read the leading French books, he focused on those in English. He then turned to the financial pages of the papers, which he started to find fascinating, and when in London he discovered The Financial Times, he arranged to have it delivered to him at home every day.

It was one evening, when articulating to Juliette his reasons for believing that anyone who had invested in a US company, whose share price had suddenly collapsed, deserved to lose their money, that the scales fell from his eyes.

"Joe advised us to invest in that stock," said Juliette, casually.

"Are you sure?"

"Yes, of course. I remember the name. I also remember being told by Papa's lawyer that if Kennedy recommends you buy a share then you sell it, and if he says sell then you buy. They said that you could almost guarantee that Joe Kennedy would be doing exactly the opposite to what he recommends, so I ignored it."

"You know, if we had conducted our military campaigns with the same lack of critical analysis as the financial markets apply, then we would have been charged with negligence," said Étienne, with real anger in his voice.

Juliette nodded obligingly.

"The stock market doesn't base its decisions on facts, or even sensible predictions. It's a market of gossip and rumour, with only a very few, those with inside knowledge like Joe, who make the money. The rest of us are just their patsies." As he spoke, he got more agitated at the immorality of it all.

"Do you own any shares?" asked Étienne.

"In my Trust, of course."

"Then sell them."

"Why?"

"Because, we should only trust ourselves and no one else." There was a touch of irritation in his voice. "We should only invest in businesses which we know. Why should we trust putting a franc into anyone else's business? It's foolhardy."

At first, Juliette disagreed, pointing to her father's success in investing. When Étienne pointed out the control features which her father exercised through his private equity investment agreements, and the lack of control she had over her stock market investments, Juliette reluctantly agreed, more to keep the peace than in any conviction, that Étienne was right. So early in May 1929, Juliette wrote to her Trustees and financial advisers giving them instructions to sell everything they had invested in. Apart from £5,000, which they were to keep in cash, the rest was to be spent in buying gold, for it was the only asset which appeared to Étienne to be inflation proof.

Juliette's advisers argued back pointing out how much money their advice had made for her in the past and imploring her not to sell, or at least to keep the gilts. She and Étienne talked through the night on what to do. Eventually she demanded that they sell everything, and so it was that, when the Stock Markets around the world crashed in October 1929 and the Great Depression started, Juliette's wealth, including that which had been gifted to her by Penrose, had been protected. Some would later say that they were lucky, not realising how hard Étienne had worked at understanding finance so he could make that luck.

The question before Étienne and Juliette now was whether they should cash in some of her gold and buy the vineyard which was directly opposite them on the other side of the river. It had been owned by an American bankrupted in the crash. When Étienne left de Gressier to join the army, the valley hills on the other side of the river had been a picture of growing vines under a clear sky. Then its new American owner built a huge white ranch-style house on the brow of the hill; a property more in keeping with the southern states of the USA than the vineyards of France. The house was called La Maison de Louis, as the American came from Louisville, but as a sign of their disapproval, Étienne and Juliette nicknamed the house 'La Bête Blanche'.

Before Étienne's trip to London, Juliette and he had decided that they shouldn't buy La Bête Blanche and his trip to London had confirmed the wisdom of their decision. However, in the loneliness of his hotel room, the thought of the fields of La Bête Blanche being owned by anyone else niggled Étienne, causing him to toss and turn. It was 60 hectares of land which he knew he could make profitable. It was late in the evening when he got the hotel to telegram the seller's agents with a proposal that he would rent the land for a period of seven years with an option to buy at any time over that period. A telegram had come back by return saying that the offer was accepted provided he paid a 10% non-refundable deposit for the option.

Étienne hadn't shared his proposal with Juliette, and it was this which had been making him anxious as to what she might say, for they had always discussed everything like this. He consoled himself with the fact that, if she didn't agree, he could always withdraw from the transaction by refusing to accept the seller's revised terms.

On his arrival at Gare Saint Jean in Bordeaux, Étienne took a taxi to Château de Gressier. Instead of going straight there, he decided he would turn into La Bête Blanche's vineyards. He wanted to see exactly what was on the land. In all the years he had lived at de Gressier, he had never been onto La Bête Blanche's land; not even when swimming had he climbed onto their side of the riverbank.

As the taxi bumped its way along the drive towards the white house, Étienne tapped on the driver's shoulder to stop, for there, working in the fields, were three of his workers. What the hell were they doing here, he wondered. He started to get out of the taxi to remonstrate with them, but a sixth sense told him that there was something most odd about what he had seen. He abandoned the idea of an immediate scolding. There were too many of them for this to be an accident. It was a matter to be discussed with Hugo Coudace in the morning.

That evening Étienne shared with Juliette his proposal for La Bête Blanche. He was relieved when she agreed they would do the deal on offer. There was only one condition laid down by Juliette, on which she was emphatic. The wine from La Bête Blanche was never to be mixed or branded with the wines of Château de Gressier. Étienne agreed without hesitation, suggesting the name Château Auberre for the wine from these 60 hectares, not admitting where the name had come from. It was only when he had made a solemn promise to that effect, was Juliette truly satisfied and she approved the deal.

Étienne said nothing to her about their Estate workers working in the fields they did not yet own. Instead, he sent a letter to the seller's agent with a long list of questions regarding the vineyard. In particular, he wanted the name of its current manager and the names of all its employees.

Two days later Étienne had some answers to his questions. Others would follow later, but he got the two important ones he needed. The General Manager was Monsieur Delors, and the vineyard had no employees. They had all been laid off. Still Étienne said nothing to Juliette. Instead, braving his aqua-mysophobia, he quietly toured his Estate to identify and count the men working on his land. Day after day he found there was always one man missing, sometimes two, may be three, but it was never the same men. Étienne drove around looking for the missing men, expecting them to be at La Bête Blanche, but there was never any sign of them there, or anywhere.

Late each Wednesday night, Coudace left Étienne the week's time sheets which calculated the wages to be paid to the men. It paid everyone for the work they had done and would be doing that week through to the Friday, adjusted for any overtime or time off in the week before. For the first time in a long time, Étienne studied the sheets carefully. There were no adjustments for the men who had been absent. Étienne decided it would be premature to say anything, because if, as he now suspected, he was paying the wages of men working elsewhere, Coudace could have reasonably argued that the adjustments would, as normal, be made in the following week's calculations. He had no option but to watch and wait and hope that he was wrong.

Étienne's audit of his men continued quietly over the next week. It almost became an obsession for him to observe, undetected, where they were during the day. Every day there was either one or two men missing, and he had no idea where they were. Ever since he had taken charge, those eleven years ago, he had trusted the men to go about their daily duties. Now he felt most aggrieved, almost angry, that they might have been abusing his trust.

Still Étienne said nothing to Juliette about the absconding men. However, she could not fail to notice how something unsaid was troubling him, for he went into a shell, rarely concentrating on the subject matter of their conversation.

When Coudace submitted the wage sheets on Wednesday night, with no adjustments for the week before, all of Étienne's fears where confirmed. He was being cheated, and he hated it. What he didn't know was whether it was just Coudace involved in the deception, or the men as well. He puzzled about this for some hours. Eventually, he decided to pay the wages in full per the claim sheet, except this time he would hand out the payslips personally and not leave it to Coudace. It was, he concluded, only when they had the money in their hands, for some time, that he could prove he had been defrauded, and not just an attempt made to defraud him. It was then that he would make his challenge, on all of them!

With the wages sheet tucked under his arms, it was a very agitated

Étienne who mounted his motorbike for his weekly trip to the bank. He only used his car on wet, rainy or icy days as he preferred the thrill of racing through the lanes with the wind rushing through his hair. He also found that by riding his bike fast he couldn't think of other things, whereas in the car he found his mind would wander. He didn't want that happening today.

As he drove out of the village, over the river bridge and towards Bordeaux, Étienne had a change of plan. He suddenly turned left onto La Bête Blanche's drive, proceeded up to the white house and parked. He found Monsieur Delors on the veranda, wrapped up and sitting comfortably, reading the previous day's paper, and supping at a cup of coffee.

Étienne introduced himself. Delors said he knew who he was, which Étienne found strange because they had never met. It was when Delors revealed that he knew about the offer Étienne had made that it became clear that Delors worked for the land agent who had looked after the estate for the owner.

"Can I ask about the men who work here?" said Étienne casually, "I am worried about their jobs."

"Did you not see our letter?"

Étienne nodded to signify he had.

"As we said, there are none. Not for the last five or six years. We do the same as you. We hire our workers through Monsieur Coudace."

"Do you pay Coudace for these workers or do you pay them directly?"

"We pay him each week. His staff sign time sheets and we pay him against those."

Étienne's body turned to steel as it dawned on him for how long he had been cheated.

"He also gets twenty cents for each bottle of wine produced at the end of the harvest as his fee. Is this the same for you?"

"No," said Étienne abruptly. "He just gets paid. Do you have all your worker's wage sheets?"

"Yes, Why?"

Étienne didn't say what he was thinking. He just knew that these sheets would be essential in proving Coudace had been stealing from him.

"Are they signed by each worker?"

"Yes, I think so. In any case everyone has to sign in and out."

Monsieur Delors had been leaning back in his seat, treating Étienne's visit casually but with the obvious change in his visitor's demeanour, Delors started to lean forward and engage more closely.

"What are your plans?" asked Étienne.

"I work for the agents selling the business," answered Delors. "There is no profit for us in the deal you've done so I am off site tomorrow."

"Oh, I'm sorry," said Étienne, feeling guilty that he was putting people out of work. "Could I come and see you then, before you go, to find out more about the Estate?" he asked

"Yes, but I know very little. I have only been here a couple of days a week for the past few months. The man to ask is Monsieur Coudace."

Étienne repeated Coudace's name and grimaced. "Does he know you're leaving?"

"Not yet, but it's not a conversation I am looking forward to having because I can't see him getting his per bottle fee; not unless you agree to give it to him."

"Are all the wage records here?" asked Étienne, at the same time shaking his head to suggest that no per bottle fee would be paid to Hugo Coudace.

"Yes," said Delors, frowning slightly at the fact that Étienne was returning to the same subject. "Look, it would be helpful if you didn't mention our conversation to Monsieur Coudace until I've spoken to him," said Delors. "Would that be all right?"

"Of course," said Étienne having no reason not to agree. "I am going into Bordeaux now and won't be back until late evening," he continued.

Monsieur Delors handed Étienne his business card, saying he would be pleased to be involved in the future of the Estate in a professional capacity. Étienne liked the way Delors had emphasised the word 'professional', making it clear he expected to be paid for his advice. As Étienne left, both men were comfortable in the relationship they had forged.

The moment Étienne mounted his motorbike to continue his

journey, he felt sick to the stomach. The sacking of Coudace was not a subject he wanted to discuss with Juliette. He knew her first reaction would be to defend him.

Chapter 84

Bordeaux November 1930.

FROM THE START, Dominique knew there was something different about the day. She could sense it.

"Is there something wrong at home?" she asked Étienne as she served lunch, worried that there might be a problem with Juliette or the twins.

"No," he replied briefly, "but there's a problem at work which I have to sort out." He paused, "It's not going to be nice. It made me forget about Juliette's reading list, so she's going to be cross with me for bringing back the same books as she gave me."

Dominique instinctively knew from the way Étienne deflected from his work problem to Juliette that, if he wanted to explain further, he would, so she said nothing more. Instead, they both sat looking over the estuary, holding hands over the small dining room table in virtual silence; each relaxed in the other's company, knowing that the other was there for them. Nothing else had to be said, each was content in their relationship, except it was obvious that something was on Étienne's mind.

When Dominique was in the kitchen area clearing away the lunch things, very unusually Étienne joined her. Dominique was still in her school clothes. Long had gone the day when she rushed home and changed before he got there. By the kitchen sink, he started to undo the buttons on the cuff of the sleeves of her long blue buttoned-down dress and, as she tried to wriggle and slap him away, he undid the front, freeing it over her shoulders to fall to the floor. There was a serious, purposefulness behind Étienne which was unlike him.

While it was nearly always Étienne who initiated them going to bed, there had always been a mutuality about when they made love, but not today. Étienne was being determined, masterful even, and there was something about it which Dominique found both disturbing and arousing. Stripped naked and bent over, with her head resting on her arm which lay on the kitchen table, she was entirely ready for him when he took her from behind. What she was not ready for was his animal-like behaviour. He was not thinking about her at all as he pounded into her, pulling on her hips, and pushing down the small of her back, then slapping her buttocks and pulling her head right back with her hair. He was being completely dominant, and yet she found she liked the feeling. He was filling her completely until his dam broke and he twitched and pulsated inside her. At this point, she felt his legs go weak and he collapsed breathlessly, lying completely still along her back.

Not once, since they had returned from Québec, had they had sex without taking precautions. It meant that Dominique was now overcome, confused at what had happened. Not just by the sensation, which she had found amazing, but she had trusted him to withdraw on time, and he had not. Now, bent over, her eyes closed, with her head still resting on her arm, with his hot breath panting on her neck, Dominique's immediate thought was whether she might be pregnant. She stood up, turned around and he wrapped her in the comfort of his arms. She cuddled up to him very tightly and looked into his eyes Then, she did something which, she thought afterwards was odd. "Thank you," she said. His smile would be the one she would remember forever.

As with every Thursday, Étienne was gone by 4.30pm. It was so, by the time Dominique's son came home, there was nothing to show he had been there; apart from a small envelope with the name Stephen B marked on it which he always left behind.

There was a sharp bite in the air when Étienne left. He descended the stairs, and as he mounted his motorbike, he wrapped his scarf around his face and neck. He pulled on his gloves and looked up to the top of the stairs, but she had gone. Dominique had moved to the balcony to see him off, but he hadn't noticed. He pulled down his goggles and drove away. She waved and was disappointed he didn't wave or look back.

At the end of her short drive, Étienne stopped at the junction before taking the road towards Bordeaux. He thought of Dominique and how much he loved her. He wanted to turn back and tell her, to convince her that she meant the world to him. Did she really understand how important she was to his very being, he wondered. As he rested there, the engine purring idly between his legs, he realised that he wanted to say precisely the same to Juliette. He wanted to go both forwards and backwards at the same time and so he stayed still, incapable of deciding. Why was his life so complicated, he wondered, as his tummy churned with anxiety. He was filled with a dread that something might be lost.

It was the word 'complicated' which moved Étienne's thoughts to the conversation he knew he must have tomorrow. It was this which caused him to rev up his bike and pull away. As he gathered speed, Étienne started to rehearse what he was going to say, knowing that when the time came, none of his pre-planned words would be used with the same neatness that they currently sat in his mind.

Dominique moved to the settee where she played with the wage packet Étienne had left behind. She could never take this money for her, but money from an officer of her husband's Regiment for his son's education, that was something quite different. For the first time ever, she wondered whether he was using her just for sex, and this was her payment. No better than a common prostitute, she wondered, while knowing, deep down, it wasn't the case. However, she knew it was something which she needed to think about. So this week, as with every week before, the envelope went into a basket in the drawer at the bottom of her wardrobe, where it lay unopened, with all the others. Uncharacteristically for Dominique, the thinking was always something she was going to do tomorrow, but that tomorrow never came.

What Dominique was certain of was that something strange had happened that day, and it worried her. It wasn't that she might be pregnant. It was that she had the most frightful premonition that something bad was about to happen. What, she did not know.

Chapter 85

Latoire Village November 1930.

THE MAN DROVE the length of the road two or three times before he chose his spot. He was looking for two trees either side of the road and opposite each other. He had been here many times before selecting exactly where, but now he had to be certain. A little further on, he drove off the tarmacked road onto a track, only three or four metres deep, towards a gate. There he stopped as he now had a perfect view of the field directly ahead and, most importantly, the road which ran adjacent to its right-hand edge. He moved as close as he could up to the fence, so that his van was hidden from those approaching down the lane he had come.

The man took a bundle of wire and some wire clippers from the back of his van and walked quickly to the other side of the road. He expertly secured the wire around the tree trunk taking great pains to ensure it was just the right height for the task it had to do.

He unwound the coil and moved to the tree across the road and directly opposite, and after measuring to make sure the other end of the wire went around this tree trunk twice, he cut it with his wire cutters. He then walked diagonally across the road with the end of the wire in his hand and laid it on the verge adjacent to the road. Once he had picked up the unused roll of wire, the man returned to his van, threw it in the back and settled down to wait. In the shelter of his van, he was protected in part from the autumn chill. He kept his window open as he listened intently for any sound, his eyes fixed on the road running to the right of the field opposite him.

The sun had set about an hour before, but with heavy grey clouds drifting slowly in the sky, dusk had come early. The air was still and there was an eeriness in the trees until some way off in the distance, he could hear the pop-popping sound of a motorbike. The man sat up attentively and reaching for his binoculars studied the road looking for a moving light. In the half-light they failed to work, so he threw them away angrily into the passenger's footwell. Suddenly, a motorbike came into view. While the man tried hard to identify the rider, the bike kept appearing and disappearing behind trees and bushes, denuded by the autumn winds, such that he couldn't be sure it was his target. "It has to be him," he told himself. "It has to be him," he said, this time out loud by way of reinforcing his hope that this was his prey.

The man scampered out of the van, found the end of the wire and was rushing to the opposite tree when it became apparent that the sound was not coming closer but fading away into the darkness. The man retraced his steps with the wire and returned to the van. His nerves were completely on edge. His breathing was hard and laboured. He could feel the adrenalin rushing through his fingers, causing a build-up of lactic acid so that he had to keep stretching and curling them to remove the discomfort.

He listened carefully once again; this time closing his eyes in concentration, for now he knew that his first warning would be sound and only then sight.

In the distance, there was the sound of another motorbike. This time the man was certain that this was the one. He had heard it before. It had the deep throaty purr of a 750cc engine working at only a fraction of its capacity. He climbed out of the van and moved to the gate where, holding the top bar, he stared for the light of the bike. Suddenly, the bike's headlights flashed through the trees. He found he could not see the rider but nevertheless he was certain it was his quarry.

This time the man rushed to the end of the wire, and holding it tightly with two hands, he pulled it to the opposite tree. Again, making sure the wire was level and at the right height, he wrapped the end twice around the trunk, and with his clippers in hand, he expertly secured it. The length of the wire now stretched tautly across the road.

Étienne didn't stand a chance. The wire caught him around the mouth and as he travelled on so it flicked his head backwards slicing his brain straight off. He was dead in an instant, and therefore completely oblivious to his body scraping along the ground, tearing his skin into shreds as he travelled, first entangled, and then disentangled from his bike.

The man's first job, after the bike had hit the ground, was to cut the wire free from the trees at both ends and roll it up. His first reaction was to throw it far into the ditch, but realising it was incriminating evidence, he threw it into the back of his van, determined that it would be gone from there in the morning.

His second job was to get the satchel. He approached Étienne's body carefully trying not to step in any of the blood or brains spread along the road. He started to cut the strap with his pruning knife, and although it was very sharp, it took time with a slow sawing action before it was in two and could be pulled away.

With the satchel safely recovered, the man returned to his van and placed his gloved hands on the steering wheel. He stared straight ahead as, once again, he stretched his fingers wide open and then closed them again. Fighting every sinew in his body to flee, he sat still and forced his breathing to slow down as he emptied the contents of the satchel onto the passenger seat. Once he felt he had his body under control, he pulled the starter button on the van and immediately the engine came to life. He reversed out of the siding and drove off in the direction from which the motorbike had come. He made a point of not switching on the van lights for his eyes were already acclimatised to the darkness and he didn't want to attract attention to his movements.

At the 'T' junction, three quarters of a mile from where Étienne's body lay, the man turned in a circle, mounted the grass verge as he went, and returned down the road from where he had come. Three hundred metres from the site of the execution, the executioner launched the satchel out of the window, past the grass verge and deep into the hedge.

All his efforts were now focused on a successful getaway. Using what little natural light was left, the man slowly and carefully manoeuvred his way past Étienne's body and the blood and gore spread down the road. The front wheels of the motorbike had stopped revolving, while those at the rear continued to be driven by the engine which was still ticking over. With his heightened senses, the noise seemed much louder than it actually was and increased his worry of discovery. He took care to make sure he did not drive on the grassy verge and then, with his eyes peeled wide, he made his way as fast as he could down the road which was well known to him.

The man had one more task to achieve before he could retreat home, and that was to create his alibi. So, at the point where the road ran downhill, he switched off the engine and allowed the van to freewheel. He braked so as to turn left into Château de Gressier's courtyard and then allowed the momentum and the slope to take the van silently down the tarmacked road to the machinery shed where all the château's vehicles were always parked. There was just enough momentum to get the van into the shed where he brought it to a stop. He gathered up the wage packets which he threw hurriedly into his day bag. But it was the sound of his feet crunching on the cobbles, as he walked away from the van and into the vineyard's office, which seemed to him to be, at that moment, the loudest sound in the world.

In the office, the man phoned the telephone exchange to make his second call of the day to Paris. The time between the two calls, as recorded by the exchange telephonist, was 37 minutes. He then went into the kitchen to see Juliette's cook, staying for just a few minutes saying he had to leave to make a phone call to Paris; a call which he had just made.

His alibi set, the man headed for home where he spilled all the wage packets onto his table. He counted them once and then counted them again. He needed to make sure every package was accounted for. He then ripped into them rapidly, sorting the cash from the envelopes and wage slips inside. He methodically piled the notes into their different denominations, not noticing that they were brand new because they always were, and placed them on his table top. He threw the envelopes and payslips into the grate to burn in the fire which had previously been the home of a few burned embers, but now started to flicker with flames of different colours.

The man counted the money and placed it into a brown paper

bag. He then climbed down the stairs which took him deep into the basement. There, hidden high in an old chimney breast, he removed a beautifully polished handmade wooden box wrapped in a green felt cloth. He unwrapped the box carefully and reached for the key which was dangling from a nail secured into a timber beam directly above his head. He unlocked the box, and as he opened it and saw the cash inside, he smiled.

The man removed the money from the paper bag and added his new gains to the wooden box, bundling similar denominations together, as if he were a cashier in the bank. He locked the box, re-wrapped the felt cloth around it, and replaced it, back high into the chimney. It was as safe a storage place as had ever been made.

The man climbed the stairs, turned off the light and shut the door to the basement. He picked up a bottle of cognac and moved to sit in a hard, wooden chair close to the window. He took a sip of the brandy and smiled. He closed his eyes, and in the darkness his mind repeatedly showed the crashed motorbike with the wheels going around, but no sight of the body or the decapitated head. He breathed heavily and with contentment, for there was no remorse. Far from it, the path was now clear to get what he really wanted. Something far more precious than money or power, it was a possession he had dreamed of and yearned for; something he had to have. It was an obsession that had dominated his dreams ever since he saw her. Now he was going to make her his, however long it took. He knew it would start with a phone call. All he had to do was wait.

Chapter 86

Latoire Village November 1930.

IT WAS HUGO Coudace who found Étienne's body. He had received a telephone call from an anxious Juliette; it was nine o'clock and her husband still wasn't at home. He was, she exclaimed, never later than their supper time. Coudace waylaid her concerns, but by ten o'clock, with her voice breaking in high-pitched anxiety, Juliette demanded he do something. Coudace called at Château de Gressier to find Juliette, in a cream silk dressing gown, pacing the floor as though she were a caged tiger. Coudace calmed her down and then proceeded to make phone calls to the police, the hospital, the doctor and even the local restaurants and cafes to see if he could track Étienne down. As he spoke, he delighted in watching her every move. With the light of the fire radiating behind her, he could see her slender legs and the fact that she was wearing nothing under her dressing gown. It was this sight which made his heart beat faster.

"I'm sure his motorbike has broken down and he's pushing it home," said Coudace to Juliette in words of comfort. At eleven o'clock, in response to Juliette's pleading, Coudace ventured out to go and search for Étienne.

Coudace turned left out of the gate, and as he was accelerating towards the main road, he was late in seeing Étienne's motorbike in the middle of the road. He braked hard and swerved to miss it. With the van out of control and failing to respond to his turn of the wheel, it careered into Étienne's body dragging it along the road as it disappeared under the wheels and engine.

Coudace reversed, allowing Étienne's body to unroll from beneath the van, and it was only when it was visible in his car lights did he stop and look. He didn't get out. He didn't want to for, from where he was sitting, he could see that Étienne was dead.

Coudace turned the van around slowly and drove back to the Château, carefully preparing his words to tell Juliette she was a widow. Instead of going into the house, he went to the vineyard's office and there, just before midnight, Coudace phoned the police to report a dreadful accident, and the death of Étienne Guégan.

Chapter 87

Latoire Village November 1930

INSPECTOR HENRI HILAIRE listened carefully, writing a few notes in the note book he kept by the side of the phone. The conversation ended with him asking that they instruct his driver to come and collect him immediately. He looked up at the clock and, as always, noted the time. He was pleased, really pleased, for, as a Judicial Police Officer of the National Gendarmerie, he was authorised to investigate cases of possible murder, and he had a probable new case.

Hilaire was not particularly popular with his colleagues. It wasn't that he was liked or disliked. They simply found him a little strange. Everything he did had an unnatural precision and efficiency about it. His desk had an order rarely found in a police station. His pen, pencil and papers were always placed neatly on his desk. If he found a file out of order, he would have to refile it in accordance with the set procedure. Some found his behaviour both obsessive and tedious, while respecting his output, for he was a prodigious worker. He never went for a drink or associated after work with his colleagues. He was a man who was happy to be on his own.

As a detective, he was expected to wear civilian clothes, but Hilaire never did. He was always immaculately turned out in his uniform. Some claimed he did it to show off his bravery medal, but Hilaire never thought getting shot was a particularly brave thing to do. It just happened to him because he was in the wrong place at the wrong time. To Hilaire it was only common sense. He wore his uniform because he looked much younger than his years and it gave him an immediate authority in every circumstance. Further, it was more efficient as he didn't have to waste time explaining who he was and what he did. Most importantly, he didn't have to choose what to wear each morning.

Another thing that set Hilaire apart was his incredible politeness and courtesy. Rare for a policeman, he never swore. He never joked either but always politely joined in the jokes of others. It was for these attributes that his colleagues accepted and were happy to work with him.

As Inspector Hilaire was driven to the crime scene, he was bothered by his delight at the job in front of him; for hadn't a man died? It had been over a year since he had been sent on a murder investigation course in Paris, and in that time, he had only investigated one murder - a crime passionnel which he didn't think counted because the wife immediately admitted stabbing her husband.

As an Inspector, Hilaire was given a chauffeur but more often than not he preferred to drive with his driver in the passenger seat. Not so at this ungodly hour of the morning. Hilaire sat in the back, his briefcase on his lap, as he scribbled away, reminding himself of the key points he needed to deal with at the crime scene. His course had been a long time ago and he was worried he might forget something important.

It was just after four o'clock in the morning when Hilaire's car stopped behind a crowd of people lined up against a rope which had been placed as a barrier across the road. He got out, leaving his briefcase behind in the car, put on his cap, pulled down his jacket and then stretched himself to his full 1.9m height. He stood still for a moment and then paced off towards the crowd, which parted like the Sea of Galilee, as he made his way towards Étienne's body. What were so many people doing here at this time, he wondered?

Hilaire immediately noticed that the local gendarmerie had done a good job of securing the area. Two policemen instantly arrived in front of him. One young and green behind the gills, the other elderly who had clipped the ears of more youths than Hilaire had even encountered. Both spoke at once, telling the same facts until they started taking a sentence in turn. They acted like young children trying to tell an exciting story to their father.

The body was that of Monsieur Étienne Guégan, owner of Château de Gressier, they said. His wife had reported him missing to Monsieur Coudace, the General Manager of the Estate, who late in the evening had gone to look for him. Monsieur Guégan had been in an accident. He had come off his motorbike and was lying on the road. Unfortunately, Monsieur Coudace didn't see Monsieur Guégan's body and drove over it by accident in the van he was driving. They had attended, as a result of a phone call from Monsieur Coudace to what he reported was an accident, but it was the priest, when saying the prayer for the dead, who noticed that Monsieur Guégan's head had been sliced clean in two. He had been decapitated with a wire which had been strung across the road. Every Thursday, Monsieur Guégan went to the bank to collect the wages which are then paid on Friday morning. He always used the same satchel, and this was missing. It was obvious to them that Monsieur Guégan had been murdered for money. To the two officers, this was an open and shut case. The motive was money and the culprit would be someone who knew of Monsieur Guégan's routine.

"Why are all these people here?" asked Hilaire, pointing to the crowd which had gathered at the village end of the road.

They're from the village, mostly estate workers, wanting to know what's happening, when they're going to be able to go to work and, of equal importance, when are they going to get paid," replied the elder of the two policemen.

Amongst the crowd, Monsieur Ergral, the local photographer, was snapping away, trying to get the shot of the day to sell to the local, and maybe a national, newspaper. Inspector Hilaire spotted him, not by some magic of detection or observation but merely by the fact that the photographer's pushing, shoving and occasional explosion of a flash bulb was causing a discombobulation in an otherwise silent and mournful group. Hilaire told the youngest of the policemen to bring the photographer to him.

Efficiently, Hilaire explained to the photographer what he wanted. His appointment was to be the official crime scene photographer, paid for by the gendarmerie. The photographs were to remain private until after a trial and a conviction; only then could he do what he liked with them. Hilaire stressed the word conviction. He rapidly dictated to the elder policeman, who quickly wrote in his notebook, the terms of the deal struck as evidence of the contract which had been made between them.

Hilaire then took a torch and moved forward to examine Étienne's body and the remains of his head which was smashed around the tarmac. He studied the crashed motorcycle and instructed the photographer of the pictures he wanted taken as he went. He then moved to each of the two trees where he had been told that a wire had been wound around. He noticed that, while the wire around each trunk was still in place, the wire which had gone across the road and acted as the guillotine was missing. "Where is it?" Hilaire asked. Neither of the policemen knew. Whoever had it would be an interesting suspect, he thought.

"Let's move everyone out of here," commanded the Inspector. "I want the road emptied from here, all the way down to the junction this way and then past the entrance to the Château at the other," he said. The two policemen looked at him, each expecting his instructions to have been given to the other. "Now, please," said Hilaire, placing emphasis on the word now. "Each of you take one side and deal with it, now." The word now re-emphasised.

"Where's the doctor?" Hilaire asked them, as they were leaving.

"He has certified death and is with Madame Guégan," replied the younger policeman.

"And the priest?"

"He's there too," said the elder policeman, as they continued to play their ying and yang roles. "The ambulance is also here, waiting to take away the body," he continued, in an attempt to be helpful.

"Please tell everyone they are to go back to their homes. There is nothing to see."

"They are all worried about their wages," said Hilaire's driver, having heard some of the murmurings.

"I am sure they are," replied Hilaire, and after a while he added, "but that's for later, right now we have a crime scene to examine."

Once his audience had gone, Hilaire began to relax into the job he had been trained to do. Everything now had to be done in an orderly manner.

He summed up. "We are missing two things from the crime scene, wire and the wages bag. Anything else? What about his wallet?"

Neither had checked, so Hilaire went to Étienne's body and started to check through his pockets. His wallet and personal possessions, a watch and signet ring, were still there. His wallet was full of cash.

"This was not a professional robbery," he concluded. "Professionals would never have allowed such an opportunity to be missed, unless they were disturbed, and there is no evidence of that, well at least not so far."

Hilaire gave instructions for the remaining wire around the trees to be carefully photographed and then started to pace up and down the road. Daylight was just starting to fill the red sky, now empty of the storm clouds from the previous day.

"They waited here," announced Hilaire, pointing to the gateway where the man had parked.

"They?" asked the young policeman who had been following Hilaire around while waiting to be told what to do.

"Humm," Hilaire exhaled. "He, she, they, it's where the person or persons and the car waited," he said, allowing the car to come into his definition of 'they'.

"Can we cover the body?" asked one of the ambulancemen, as no one had yet given Étienne his dignity in death for fear of upsetting anything.

"Monsieur le Photographe," yelled Hilaire. "Have you taken all the pictures of Monsieur Guégan I asked for?"

"Oui," came the reply.

"Then the body can go to the mortuary for an autopsy."

"You want an autopsy?" the ambulanceman enquired. "Isn't the reason for death obvious?"

"Oui, I suspect it is, but, there will be an autopsy. It is the law and we don't know what else we will find. Was Monsieur Guégan drunk? Until I have the report there is no way we can know this kind of thing."

Hilaire didn't dismiss the ambulanceman, he simply moved away to his former task of studying the car tracks in the gate entrance. He called the photographer over to take pictures as he was sure that these were important clues.

"Please, be very careful and very accurate," he demanded, "these are important. All the way around, three hundred and sixty degrees," he added, to make sure he was properly understood.

"Where's Monsieur Coudace?" Hilaire asked suddenly.

"He's with Madame Guégan," replied the older policeman.

"For God sake, go to him now and take his statement, but nowhere near Madame Guégan. Do you understand?"

The elder policeman was shocked by the ferocity of the order.

"I want you to watch and note carefully everything she does ... they do," he said. "Everything," he stressed.

"You don't suspect Madame Guégan, do you?" asked the elder policeman.

Hilaire's expression said what he did not need to say. Did they not all learn in police basic training that you trusted no one and suspected everyone until you had proved it was not them?

Hilaire called to his driver to bring over a tape measure and for the first time the young man moved away from the car, delighted at last to be included in the investigation.

"Measure the width of the tyres, and the distance between the tyre tracks, and make a note of them in your notebook. In fact, sketch them with precise dimensions." Hilaire ordered.

"We must search the verges from here to the junction," declared Hilaire, as he pointed to the young policeman to take the other side of the road from where he had decided the car had waited for its prey. Hilaire took the opposite side. Their search was thorough but far from fingertip. Each used a stick collected from the ground to bash back the undergrowth. About 500 metres along the road, the young policeman found a satchel. He yelled of his find as he picked it up warily on the end of his stick and laid it on the verge.

"Why did you move it?" Hilaire yelled crossly. "Monsieur le Photographe, here please."

"Where was it exactly?" The young policeman put it back almost exactly as he had found it and the photographer snapped away. "Are you sure it was like that?" questioned Hilaire.

"Oui, just like that," said the young policeman.

"What's your name?" asked Hilaire abruptly.

"Tobie Baume," said the young policeman.

Hilaire repeated his name a couple of times then asked, "What do you make of that, Monsieur?"

"It's been thrown in the getaway," said Baume. "I think the arm that threw it was outside of the vehicle so they could throw it high."

"Why do you think that?"

"Because it landed on the top and not into the side of the bushes."

Hilaire was impressed.

"You know it means that there were two of them, sir," said Baume.

"Why?"

"Because the bag was thrown out of the nearside window as they drove away. It means that someone was driving and someone else was doing the throwing."

Hilaire was even more impressed.

After the sack had been photographed, Baume retrieved it once again and laid it back down on the verge. Hilaire opened it up but, as expected, there was no money inside just Juliette's returning library books. He examined the way the strap had been sliced through, at the same time making a mental note to do some trials to see how long it would take to cut through in practice. His instinct told him it would not be a quick job.

Baume's comments about there being two of them made Hilaire retrace his steps to where the murderers' car had been parked. He placed Étienne's bag on the back seat of his car as he went.

At the gate entrance, Hilaire looked again carefully at the footprints both to the left and right of the car tracks. There were clearly footprints on the right-hand side grouped together, but far fewer on the left-hand side where the driver would have sat. Perhaps Baume was right? The footprint pattern suggested that it was the passenger who had got in and out several times. Then it dawned on Hilaire that the car might have been reversed into the gap, blowing away any other theories.

Are those the same shoes wondered Hilaire before calling out to Baume: "I want you to measure, sketch, and map to scale that area precisely; every step, tyre mark, twig, everything," strangely repeating an order he had already given his driver.

"Did you have a scale in your photographs of this area?" yelled Hilaire to the photographer, who looked back nonplussed at what he was being asked. "A ruler, a pen, anything so we would know the distances later?" The photographer shook his head. "Please do it again, but with a measure in each photograph," instructed Hilaire, as the photographer looked on visibly upset at the obvious reprimand.

Hilaire moved to the trees around which the wire had been tied. He carefully studied the wiring, noticing the way it had been neatly wound back around the main line in order to tie it off. He walked backwards and forwards several times before concluding that it had been tied by the same person, and an expert hand at that. But where was the missing wire, he wondered, for it would almost certainly have deposits of Monsieur Guégan's blood and brains on it? Had the force of his hitting the wire broken it into two parts? He had no idea.

Realising that they had no way of cutting away the wire still wrapped around the tree, Hilaire sent his driver off to borrow a pair of wirecutters. Hilaire resumed the search of the hedgerows and verges on his own. He found nothing else.

At the 'T' junction, the rope blocking off the entrance to the road was still there, but no one was around. There was nothing for them to see, and so the excitement had moved to the village café where almost everyone had congregated, and speculation was rife. Of one thing they were all certain. This was an outside robbery for everyone knew where everyone else was.

Hilaire stood and stared. He looked one way and then the other. Which way did they go, he asked himself. He wandered around a little aimlessly contemplating this problem when, on the verge, he saw some car tracks very similar to those he had been studying just a few moments before. He went to the opposite corner where there were similar tracks. He went over the road and to his delight found another single car track but this time in a curve.

Hilaire walked back to his car where he found his driver waiting patiently for his next instruction. As Hilaire climbed in the back, leaving the door open, he asked his driver to gather his small investigating team around him at the crime scene, which they now had all to themselves. Étienne's body had gone, but the motorbike still lay in the road, exactly where it had come to rest.

"I think we are only looking for one person," said Hilaire to his audience of three people, after he'd stopped writing in his notebook. He knew it was far too few policemen for a murder of this sort. "We'll have to check but I think there is only one set of shoe prints at the gate, and we have the shoe size and sole shape. We have his car tyres and we know he went off in that direction," he added, pointing towards Château de Gressier. "We just have to find them together, and we have our man. If he's still got the money and the missing wire …." The sentence wasn't finished.

Hilaire set his listeners to their tasks which he described with pedantic thoroughness. It was when the photographer seemed more interested in getting away, rather than photographing the car tracks at the 'T' junction, that Hilaire reminded him, most firmly, that all his photographs belonged to the police, and if he showed them to anyone else he would be guilty of impeding a police enquiry. In a strange moment of frailness, Hilaire admitted to not knowing the maximum time in jail for such an offence, but he assured the photographer it would be for an awfully long time. The photographer, convinced of the threat, agreed to take more photographs as ordered and promised to develop the films personally that afternoon and would have them at the police station in Bordeaux before he went to bed.

Hilaire drove himself to Château de Gressier, with his driver in the passenger seat. As they stood under the Gallery with Étienne's bag in Hilaire's hand, they, like every new arrival, had no idea which, of the two identical front doors, they should knock on, The Cottage or The Cellars? This was the bit which Hilaire was dreading for he had heard that, after dealing with the body, dealing with the relatives of murder victim was the worst part of the job.

As Hilaire was contemplating his options, the door to The Cellars was opened by a tall, thick set man with a neat but very heavy beard.

"Madame Guégan, please?" Hilaire asked, his uniform avoiding any need for an introduction.

"Oui" said the bearded man, who had been expecting him.

"And you are?" asked Hilaire.

"I am Hugo Coudace, the General Manager of the Estate of Château de Gressier." Hugo puffed himself up, wanting the Inspector to know the importance of his position. "I look after everything around here when Monsieur Étienne is away. I was the one who found his body."

Hilaire was led through into a large drawing room beautifully decorated with the finest of French furniture carefully collected over the last 100 years. There were a few large paintings, but none were portraits. They were all views either from, or of, Château de Gressier. It was a room hardly ever used, apart from when they had guests.

Juliette had dressed and was now sitting on the couch with her back straight and her head held high. Her face muscles were tight from the strain, but she was determined to show no emotion, certainly not in public. Standing erectly in the corner with his notebook and pencil in hand, looking decidedly uncomfortable, was the elder policeman.

"You have heard the news, Madame?" for Juliette's composure made him uncertain.

'Oui," she replied strongly. Her tone indicating that it was a silly question.

"I am very sorry," Hilaire continued, "but I have some questions I have to ask."

"Of course."

"Do you recognise this?" Hilaire held up Étienne's bag.

"Oui, that is Étienne's. He used it each week to go to the bank and collect the wages."

"I am afraid it only contained some library books when we found it. They were date stamped last week."

"Does this mean we don't have the money to pay the men their wages?" Juliette asked.

Hilaire was thrown by the question, for it was as though the reality of Étienne's death had not registered. But this was a failure to recognise Juliette Guégan was first and foremost a Dovingdon, and in a crises the first thing a Dovingdon does is make a cup of tea and write a list. Paying her men their wages was a job she would instinctively place on the top of that list.

Hugo stepped forward from the shadows. "It does Madame," he said, choosing a formal address which he thought more appropriate in such circumstances.

"Please go to the bank at once and get some cash to give to everyone, today, now," she said, clearly addressing Hugo. "They must have money for they will need to shop today. We can sort out how much we owe everyone later."

Juliette rose, "Excuse me Monsieur, but I need to attend to the living." On those few words she left them to retrieve pen and paper from the library, where she wrote and signed a cheque for cash, leaving the amount blank. On her return to the drawing room, Juliette scribbled a note to the bank manager, explaining the circumstances. She handed the note and cheque, without an envelope, to Coudace and instructed him to take it to the bank and, more importantly, to take care." It was as cold, clinical, and unnatural behaviour as Hilaire had ever seen.

"Madame, I think we should accompany Monsieur Coudace to the bank," said Hilaire. "We don't want another robbery, and to be frank, we need to talk to the manager there." He could not explain himself, but he no longer wanted to be in that room with Juliette and Coudace. He would come back later and interview each of them on their own.

"Monsieur Coudace do you have a van or lorry available which might collect Monsieur Guégan's motorbike from the road and deliver it to the police station?" asked Hilaire. "I imagine you have a vehicle and some men who could do this task. We need to examine it," he explained.

"Oui Monsieur," said Hugo. "I will arrange it."

"Not yours, of course. I gather your van ran over Monsieur Guégan so it mustn't be touched until we've examined it. It's to stay where it is." Hilaire paused for thought. "I need to use the phone, please," he said. "There is much I still have to arrange."

Hugo nodded.

Hilaire was led to the hall and the phone by the front door where, demanding privacy, he phoned his police station to report what he had learnt so far and demanded more manpower.

Hugo and Hilaire left the Château at the same time but travelled independently to where Étienne's motorbike lay; Hilaire in his police car, and Coudace in Étienne's van. The elderly policeman was left at the Château not knowing what he should be doing, except standing guard and observing. What he was guarding and what he was observing, he was not exactly sure.

At the scene of the motorbike, Coudace dipped a couple of buckets in the wine barrel he'd put in the van and filled with water so as to swill Étienne's blood and brains from the road, for until then it was too gruesome to let anyone pass.

"No, no, no," yelled Hilaire, as the first bucket of water hit the tarmac. "We must have casts of the tyres and footprints before anything else, monsieur."

There followed a negotiation between Hilaire and Coudace where the two men agreed that the road could be washed, provided the water was kept away from the area where Hilaire was convinced that the murderer had sat in wait. The nearly empty wine barrel was unloaded and left at the side of the road and Étienne's motorbike was loaded into the van.

Hilaire cursed, for he did not have enough men on site.

"Constable," said Hilaire, addressing Baume. "You are to accompany Monsieur Coudace to the police station, first to drop off the motorbike. You are then to go with him to the bank." His instructions were typically short and precise.

"And my bike?"

"Is it not obvious that you will be coming back here?" replied Hilaire, irritated.

Baume said no more. Suddenly he sensed he was being invited to work as Hilaire's assistant.

Coudace and Hilaire arrived at the bank at roughly the same time. Coudace and Baume had dropped off the motorbike at the police station, while Hilaire had gone back to the Château to change the elder policeman's point of duty to the crime scene. He wanted to make sure it was not disturbed.

At the bank Coudace, Hilaire and Baume appeared as a delegation. The staff knew Coudace as an important customer and, accompanied by a police inspector in full uniform, they sprang to attention. They were rapidly taken into the manager's room, where the existing customer was quickly ejected.

Hilaire briefed the manager on what had happened and what needed to happen. The manager had obviously been identified for rapid promotion. He was far too young to hold such an important position unless he had something special, and that something was immediately shown as he organised his staff. Étienne's wage sheets from the day before were found and staff scurried around making up the same wage packets. There were problems because they did not have enough notes of the right denomination. His staff were despatched to other banks with cash in hand to change the larger notes into smaller ones, and with each visit the news of the murder spread.

Once instructions had been given to make up the new wage packets, Hilaire dismissed Coudace from the meeting. He didn't want him to hear his questioning of the bank manager.

"How much did the wages come to in total?" asked Hilaire.

The Manager looked at the bottom of the third page of his bank's records. "Just over one thousand seven hundred francs, monsieur." He handed over the book for Hilaire to see for himself. "It is a lot of money, but Monsieur Guégan employed a lot of people."

Hilaire studied the sheet and was puzzled for Coudace's name was not on the list. He was about to ask why when the manager said: "But that figure excludes Madame Bellanger. Do you want us to make up an envelope for Stephen as we always do?" the Manager asked.

"Pardon me?" said Hilaire puzzled.

"In addition to the wage packets, we always make up an envelope containing one hundred and ten francs for Madame Bellanger."

"Madame Bellanger?" repeated Hilaire.

"Oui, the English and music teacher at Sacred Heart School. The lady who organises...." His words were cut short by Hilaire who brusquely said, "No thank you, but I will have her address, please."

"Make sure you report to me tomorrow morning at 7 o'clock sharp," said Hilaire to Baume as he studied the address of Madame Dominique Bellanger. He chose to ignore the perplexed look on Baume's face as he was instructed to ride shotgun for Coudace as he returned to Latoire Village where they were to go from home to home delivering the newly prepared wage packets.

Chapter 88

Bordeaux November 1930.

HILAIRE GAVE DOMINIQUE Bellanger's address to his driver and instructed him to get there as fast as possible. As he sat in the back seat, he took out his notebook and recorded all the salient details of Étienne's visit to the bank yesterday.

Hilaire's notes were normally a matter of neatness and precision but the jolting of the car on the road made his writing almost impossible to read. Before he had finished scrawling, his car stopped outside Dominique's delightful fisherman's cottage. Hilaire climbed the stairs with his driver by his side. He knocked on the door and waited. He took time to notice how well painted and spotless the cottage was and how the staircase was lightly decorated with simple seasonal flowers, carefully nurtured to still be in bloom this late in the season.

The door was opened cautiously for Dominique was not used to visitors and certainly not at this time of day. In fact, it was unusual for her to be at home and not at school.

"Madame Bellanger, I'm Inspector Hilaire. May I come in?"

Usually Hilaire would not wait for an answer. He had learnt that, by walking straight in on making his announcement, he could take command of the situation from the start, but not this time. Like everyone, he was instantly enchanted by the delight before his eyes, but it was not this which threw him. It was the fact that he had seen and admired her before but could not place where, so he stood where he was.

She recognised him instantly, "Ah, our occasional trumpet player."

"A very bad trumpet player, madame" admitted Hilaire.

"I fear so," teased Dominique, "but not as bad as some of the others," at which she smiled and tossed her head to show that she was paying him a back-handed compliment.

"I am sorry, madame but I have come on business," he said, frustrated that she had been able to place where she had seen him, but he had not.

"Oh dear," said Dominique, not unduly concerned, for as a schoolteacher she was used to dealing with the police and the troubles caused by miscreant pupils.

"Do you know Monsieur Étienne Guégan?" asked Hilaire, still standing on the doorstep.

Dominique paused for just a second before answering, "Oui, I know him well. Why?"

"I am sorry to say he has been killed. I am investigating his death." It was a blunt announcement.

Dominique stared at him. Her face tilted slightly to one side with a quizzical look as she tried to process what she thought was an unbelievable statement. Hilaire studied her face carefully. He watched as her brow furrowed and her mouth widened but still her overall aura was of happiness. Then, as her brain slowly processed the news, he saw her visibly shrink in size, her mouth drop, her eyes fade, but otherwise she stood perfectly still.

Hilaire waited for her to speak but she said nothing. There was a silence as both continued the study of the other. For a moment she wondered whether this was some practical joke, but she knew instinctively that it was not. Suddenly, an overwhelming fear came over her whole being. Adrenalin poured through her veins, but still she did not move. It wasn't that she couldn't, it was more that she had a feeling of such hopelessness that she didn't know what to do next. It then dawned on her. What had once been very private was about to become very public, and the thought filled her with dread.

Hilaire was cross with himself for the clumsy and unprofessional way he had broken the news on the doorstep. "Madame, may I come in?"

"Oui, of course," whispered Dominique shakily.

Dominique led Hilaire and his driver through and sat them at the dining room table. Perfunctorily, she sat down opposite them.

"Étienne's dead you say?"

"Oui."

"How did he die?"

"He had an accident on his motorbike."

"He always drove that damn thing too fast," she responded angrily.

"When did you last see Monsieur Guégan?" asked Hilaire.

"Yesterday," she paused. "He left at about 4.30pm, may be five o'clock," she continued shaking her head.

"When did he arrive?"

"At his usual time."

"Which was?"

"Just after noon, say 12.15pm."

"So Monsieur Guégan was with you from 12.15pm until 5.00pm?"

"Oui."

"That is a very long time, madame."

Dominique chose not to respond.

"Did he bring anything with him? Did he give you anything?" Hilaire asked.

"No, monsieur," she replied innocently.

"No envelope?

"Ah, oui," she said, not offering an explanation as to why her earlier answer could be wrong.

"Do you still have it, the envelope?" he added for clarity.

"Ah, oui," she said. At that, she got up from the table and went to her wardrobe drawer.

On her return, Dominique placed the basket, full to the brim with unopened envelopes, on the table. She selected the one on the top with yesterday's date stamp and handed it to him. He saw her name was beautifully written in black italics.

"Is this Monsieur Étienne's writing?" he asked.

"No monsieur, this is," said Dominique, as she pointed to Étienne's writing of the word Stephen on the same envelop.

"May I open it?"

"Oui monsieur."

Dominique got up, went to the dresser drawer, and removed a long-bladed penknife, which she used to open her envelopes. She handed the knife to Hilaire, and sat down next to him again, as he sliced open the envelope and put the contents on the table.

"Do you know how much is in here?" he asked

"She shook her head."

He counted the money in front of her. "It's a lot of money," said Hilaire when he had finished.

"It is," she replied, "but it is not mine."

"Not yours, but your name is on the envelope."

"It is for my son." It was a simple reply which she decided required no further explanation.

"Monsieur Guégan gives money to your son; why may I ask?" The innuendo in his voice was too obvious to ignore.

"My son is my husband's child," said Dominique, firmly putting Hilaire in his place.

"Then why?"

"It is a question you will have to ask him," she said, realising as she spoke that this could now never happen. "You will notice not one, not one, has ever been opened."

Hilaire studied the bank notes. They were all new. Not a used one amongst them.

"May I?" said Hilaire, as he opened another of the wage packets. It, too, contained new notes. He opened a third. It was the same.

"Madame, this is an awful lot of money," said Hilaire, with emphasis. "You should put it in the bank for safety. It's dangerous for you to have so much money here."

"No one else knows," she paused, "except now you." Her voice showed frustration both from being told the obvious but also by the fact that she now knew she had to do something with the money; something which she had been putting off for so very long.

"How long has Monsieur Guégan been giving you money?"

"Not me, Inspector," said Dominique, "Stephen."

"Yes, Stephen, I'm sorry."

Dominique paused as she thought. "Since December 1920."

"That's nearly ten years?" There was surprise in his voice.

"Oui."

"But there aren't five hundred wage packets here?" said Hilaire, trying to reconcile her statement that she had not spent any of the money to what was in front of him.

Dominique got up silently, went to her bedroom and returned with a hold-all. "It's all here, every centime. None of it's been spent, ever!"

"What happened when you last saw Monsieur Guégan?" asked Hilaire, seeking to change the subject.

Dominique told how Étienne arrived and left at the normal time. She described any one of his visits when they just sat and chatted. She left their intimate moments to herself, not to be shared with anyone.

"There was something wrong at Château de Gressier," she said. "He had a problem to deal with and it upset him. He didn't say what, but it made him very pensive and a bit angry. I'm not surprised he had an accident as his mind would have been on that and not his driving."

"Madame," said Hilaire. "I've missed out on telling you one important fact. Monsieur Guégan was not killed in an accident. I am quite certain he was murdered."

There was a pause as Dominique digested what she was being told, and then she asked very quietly: "Why? How?"

"I cannot say."

"Cannot or will not?"

"I don't yet know why, and I'm not allowed to say how," said Hilaire.

On hearing of Étienne's death, Dominique could not think or feel. Slowly her senses had started to return, but the news he had been murdered shocked her. She was numbed to the core only functioning through her sub-consciousness.

"Why?" she mouthed, then looking straight into Hilaire's eyes, she asked: "Why? He was good to everyone, even to his farm manager, and oh, how that man played him up."

"Monsieur Coudace?" asked Hilaire.

Dominique nodded.

"We think the motive was robbery. All the wages money was missing when Monsieur Guégan was found."

It was an explanation which made sense to Dominique and to a certain extent it gave her some solace against all the other alternatives which were swimming through her foggy mind.

Very gently, Hilaire quizzed Dominique as he got her to tell her and Étienne's story. He listened intensely as, with his notebook away, he noticed she talked more freely.

"It's the first time I have told anyone about him," she confessed. "I have never mentioned him to anyone. He was my secret and I was his; but I suppose not anymore?" she said, in a way which was both questioning and wistful.

After a long while, Hilaire knew it was time for the interview to end. He could spend all day talking to her. Hilaire was not a man prone to envy, but as she spoke, he thought how easy it would be to fall in love with her and how lucky Étienne had been. She was, he concluded, an exceptionally rare French mistress for she appeared to seek little from her relationship, and whatever she had been given materially she had not used.

Hilaire gave Dominique a receipt for the last pay packet she had got from Étienne for Stephen. He promised he would be back, not to interview her but to keep her informed. But this was just an excuse. He wanted to see her again.

Hilaire returned quickly to the bank, banging on the door as it was now shut. The messenger answered the door and, seeing who it was, took Hilaire straight to the manager.

"Did Monsieur Guégan always have new bank notes?" he asked urgently.

"Oui Monsieur, he insisted on it. He said it was a way he could show respect to those who worked for him."

"Can you give me the serial numbers of the notes which went into the pay packets?"

"Oui, not today, monsieur, but I am sure I can get them for you tomorrow."

"Good, I need them first thing," he replied. "It's very important."

"Did you put new notes in the replacement pay packets?"

"No monsieur, well maybe a few. I will try and find out exactly."

Hilaire and his driver returned at full speed to the police station. It was one of the rare occasions that Hilaire allowed his driver to ring the warning bell. He needed to see the photographs taken that morning, so he was relieved to find the photographer was waiting for him at the gendarmerie.

They both went and sat at Hilaire's desk studying the photographs in detail. The photographer pointed out features which only a trained and artistic eye would see. Hilaire was impressed. He would remember it as his first lesson in how to look at a picture. It was, he discovered, a skill which could be taught. The pattern on the car tyres was all too common, but as the photographer pointed out, the balding on the edge of two of the tyres would make them uniquely identifiable.

Hilaire rocked back on the two legs of his chair in a rare act of ill-discipline and smiled. "All we have to do is match the two car tyres, the shoes and the new bank notes to a man, and we will have our killer," he said. A feeling of self-satisfaction came over him, as it was now a man chase and tomorrow it would start. First, he needed to interview Madame Guégan alone for he needed to know whether there might be another motive, one which was more than about money.

It was just after midnight when the photographer got back to Latoire Village. The village café was still open as no one seemed to want to go home. There was a solace in being together, but also, they didn't want to leave in case they were to miss anything new. The photographer called in at the café for a night-time aperitif as he, too, wanted to share in the excitement of the day. His new exulted position as police photographer gave him a kudos which he rarely enjoyed. The photographer took on the status of a minor celebrity as his audience was held in rapture as he described, detail by detail, every scene in every photograph. "The police only have to match the front two car tyres and footprints from the crime scene to the man with the new bank notes and we will have our murderer," he announced, including himself as part of the investigation team.

In the corner of the café sat a man on his own, for he was not one to mix with anyone else from the village. He was unusually pensive, working out what he was going to do next, but the photographer's news had added a complexity which, if not dealt with quickly, would hamper his ambitions. When he left without saying anything to anyone else, no one was surprised for this was the custom of the man who was said to 'walk with God'.

Chapter 89

Bordeaux November 1930.

HILAIRE STARTED THE next day incredibly early. The murder of such a prominent member of society had created a lot of frisson, not only with the press but throughout the gendarmerie. It meant that this Saturday was turned in to one like every other working day. Everyone in Hilaire's unit had been stopped from whatever they were working on, and with his team expanded by five detectives from other units, it was a large group of people who were assembled for what would become a routine early morning briefing. Hilaire's first instructions were to get formal written statements from Madame Bellanger, Monsieur Coudace, the Bank Manager and everyone who worked at Château de Gressier or lived in Latoire Village. He also set a team the task of establishing Étienne's exact movements, minute by minute, throughout the day. Hilaire reserved for himself the task of getting a formal statement from Madame Guégan; a task he was not relishing.

Baume was instructed to accompany Hilaire and told, in no uncertain terms, that at the interview he was to be unobtrusive, out of view and say nothing. He was just there to take notes which he could later turn into a statement. Hilaire wanted the interview to be private, an intimate conversation designed to build trust.

As Juliette and Hilaire sat down to talk, not in the drawing room but in the comfort of the library, the first thing that surprised him was how good her French was, for there was no trace of a foreign accent. If anything, it was a little too formal, but he put that down to her being English. He studied what she was wearing, for while her clothes had the style of Paris haute couture, they were worn with a casualness which belied any French upbringing. It was as though they were incidental to her being and not part of what made her a remarkably beautiful woman.

Very slowly, Hilaire took Juliette through her day from the moment she awoke to the moment she heard of Étienne's death. Her husband had kissed her on the cheek just before he left at about 8.00am to go to Bordeaux, and that was the last time they saw each other. Hilaire was surprised at how unemotional she was as she described their last goodbye.

She spoke of her day in detail trying hard to provide supporting evidence for everything she said she had done. There was beginning to be a helpful innocence about Juliette's replies and so, having reached a level of comfort where Juliette was no longer on guard, Hilaire decided to pounce.

"On Thursday, Monsieur Guégan spent from 12.30pm until about 5.00pm with Madame Dominique Bellanger at her house. He was a very regular visitor. In fact, he'd been going there at the same time each week for about the last ten years" he said. "There was a gap of about two years after your children were born, but otherwise, it's been a very regular liaison."

A look of unconcerned puzzlement came over Juliette's face, for she knew it could not possibly be true.

"Who told you this?" asked Juliette, being sure that the source would give her some clue as to the situation.

Hilaire chose not to answer. Instead he asked, "What do you know of this relationship, madame?"

"I know nothing," she answered firmly. "Who is this Madame Bellanger?"

"Madame Dominique Bellanger is a school teacher at Sacred Heart School in Bordeaux. You will know of her as she organises the summer orchestral concerts in Bordeaux," said Hilaire in the hope that it would aide her identification

Juliette shook her head, for she still didn't recognise the name. She was in shock at the news that Étienne was with another woman. It could not possibly be true.

"Apparently, they have been friends since they were teenagers," said Hilaire.

Juliette shook her head once more.

"Your husband has been giving her, or I should say her son, Stephen, just over one hundred francs each week for the last ten years. Why would this be?"

Juliette's mouth fell open. She was going to say: 'Don't be so ridiculous,' but the look on Hilaire's face told her that what he was saying was true. Not only did she have no knowledge about her husband's relationship with this woman, but she had no explanation for the gifted money; and this made her feel truly foolish.

With her brain in turmoil, Juliette did not hear Hilaire explain that Étienne and Madame Bellanger's husband, served together in the same regiment, and that Monsieur Bellanger was killed in the war. There was only one question screaming in Juliette's mind. Was Étienne the father of Stephen? The thought made her feel sick.

Seeing Juliette's visual distress, Hilaire very gently changed his line of questioning. "Madame Bellanger said that Monsieur Guégan was terribly upset during the afternoon of the day he died. She said he was distracted. He had a problem he knew he had to deal with, but she didn't know what it was. Can you tell me about this problem, madame?"

"Problem, what problem?" repeated Juliette, now visibly agitated. She knew nothing of a problem. How did this damn woman know of a problem when she did not? Her thoughts raced in confusion, such that she was unable to arrange her words in proper order to speak coherently. She simply shook her head.

"Madame, the motive for your husband's...."

"My husband," interrupted Juliette. "It appears I know nothing of my husband."

"The problem might be the motive for your husband's murder, and we know from Madame Bellanger that the problem is here, with the vineyard," said Hilaire forging on.

On hearing the word vineyard Juliette closed her eyes and gently shook her head. It had been true, Étienne had been distant, but only for a couple of weeks, ever since he had returned from London. There could not be a problem with the vineyard as she was sure she would have known. In fact, Juliette was so sure nothing was wrong she told Hilaire about how they had made a bid to buy La Bête Blanche.

"Madame, we need to examine all your husband's papers. We need to search the whole house. We need to establish if there is another motive other than robbery."

"Oui, Inspector, please search away," said Juliette. "I know of no secrets. Our house is our office. Everyone comes in and out. Everyone sees everything. It is all open. In fact, I would have said that it was impossible to have a secret here, but obviously that is not true. Please look, please look everywhere." The despair in Juliette's voice was palpable.

"Thank you, madame," said Hilaire. "If I may I will start with the safe."

"What safe?" said Juliette for she knew of no safe. Had 'that' woman told of a safe she knew nothing about. "We have no safe," she affirmed.

"No safe, madame?"

"No safe," replied Juliette, her tone sinking as she said it.

"I just presumed that you must have a safe," said Hilaire.

"No safe," replied Juliette sharply, now feeling embarrassed that they didn't have something which they obviously should have had.

"Then we should start in the office," said Hilaire.

"Oui, that sounds a good place. My father said that you only really know a man when you know how much he owes and by reading his cheque book stubs. Perhaps we should go and read those together," added Juliette sarcastically.

Juliette took Hilaire and Baume through the rest of The Cellars and across to the barn where the winery's office had been established. She pointed to a large desk against a wall with chairs that sat opposite each other and said: "That partner's desk is where Étienne and I worked. It is yours to use." She then excused herself, saying she had two very distressed children to look after.

Hilaire sat down at Étienne's desk and looked around. The room was oblong in shape with large windows at either end. There were two other partners' desks all of the same make and style in a row against the wall. Filing cupboards went all the way down the other side of the room. There was an order about the place. It was neat, clean, and tidy. Hilaire wondered what all the people who worked here actually did, and there was no better person to tell him than the General Manager. It was time to interview Hugo Coudace.

Juliette did go to her children, but she only looked in on them for a few minutes and found that they were being well entertained. They would be back to school tomorrow, she decided. Instead, she climbed the stairs to the Gallery where she sat at Étienne's desk She picked up one of the silver maple leaves, not knowing it was a present from Dominique and admiringly stroked it before she opened each of the drawers and stared in them mindlessly. There was nothing of note in them. Just the accumulation of stuff that you don't want to throw away in case one day it might have a purpose; but of course, it never does.

Juliette's words of earlier, that they had no secrets, were beginning to haunt her. Of course, they had a secret! They were wine suppliers to one of the USA's biggest bootleggers, not only of Château de Gressier wine, but for half a dozen of the biggest vineyards around. Yes, they sold the wine to a UK company, and it was always shipped, via the UK, to Canada or Bermuda. But they knew exactly where the wine was going. Their secret, as she and Étienne had discussed many times, was that they were involved in a conspiracy to import alcohol into the United States contrary to that country's prohibition laws. Was this the problem which had been worrying Étienne, Juliette wondered. If it was, then she should tell the Inspector, but if it wasn't, then she would be silly to raise the matter. How was she going to find out what it was that had been worrying Étienne?

Late that night, Juliette lay awake wondering whether it was all Étienne's fault that it took her so long to get pregnant. Was 'that woman' taking what was rightly hers, she wondered. Suddenly Juliette felt an overwhelming hatred for a woman she did not know, and anger at Étienne for his betrayal. With these thoughts racing through her brain, Juliette was unable to sleep. She knew she had to do something about challenging her rival; but how and when and where?

Chapter 90

Château de Gressier November 1930

IT WAS SATURDAY afternoon when Hugo Coudace arrived in the office at Château de Gressier and took his place at the partner's desk furthest away from that which Étienne and Juliette used to share.

"May I ask where you have been?" said Hilaire rather huffily, as Coudace walked through the door. "We've been looking for you since mid-morning."

"May I ask what you are doing in here?" responded Coudace, his tone less than welcoming.

Hilaire ignored him and instead asked his question again, this time in a more direct, less polite, manner.

"I have been at La Maison de Louis."

"Where is that?"

It's the white house directly opposite. Madame and Monsieur Guégan call it La Bête Blanche."

"Why?"

"Why have I been there or why do they call it that?"

Hilaire never swore but this did not stop him cursing in his head, which is exactly what he did as he realised, he had in front of him a man with the ability to be extremely obtuse. "Why did you go there?" he asked.

"Because it's for sale."

Hilaire nodded, and then asked, "All day?"

"I then went to see Monsieur Peltier to discuss the acquisition of three of his fields."

"Are they for sale?"

"They are to me," replied Coudace tartly.

"And why not to anyone else?"

"Because they won't pay what we will pay for them."

"Who's we?"

"Château de Gressier, of course."

"You still think the Estate will buy them?"

"Yes, of course," replied Coudace, in a detached manner.

"The King is dead; long live the King," commented Hilaire, wondering if it might get a reaction but it passed Coudace by.

"Where are these fields which are for sale?" asked Hilaire. In a lengthy conversation Coudace explained that it was the land which was between the Latoire Church and the road on which Étienne had been killed.

"You know," said Coudace. "Where Monsieur Guégan was killed was exactly where he would have stopped and looked over the gate at those fields, wishing one day he could buy them. Without them he never felt the Château was complete."

"Why didn't he buy them?"

"'Because Monsieur Peltier wouldn't sell. He didn't like Monsieur Guégan."

"Why?"

"I don't know, you'll have to ask him."

"So why will Monsieur Peltier sell now?"

"Because Monsieur Guégan is dead and Peltier needs the money."

Coudace and Hilaire boxed and coxed for the next hour as Baume sat quietly taking extensive notes.

"Do you know Madame Bellanger?" asked Hilaire.

"No, who's she?"

Hilaire didn't answer, instead he paused and theatrically studied his notebook to allow the next question to appear random.

"I'm told that Monsieur Guégan was worried about something to do with the Estate. Do you know what it was?"

"No, there's nothing I know of," and, as it was said, Hilaire instinctively knew Coudace was lying.

"Come now, we both know that is not true."

"What has Madame Guégan said? She will know more about the business side than me," said Coudace very calmly, as internally he began to panic as his conversation with Monsieur Delors on the day of Étienne's murder came flooding back.

The Lands of de Gressier

"She was too distressed to talk," said Hilaire, untruthfully.

"The financial collapse has meant we have lost an awful lot of customers. Monsieur Guégan's last sales visit to London was not good. That could have been worrying him."

"It's not that, the vineyard finances are sound. You know that."

"He could have been worrying about the purchase of La Bête Blanche," offered Coudace.

"Maybe, but Madame Guégan doesn't think so. As you also know, they were only renting it, with an option to buy. It was something they were both very relaxed about."

There was a long pause as Coudace thought quite deeply. "We've been shipping wine into America in breach of their prohibition regulations. We send it via Liverpool, but its destination is Quebec for onward transmission in to the United States." he said. "If the reason for Étienne's murder is not robbery, then it will be found there because some of those people have a reputation of being pretty damn nasty."

Hilaire looked carefully at Coudace as he knew, if what this man was saying was true, then his case had suddenly got much bigger. Mentally he settled down for what he knew would be an extended interview. "Let us start again, he said. "Firstly, please let me have a list of every man who has worked here, let us say for the last five years."

"Now?" asked Coudace, puzzled.

"Yes, now please," replied Hilaire.

Chapter 91

Bordeaux November 1930

DOMINIQUE OPENED THE door and her heart immediately froze.

"Madame Bellanger." It was said as a statement not as a question. 'I am Madame Guégan. I'm Étienne's wife," she paused, checked herself and added, as her voice quietened, "or more properly, I am Étienne's widow." It was the first time she had used the word widow and it seemed strange on her lips. "I believe you were the last person to see my husband alive."

"Oui Madame, I am Dominique Bellanger. We have met before." There was a silence as Dominique offered Juliette both her hands, which she took with a puzzled expression. Very slowly Dominique walked backwards guiding Juliette across the threshold, as a parent guides a child as they are beginning to walk. Inside they stopped, for what seemed an eternity, as they studied each other, not knowing what else to say. Juliette had rehearsed her script so many times she should have been word perfect, but now, with her rivale d'amour standing before her, she was completely disarmed. Immediately on seeing Dominique, Juliette knew, because her stunning beauty was unforgettable, that they had met before, but at that moment, she could not remember where.

Juliette had dressed for their encounter very carefully. She had one aim; to show that it was she who deserved to have been Étienne's wife and have him in her bed; not some tart of a school mistress. She had chosen a beautifully tailored royal blue coat with black fur collar and cuffs which she adorned with an exquisite platinum and diamond brooch pinned to the large lapel. Her hat was simple and unfussy, made of crushed velvet in the same colour and shade as her coat, but around the rim Juliette had added a small black band of mourning.

The shape of her hat enhanced the natural beauty of Juliette's face, but above all else, Dominique noticed the beauty of her deep hazel eyes set against the whitest of sclera she had ever seen.

Juliette's dress had precisely the effect she wanted, for Dominique was immediately disarmed, not just by the fact that Juliette was there but by the beauty, elegance and poise of the aristocratic English woman now before her. To make matters worse for Dominique, she was still in her school clothes and the chalk dust from her morning efforts was still in her pores. It was one of the very rare moments in Dominique's life when she felt both very inferior and very guilty. She should not have worried, for what Juliette saw in her opponent was a delicate, petite woman whose face was flawless, not a line to be seen, with similar deep brown eyes. It was on seeing the way her opponent looked that Juliette's feelings of righteous confidence of the woman scorned, immediately evaporated.

The difference and sameness between them were immediately obvious. The English woman was stiff and proper, with a correctness and efficiency of touch, while the French woman was natural and loose, with an air of freedom and lightness of touch. It was as though each offered Étienne something which the other could not. There were some familiarities. Each had a delicate bone structure, but it was the bright sparkle in their eyes, which offered a smile to anyone who wanted to accept it, that was their most common feature. Even in the hardship that the two women found themselves, they could not stop their eyes radiating an unintended warmth to the other.

Slowly the two women composed themselves, and after some time Dominique said, "Please come in. I am so sorry about...." She checked herself because she was about to say Étienne. "I am so sorry for your loss. Monsieur Guégan's parting is a very big shock. Please come through," she continued.

After closing the front door Dominique led Juliette through to her large sitting room, with the panoramic views over the river, and offered her a chair. The chair was the same one in which Étienne would sit as he contemplated the day.

"I believe you were the last person to see my husband alive, madame. Is that true?" asked Juliette refusing to sit.

"Dominique, please," she replied.

Juliette gave a weak sarcastic smile in acknowledgment before she started her tirade: "How come you were the last person to see my husband? Why was he with you from lunch time to early evening? What were you two doing all that time? Ten years he's been coming here, ten years!" she yelled, "and the money, why the money? What kind of woman are you to be having a secret affair with my husband for so long?" The anger in Juliette intensified, as she spoke louder and louder.

"Those are many questions," said Dominique, very softly.

She could have responded in kind. In fact, long ago, she had worked out her line of counter-attack should this moment come. It was exactly what her grandmother used to say, when discussing the affairs in their village: No man seeks companionship elsewhere if he has it at home. A husband only ever strays if his wife is failing to please him mentally or physically. Depending on the company she would sometimes crudely add: Every wife must empty her husband's tank first thing in the morning; otherwise he'll only spend the rest of the day thinking about other women and sex, and if he strays, well, is it any surprise?

Dominique's retort, in simplified form, was that Juliette could only have herself to blame. If Étienne preferred her company to his wife's then that was a matter for Étienne and Juliette; not her. Étienne was her friend, and as far as she was concerned, she was never going to forsake him if he needed her; never! But this was never said. Dominique knew that, in the strange circumstances the two women found themselves, it was not the proper thing to do.

"Would you like something to drink?" Dominique asked, continuing to speak in a disarmingly gentle tone. "A coffee or perhaps a little cognac. I think we are both hurting in our own way and have much to discuss. It would be better if we did it ...."

"A little cognac would be perfect," replied Juliette, cutting Dominique off before she'd finished the sentence. The aggression in her voice was still obvious to hear.

Once Juliette was seated, Dominique made her apologies, and in her bedroom, she fought her wardrobe, frantically discarding item upon item on the bed. She first selected a pair of navy tailored trousers thinking of matching them with a white pressed blouse and then at the last moment she chose a blue frock with small white dots and a white collar and cuffs. It was simple but smart and, as she tightened the small white belt around her waist, she knew she had made the right choice. It was the dress she wore on her first date with Étienne. She added a single strand pearl necklace which he had given her. She then pressed a damp towel around her face and, with no change to her make-up or hair, stopped for a second to compose herself. She took comfort in knowing that, even if she did not wear Étienne's wedding ring, it was her he truly loved.

Dominique returned to where Juliette was sitting, bringing with her a bottle of cognac and two cut-glass brandy glasses. Slowly and in silence she poured a glass and handed it to Juliette. It was only now that Dominique was ready to answer Juliette's question: "That is what I have been told," she said firmly.

Juliette looked puzzled, for she had forgotten her question, so Dominique repeated it; "That I was the last person to see Monsieur Guégan alive."

Juliette smiled weakly and whispered the word "Étienne" giving Dominique permission to use his first name. She then took a sip of her cognac. She could wait no more. It was the question she had been desperate to ask. "Were you and he lovers?" she asked. The words seemed clumsy, so Juliette repeated the question slightly differently. "Were you and my husband lovers?" It was clear from the stress in her voice that she was desperate for an answer, but now the words were out, she felt humiliated and degraded, as challenging Dominique was only part of the reason for her visit. The most important thing was to find out what had been worrying Étienne about Château de Gressier.

Dominique paused, for she didn't want to say yes. Such an admission would make their love seem sordid and shameful. Instead, she let Juliette's question hang in the air as she raised her glass and said in a formal toast, "Monsieur Étienne, may his soul rest in peace". Juliette raised her glass in response and slowly poured another few drops of cognac into her lips.

"Étienne was very kind to me and my son," she paused. "Yes, I did love him". Dominique had never admitted this to anyone else before, and with those words tears gently rolled down her cheeks.

"Madame Bellanger," said Juliette purposefully, and then she paused. "Is my husband the father of your son?" The words burst from her lips, and although they were carefully pre-planned, she knew immediately that the tone was wrong.

"No, madame," replied Dominique, almost spitting out the words in anger. "My husband is my son's father." She paused and then added, "He was killed by the English during the war." She stressed the words killed and English with the same accusatory emphasis with which Juliette had asked her question.

"Madame, if you had thought for a moment you would have known it was impossible," Dominique continued in a tone designed to make Juliette feel foolish. "Your husband and my husband served together in the war, in the same regiment."

"I didn't know," said Juliette who suddenly remembered where she had first seen Dominique – at the Remembrance service.

"There's a lot you don't know," bit back Dominique. "I suppose you don't know that Étienne," she deliberately used his Christian name, "knew the English Major who killed my husband."

Juliette's blood chilled, and then drained from her face, for she instinctively knew where this story was going, and she didn't want to hear it.

"They said it was an accident. Étienne said it was an accident, but still the British tried the Major and found him guilty of murder. Except they never ... He was blown up in jail, wasn't he. I believe you knew this Major too, Madame."

"Yes, I am really very sorry," said Juliette, who composed herself and returned to the stiffness which was her British default position.

"The Germans broke through the lines," said Dominique. "My husband was sent to counter-attack, except the British fired on them, didn't they?" They overshot, missed their target, and hit the French troops fighting in the field instead. They killed Georges, along with many of his colleagues. I think the history is well recorded, Madame."

Juliette knew the story. In fact, she knew more than the story. She knew all the facts, for she had studied them as though she was a barrister preparing to defend an accused man at trial. She decided to say nothing, for whatever she said it would make no difference to Dominique. Instead, she sat still in the chair, sipped at her cognac, and drifted into her own thoughts. As she did so, tears started to fall delicately down Juliette cheeks as she suddenly felt very lonely and lost.

Dominique watched Juliette, and seeing the pain on her face, tears started to form in her eyes too. Slowly her grief for the loss of two men, her husband and her lover, became overwhelming. She had loved both with all her heart, and now they were gone and realising this once again, Dominique broke into heavy, wet, breathless sobs.

"He was never totally mine," said Juliette, being the first to gather her composure sufficiently to be able to speak. "He shared himself with everyone. He was always there whoever you were."

"I know," said Dominique. "He was exceedingly kind, very special, and very generous. He did so much for so many people, especially for those in his regiment. He took responsibility for everyone and everything. He never stopped."

"Yes, he was a natural leader," said Juliette.

"And to live each day with his fear, proved his bravery beyond his medals."

"What fear?" asked Juliette innocently.

"His fear of mud," replied Dominique.

Juliette looked puzzled.

"His fear of drowning in mud," affirmed Dominique.

Juliette shook her head, not knowing what was being talked about.

"Did you not know that after his time at Verdun, it was only with you that Étienne could walk the Estate without the sight of mud bringing back memories of the war? He said that each mud pool virtually paralysed him with fear."

"No," said Juliette, surprised.

"Did you not notice his obsession with the drainage systems on the estate?" asked Dominique. "He knew it was illogical, but he was scared stiff of drowning in mud. I think he saw too many people die this way during the Battle of Verdun."

It was only when Dominique mentioned it that Juliette recognised this truth and then felt truly dreadful at the revelation, for was she not the nurse amongst them; had she not seen the effects of shell shock?

"It was only here, and when he was with you, that he was free from his phobia. We each gave him a moment to escape his nightmare," said Dominique trying to rationalise something which was not rational.

The two women sat and chattered about the man they knew. During parts of their discussion each felt bouts of jealousy and anger at the knowledge the other had of the man in their lives, but this was tempered by the comfort of being able to talk about him with someone else who really knew him. They talked about his habits, both good and bad.

Juliette talked of her son and daughter and how each had inherited characteristics and mannerisms in the way he sat or stood. Dominique talked of her son, and although they saw each other rarely, how Étienne provided Stephen with an important male role model which his own father was not able to provide. They even started to laugh together as they each remembered the good times.

They then talked of Étienne's murder. Juliette said that the police thought the motive was money, but Dominique was not sure. "He had something else on his mind," she said. "I know he had something unpleasant to deal with concerning the de Gressier Estate, but he didn't say what. He was bottling it all up."

Juliette quizzed Dominique hard on what the problem might be, for she had heard the police say the same thing. Could it be the depression or the possible purchase of La Bête Blanche? But none of these were identified by the two women as the problem.

"It could have something to do with the shipping of wine into Quebec," offered Dominique. "I know Étienne was terribly upset by what happened to him there." She deliberately remained silent on the fact that she had accompanied him. "He said Mr Kennedy's pals were thugs who stole some papers from him in some kind of nonsensical industrial espionage. Those were the words Étienne used: nonsensical industrial espionage. He was sure he was being set up for some scam or something."

"Yes, I know. We immediately changed our trading terms with

Joe Kennedy on Étienne's return, so I'm sure it's not that. Did you mention this to Inspector Hilaire?" asked Juliette.

No," answered Dominique. "I've only just thought of it."

"It's just the Inspector has made it an important line of his enquiry. I don't know why but he is digging everywhere."

Dominique shook her head. "If I was doing the digging it would be into Hugo Coudace," said Dominique. "Étienne never really trusted him." But these words were immediately lost on Juliette, for on this matter she was certain that Dominique was surely wrong.

Slowly the enmity which both had felt towards the other at the outset began to disappear and a bond started to be created – a friendship brought about by cognac and a common grief. They then shared a pot of tea and each talked of their lives, one as a teacher and the other as a former nurse and now farmer's wife, both with hectic schedules, as they equally found that their lives were open to all those that they worked with or for, rarely finding that they had a moment to themselves. They both found, in a strange and yet comforting way, that while outwardly their lives appeared quite different, there was so much that they had in common.

Dusk was heavy in the sky when Juliette left. Her chauffeur, who had heard the gossip and had guessed at the nature of the meeting, was surprised both at its length and the change in Juliette's demeanour from being sharp, intense, and prickly, to being both exhausted and satisfied.

Once the door was shut, following Juliette's departure, Dominique placed her head heavily against the wall and closed her eyes. She felt overwhelmed by the guilt of being the mistress of a man with such a lovely wife. How could she have betrayed Juliette in the way she had done? The answer was an easy one. Étienne needed her, and she loved him so. There was nothing more to it than that.

Dominique went into the bathroom and started to wash the dried salt of her tears from her face. As she stared at herself in the mirror, she started to imagine Étienne was behind her, just as he was the last time they were together. She undid a few buttons of her dress and moved her right hand over her breasts touching and squeezing them just as he had done. She leaned forward, rested her left arm on the ceramic basin and then rested her head to lie on her arm. She spread open her legs and lowered her back, sticking her bottom in the air. She was remembering the last time they made love. The way his fingers dug into her hips. The smacking sound as his thighs hit her buttocks. Her feeling of joy as she surrendered herself completely to the power of his body. She tried to remember the feeling of him inside her but there was a void in her memory.

"Oh God," she said out loud, as she started to wish, nay pray, that she was pregnant. "Please let me be...." but the words trailed away as she said them, saying only to herself the final word "pregnant." "Let it be, let it be," she again said out loud in desperation. He was always so careful, but not the last time. Suddenly, Dominique was a woman on a mission. She rushed to her handbag and found her diary and counted the days. She counted them again, just to make sure. Yes, it could just be. "Please God," she asked. "Let it be so".

That night, despite being totally exhausted, Juliette could not sleep. It was not surprising for there was so much still to do, and the gap in the bed, where Étienne would sleep was shouting his absence at her.

The autopsy was tomorrow, after which Étienne's body would be released by the police for burial. There was now a funeral to arrange. But none of this really weighed on Juliette's mind. Time and time again she went through the conversation earlier that day with Dominique.

She felt guilty at never having noticed Étienne's fear of mud, but now it had been pointed out it was obvious. Juliette could understand him turning to Dominique, with the view from her house over the river estuary, to help ease such fears. Except, did she not say that, when he was with me on the Estate, he did not have those fears? It was so confusing.

She blamed and cursed her brother, for she was in no doubt, it was because he had killed Dominique's husband that Étienne had felt it necessary to take her, and her, son under his wing. It was as predictable as tomorrow's sunrise that, in these circumstances, she would become his mistress. Juliette knew that, if the tables were turned, she would, almost certainly, behave in the same way, for was Étienne not irresistible!

Instead of hating Dominique as she intended, she had found she liked her. If a man was to have a mistress, she concluded, then Dominique was a good choice, for it appeared that their relationship was not based on sex for money, as she had first feared, but on Dominique's deep love of her husband.

Juliette wondered if Dominique loved Étienne more than she did, but these thoughts got her nowhere as her scientific mind turned to consider a formula to measure love and the factors which went into it. No sooner had she dwelled on this proposition than her mind returned to Dominique's son and the fact that he had been made fatherless because of her brother. It explained why Étienne had been paying Dominique maintenance each week for Stephen. It was old fashioned blood money; except Hilaire had said that Dominique had never touched a centime of it. Did Dominique see it in that way, as tainted money? Is that why she hadn't spent any of it, Juliette wondered.

Juliette rose from her bed and, wrapping herself in a gown, she went to the small writing table placed in front of one of the windows in her bedroom. She turned on the light, sat down and searched for some paper and a pen in the drawer. On the top was the last letter from Judith Perfett which Juliette still had to reply to.

Seeing Judith's writing, reminded her of something she had once said on the subject of marriage. "Never marry outside of the clan," Judith had warned, when she was talking about a Welsh soldier who was pursuing her with ardour. There will be things about them, and things about you, which you will never be able to share, for your cultural attitudes, right from birth, will be so very different. Was this part of the explanation, Juliette wondered. She then thought of her friendship with Jack Morris. It was true. There were things unsaid which united them by just being English. Did Étienne need Dominique in her life simply because she was a French woman?

As she was pondering this question, Juliette opened Judith's letter and started to re-read it. Once again it was written with such fun that it lifted her heart, putting her in a better frame of mind to write the letters she had come to the table to write.

The first letter was to the Bank Manager instructing that, on the first day of each month, the sum of four hundred francs was to be paid to Stephen Bellanger. As she wrote the name Stephen she realised it was the English equivalent of Étienne. Had Dominique named her son after Étienne because he was his real father, she wondered. Then she realised there was no point in her caring. It was what it was.

Her second letter was to Dominique inviting her and Stephen to Étienne's funeral. She wrote saying it would be a real honour if they would sit in the front row at the service alongside Victor, Victoria, and herself. Juliette was determined that these five were going to stand together against the rest of the world whatever problems there were at Château de Gressier.

As Juliette drifted into the first sleep she had had for many hours, her final thoughts were of Penrose. He needed to come back and marry Dominique immediately. In fact, he should have married her and never left. She thought of him again immediately she awoke. The one person she wanted to write to was Penrose, but she could not, for she did not know where he was. The war had been a long time over and surely, she thought, he could let her know he was alive and well, but he didn't. She knew that Étienne's murder had become international news, so she hoped that this would cause him to write, but it hadn't. Every time she thought about her brother, Juliette's anger grew just a little deeper.

Chapter 92

Latoire Village December 1930

THE LOSS OF Étienne made Juliette feel incredibly lonely. It wasn't that she was alone. It was just that she had no one to share with. The day after she had seen Dominique, Juliette reflected hard on her friendships. There were only two people in her life whom, deep down, she felt were there for her whatever happened, Judith Perfett and Jack Morris.

Judith and Juliette had corresponded regularly, but they had not seen each other since the end of the war. Judith's letters were always full of calamity and joy and brought much laughter as she described the disasters of her campaign for equal suffrage of women, bringing the voting age down from thirty to twenty-one (the same age as for men) and the embarrassment, but secret pride, of her husband at her shenanigans.

Judith's letters told how, as the rector's wife, she had become the resident volunteer midwife, as this was the role of the previous rector's wife, the joy each new life gave her and how she questioned the existence of God at the death of every child. She wrote amusingly of their struggles to find money, either for some need of their children but mainly for some new humanitarian cause which was their passion of the moment. It was in great distress that Juliette replied to Judith's last letter and told of Étienne's death, and her meeting with his mistress. It was two days before Étienne's funeral that, with overwhelming emotion, Juliette welcomed Judith to Château de Gressier. The two re-coupled as though they were two sisters who had never been apart.

Juliette had not seen or heard from Jack since his visit five years ago when he brought Col. Dovingdon's gifts of gold pocket watches for his grandchildren. She could not say why, but she had a need for him to know that Étienne had died. Deep in her subconscious she wanted him to come to her, just as he had done when they were young children. So, in hope rather than expectation, she wrote to him telling of her tragedy. Jack, doing his duty by Col. Dovingdon, showed him Juliette's letter and once again, for a generous fee, he was despatched to Château de Gressier to be at her side for Étienne's funeral. He was commanded to do whatever was required to make sure Juliette was safe.

Immediately they met, Juliette and Jack resumed their unspoken, unconsummated, love affair for she was always excited by Jack's masculinity of purpose and he by her sexuality. The way he could make her laugh and find fun in any circumstance. For Jack, Juliette was like a beautiful film star; an illusion which was to be seen and known but only in the way she wanted you to, and never to be touched. What made them special was a telepathy where each knew what the other was thinking and feeling. In different circumstances they would have been happily married, but not pre-war when they were young and not now as, each with their history, it was just too complicated to even consider.

Juliette thought hard about what she might put in Étienne's grave as a token of her love. It was the words, *'we come into the world with nothing and leave with nothing'* which acted as her inspiration. Taking a long lock of her hair, together with those from Victor and Victoria, she very carefully pleated strands of hair from each of them into a delicate string which, using a short broken needle, she then wove into a fine ring with not a single hair end showing. Just after midnight on the day of Étienne's funeral, and before his coffin was shut for the final time, Juliette climbed the stairs to the Gallery where Étienne's body was lying at rest. It was, she had decided, the place he would like to spend his last few hours. There, with just the light of the fire and the candles placed around the room, she opened the lid.

Juliette moved cautiously, at first peeping, worried at what she might find. She had heard the graphic reports of the way Étienne had died and expected to see the kind of injuries she had seen in the war. Carefully, she looked at his face. The undertakers had skilfully made him look human and reasonably peaceful. Unquestionably it was him, at the same time it wasn't. He was no longer there.

Very slowly and carefully, she slipped her ring of hair on to his wedding finger, for he had never worn a wedding band. Very gently she closed his fingers together so that his regimental signet ring and her band of hair touched. Then, she took the two goodbye letters written by Victor and Victoria, with their drawings of their father and how they remembered him. Undoing his dress tunic, she tucked these under his shirt against his heart and the autopsy scars. Very carefully she redressed him, making sure everything was precisely in place before slowly raising his arms and placing them across his chest. As she shut the lid for the very last time her face tightened as, without a sound, her throat choked as the tears poured from her eyes.

Dominique was initially uncertain as to whether she should go to the funeral, but Juliette's letter caused her to change her mind. Her plan was to sit quietly at the back of the church, but Juliette did something which Dominique had not expected. Remembering the kindness Mrs Winifred Bennett had shown her and Judith at the dinner with General French, Juliette made a point of escorting Dominique and Stephen to sit in the front pew to be alongside them. The loyal support which Mrs Bennett gave General French during the war, at the cost of her own reputation, was something which Juliette had secretly admired. By defying convention, and formally recognising Dominique, was her way of saying thank you for giving Étienne the support he had needed when she could not. When Juliette, Victor and Victoria came into the church later, following Étienne's coffin, the two families sat side by side, united in an inconsolable grief.

Juliette's acknowledgement of Dominique's importance to Étienne was a kindness Dominique would never forget. It touched her beyond all measure. Nevertheless, the gossipers, who ensured that the two women were the focus of public ridicule, saw Dominique's positioning in church as proof that Stephen was Étienne's son.

The funeral service was long, with much of it said in Latin. It gave time for the mind to wander. The walk from the church to Étienne's final resting place was too difficult to bear, but with Victor and Victoria holding Juliette's hands, the three of them walked with a stoicism they knew Étienne would have expected. Dominique and Stephen walked behind; her tears obvious for all to see.

At the wake, the two women sensed an atmosphere of animosity towards them. "It was her own fault he had a mistress," Juliette overheard one elderly village woman say, before adding: "Why an English woman think's she could keep a Frenchman satisfied is beyond me."

The mood meant that Juliette and Dominique circulated for a little while and then returned to each other for solace. Not to talk about Étienne, but through a feeling that everyone was judging them, which they were. Juliette, the English woman and wife, and Dominique, the French mistress, were the outcasts at the funeral of the village's local boy, their hero and leader.

Did Juliette not understand that by Dominique taking a married man as her lover, she had to be cast out of society? It was Juliette's place to make sure that, in defence of the sisterhood and marriage, not only should Dominique be outcast, but she had to stay there. The fact that Juliette had defied convention, and therefore the sisterhood, meant she had to be expelled too. But neither woman really cared, for they found comfort and a common cause in defending themselves against the enmity of their fellow women, and as a result, Juliette took a third lifelong friend into her life.

That night, sitting alone in her cottage with Stephen tucked into his bed, Dominique was feeling very mournful. Not only was there the pain of Étienne's death, but her hope for his baby was also not to be. She always felt that she could cope with Georges' loss because she had Stephen, his father's walking embodiment, but with Étienne she had nothing but her memories. She gathered together her sewing things and very neatly hand sewed a small cushion of silk in emerald green. Then, she took off the cut diamond ring she was wearing. It was clustered with small diamonds to make it oval in shape. Apart from the pearl necklace, it was the only present Étienne had ever given her. She had worn it that day of his funeral, for whenever they were together, she had worn his ring next to her wedding band; leaving off her husband's engagement ring, which she always otherwise wore.

Picking up her husband's diamond solitaire engagement ring, she placed them both on the cushion she had made, taking great care to ensure that the shanks overlapped. She played with the way they looked and decided that rather than the stones being opposite each other they would lie side-by-side and touch. Georges and Étienne had both been soldiers. They fought side-by-side. It was only right, she thought, that their rings should forever rest that way. Very slowly and neatly, she sewed the two rings onto the cushion, never to be worn again. She decided that one day these rings would be buried with her. The three of them were never to be parted, even in death.

Chapter 93

Bordeaux 1931

VERY SHORTLY AFTER Étienne's funeral, Dominique lost her job as a teacher on the grounds of immoral probity; the headmistress told her, in no uncertain terms, that her relationship with a married man set a bad example to the girls. There was no appeal.

The orchestral numbers quickly fell, as what wife wants her husband playing in an orchestra where the organiser was an attractive woman of now known loose morals. Everyone in the orchestra talked of the dilemma of falling numbers but no one had the strength of character to raise the issue with Dominique, or formally amongst themselves, for they all knew it was as a result of her efforts that they had an orchestra at all.

Thankfully for Dominique, memories are not that long. On hearing she had 'left' Lormont School, the headmaster of a boys' elementary school in La Bastide, on the other side of the river to Bordeaux, took her on, at first temporarily and then full time, perhaps in the hope, but to no avail, that she would become his mistress too.

Dominique knew she was going to be teaching in one of the roughest and toughest areas, but she had no idea of the extent of the challenges, made even worse by the difficulties in recruiting teachers. They were always short staffed. It was in this new community that Dominique found the new talent to rebuild the Lormont orchestra. Perhaps it was not as good at it had been, but she convinced herself that each new member had the ability to surpass those they replaced, and this gave her a goal. She would darn well show them!

One of the new members to Dominique's orchestra was Henri Hilaire. She conscripted him at Étienne's funeral, even though he protested that, while Étienne's murder remained unsolved, he could not spare the time. He also argued that his playing was truly dreadful, but it was his desire to see her again which caused him to overrule his own objections.

Juliette suffered from the usual suitors, inappropriate playboys after the pickings of a rich widow. It was a problem made worse by the slaughter of young men in the war. It meant that the gene pool of suitable men had been dramatically reduced. It was a fact that there were simply not enough good, eligible men to go round for the nubile women of the Gironde; let alone for those that had been married and now had children. Thankfully for Juliette, anyone who was interested in crossing the threshold into her life was quickly and efficiently evicted by Hugo Coudace just as any father might dismiss an inappropriate suitor for his daughter's hand. As far as Hugo was concerned, there was only one successor to the amour of Madame Juliette Guégan, and that was him.

After Étienne's death, Hugo made sure that he was always sitting in the kitchen of The Cellars waiting for Juliette as she came downstairs in the morning. Over an early morning cup of coffee and with the children at school, he would, in a slow, calm, and hypnotic way, discuss nothing in particular. Any problem or issue Juliette mentioned he quickly volunteered to deal with ensuring they quickly disappeared from her agenda. Once again, Hugo became completely inveigled into the operations of Château de Gressier, just as he had been immediately before she and Étienne had returned from the war.

There was only one thing over which Juliette kept control: the bank account. It was in this way she thought she was protecting the heritage of Château de Gressier for her son and daughter. However, it was just a gossamer of good governance, for as she paid every invoice and bill Hugo told her to pay, without question, she was leaving the till wide open for him to help himself.

Hugo helped Juliette complete the lease of La Bête Blanche and manage the vineyards. No mention was made of his per bottle commission. Very quietly, he bought for himself the three fields between the church and the road on which Étienne had been killed. Juliette knew that Étienne coveted the buying of this land, but Hugo chose not to tell her that it had come on the market or that he had become its owner. He would allow it to go fallow; an ace up his sleeve to be played at a later date.

The death of Étienne brought a noticeable change in Hugo, for he became much more relaxed. It was as though, without a boss, a great pressure had been released from him. It was this new laissez faire Hugo that Juliette started to see. For as long as she had known him, Hugo had set out to impress her. In doing so, he had always been clumsy in his application of the social graces. These skills normally handed down from one generation to another, such as good etiquette and decorum, were facets missing from his lineage. While there were many examples of the good manners to which Hugo aspired, he was incapable of observing them. The servants working in the house, who had long been schooled in the appropriate behaviour, felt embarrassed by his awkward, snake-like efforts. On each failure they mocked him unmercifully behind his back. While it was obvious to others, Juliette never saw in Hugo what they would describe as an unctuous and obsequious manner. To her, he was kind and attentive and she was truly glad and thankful to have him around.

There was a simple explanation for Juliette's liking of Hugo. She found, as others had done, that when you looked into his eyes, everything in your life calmed down. It gave her a warm, ghostly, almost light-headed feeling. It was precisely this which made others describe Hugo as having an ability to walk with God. For Hugo, the mild affection Juliette showed him was sufficient to keep his battery of ardour fully charged, for he was determined that, now free, she would one day become his wife.

Chapter 94

Bordeaux 1931

HILAIRE WAS CONFIDENT that, with the evidence from the crime scene, Étienne's killer would soon be caught; and so he set about his work in the methodical and logical manner he had been taught.

Everyone over the age of 16, who worked on the Estate or lived in the village, was interviewed, and the footwear of every man was examined as they looked for ex-army issue boots. Those who had the same size as the footprints at the scene were added to a list of possible suspects, but none had the unique markings which were clearly visible from the photographs taken at the crime scene. The list was long, for there were many boots of the same size, as many men on the Estate wore boots that were too big for them, filling the extra space with newspaper and additional socks.

An examination of the car tracks identified the tyres as being Michelin, but these were common to both Citroen and Peugeot vehicles. These cars had different axle widths and so a lot of work was done in trying to accurately estimate the width between the tyre tracks to identify the make of vehicle.

To Hilaire's chagrin, the photographic evidence, and the measurements they made at the scene, albeit they were made by two separate people, conflicted. They were not precise enough to identify the make or model. What Hilaire did know was that if they could find the vehicle's front tyres then he would have the car, for the rubber had worn unevenly on both with the inside rim still having almost a full tread while the outside rim was worn almost bare on the near-side tyre. It was a mirror image on the off-side tyre. An examination of every car and van on the Estate, and in the surrounding villages, eliminated all of these from Hilaire's enquiries.

Every known villain in the area was interviewed, their statements taken, and location corroborated. Hilaire focused at first on all those whose modus operandi included wage snatches, but it soon became apparent that those who chose to earn their living this way had not yet identified vineyards as a thieving opportunity. As a result of eyes being opened, the police had to invest in a huge crime prevention effort designed to protect other vineyards and this took up more valuable time.

The paperwork of Château de Gressier's sales to Joseph Kennedy, and his company Somerset Importers Inc., was examined in the smallest detail. Apart from the fact that the wine was ending up in the US underworld, there was nothing to suggest this relationship was the motive behind Étienne's death.

After the first four weeks of evidence being gathered, there was no obvious suspect and, with a mass of statements, Hilaire felt he was being overwhelmed with data. The procedure of carding every person who came into their investigation, and why, was meticulously followed, but once the information was filed away Hilaire, found it became invisible and, in effect, lost from his enquiry.

Hilaire decided what he needed was a cross-referenced timeline to see exactly where everyone was and when. It became an obsession with him as he worked non-stop for twenty hours each day, for days on end, until he was past exhaustion. After half a dozen false starts, he had a wall of paper nine-foot-high and twenty-four-foot long on which every person who came into the enquiry was listed. It was split into two halves to make it manageable and between them they covered the time from sunrise on Thursday morning to sunrise on Friday morning. There was a much bigger, minute by minute, scaled timeline covering the period from 3pm to midnight on Thursday, just after Étienne's body was found. On this timeline Hilaire, using a multitude of colours, meticulously plotted, and cross-referenced everyone's statements proving, as best he could, where everyone was. The fact was that everyone on the Estate, and in the village, did what they always did every Thursday, keeping to the same routines. There was only one difference, Étienne was over an hour late arriving at the bank and there was no explanation. The man who could have explained that gap, Monsieur Delors, left La Bête Blanche for the last time on the day of Étienne's killing and so his evidence never came in to the timeline. The fact that Delors's business card was found amongst Etienne's posession did not raise the enquiries it should. The investigation would have been different if he had been interviewed, but he was not.

As a piece of work, the timeline was a masterpiece. It brought into visual context what was hidden in the cardex. However, at the end of the exercise, it did not give Hilaire what he wanted, for he realised what he needed was the negative of what he saw. His timeline showed where everyone was. It did not show the gaps; and it was in the gaps that he knew he would find his answer. Ultimately, he was no further forward.

There was case review after case review by external policemen brought in from Paris, but these resulted only in praise for the way Hilaire had tackled the investigation, with some of his investigatory innovations being taken back to the capital. Very slowly, the avenues for examination started to dry up, and the pressure to concentrate on other crimes, which could be solved, started to take precedence. The Étienne murder case eventually became a mass of papers in a series of filing cabinets to be almost forgotten by everyone other than Hilaire, Juliette, and Dominique.

Just as Étienne's murder was locked away in filing cabinets in a Bordeaux police station, so was the Gallery between The Cellars and The Cottage. Juliette shut and bolted the doors from each of the houses, so it became fossilised; a shrine only to be re-opened when Étienne's killer was caught.

Chapter 95

Château de Gressier August 1933

THE BOY DIVED from the riverbank. A long shallow dive, as though he were a stone skimming across the surface of the water. Two or three strokes of crawl and he was in the middle of the river. Taking a deep breath, he ducked deep underwater and headed back to the riverbank. None of his friends saw the eight-year-old disappear and none of them saw his desperate struggle to free himself from the weeds he had swum into. Trapped, panic set into his body making his need for oxygen even more urgent until he could hold his breath no longer. The air burst involuntarily from his lungs and by reflex he breathed in the water. Very slowly, as the oxygen in his bloodstream was used up, the boy drifted into unconsciousness.

The first warning sign that Victor's friends had that he was in difficulties was the burst of air from his lungs as it exploded onto river surface. They swam to where he was lying but the weeds were trapping them too. It was the boys' yelling which brought the vineyard workers to the riverbank. Wading up to their necks with their scythes, they released his lifeless body and brought it to the riverbank. Just at that moment, Hugo arrived. He picked up Victor's little, wet, lifeless body and tried a few compressions of artificial respiration, but it was obviously pointless. Taking the boy's precious frame in his arms, he carried Victor up the hill and into the kitchen where he laid him on the kitchen table, as though preparing for a lifesaving operation; but there was no life to save. Hugo took a warm towel from the range and covered Victor's face and the top half of his naked chest. There were cuts on his arms as the men, in their desperation and unable to see, had slashed their scythes deep down in the river weed to free his trapped body.

Juliette was in her bedroom when she heard the shouts for help, and then the noise of feet crashing on the gravel. Instantly she felt a chill. It travelled throughout her body. Instinctively, she knew something was horribly wrong. She thought of that moment many times later. She identified it as the time when she felt her soul leave her body, just as Victor's had left his, and she started a living death.

Juliette arrived in the kitchen just as Hugo was covering Victor's face. It was as white as a sheet and his lips were purple. Little drops of water were still falling from his hair. In silence, but with steely determination, Juliette grabbed the towel and started to shake Victor in a frenzy. "Wake up!" she yelled. "Wake up, wake up!" she shouted even louder. Her command was so stern and violent, no one living would have dared disobey.

Hugo moved between Juliette and Victor's body, and facing her, he grasped her strongly by both arms. He looked straight into her eyes, and guided her backwards, her feet hardly touching the ground, as he placed her in an old kitchen rocking chair, by the side of the range. It was notorious for always being warm whatever the time of year. Juliette was now silent. No tears. No reaction.

The kitchen started to fill up fast, as people from all around rushed in to see what was happening, but immediately each fell silent as their eyes fell on the scene.

Hugo turned, picked up Victor's lifeless body, and carried it over to where Juliette was sitting. He slowly placed him on to her lap and into her arms. Victor's body was cold and wet and so, more by reaction than thought, Juliette squeezed her son tight and rubbed his arms trying to put heat into his limp body.

Looking into Victor's face, she very carefully lifted his right eyelid to look into his eye. There was nothing. Victor's soul had departed. She knew then that he was dead, and with this Juliette started to weep, and then sob, and then, as she pulled her child into her breast, she howled, the prolonged howl of a lonely wolf. The unbearable howl of pain. All those who heard that screech felt a shiver in their spine. It was a sound they would never forget.

Hugo moved to the door and guided everyone out. He left Juliette alone serenely swaying in the rocking chair as she cradled Victor in her arms, his head resting just under her chin. She was talking to him, asking what had happened, softly scolding him for being stupid, and asking how he thought Victoria was going to manage without him.

Hugo stood guard at the closed door. His huge frame acted as a block. Everyone knew better than to challenge him. He gave his instructions in a crisp no-nonsense manner, pointing to each person to whom he gave an order. He felt no need to explain. "Fetch the doctor, fetch the gendarme, fetch the priest, fetch the undertaker, fetch Monsieur le Maire, and find Victoria and bring her here."

Each person charged with their task set off towards the village. No one noticed at the time, but this was the moment that Hugo Coudace's takeover of Château de Gressier was complete, for from that moment on he was solely in charge.

With a lock of Étienne's hair taken after his death and with strands of her own and Victoria's hair, once again Juliette painstakingly weaved a band for Victor to wear on his ring finger. It was smaller in circumference this time and therefore more delicate to work. So it was that, in her concentration for perfection and with her heart completely broken, Juliette's soul went into deep hibernation. She was thankful for just one thing. Étienne had not seen his son die. She knew his agony would have been so profound that she could not have bourne that too.

As Juliette and Victoria stood at Victor's graveside, the animosity which the villagers had held against Juliette for three long years, evaporated in wave after wave of sympathy as the two of them stared at the polished wooden coffin deep at the bottom of the grave. To Victoria it looked lonely and so small. Her mother's hand was clasped over hers and, although she was holding it tight, there was no hiding Juliette's visible shaking as she fought to stand straight. The urge not to bend double, to relieve the pain in her chest and stomach, and drop to the ground, was overwhelming. She wanted to scream out loud, but no sound or movement was possible, even her tears were now choked so that they couldn't fall. All this pain transmitted itself from Juliette to Victoria in such a way that, years later when she remembered the moment, the fear and bewilderment Victoria felt then would recur as it was indelibly seared into her memory.

As Victoria stood over Victor's unfilled grave, she listened intently for any sound from his coffin. She was willing her brother to bang out loud, to reappear and bring to an end this long game of hide and seek, but as the earth was thrown on to the coffin top, with the clods of clay bouncing on the polished wood before landing, Victor's final resting place disappeared before her eyes.

That night, when the house was sound asleep, Victoria, dressed only in her nightie and with bare feet, crept through the kitchen door and out of the house. She took her brother's pillow with her. The moon was bright as she moved silently to his grave, taking the same route her father had taken to visit his father's grave all those years before, when he had returned from the war.

Victoria paused for a moment by the river where Victor had drowned and looked at the reflection of the moon as it shimmered softly in the darkness of the water. As she climbed over the wall and into the graveyard, she felt no fear of the night, for this was where Victor lay, and she knew that he would keep her safe. He would protect her, as he had always done.

At the graveside, Victoria placed Victor's pillow at the end with the small wooden cross and lay face down on top on the cut turf, which had been placed on the mound of bare earth. With her head resting on his pillow, and with her arms wide apart, she could smell and taste the soil. She reached across to touch her father's grave which was beside Victor's. She knew Victor was under her, asleep, and would never wake up, but she was worried for him. She wanted him to be warm and comfortable with his head rested on his pillow, and as she cuddled its softness she felt as though she was cuddling him. The fact that Victor didn't have his pillow with him in his coffin was something which would bother her for the rest of her life.

Victoria started to whisper to her brother. It was the same one-way conversation they often had late into the night, after she had climbed into his bed for comfort, when she would speak and he would say nothing. Firstly, in an effort to comfort him, she told him everything was all right. She recounted the day, telling him who came and said what. She told him how upset Mummy had been, and with this Victoria could speak no more. She was suddenly overwhelmed with anger and rage so, with her fists clenched tight, she beat down on the mud, intent on hitting her brother deep below. The thumps on the soil started to subside, as her tears and sobs took over, until exhaustion meant she could cry no more.

As Victoria lay flat, prostrate, with her head turned to the side and her eyes wide open, she saw him, running and skipping through the churchyard. In the strangeness of dreams, he morphed to sit on the church wall, his legs swinging with a huge beam on his face. At that moment, Victoria knew she had Victor with her for always. He would never ever leave her.

Chapter 96

Château de Gressier August 1934

AFTER VICTOR'S DEATH, Juliette became a recluse in her own home. She could not bear to go into the village knowing that people would stare, and once their gazes met, she would look away in embarrassment not knowing what to say. She wouldn't cross Latoire River Bridge as it took her close to where Victor died. If she wanted to go into Bordeaux, then she would take a different route which added an extra thirty kilometres and nearly an hour to her journey.

Dominique and Stephen were at Victor's funeral. They did not sit in the front row, not because Juliette didn't want them to, she did. It was just that she forgot to ask. Dominique visited as often as she could, but the meetings became hard work. Slowly the time between them lengthened until they eventually stopped. Importantly, Dominique would, every now and again, phone Juliette for a chat, just to make sure she was alright. These calls were usually late in the evening when everything was quiet, when Dominique knew that the black dog of depression could easily appear.

Judith Perfett had travelled to Château de Gressier the second she heard of Victor's death. Without hesitation she knew she had to be at the funeral and Juliette's side. It was Judith's presence which kept Juliette going through those dreadful first days. On her return to England she wrote incessantly. She wanted her friend to know that she was there for her. They were the most wonderful letters. Each contained a neatly written copy of a poem which was uplifting and encouraging in a variety of different ways. Judith had learnt a lot from being a vicar's wife. Although her life was full of routine, as was Juliette's, she found fun in the smallest of things and these would be lavishly spread throughout her letters.

Jack came to see her, carrying a letter from her father. It was the first letter from him that she opened since she had married Étienne. It was a beautifully crafted letter which had taken her father hour upon hour to write, but its reading left her cold. As before, Jack and Juliette renewed their friendship as though no time had passed. She wanted him to stay forever, but knowing it was impossible, she never asked.

Although the magistrates exonerated Juliette from any blame, the inquest gave her no comfort. Victor's death, they concluded, was an accident indirectly caused by the heavy rains which had poured throughout the whole of the Garonne region in the spring.

These rains had resulted in Bordeaux being badly flooded. They also devastated many vineyards in the region. When Château de Gressier's river, a tributary of the Garonne, had burst its banks, it destroyed the maize and tobacco crops which were traditionally planted on the lower fields of Château de Gressier and La Bête Blanche. However, thanks to Étienne's obsession with mud, Château de Gressier's drainage system worked well and their vines were protected from the worst of the ravaging rain. It was not the same for La Bête Blanche, where the rain washed away the soil, taking vine row after vine row with it.

The heavy rain had created circumstances which, said the magistrates, no one could have reasonably foreseen. The force of the swollen river had carried a number of boulders downstream which lodged just before the river bridge. This slowed the running water, which together with the soil leached from the vineyards, allowed the riverbed to silt up, making it an ideal home for weeds and, in turn, a death trap for any young swimmer.

As Juliette receded into her shell, the relationship between Juliette and Victoria degenerated into a negative spiral of despair. They were both hurting so much that neither had the strength to help the other. Instead, in their need, they each sucked from the other whatever energy they might have had, such that mother and daughter became estranged, one from the other.

Although Victor and Victoria were obviously not identical twins, for a long time the similarities between them gave the impression of being so. What was particularly remarkable was the similarity of their eyes and face, such that even Étienne and Juliette would, on occasions, struggle to tell them apart. Their earliest solution was to grow Victoria's hair long and, each morning, dress them as boy or girl, as their sex determined.

On the anniversary of Victor's death, convinced that Juliette loved her brother more than her, and certain that she would prefer him to be alive, Victoria cut her hair short to mimic her brother. At first, she hacked at its length and then cack-handedly worked at cutting the sides as she tried to layer it in the way that Victor's hair had been cut. After half-an-hour of arm-aching work, she looked like a bird which had been half-plucked with feathers sticking out in all directions. Then, going into Victor's bedroom, which had not changed since his death, she chose his favourite shirt and jumper and put them on.

Juliette's shock at seeing Victoria dressed as Victor caused her to explode in an anger which her daughter had never seen before. Not once did she consider the reasons behind Victoria's actions. Instead, with the strength of a woman possessed, Juliette forcefully stripped her daughter of Victor's clothes. In that moment, the alienation of mother and daughter was complete.

Chapter 97

Château de GressierAugust 1934

VERY GRADUALLY, JULIETTE became less and less involved in the running of the Estate as Hugo assumed responsibility for all the decisions. He continued to call into The Cellars every morning and say hello to Juliette, just as he had done since Étienne had died. But now, he would also stay in the office, late into the evening, always calling in before he went home. Slowly, he made himself indispensable, always doing Juliette's bidding, while at the same time adding to the insecurity she was already feeling by questioning her every decision.

Rather than exploiting his position as he had done before, Hugo now moved to ruthlessly consolidate his rule. To everyone else on the Estate, and in the village, Victor's death had been the moment when Hugo's Svengali-like training of Juliette became complete; only she, in her helplessness, did not see it that way.

What Hugo wanted above all was to bring Juliette back to her old happy self, for he was certain that, with her depression lifted, she would come to him. For this reason, Hugo was desperate to find a way of impressing Juliette which went beyond the routine. He knew she thought of him only in respect of work, and he was desperate for her to think of him as her potential lover. Hugo first thought of impressing Juliette by building a shrine to Victor, but he didn't know what form it should take. It was when he noticed that she talked incessantly about the dangers in the river, and mithered about another drowning, that his plans developed.

Very secretly, over the winter months and into the following spring and summer, Hugo used the staff on the Estate to reshape the river on each side of its banks and for the length of the Château de Gressier and La Bête Blanche's land. In a feat of engineering, he made the river straight and the banks parallel, as though it were a stretch of canal. He lined the river sides with old railway sleepers, which he piled deep into the riverbed giving it a straight edge. He then arranged for the river to be dredged, putting the silt in the gaps between the railway sleepers and the original riverbank and, at the same time, making the land the same height all the way along. Everything was designed to cause the river to flow faster, and in the process, stop it silting and growing deadly weeds. On the de Gressier side, nearest the bridge, he built a set of concrete steps and a slipway which enabled a swimmer to walk deep into the water in safety.

It had been the practice to farm either tobacco or maize on the flat flood lands on both sides of the river, from its edge up to the bottom of the hill slope where the vines had been planted; a distance of between one hundred and a hundred and fifty metres. Coudace decided that, for a distance of thirty metres from the riverbank, both sides would be laid to grass. On the de Gressier side of the river, about three metres from the river's edge, he planted a row of plane trees, like those renowned for running the length of the Canal du Midi. Between the trees, Hugo placed two wooden bench seats so that Juliette would be able to sit and enjoy the tranquillity and remember her son.

Juliette knew that the work was taking place, for she could see it from the house, but she would never go down there. Every time she asked what was going on, Hugo would explain that they were dredging the river of boulders and silt to stop anyone else from drowning. It was enough to satisfy her curiosity.

On the anniversary of Victor's death, knowing Juliette would not want to walk the quickest way to the village church, as it would take her by the river where Victor drowned, Hugo insisted he take her by car to visit her son's grave. Juliette spent many minutes alone sitting on the burned summer grass, her hands reaching out to touch the two graves simultaneously. Étienne's grave was now completely flat, with its headstone in place, but there was still a mound from Victor's grave as the earth had yet to fully settle. She said nothing. What could she say? She tried to find comfort in her dream that Étienne and Victor were together again in a celestial heaven, that Étienne was once again looking after their son; but she found it was all too impossible to really believe.

Hugo waited patiently in the shade just a few metres away from the car as the sun rose higher and higher into the azure blue sky, empty but for a few puffs of high white clouds. It was the most perfect day and he felt nervously confident that it was going to get better. Slowly Juliette returned to the car. Nothing was said between them as they drove back to the Château. Hugo didn't stop there as he normally would, but instead of turning left into the drive, he continued past the house between The Cellars and The Barn, and with the vines laid out like a carpet on their left, he drove down the hill towards the river. Juliette froze when she realised where he was taking her. Still nothing was said.

Hugo stopped just a few metres back from the river's edge. He didn't look at her. Instead he quickly got out, stepped around the car to open her door, and offered Juliette his hand. She had no expression on her face as she looked up into his eyes. Dutifully she accepted Hugo's hand as he tentatively led her from the passenger's seat.

Nothing was as she remembered it. Only the bridge and the sparkle of the river water remained the same. The wildness which formerly surrounded the river edge of her working farm had gone. Both sides of the river had been replaced with a manicured landscape, which gave a neatness and uniformity to nature.

In silence, Hugo led Juliette to two bench seats which had been placed equidistant apart under the row of newly planted trees. One was engraved Victor and the other Victoria. Juliette looked at the wording and then into Hugo's eyes. To his delight, he saw her yield her first smile for over a year. Very slowly, almost daring not to, Juliette sat down on the bench engraved Victor. She touched his name with her thumb as she wriggled slightly, for she felt uncomfortable sitting on a memorial to her son. In complete silence, Hugo retired to stand some way behind Juliette, leaving her alone to her thoughts.

Juliette was overwhelmed with the perfection of what she saw. Not only had Hugo made the river much safer, but there was now peace and tranquillity in a place where it had been absent before. It was, she concluded, the perfect shrine to her lovely son. So much better than his grave, which lacked any kind of personality about who he was. This was where his soul was. It was where she wanted to be.

Slowly, in her imagination, and as though it were true, she saw Victor and Victoria in the middle of the river laughing and splashing. In their fun, they were joined by the children from the village, as used to happen. Slowly Juliette lost the image, which was giving her so much joy, and came back to reality.

Juliette turned around and saw where Hugo was standing. Although he was watching her, he did not move. She got up with a bounce in her step, which Hugo hadn't seen since Étienne's death, and walked towards him. This time it was she who took his hand. "Thank you," she said, looking deeply into his eyes. "Thank you," she repeated, emphasising the word, before gently kissing him on his bearded cheek. "I think it is perfect. It's strange," she continued, "but there is a feeling of happiness here."

Hugo could only agree, for her reaction had made him the happiest man in the world. It was later that afternoon, when Juliette saw Victoria with her shorn hair, that her depressive temperament returned with a vengeance.

Chapter 98

Château de Gressier December 1934

JULIETTE AND VICTORIA both dreaded the thought of Christmas for they remembered the agony of the Christmas before when they sat at the table, just the two of them. The absence of Étienne and Victor from their places had an effect as chilling as a ghost. Since the anniversary of Victor's death, the relationship between mother and daughter had deteriorated such that contact between the two of them became virtually non-existent. The thought of each buying a Christmas present for the other was more than each could actually bear.

On Christmas Eve, Juliette and Victoria went to church for the service of nine lessons and carols, as they had always done. Beforehand, they placed winter wreaths on Étienne and Victor's graves where both wished fervently for the life they had before Étienne died; a life when they remembered being happy. Instead the damp, dark chill of the graveyard was a simile for the sadness which pervaded both of them.

The chilly atmosphere in The Cellars on Christmas Eve continued through to Christmas morning. Juliette had organised a Christmas tree and decorated it, having insisted, ever since she was married, that Christmas at Château de Gressier would be English in its character. This gave the setting for a perfunctory exchange of presents between mother and daughter before they left for the church.

At the church, Juliette and Victoria were met by Hugo who was waiting patiently for them. Victoria shivered as she always did when she saw him. There was something about the way he looked at her which made her feel uncomfortable. Her instinct was to keep out of his way. Unusually, Hugo was very smartly dressed. There was not an item of clothing which was not brand new and, amazingly for him, very cleverly coordinated. Juliette's instant reaction was to compliment Hugo on his looks and with these words he rose in magnificence. This gave him confidence and so he escorted Juliette and Victoria to their seats in the front pew, before retiring to the side pew where he always sat on his own. However busy the church, no villager would sit next to him, nor would they presume to sit in the front row where the Guégan family had worshipped for the last 200 years.

It was the same very smart Hugo who presented himself at the front door of The Cellars about half an hour after the service. He'd had several swigs of brandy to give him the courage he felt he needed. He pressed the bell which he heard ring deafeningly inside. He stood back and waited. Although it was now past mid-morning, the day was still cold, damp, misty and dark. It was difficult to see the vines in the fields at the front of the Château. By chance, Hugo looked up at the roof beneath where he was standing. He saw, for the first time, where the buckshot had embedded itself into the wooden timbers when his gun had accidentally fired in the tussle with Étienne. At first he wondered why he hadn't noticed this before, but these thoughts disappeared as the door opened, and he saw before him, just as he had seen all those years ago, what he believed to be the most beautiful woman in the world.

The sight of Juliette knocked Hugo off his stride, for he was expecting it to be opened by the maid which, on any other day of the year, it would have been.

"Hugo, what are you doing here?" asked Juliette, startled at seeing him. "You don't usually come to this door."

"I wanted to see you about something special, something important."

Juliette frowned slightly for she detected a nervousness in his voice. "You're not planning on leaving me, are you?" she joked.

"Er, no. Why do you say that?" asked Hugo, defensively.

"Come through to the kitchen," beckoned Juliette. "I have mulled some wine, although there's only me to drink it."

"Can we go somewhere else, rather than the kitchen?" asked Hugo.

"Of course," said Juliette, now quite puzzled. "Let us go into the Library." It had always been Juliette's favourite room in the whole house and today, with the huge fire burning in the grate, there was a warmth and cosiness about it.

"Come, sit," she said, trying to make him as easy as possible. She pointed to a settee where her guests would normally sit, if she had any.

"I'll stand if I may?" responded Hugo, as he moved to place his back to the fire unaware that, in doing so, he was blocking out the heat.

There was an unusual tension in Hugo's body, and so immediately after she had sat down Juliette changed her mind and stood up again, for she felt uncomfortable about the way he towered over her.

"Juliette," said Hugo, after a little pause. "I think we should get married."

For the first time in a very long time, Juliette could not think what to say. Not a muscle on her face moved to change her expression. She had not expected the statement and did not know how to respond.

"Do you not agree, it would be good for us to be married?" continued Hugo, uncertain how to interpret Juliette's lack of reaction.

"Are you asking to marry me?" said Juliette, her voice becoming softer and quieter in its uncertainty.

"Yes, I think so," responded Hugo cautiously and then, more confidently, he continued, "yes, I am."

"But why?" she asked

"Because you need me and it would be good for both of us," he said. As soon as these words were out of his mouth, Hugo regretted saying them, because they were a long way from the script he had prepared and rehearsed very many times for this moment.

"Is there not more to it than that?" asked Juliette, who by now was sitting down and looking up at Hugo, who was still in front of the fire.

Hugo stepped forward and slowly picked up Juliette's left hand which was rested on her knee. She could not remember him ever having touched her with such familiarity before. It had always been so very formal, and now he held her hand very gently.

"I don't think so." He paused. "I want, no, I would like you to be my wife." His voice, while still gravelly in tone, had become soft, warm and inviting.

Juliette looked up into Hugo's eyes and in his gaze she felt a power wave surge from him to her in a way she had never felt before. It was hypnotically overwhelming in its effect. Once again, he was walking with his mysterious God.

"It's not something I've thought about," said Juliette defensively, adding "getting married again is not something I'd ever contemplated."

Very graciously and still holding her hand, Hugo knelt down opposite her. With his other hand he reached deep into his jacket pocket, and simultaneously opening the lid of a dark blue velvet box, he presented Juliette with an oval cut emerald engagement ring. It was quite beautiful, for the emerald had a colour and clarity which was exquisite. It was set in a surround of large diamonds that shone brightly even in the dullness of the room. Its sparkle spoke, as all engagement rings should speak, of the brightness of their future together.

If Juliette was in a state of confusion before, she found the presentation of such a beautiful ring completely disarming. She offered no resistance as Hugo gently removed Étienne's engagement ring, and keeping it tightly in his hand, he slipped his own ring next to her wedding band. As she looked at her hand, her eyes focused, not on Hugo's ring, but on Étienne's gold wedding band now scratched and worn. Not once, since their wedding day, had it come off her finger and suddenly she felt she was betraying everything that she and Étienne had together. The answer would have to be no.

But at the moment she was making up her mind, Hugo placed Étienne's engagement ring on the fourth finger of her opposite hand and in that moment she knew Étienne would be with her, whatever happened.

Still kneeling and holding both her hands, Hugo very quietly and gently asked, "Will you marry me, please?"

There was a long pause as Juliette thought of her answer. She could find no reason to say no. Love and lust were things of youth, she thought. Perhaps companionship was a good enough reason to marry. It was on this thought, and this thought alone, that Juliette said, "Yes," and with, her response Hugo's heart danced a jig of joy and a huge smile brightened his whole face.

Chapter 99

Latoire Village and Bordeaux April 1935

VIRGIL BEAUVAIS PACED up and down outside the police station. He had not slept all night as he had argued with his wife. Even as he took the early bus into Bordeaux, he really didn't know whether he was going to go through with their agreed plan or not.

Virgil was one of those salt of the earth people; honest, proud, hardworking and loyal. He had not been educated, nor did he have a fine intellect, but he had been given the power of observation. It was this that made him such a valuable member of the de Gressier land team. He could spot disease long before it showed up, and his ability to forecast changes in the weather hours ahead of anyone else was legendary.

Virgil's troubles had started just two days before, when, as he was bent over, tending to his vines, Coudace suggested that it was time that Lily, his eldest daughter, should visit him at Maison Presson, his home. A suggestion from Coudace was not an invitation which could be rejected; it was, in these circumstances, an instruction.

"Why's that, Boss?" said Virgil, innocently.

"How much do you owe me?" asked Coudace, deliberately not answering Virgil's question.

"I don't know precisely," said Virgil, "about three hundred and fifty francs?"

"Five hundred and forty francs," said Coudace, matter-of-factly.

"But that will be easily paid off with summer overtime," said Virgil.

"That's if you're working here this summer," Coudace retorted, threateningly.

"Shall we say Thursday, 6pm?"

"I'm not sure," said Virgil, "I'll have to check with my wife."

"You have an Estate cottage, don't you?" asked Coudace.

"Yes."

"Then, I imagine it will be a very short discussion."

The conversation between Virgil and Beatrice, his wife, later that evening, when Lily was asleep in bed was not easy or comfortable and it was certainly not short.

"No," said Beatrice, emphatically "when she was told of Coudace's demand. She will not go." Beatrice didn't need to ask why he wanted to see Lily for, like Virgil, she already knew.

Virgil repeated the conversation about the money he owed, the implied loss of his job and their cottage. There was no anger in the way he spoke, he was merely repeating facts.

"It makes no sense. He gets married on Saturday, to Madame. We have an invitation, all of us," continued Beatrice.

"I know, perhaps he thinks it's a 'last time' kind of thing."

"What, 'le droit du seigneur?' That's ridiculous. Its medieval nonsense," Beatrice chided before adding, "the same happened to Monica's little Clara."

"You never said," said Virgil.

"No, of course not. Monica was too ashamed and wanted it kept quiet. But it was the reason she gave me for Clara running away."

Virgil said nothing for, without anyone saying anything to him, he already knew the reason.

"Clara went up to his house three or four times, because Jean told her she had to go.

"What, her father made her go?" asked Virgil, feigning surprise.

"Yes, little Clara told her mum what he did to her, so as to stop her from having to go, but still Jean insisted."

Still Virgil chose discretion and not to comment.

"She was only thirteen too, just like our Lily," said Beatrice. "Then there was little Zoe, she went up to Maison Presson to be with him, and she was never right afterwards."

"Little thing was only about twelve or thirteen too," added Virgil, "but she looked much older."

"She never left the house after she'd been there. Her parents sent her away to live with an aunt somewhere, perhaps that's what we should do with Lily."

"No," said Virgil firmly. "We have to stop him. He'll keep going after other young ... until he's ..." He didn't finish his sentence.

"How are we going to do that?"

"Will Clara and Zoe report him to the police for what he did?" asked Virgil.

"No, why would they want the shame? Who's going to believe them?" replied Beatrice before adding, "What about Madame? Why don't we tell her, then she'll stop it."

"No, she's so infatuated with him since Étienne died, that she hears nothing but what Coudace wants her to hear. As we've all said, she's under his spell."

"No, it was after Victor drowned, that's when he really got his hooks into her," corrected Beatrice. Virgil nodded his agreement. "Well, she's not going," said Beatrice firmly. "You can tell him. Tell him we know what he did to Clara and Zoe and it's not going to happen to Lily."

"Yes, yes," said Virgil anxiously.

"You know what he did, don't you....to Clara and Zoe?" continued Beatrice, pressing the point.

"Yes, yes," continued Virgil, not wanting the ugly details to spoil his train of thought.

"Well, the same is not going to happen to Lily," repeated Beatrice, so as to make her view clear.

There was silence in the room, only broken by the occasional crackle of the fire, or a spout of steam from the kettle as the pressure was released from the lid.

"I'm fairly certain he killed Étienne," said Virgil very softly and after a long pause.

Beatrice looked at him but said nothing for she instinctively knew he would resent it if she asked questions. He had to be allowed to speak in his own time, as he uncovered his thoughts.

"I think I can prove it too," he continued, after a little while.

"How?" prompted Beatrice, very gently.

"There's only one of us on the Estate that's left-handed, that's the boss. Everyone else is right-handed. He has special wire-cutters. They come special from Paris. We all turn the wire around itself one way. He turns it around another. It's just as neat. Also, his cuts are different, because his blade is upside-down to ours."

Still Beatrice said nothing as she sensed there was more.

"It was all a bit odd 'cause the day after Étienne's death, the Saturday, the wheels on his van were swapped with the wheels on Étienne's van for no good reason. Why would you do that?"

Suddenly, the discussion was no longer about Lily, but whether Hugo Coudace was a murderer. Like most people who worked on the de Gressier Estate, Virgil and Beatrice did not like Coudace, nor did they trust him. His aura was always threatening; unless he wanted something in which case his charm was devastatingly effective. As they had done many times, they discussed the common description of Coudace 'as walking with God' and once again they agreed it was fair, for he had the ability to materialise out of thin air, in a hush, and in doing so he created a strange, mesmerizing, bewitching presence.

Beatrice, on hearing Virgil's theory, did everything she could to suppress the anger she felt at him for not sharing something so important for so long. She knew it would be no good if she complained. Instead, steeling herself, she said very firmly, "Virgil, you have two choices. You can go to the police in Bordeaux in the morning and tell 'em what you have told me, or every night for the rest of your life you will have to explain to me why it took you so long to say anything, and then you did nothing."

It was, as they say, a no-brainer. Virgil would be at the police station in the morning; but as for Beatrice meeting her side of the bargain, depressingly, he knew it was never going to happen. By sharing his thoughts, he knew he was in for a prolonged period of serious mental pain.

Chapter 100

Bordeaux April 1935

IT WAS WITH the memory of Beatrice's scolding that Virgil walked into the police station and asked for Inspector Henri Hilaire. "I need to see him about Étienne Guégan's murder," he said.

On seeing Virgil, Hilaire instinctively knew there was something special about this moment for there was a shyness and hesitancy from the man in front of him. His first thought was that Virgil had come to confess.

In the interview room, Hilaire removed his uniform jacket and tie so as not to appear imposing, and, deliberately sitting adjacent to Virgil rather than opposite, he offered him a cup of tea. This was going to take a long time, as long as it takes, he thought, before he got his confession.

At first they talked about Étienne, what a lovely man he was, and how pleased they all were to have worked for him. How surprised Virgil was to learn that Étienne had a mistress in Bordeaux, because Juliette and he had made such a perfect couple. Hilaire was impressed, for there was not a detail of gossip or story on which Virgil was wrong. It was therefore quickly into their conversation, that Hilaire dismissed from his mind any idea that Virgil was Étienne's killer.

"So, what information do you have on Étienne's death?" asked Hilaire, changing the subject.

"I think you're looking for someone who is left-handed, are you not?" said Virgil.

"What makes you say that?" asked Hilaire.

"Because of the way the wire was twisted back on itself, right-handed people do it one way, left-handed people do it another."

"Did you see the wire?" asked Hilaire.

"Yes, when it was around the tree. I was one of the first there. If you remember, we were all stopped by the tree with the wire on it, until you came and sent us back up the road."

Hilaire wrote in his notebook.

"Do you still have the wire?" asked Virgil.

"Yes, of course."

"Then you will be able to examine the cut of the wire. It will be different if it was cut by left-handed wirecutters as opposed to normal right-handed ones."

"Is there a difference?" puzzled Hilaire.

"You may have seen left-handed people try to use right-handed scissors upside-down, but they never cut well. It's the same with metal shears."

"Let me be clear," said Hilaire. "You believe the evidence shows that the murderer is a left-handed person, owning left-handed shears?"

"No," said Virgil, wanting to be very precise. "What I'm saying is that if the evidence you have shows that the murderer is a left-handed person, then you should be questioning Monsieur Coudace."

"Hugo Coudace?" repeated Hilaire, just to make sure. "Why?"

"Because he's the only person on the Estate who's left-handed."

"And he has special left-handed shears?" asked Hilaire.

Virgil nodded.

"Is there anything else?"

"You've been unable to match the tyre tracks to any tyre, haven't you?" said Virgil.

"To any car, yes," Hilaire acknowledged.

"That's because, between late Friday night, after Monsieur Étienne's death, and early Saturday morning. Monsieur Coudace swapped the wheels on his van with those of Monsieur Étienne's, and then had the tyres on Monsieur Étienne's van changed for new ones."

"Eh," said Hilaire, not understanding exactly what he was being told.

Virgil repeated his statement.

"Did you see him do this?"

"No."

"What makes you say it?"

"Because it happened."

"How do you know it happened?" asked Hilaire, perplexed.

"Monsieur, I have little read'n and write'n but I see things, ask any one." Virgil's voice was getting strong and more determined as he spoke. "It's what keeps me in my job. I know and remember things. Show me a picture for a few seconds and I will describe it back to you forever."

"So what makes you say it happened?" asked Hilaire for a second time.

"I know it was Monsieur Coudace's van what hit Monsieur Étienne. You could see from the bang in the fenders. Now Monsieur Étienne always paid to have his windscreen, headlights and wheels washed whenever he filled up with petrol. It was why they were always shiny black, whereas Monsieur Coudace's were always dirty."

"But we know Coudace's van didn't leave the garage at Château de Gressier that morning. My policemen examined it in the barn there."

"Yes sir, but the vehicle they examined had Monsieur Étienne's wheels on it. I'm certain they were changed during the night."

"You're telling me that the van Monsieur Coudace drove on the Saturday was Monsieur Étienne's but with his wheels on it."

Virgil nodded.

"Were all four wheels swapped, do you know?" asked Hilaire.

"Yes, sir."

"Were the vans identical?" asked Hilaire, wanting to check that the wheels could be swapped.

"Yes, they were bought at the same time, just a few weeks apart."

Hilaire paused as his mind raced back to the Saturday after Étienne's death and he remembered that it was not until late afternoon that Coudace appeared in the Estate offices. He racked his memory to recall what he said he had been doing earlier but could not remember. He would have to go back through his notes. He mentally cursed, for Saturday was not in his timeline and therefore Coudace's statement of what he had been doing was outside the verification period.

"So we are dealing with four swapped wheels," said Hilaire seeking to confirm his understanding. "Where did they go?" he asked.

"Maybe six," replied Virgil, "'cause I'm sure the spare wheels had been swapped between the vans."

"I'm sorry but I don't understand. Why? How do the spare wheels come into this?" asked Hilaire.

"I don't know," said Virgil, getting frustrated. "Probably because Monsieur Ergral told everyone in the village, the night immediately after Monsieur Étienne had died, that you were looking to trace two front car tyres. Monsieur Coudace heard this. Perhaps he decided, then and there, to swap his front wheels with the spare wheels to immediately hide the evidence. How would I know? I'm not the detective," he pleaded.

"Monsieur Ergral, the photographer?" asked Hilaire, concerned.

Virgil nodded. Hilaire's stomach tightened but his face gave no clue as to his feeling of anger. Trying to match the car's tracks to its originating tyres had been a major thrust of his investigation.

"So where did the wheels go?" asked Hilaire, repeating a question he asked earlier.

"They went so the tyres could be changed," said Virgil, in a tone which suggested he was answering a stupid question with an obvious answer. "But they weren't done at the garage in Libourne where they would normally go. I think they were done in Bergerac."

"What makes you say that?"

"'Cause two of the new tyres still had Firestone delivery labels on them, well part of them anyway, and the address on one of the labels was for the garage in Bergerac."

"Are you sure?"

"Yes."

Hilaire made a note in his notebook to check.

"How do you know the spare wheels were swapped?"

"Cause Monsieur Étienne's van had the dirty spare wheel put back on it when it was clean before," said Virgil.

"Can I get this right?" said Hilaire. "You're saying that, by the Saturday night, after Monsieur Guégan had been killed, of the ten tyres on the two vans, there were four brand new ones."

"Yes," said Virgil, his voice expressing concern that he was not being believed. "There were four brand new tyres on Monsieur Guégan's van. I'm sure of it."

"Sorry, I'm really not getting this," said Hilaire, apologetically.

"Let's draw a diagram of two vans each with their wheels and you show me how you think the wheels and tyres changed."

The two men pored over a piece of paper as Virgil drew lines showing how he thought the tyres and wheels had moved. At the end, Hilaire looked up wide-eyed. It was as though he had seen the light. It left Virgil feeling perplexed, for although he was the one who had no reading or writing, it seemed to him that he was the only one showing any common sense.

Hilaire's expression of delight gave Virgil confidence to continue. "I don't get it," he said. "For some reason you examined all the tyres of all the cars and vans on the Estate and in the village but not Monsieur Étienne's which Monsieur Coudace had started to drive. Isn't that very strange?"

Hilaire paused as he contemplated the consequences of this lapse in their investigation.

"Why are you mentioning all this now?" asked Hilaire casually.

Virgil said nothing as his eyes visibly narrowed in a determination that put Hilaire on edge. "Coudace is a child molester," he said angrily, after a long pause. "His next victim was to be my daughter. He has already attacked many girls in the village."

Hilaire paused. He put down his pencil, leant back in his chair, and stared at Virgil. Was the first part true or was this the real story, he wondered.

"Can you name the girls he attacked?"

Virgil listed six girls' names including those of Clara and Zoe whom he had discussed with his wife the evening before. As others acknowledged, Virgil knew things which came to him through his power of observation.

"What evidence do you have?"

"None," said Virgil, feeling very stupid, "but each of those girls has, and if they will agree to give evidence, then you've got him for this too."

Coudace had been one of Hilaire's earliest suspects but there was nothing concrete which had linked him to the murder. In fact, the log of the telephone operator had given credence to Coudace's statement of where he had been and what he had been doing. Eventually, Hilaire had concluded that Coudace was only a suspect because he didn't like him, and his controlling ways. In recognition of his own prejudice, Hilaire had struck him off the list of suspects.

With Virgil putting in place some important pieces of the puzzle, Hilaire had a sudden sense of excitement. He was now sure he had his man for one crime and perhaps many more. Unusually for Hilaire, he started to ask a series of disjointed questions about both Étienne's death, Juliette, and the girls of the village.

Virgil kept slowing Hilaire down so he could be very precise for, without doing so, he found he got confused. He was anxious that a clever man was twisting his words and he was not going to be caught out that way.

It was early afternoon when the interview ended. There had been copious amounts of coffee and water drunk but no one had eaten. As they both stood up, Hilaire could have sworn that Virgil had visibly shrunk from when they first met. There was a difference between the way he had presented himself then and now. At first, Virgil had made every effort to hold himself tall and erect, but now he had been believed, his body form returned to its usual curved, timid shape, formed by years of suppression.

Hilaire shook Virgil firmly by the hand and promised, as had been requested at the start of their meeting, that their conversation would remain private unless and until a written statement was required. He also did something which he had never done before: he made a point of thanking Virgil for doing his civic duty in immensely difficult circumstances.

Virgil walked down the road towards the centre of Bordeaux and the bus station. He stopped for a glass of cold lager at an insignificant café on the way. He couldn't remember when he needed a drink more.

Immediately the meeting was over, three things happened. Firstly, Hilaire instructed his Sergeant to find the garage in Bergerac, interview the garage owner and get the name of every person who had their car tyres changed on the days immediately after Étienne's death. Then, he called back from storage the evidence box of the Guégan murder. Finally, he did an all stations enquiry asking whether there was any record of any complaint of any nature being made against a man known as Hugo Coudace.

As he sat at his desk reflecting on the day's work, Hilaire had a real hope that the Guégan murder had at last been solved for, in addition to his professional pride, he had a very personal reason for wanting the file closed.

Chapter 101

Château de Gressier April 1935

JULIETTE WANTED HER wedding to be a modest affair for she was concerned that those on the Estate would be reminded of the wedding she and Étienne had denied them all those years ago. She thought of inviting her father and quickly dismissed any rapprochement from her mind. Oh, how she wished her mother could be there, but then she knew she would do nothing without her husband's consent, so it was not to be. She had only one member of her family left, her daughter Victoria, who so hated the idea of her mother being married to Hugo that she made it clear she did not want to go.

Juliette's biggest concern about getting married was that the de Gressier Estate belonged to Étienne's family, not hers. Her money might have saved it a long time ago and made it good, but it was Étienne's line she wanted to benefit. She spent long hours making sure that, in a prenuptial agreement, Château de Gressier would pass through to Victoria and then her children. It was an absolute, and without Hugo's agreement there would be no marriage.

While Hugo had no Estate, over the years he'd acquired many parcels of wine and farmlands around the area which he harvested on his own account. There was also his share in 'La Bête Blanche', on the other side of the river, which he and Juliette had purchased in a fifty-fifty partnership long before the lease came to an end, just so they could stop paying rent. Their prenuptial agreement made it clear that Hugo's assets would pass directly to any children they had, and if there were none then they too would go to Victoria and her heirs and descendants.

Hugo and Juliette's wedding was held on a nondescript day in the village church. Juliette wore a long, cream, silk dress and matching bolero jacket with a high turned-up collar which showed off her long, slender neck. Her cream silk shoes, and veil were both embroidered with hand-made silk daisies.

Immediately before the service, supported by her daughter as reluctant bridesmaid, Juliette walked to Étienne's grave. She stopped, took a stem from her bouquet and, bending down, she placed it diagonally beneath his headstone. For the umpteenth time, Juliette asked him secretly if he minded. She knew he would, particularly to Hugo, so after a shiver and deep sigh, she moved to Victor's grave right next door. This time she bent low on her knee and taking another stem, she did the same thing, but this time taking great care to ensure the flower head was placed just above where she imagined Victor's heart would be. She swept the damp grass with her hand, before feeling her mouth go dry and tears fill her eyes.

Rising to stand by the side of her daughter, Juliette looked down to the two graves, as did Victoria. Each felt a deep and desperate loneliness, so they held hands in an attempt to assuage their grief. Without saying anything to the other, both wished in earnest for their life gone by, in which these two played such an important part. Neither of them wanted to turn around and go forward with their new lives, which the wedding had now ordained.

Juliette first thought of Jack Morris giving her away but decided against it, for if he were there then she knew it would be him that she would be thinking of marrying. No, the only people who could give her away were in the churchyard. She would walk down the aisle on her own, supported by her daughter, and so the two turned and walked serenely to the church entrance, down the aisle and to Hugo's side.

The reception was a very lavish affair in a large marquee erected on the front lawn of the Château. Everyone from the Estate, the village, their customers, and professional advisors were there. There was just one thing lacking. Neither Juliette nor Hugo had any friends. Dominique was invited to the wedding but decided to stay away, as did Virgil and his wife. They had thought that the evidence he had given would have meant that Hugo would have been arrested by now and the wedding cancelled. Perhaps, he wondered, he'd got it all wrong.

While the wine was freely flowing at the wedding, Hilaire was at his desk with four different types of wirecutters, all right-handed, supervising the cutting and winding of rolls of wire. Everyone in the police station was forced into having a go. There were no left-handers amongst them, and they all did it the same way, clockwise, whereas the wire which had killed Étienne was wound around in an anti-clockwise direction.

Hilaire had moments of doubt about which way up the actual wire on his desk had been attached to the trees, but several of the photographs, taken as evidence, showed that the wire had been tied just as Virgil explained.

Hilaire studied at great length, and with the aid of a large magnifying glass, the way the wire was cut. He was sure there was something unusual about the cut but could not define what it was. It would have to go to a laboratory to be forensically examined.

It was early evening, just as he was leaving the police station that Hilaire met his Sergeant coming back. He was dragging in with him two filthy dirty tyres grubby with a lime whitewash.

"These are from Coudace's van," shouted the Sergeant with a huge grin.

"You're sure?"

"I'm certain. They're from a garage in Bergerac just as you said. It was the third one we visited. I've got a witness statement and everything. Coudace swapped four tyres, two of which were in good condition, for new ones. The two good tyres were sold on almost immediately, but the garage owner used the other two as flower plant pots at the front of his garage. He remembers it all very clearly as the tyres had worn unevenly and couldn't be sold. Also, he didn't have enough tyres in stock to do the whole job, so his wife had to traipse around two other garages to get them."

"Are you saying that those tyres have sat there for the last five years?"

"Yes, I've got both the owner and his wife to give me a statement as it was her who planted the flowers and maintained them."

Hilaire raised his eyebrows in amazement.

"You can't believe the fuss she made when I insisted on taking them."

Hilaire then smiled in appreciation of his Sergeant's tenacity. Little did he appreciate that his Sergeant had expected nothing less than a full interrogation if, having found the tyres, he had turned up at the police station without them. A polite interrogation it may have been, but nevertheless an ordeal far worse than that involved in upsetting the garage owner's wife.

Back at Hilaire's desk, there was a scurry as they found the photographs of the tyre tracks and pored over the detail trying to compare the tread marks with the patterns in the mud. To the bare eye it looked as though they matched. Again, they would have to be forensically examined with the castes they had taken but, prima facie, Hilaire was certain he had enough for his immediate needs: a search warrant.

Hilaire first had to make a case to the Procurer and then, with their approval, get a Judge d'Instruction to grant a search warrant. It was close to 10pm that evening before Hilaire had the documents he needed. Tomorrow morning, first thing, they would arrest Hugo Coudace on the suspicion of the murder of Étienne Guégan and search his house. It was going to be an interesting day.

Chapter 102

Dordogne, France April 1935

HUGO AND JULIETTE Coudace booked into the luxurious Michelin starred hotel, near Saint Michel de Fronsac, with its spectacular views over the River Dordogne. At the same time, Hilaire was being issued with Hugo's arrest warrant. By coincidence, it was the hotel where Étienne had seduced Dominique for the very first time; a point not lost on a coy and embarrassed Dominique when she heard where they had stayed.

By the morning, Juliette knew she had made a terrible mistake in marrying Hugo, for he had come at her all night and then again in the morning without showing a single thought for her and her needs. She was treated as his possession, to do with as he wished. He'd moved her around the bed, bending and moving her arms and legs as some child plays with a toy, all for his enjoyment and nothing for hers.

Hugo was sound asleep as Juliette sat in the chair by the window, wrapped in her dressing gown, looking over the lawns and then the river in the distance, as the sun rose. She was thinking about Étienne and the pleasure he had always given her when they made love.

While Juliette was deep in thought, Hilaire was breaking into Maison Presson, Hugo's house, leading a team of police searchers. He was surprised that Hugo was not there for he was certain that this was where he lived. He sent one of his officers to Château de Gressier where he learnt of Hugo's marriage to Juliette the day before. Why hadn't Virgil mentioned it, he wondered. More importantly, was she an accomplice?

Hilaire demanded that the search be precise. He ordered every room was to be slowly and methodically searched. Everything was to be pulled out and put back. A large number of wire cutters were found, and each was taken into evidence. There was a search of the barns and the roof space. After a little while, a search becomes routine, particularly when nothing incriminating is found early on. The excitement ebbs and it loses its edge. They were into the fifth hour of their search and the last place left was the basement. It was cold and dank with poor low-wattage light bulbs which Hilaire insisted on being replaced with something much brighter. As his men searched, Hilaire casually picked up one of three biscuit tins stacked on top of one another. Lifting the lid off the top one, he immediately shouted out in excitement "We've got him, we've got him," while simultaneously holding up several pairs of girls' knickers for everyone to see.

The team stopped and looked completely puzzled. They didn't know what knickers had to do with Étienne's murder. In his focus on catching Étienne's murderer, Hilaire had forgotten to mention to his team the allegations of sexual assault and paedophilia.

The three biscuit tins revealed pairs and pairs of young girls' knickers crunched inside.

"There's more stuff like that upstairs," said one of their number. "All a bit kinky."

The find, although nothing to do with their original reason, gave the search team a new lease on life. Hilaire instructed two of his searchers to start the search from the top again, but this time to look for anything which might be related to any kind of sexual activity, leaving just a few of their number in the basement.

Eventually, the search team made its way to the basement fireplace. With the aid of a torch and a tug on a dirty felt cloth stuffed into the chimney, a polished wooden box fell into the hearth. A screwdriver and brute force broke the lock and with that Coudace's fate was sealed. Inside, amongst tens of thousands of francs, were some brand-new bank notes. Hilaire looked at the numbers. He was sure, but not a hundred percent certain, that the numbers matched those which had been in the wage packets which Étienne had withdrawn from the bank on the day he had been killed.

Chapter 103

Dordogne, France April 1935

HUGO AND JULIETTE had a lovely relaxing Sunday. Juliette resisted Hugo's suggestion that they should go back to bed in the afternoon. Instead, they walked the fields and found many things to laugh at. It was not something they generally did as theirs was a serious relationship. At bedtime, Juliette decided that she would have to teach Hugo how to be a good lover, how to please her and how these moments should be shared. All her efforts failed, for every one of her words was taken as an affront to his masculinity, which meant that he was even rougher, harder, and more selfish than he had been the night before.

As Hugo slept the sleep of the exhausted, Juliette, not only physically but emotionally hurt from his bruising, knew she could not share her bed with this man again. She had, she decided, made a terrible, terrible mistake in getting married.

Hugo and Juliette returned to Château de Gressier just after lunchtime on Monday morning. The marquee was already down and being loaded onto a van. Both took little notice of the parked police car for it was not an unusual sight. Hugo carried Juliette across the threshold as is customary for a newly married couple. They kissed modestly as he put her down, both unaware that they had been joined in the hallway.

Hilaire was standing there very smartly in his uniform. "Monsieur Hugo Coudace, I'm arresting you for the murder of Monsieur Étienne Guégan." He then turned to the accompanying policeman and said very politely, "Please handcuff him and take him to the police station. I will join you later."

Not a single word was said by Hugo as he was led out of the house. Juliette, surrounded by unopened wedding presents, said nothing either, for she was totally stunned.

"Madame," said Hilaire, "can we please go through to your drawing room? I need to ask you some questions."

As Juliette sat down, she knew immediately she was a suspect in Étienne's murder.

"It is an indelicate question, madame, but when was the first time you went to Monsieur Coudace's bed?"

"Two nights ago, on our wedding night."

"Really?"

"Yes! Since my late husband died, I have only ever slept here, and the staff will confirm that I have only ever slept on my own."

"Monsieur Coudace has never slept here?" asked Hilaire.

"No, of course not. Tonight, would have been his first night sleeping here with me. Except in 1919, he did have flu, and we nursed him here then."

Hilaire looked carefully at Juliette. If she had been French, he decided, he would not have believed her, but he suspected that there was something puritanical, almost buttoned-up, about the English which made her protests of chastity almost believable.

"When was the last time you were at Monsieur Coudace's house?"

"Maison Presson?"

"Yes."

"About a year ago, maybe two, why?"

"Why did you go?"

"I can't remember. I can tell you I've never been inside."

"Never inside, why?"

"Probably because I wasn't invited," said Juliette, getting very uncomfortable, as the enormity of what was happening began to dawn.

"We have reports of Monsieur Coudace committing a large number of sexual assaults on young girls at Maison Presson which we are investigating too."

"What do you know about Monsieur Coudace entertaining young girls at his house?"

"What? Nothing!" protested Juliette, "Nothing at all," her voice rising in pitch.

"We found a lot of incriminating evidence during our search of his house."

"Like what?"

Hilaire didn't answer. He was studying Juliette's behaviour, for her mind was leaving the world she was in to one where, as the slave of Hugo's sexual appetite for two days, she was certain that, even if he was not guilty of Étienne's murder, he was guilty on these charges.

Chapter 104

Bordeaux July 1935

COUDACE ADMITTED HIS guilt to Étienne's murder a few minutes after the biscuit tins full of young girls' underwear were shown to him. It was when Hilaire told him Juliette knew about the sexual assaults that his fight for freedom, and his life, left him. He knew then that Juliette would never have him back. He was prepared to be judged as a murderer, but to be tried as a paedophile was a disgrace he could not bear to countenance.

Once Coudace had confirmed to the Procurer and the Judge d'Instruction that he would plead guilty to Étienne's murder, Hilaire decided that the cost of investigating and bringing sexual assault charges against him was not in the public interest, particularly as there were, as yet, no complainants. These charges were quietly dropped, only to be resurrected if Coudace changed his plea to not guilty for Étienne's murder.

Coudace's trial was very brief. If he was in any doubt about Juliette's feelings, these were made clear by her refusal to see him either while on remand or during his trial. Although, as a member of the family of the murdered person, Juliette had a right to be represented in court, she decided not to be so. There was nothing she wanted from this man, except for him to be gone forever.

In the plea of mitigation against the death sentence, Hugo's lawyer told of a man who laboured to make the wines of Château de Gressier which he passionately loved. He told of a man who, through his years of hard work, began to think that the Estate more deservedly belonged to him than to Étienne. He told of a man who had become infatuated for the love of another man's wife. His was not a crime for money but, said his lawyer, a *crime passionnel,* for which an indeterminate prison sentence would be appropriate.

It was as a crime passionnel which saw Hugo given the privilege of being executed privately within the walls of Bordeaux Prison. It avoided his last frightening moments being in public humiliation as he knelt in front of its guillotine.

Coudace had not one visitor from the moment of his arrest to the moment the blade dropped. Not a single person mourned his passing. Whether he went to his death bravely or as a coward, no one at Latoire Village or Château de Gressier knew, for no one cared to ask.

For Hilaire, finding Étienne's murderer was a bittersweet moment, for when interviewing Coudace, Hilaire asked him how he knew the van tyres were incriminating evidence, and had to be changed.

"You told me Monsieur," replied Coudace.

"How, when?" asked Hilaire, shocked at the answer.

"It was when I was cleaning the blood off the road with water. It was then that you told me you had to have casts of the tyre prints as these would lead you to ...."

Chapter 105

Château de Gressier August 1935

THERE WAS AN eeriness over the de Gressier Estate on the morning of Hugo Coudace's execution. No one spoke, as the only thing on their minds was how they would be feeling if they were him. Each kept furtively looking at their watches wondering whether the deed had been done.

At eight o'clock, Juliette got a phone call from the prison chaplain to tell her that Hugo was dead. He gave no details and she asked for none, simply thanking him for the news and hanging up. Immediately, she went outside and shouted for everyone to gather together. All the staff congregated on the lawn at the back of the Château, each embarrassed and sharing only whispers amongst themselves.

Juliette's instructions were simple: "Monsieur Coudace is dead," she announced. "There's no working on the fields today. We're going to Maison Presson. Follow me!" she shouted to the subdued throng, before marching off like a general in front of her army, expecting everyone to follow.

Victoria rushed from the kitchen, where the maids had been trying to keep her busy, to join Juliette's marching army. She did not see Hugo's death as any kind of loss. To Victoria it was a moment of triumph and joy, for she could now have her mother back.

At Maison Presson, Juliette stayed outside. She had never been in and was not going to now. "Bring everything out, absolutely everything," she instructed to all those around her. "Make sure that all his property, possessions, belongings, anything, everything is piled high in the yard. There is nothing to be left inside. It's all to be burned!"

The contents of Hugo's house were thrown out of the windows or carried out into the yard where they were stacked as a huge bonfire. Then, with the contents soaked in a mixture of paraffin and petrol, Juliette threw a flame. There was immediately a huge explosion which threw her and everyone back as the flames flew high into the sky.

Everything went onto the bonfire, irrespective of whether it was flammable or not; glass, pottery, iron, all went into the flames. There was not a picture, or a shelf left behind. The building was stripped from basement to ceiling as was the shed, outhouse, and barn. Requests that something useful might be kept by one of the men were always denied such that they eventually stopped asking.

Victoria found she was in seventh heaven. She hated this man, first for taking her father and then her mother; now with every item she threw on the bonfire she was helping him burn in hell.

To another group of men, Juliette gave instructions to clear the bushes and undergrowth around the house. Only the majestic trees along the edge of the road were to be saved. She wanted the house to be open so that it could no longer hold any secrets.

The fire Juliette built was so big that it was seen from miles away, resulting in fire engines from two separate stations attending Juliette's cathartic incineration. They stayed and watched for, despite the reasons for the day, there was quite a party atmosphere. It was as though the Estate was being liberated from a repressive ghost.

Dominique had planned for a long time that she would come and see Juliette on the day of Hugo's execution, for she too had lost someone very precious at his hands. She had first made her way towards Château de Gressier, but the flames drew her towards Maison Presson. There she found Juliette sitting calmly on a log, silently watching her men at work.

Juliette rose to greet Dominique. They kissed, they hugged and sat next to each other, arm-in-arm.

"Hugo's place?" asked Dominique.

"Yes."

"Good idea, good plan," said Dominique approvingly. They then sat in silence, mesmerised by the flames.

After a little while, Dominique added, "I'm getting married again."

"Oh, how lovely, who to?"

"Henri Hilaire."

"Inspector Hilaire?"

"Yes."

"When, how long?" asked Juliette excitedly, wanting all the news.

"We've been together since Étienne's....," she paused because she didn't want to say the word death. "Well, about six months after it, actually," she continued. "He joined the orchestra and, well, because of Étienne we started talking."

"Oh," said Juliette, not knowing whether to approve or disapprove.

"He asked me to marry him the week after he had Hugo's confession. He said he didn't think he could ask before he'd captured Étienne's killer."

"Isn't that strange?" asked Juliette.

"He thought it would be like a sword overhanging us," responded Dominique.

Juliette nodded.

"It's a good job because ..." Dominique lowered her voice. "Secretly, I'm pregnant with his baby."

"Oh, I'm thrilled, really thrilled," shrieked Juliette, genuinely delighted by the news and spontaneously giving Dominique a hug. "When, time, time?" she insisted.

"Shhh, Shhh!" pleaded Dominique. "We're not saying anything 'till after we are married."

"He's a really good man," said Juliette.

"Yes, strangely good," agreed Dominique. "I'm forty-two, I didn't think....," she added by way of an unfinished explanation.

"Quite handsome," added Juliette, ignoring Dominique's comment on her age.

"Especially in his uniform," said Dominique smiling. "He's very precise, like a scientist, everything has to be just so; while I am far more relaxed about everything."

"Is it the attraction of differences?" asked Juliette. "It often happens," she added.

"We came together over music. We both love it. He talks about the technical structure of the piece and I talk about its mood, emotion and story."

"I'm so happy for you," said Juliette, repeating her joy to make sure it had been received, for that was exactly how she felt.

"It is strange but I'm sure I love him."

"And him you?" asked Juliette.

"Yes, it's not like Georges, or you know ......" She paused. "It's more mature, more thought through. In some ways, it's much easier, less painful."

Dominique hinting about her love of Étienne struck Juliette, for it reminded her that her husband did not just love her, but the innocence of the remark meant she could take no offence, so Juliette hugged her, just like she was her best friend. It was the most fantastic news on such a dreadful day.

"Do you know, Stephen is now nineteen?" said Dominique, there being surprise in her voice.

"How's he taken your news?"

"He only knows we're getting married. We thought it best to tell him about the baby only after that."

Juliette nodded in approval. "Let's go back to de Gressier," she said getting up. "The men can finish off here."

Juliette shouted to Victoria to join her, but she was determined to stay. Although it was just a bonfire, it was important to her to that nothing, other than ash, was left. Although she was only nine years old, Victoria had heard what Coudace had done to the young girls of the village and the Estate. She felt she owed it to them to make sure that he was nothing more than dust.

Juliette and Dominique walked back down the road arm in arm.

"Do you still save the money Étienne gives you for Stephen?"

"And now you," added Dominique, confirming that she was still aware of the arrangements which were made after Étienne's death. "Yes, of course."

"Would he like to buy Maison Presson?" asked Juliette.

"Hugo's house?"

"Yes, I have to sell it," added Juliette.

"I don't think Stephen has enough saved," said Dominique. She then added, "Why does it have to go?"

"Hugo borrowed money from the bank to buy land all around the

Estate. He also had a share of the Estate de Louis opposite and he borrowed to buy that too."

"Is Estate de Louis the same as La Bête Blanche?" asked Dominique confused.

"Yes, La Bête Blanche was Étienne's nickname," laughed Juliette. "Louis is the vineyard's proper name given to it by the previous owner."

"I think I prefer La Bête Blanche," said Dominique.

"Me too," said Juliette. "The bank has agreed that they will transfer Hugo's house and all his land to me, but I have to take over the loan repayments and this is going to be … well, it might cause some difficulties for some time."

"But Henri told me that he found a lot of cash in Hugo's house," said Dominique.

"Yes, they kept it as evidence. I suspect I will get some of it back because it includes the stolen wages money. I didn't know but he'd borrowed huge amounts to buy land, all over the place. Within about two days of Hugo being charged with murder the bank foreclosed on all his loans. I was lucky as there was a prenuptial agreement in place, otherwise de Gressier would have been threatened as well."

"Really, it was as bad as that?" asked Dominique.

The way Juliette walked on in silence confirmed that it was. "I don't want to keep it," she said after a little while. "It has bad memories. I also need to make some payments to some of the girls in the village," she added. She looked at Dominique to make sure she understood. She did not.

"Hugo thought he would exercise his droit de seigneur on some of the girls in the village and working on the Estate," added Juliette.

Dominique deliberately looked at her blankly.

"Not on their pre-wedding night, as might have been the custom, but when they were young … too young," Juliette continued.

"Ah," said Dominique, giving away the fact that she already knew of Coudace's predilection.

"You knew?"

"Yes," she replied, after a long pause. "Henri told me in confidence. I would never have said anything."

"I would quite like Stephen to buy it," said Juliette, "for either what he's got saved up or for what it's worth if it's less. How old is he again?" she asked, knowing she had just been told but not remembering the answer.

"Nineteen," replied Dominique, then she added the words, "Hugo's house, Maison Presson?" just to make sure she had understood exactly what Juliette wanted Stephen to buy.

"Yes, I'll make sure it's all painted and done up inside for him."

Dominique said nothing, allowing Juliette to outline her plans.

"I will need a manager to replace Hugo and he could pay Stephen rent for it, couldn't he?"

"I will ask him about it," agreed Dominique, "I'd be surprised if he didn't think it a good idea."

"Please make sure you ask Inspector Hilaire too," continued Juliette. "He needs to agree. You're about to be a married woman!" she teased.

The two women, their arms still linked, squeezed into each other and smiled, and with this their steps started to take on extra bounce.

Late that afternoon, Juliette summoned Virgil to her house. To say that he was scared about the meeting was an understatement for he had no idea what Madame wanted.

"I hear it was you who identified Monsieur Coudace as Monsieur Étienne's killer," said Juliette.

Virgil did not know how to reply, so he said nothing.

"It's the gossip of the village. They say it was you who noticed that the wire was twisted by a left-handed person."

Again, Virgil did not know what to say as Juliette was giving no sense as to which way he should answer.

"Virgil," Juliette continued, "I'd like to thank you for what you did. It must have been very hard."

"Thank you, Madame," said Virgil, speaking for the first time and rising in stature as he did.

"Please come and sit down," said Juliette, beckoning to a chair. Virgil sat uncomfortably, balancing only on its edge.

"Monsieur Coudace was very unkind to some girls on the Estate and in the village."

Again, Virgil didn't know what to say.

"It's okay," Juliette continued, "all this has been reported to me by Inspector Hilaire."

"Did he say I said something?" asked Virgil, anxiously.

"No, did you?" asked Juliette perplexed. Then, not waiting for an answer, she went on. "When the inspector searched Monsieur Coudace's house, well, let us say they found things that they shouldn't have."

Virgil visibly breathed a sigh of relief.

"Virgil, a favour, I need ... a favour," continued Juliette, before she suddenly stopped. She didn't know how best to ask for what she wanted. "I need a list of the names of the girls he attacked," she blurted out. "Each of them will have been changed ... by the ... experience, even if it's just a little bit. You will have observed those changes."

Virgil looked at her, wondering.

"I'm one hundred percent certain you know what I'm talking about," she went on. As she was talking, Juliette saw in him a reticence and so she added "It's only right and proper that they are paid compensation, but I don't know who to pay, and I suspect you do."

Still, Virgil said nothing. He was slowly, cautiously processing what he'd been told.

"Was your daughter one of them?" asked Juliette. It suddenly dawned on her that this might be the reason for his shyness.

"No, but she might have been," replied Virgil. "He wanted her next, and me and Madame, we was having nothing of it. It was why I went to the police about the murder. It was the only way we could stop him."

"Thank you, Virgil," said Juliette, who then did something very unusual. She stood up, walked over to the sideboard and pulled out a warm bottle of beer, which she poured into two glasses, and handed one to Virgil.

"Cheers, Virgil," Juliette said, raising her glass. "Here's to you, for a job well done."

Virgil raised his glass and took a swig.

"Now, to that list of names," Juliette insisted. "This conversation is between you and me and is never to be repeated. Understood?"

Virgil raised his glass in acknowledgement of her command, took another swig of beer, wiped his mouth with the back of his hand and started to list names.

"Madame," said Virgil, when the list was completed. "I wonder if I may say something?"

"Of course," she answered, there being a deliberate softness in her voice.

"Put on the lights."

Juliette looked puzzled.

"In Monsieur Lionel's time, all the lights of The Cottage and The Cellar's was on. It was like a beacon which lit up the whole valley. It said to all around that all is right with the world. In Monsieur Étienne's time it was the same, the Gallery light never went out. It was like the lodestar shining, telling us it was safe to come home. Light up the house again Ma'am. Everyone will thank you for it and I think you'll feel a bit better for it too."

That night, with every light in Château de Gressier switched on, the menfolk of the entire village gathered with their wives in the village café. They all smelled of smoke from the bonfire, the skin on their faces was tight from being too close to the flames. For the first time since Hugo Coudace had come and taken control of the de Gressier estate, there was a lightness of touch as well as relief, for it was clear that the loans each of them had with Étienne's murderer had, along with his life, been extinguished on his execution.

Long after Victoria was in bed and asleep, Juliette went outside and, with her eyes focused on the moon, she thought of her father, her mother, and Penrose. She slowly said out loud their family poem:

"When the moon is high
and its beam shines bright.
Then think of me, for
I will think of you."

She wished beyond any wish that they could be reunited again but she knew it could not be.

She looked down the valley, past the vines, past the river and up to the silhouette of La Bête Blanche and the dark blue sky of the night. She thought of Étienne. She remembered his saying: *We must make tomorrow today.* She repeated it to herself several times and with that she knew exactly what she was going to do. She was going to make the wines of de Gressier the best in Europe, and she was going to start with this year's harvest.

Thank you for reading The Lands of de Gressier. I do hope you enjoyed it.

If you liked this book, it would be helpful if you would post a positive review on Amazon at www.amazon.com

If you would like to know more about the lives of Penrose Dovingdon and Juliette Guégan then this is told in the next book, The Vines of de Gressier.

If you would like to know when The Vines of de Gressier and the other books in the series will be published, then please follow us on social media at:

Facebook Page @DeGressier
Twitter @deGressier
Website www.degressier.com